STARVING IN THE SNOW

"It isn't much further." Daniel pointed. "There, at the Yuba."

Jessie turned, straining to see. "Surely? You aren't saying that to keep me going?"

"I promise you."

If it hadn't been for the moon, they wouldn't have been able to continue. As it was, Jessie could see only a few feet in front of her. Elizabeth had begun crying, but the baby would have to wait.

Food. The thought filled Jessie's legs with unexpected strength. Still, she knew that if Daniel hadn't carried her while she recovered a little, not even the promise of sweet cakes and honey could have kept her going now. She remembered little of that time in his arms, wished she could hold on to more.

Daniel. She felt him behind her, his bulk seeming to block a little of the wind that had dogged them for hours. She heard him breathing but was unable to tell how much strength remained in him. One moment he plodded behind her; the next, he'd pulled alongside, sinking into the soft snow surrounding the tracks. "There." He pointed toward a thicket of pine trees in a narrow valley ahead of them. "That's it."

It. The precious food that would keep them alive. Despite her urgency, Jessie allowed Daniel to step around her and plunge ahead. She clutched Elizabeth to her. "It's all right now, sweet baby. Everything's going to be all right."

Daniel ducked under a low branch, momentarily out of view. Jessie half plodded, half ran after him. She'd pushed the branch out of the way and was casting around for him when she heard him curse.

"Daniel? What is it?"

"Wild animals. They've taken everything."

Tor books by Vella Munn

Daughter of the Mountain
River's Daughter

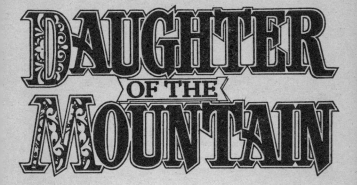

VELLA MUNN

TOR

A TOM DOHERTY ASSOCIATES BOOK
NEW YORK

DAUGHTER OF THE MOUNTAIN

Copyright © 1993 by Vella Munn

Cover art by Royo

A Tor Book
Published by Tom Doherty Associates, Inc.
175 Fifth Avenue
New York, N.Y. 10010

Toro® is a registered trademark of Tom Doherty Associates, Inc.

ISBN: 0-812-52326-3

First Tor Edition: April 1994

Printed in the United States of America

0 9 8 7 6 5 4 3 2 1

Disclaimer

Daughter of the Mountain was written as a tribute to the courageous men, women, and children pioneers who spent the winter of 1846–7 trapped by snow in the Sierra Mountains, a few desperate miles from California's lush Sacramento Valley. Their spirit and will to live may never be equaled.

Although actual members of the ill-fated Donner party, as well as other historical figures such as Captain Sutter, who offered his fort as shelter to the survivors, are mentioned in this book, it remains a work of fiction and should not be interpreted as a literal account of history.

I am deeply grateful for the diaries, letters, and log-books kept by the survivors; George R. Stewart, author of *Ordeal By Hunger*; and my mother for raising me in the shadow of that haunting mountain.

CHAPTER 1

Jessie's muscles spasmed. Weak, she nearly sank to her knees, but she'd almost reached the small, snow-trapped shelter. She hated the smells, the dark silence inside what she, her parents, and the others in the wagon train had built while snow fell all around them, but there was warmth within the wood-and-canvas walls.

Once again she shuddered. A sob pooled in her throat, but she fought it down. Tears, she knew, changed nothing.

Yet another storm would descend before nightfall. Already the clouds had turned from gray to black, sagging, building, enveloping first the mountain peak and then the already blanketed evergreens, settling finally over the thin trail she'd traveled along today. She hated seeing yet more snow fall, but hate took so much energy.

Energy she needed simply to stay alive.

A lash of wind caught her unawares, half lifting what remained of her shawl off her head. She wrapped the ragged ends as best she could around her neck, tucking her numb fingers between the wool and her throat. Her forehead ached from cold and exhaustion. She'd stopped feeling her feet not long after leaving the shelter this morning. If it wasn't for Elizabeth, maybe she'd sink to her knees in the snow and let go.

Angry now, the wind slapped her cheeks and scraped at her eyelids and nose. Jessie ducked her head, set her legs under her heavy skirts, and pushed on. Last month the final climb to the shelter huddled against a wall of rock hadn't taken this much strength, but a month ago there'd been some dried fish, what hides they hadn't given to the others, and the wolf Raymond shot after it ventured too close.

She hadn't eaten anything for four, maybe five days now and very little before that. Without food in her stomach, she wouldn't have the strength to return to the traps.

The moment she pushed aside the wind-tattered blanket that covered the small opening, she caught the hard scent of smoke. Half-angry at whoever had put too much damp, green wood into the small sheet-iron stove, she blinked, trying to make out the forms huddled around it.

There was one, Raymond Sage.

His hunched, ragged figure brought it all back—only she, Raymond, and Elizabeth remained.

Jessie dropped to her knees before the stove and stretched out her hands. As warmth returned to her fingertips, her anger at his fire building evaporated. That emotion, like tears and grief, took too much from her.

"Anything?"

Jessie started to shake her head. The movement made her so dizzy that she momentarily forgot how uneasy she felt in Raymond's presence. "The traps haven't been touched. There aren't any rabbits, mice, anything, left." The last sentence rose from her to mix with the smoke.

"There haven't been any rabbits except that one sick thing since we got here. Why you keep looking—"

Raymond knew why, when she felt strong enough and the winds didn't churn the snow around her, she checked the crude snares she'd set up near a number of deadfalls. The alternative . . .

"How is she?"

"Sleeping."

It seemed like six-month-old Elizabeth Walker slept all the time. Although she hadn't stopped shivering, Jessie backed from the fire and, still on hands and knees, crawled over to the mound of blanket and pine needles that was the baby's bed. Jessie cupped her hand close over the gray, slack mouth, not breathing until a puff of warm air reassured her that Elizabeth was still alive. Then she scooted around until she was sitting cross-legged and stared at what Raymond was doing.

Cooking. His attention now riveted on what he was doing.

She felt old, so old. Now that she was back inside the shelter, she couldn't believe she'd had the strength to walk the half mile to the snares.

Raymond was cooking, simmering something in the battered pot that once belonged to Elizabeth's mother.

The wind outside must have changed directions. It now sucked the smoke up around the stovepipe and out the hole the men had left in the cabin roof.

Before her father cut himself with his axe and died, raging until the end that her mother wasn't doing enough to stop the bleeding.

"It's going to snow," she said.

"I know. I watched the clouds building."

She swallowed and forced herself to speak. "You took Elizabeth outside?"

"For a few minutes. But she started crying. You know how I hate that. She stopped when I brought her back in."

If she'd been there, Jessie would have kept Elizabeth outside longer so the baby could breathe fresh air and a little of the weak winter sun could touch her too-thin cheeks. But she hadn't been to the traps for three, or was it four—they all ran together—days. Raymond wouldn't go. He said it was a waste of time.

He was right.

Jessie felt her head jerk forward and realized she'd almost fallen asleep. Despite the effort it took, she managed to struggle out of her damp shawl and spread it so it would dry. If she had to go outside before it did, she could wear her mother's, but she hated having to do that. It hurt so much to touch her mother's belongings.

"Don't."

"Don't what?" she asked, wondering at the rawness in her throat.

"Stare at me."

Had she? She opened her mouth to tell Raymond she hadn't been aware of anything except a weariness that went clear to her heart. But when she focused on what he was doing, she understood. She indicated their surroundings, the matt of pine branches that served as their floor and absorbed some of the moisture that continually seeped in, Mama's two beloved stick-back chairs, the washstand Papa had wanted to leave behind in Missouri, the crude pole-and-brush beds the men had fashioned so no one would have to sleep on the ground. "There's nothing else for me to look at."

"I know what you think—"

She dragged in a breath of stale air. "It isn't for me to say one way or the other, Raymond. You only do what you must."

"What we both must, Jessie. You know what they're doing—the Donners, Mr. Keseberg, the Eddys."

Jessie nodded. This wasn't the first time she and Raymond had talked about what he believed the others were doing to stay alive. He seemed fixed on the subject and that, as much as the reality, set her on edge. For a long time she, her parents, elderly Mr. and Mrs. Allsetter, Elizabeth's mother, and Raymond had fared better because the Allsetters had oxen, and a wolf pack had been drawn to them. But the animals that had hauled the Allsetters' wagon into the mountains were dead and eaten. The wolves had stopped coming. And nothing remained of the fish Raymond had pulled out of the small nearby lake even after it froze over. Much of the wolf Raymond had shot had gone to feed Elizabeth's mother so Elie would have milk for her baby. It hadn't been enough. Now Elie lay under the snow with the others.

Elizabeth. What would she feed the little one when she woke? Without saying anything to Raymond, Jessie made her way to the limp flour bag beside the cooking utensils. She reached for a small pot half-full of melted snow and shook what remained of the flour into it. It was barely enough to turn the water milky. Still, she placed it beside the stove not far from Raymond's pot.

"What are you doing? You can't keep her alive with flour water. And you can't keep yourself alive if you don't eat."

I know. Don't you think I know that? "She needs it more

than I do." Jessie glanced, quickly, at Raymond's pot. *That* would put life back into Elizabeth's limbs. Although nothing remained in her stomach, she felt close to vomiting. "There's still some coffee."

"Coffee? Jessie, don't!"

Before Jessie could think of anything to say to him, Elizabeth made a soft mewing sound. Jessie pushed herself to her feet and started toward the baby. After her second step, her legs buckled. On hands and knees, her head seeming to pulse, she crawled over to Elizabeth and clutched her to her breast. "Don't cry little one," she crooned. "I'm here. You—it's going to be all right. All right."

But it wasn't.

Elizabeth mewed again, distracting Jessie from her fevered thoughts. The baby sounded so weak, the way the others had before they died. "No, sweetheart. Don't cry. You need your strength." With Elizabeth tucked in her arm, Jessie half walked, half stumbled back to the stove. She sensed Raymond's eyes, not on her, but on Elizabeth and a terrible fear washed through her. No! He couldn't be thinking that!

Trying to ignore him, she settled herself and Elizabeth before the almost stifling heat. The moment she stared into those huge blue, somber eyes, she forgot everything except the baby and her fierce determination to keep Elizabeth alive.

"I saw the sun today," she whispered, concerned because Elizabeth didn't seem to be responding to her voice—something she'd always done. "Just for a few minutes. Then a cloud came—maybe it's going to snow again. I wish it wouldn't. Dear God, I wish—" No. Wishes and dreams were one and the same, a lie. "The mice are sleeping, hibernating. Do you know that word, hibernating?

And the rabbits and bears. Everything except the deer and wolves. Only, my papa said the deer leave the mountains in the winter. That's why we haven't been able to shoot any."

She pulled Elizabeth's tiny hand out from under her blanket and blew moist air on it. Still, Elizabeth didn't move.

"When we leave this place, when Mr. Reed brings back help and we get to the valley, I'll plant flowers for you. By then you'll be so strong, crawling, learning how to walk. We'll sit together and watch the flowers bloom. And we'll have corn, peas, potatoes. Oh, Elizabeth—" Her voice caught. "I promise you sweet peas and apples with so much juice in them that it'll run off your fingers."

"You're talking crazy."

She hated Raymond's voice. Hated his strength. "I have to talk to her. Give her a reason to go on fighting."

"Sweet peas and apples won't give her strength. Not here. Not now. We're going to die." His voice rose. "Die."

Trembling, Jessie dipped a spoon into the flour water and held it to Elizabeth's mouth. The baby made an almost frantic sucking motion, then stopped. She twisted her face as if to cry. Instead, only a whimper came out. After a moment, she took the white-colored water, eyes dull.

"I know," Jessie whispered. "I know it isn't enough. It won't—" Her vision blurred. Tears. But tears changed nothing. Only one thing would—only one thing would keep Elizabeth alive.

With Raymond's hot, dark eyes on her, she dipped the spoon into the other pot. *Stay alive, Elizabeth. It doesn't matter; nothing does. Just stay alive.*

CHAPTER 2

It began snowing before dark.

Jessie sat holding Elizabeth, straining to hear the baby breathe. The wind rocked the cabin, throwing snow against it as if angry at those inside who'd survived its strength. Raymond took a cup of what she'd fed Elizabeth and drank it, his facial muscles pulled tight. He hadn't shaved for a long time now, saying that his beard protected his face from the cold. She thought it only added to his wild look. From where she sat on the opposite side of the small stove, Jessie could smell his unwashed sweat and the smoke that clung to the only shirt she'd seen on him in weeks.

Did she know him anymore?

She bent over Elizabeth and drew in the baby's slightly soured breath. She worked hard to keep her in clean diapers so her flesh wouldn't chap. Whenever she scrubbed Elizabeth's clothes in the washing pan, she added what she could of her own things. She'd asked Raymond if he wanted her to wash anything for him, but he'd told her not to bother.

How old was he? He'd never said but her mother had thought him to be just into his thirties, which could make him ten years older than her. Today he looked closer to fifty.

Almost as old as she felt. Twenty? No. She couldn't possibly be that young.

The wind slammed into the blanket door and sent snow skittering inside. Jessie met Raymond's eyes, but neither of them spoke. She shifted position slightly to shield Elizabeth from the cold and ran her fingers through fine, limp blond hair. Her thoughts went to her own tangled hair, and the hunk her father had cut out of it before she twisted away from him.

It didn't matter. He was dead.

"Sleep, little one," she whispered. "Sleep and dream of California. Your aunt is there. And your uncle. Your mama told me they have a farm, a real farm. They—they'll give you a home."

Raymond grunted and glared but said nothing. Feeling his disapproval, Jessie nevertheless went on. She spoke of how Elizabeth had been so young that she couldn't hold her head up when she and her parents joined the wagon train at Little Sandy, elected George Donner captain, and made the decision to follow Lansford Hastings' advice to take the route south of the Great Salt Lake. "Do you remember the day Mr. Reed killed Mr. Snyder? Mr. Snyder shouldn't have beaten his oxen; what could Mr. Reed do except try to stop him? Mrs. Reed cried so, saying her husband would die in the wilderness if the men banished him. But he didn't die, Elizabeth. Mr. Stanton said he surely made it to Fort Sutter. He'll be back, little one. He won't leave his family here to die. Or us."

"Jessie, damn it, don't."

She refused to look at him. "I have to give her something to hold on to."

"Hold on? What for?"

For several minutes Jessie sat rocking Elizabeth, thinking, not about Raymond's words, but back to the day when Mr. Reed's knife put an end to another man's life. She'd been horrified and sickened, certain she'd never see anything like that again. But she had—wagons careening off the side of a mountain, animals dying of thirst and Indian arrows, the life ebbing from her mother while Jessie cried and rocked her. Snow that wouldn't end.

When the baby moved her head as if she wanted to nurse, Jessie ladled out more of the horrible broth and fed it to her. Her own stomach rumbled. She swallowed, feeling sick. The baby fussed briefly as if her little stomach was unaccustomed to food, then, slowly, fell asleep.

"You're a fool. It's the only thing that'll keep you alive."

I can't. It might be— Jessie fought to stop the thought. She hadn't asked Raymond which frozen grave he'd gone to. If she didn't know who'd made the sacrifice after death, maybe she could— But her mother was out there in the snow. And dear Mr. and Mrs. Allsetter. Elizabeth's mother. Her father.

Her stomach knotted. Her arms ached from the effort of holding Elizabeth. Trembling slightly, she placed Elizabeth on a blanket and curled beside her, her head resting on the crook of her arm. Most evenings she spent reading from the family Bible, but tonight she lacked the strength. She turned herself over to the storm, her mind rising slowly into the air, feeling the powerful updrafts, sticking out her tongue so she could catch a few snowflakes.

She used to love the snow. As a child she'd sit for hours watching it fall, waiting for it to be done so she could run outside and build a snowman. Her father never had time for such things, said that a man couldn't waste his energy in child's play, especially a girl's nonsense. But her mother, her dear, dear mother, always found time to carry out coal for eyes and a carrot for a nose. They'd stand together in front of the farmhouse, arm in arm, giggling like children.

She'd still be there, tending her garden, coaxing the soil to produce more than any other garden for miles around if her father hadn't heard about the California Territory and told his wife and daughter they were going to join the migration west.

West.

California.

Would she ever dig her fingers into rich soil again, plant the seeds she'd brought with her, ever watch new life poke through the earth and reach for the sun?

Or would she join her mother and the others out in the snow?

The wind had stopped blowing when Jessie woke up. Her body ached from having spent the night on the ground, and her mouth felt as if she'd packed it with wool fresh from a sheep. She sat up and looked around for Elizabeth.

Raymond had her. Engulfed in his broad, awkward hands, Elizabeth stared up at him while he fed her. For every spoonful he gave the baby, he took one himself. Suddenly, powerfully, Jessie feared for Elizabeth's safety.

When she rocked, unsteady, to her knees, Raymond looked over at her with dead eyes. "She cried." He indicated Elizabeth. "You didn't hear her."

Hadn't she? She always had before. "How—is she?"

"How should I know? She's hungry."

He was waiting for her to say the same thing, but even with her stomach cramping, she couldn't. Every nerve in her screamed to yank Elizabeth from Raymond's arms, but he'd never hurt the baby. If she told him what she was thinking, it would only make things worse between them. "I—have to go outside. I'll just be a minute."

"The snow's mounded up around the cabin. The wind must have been blowing toward it."

It took so much strength to stand, put on her shawl, and walk to the door. She pushed aside the blanket, looked back at Raymond, then stepped outside, her heavily booted feet instantly sinking into a soft layer of fresh snow. Although it stung her eyes and hurt her lungs, the cold air cleared her head, and she made her way to some half-buried trees so she could relieve herself. After quickly cleaning both her hands and face with snow, she stood on widely spread legs and faced the cabin. New snow lay white and clean on the flat roof. They would have to shovel it off so the roof wouldn't collapse under the weight, but, dear God, how was she going to summon the strength to hold a shovel?

The sky was clear. It was as if the wind had turned its anger from the cabin and vented it on the clouds sometime during the night. The men her father had listened to, those who'd already been to that place called California, had said the sky was so blue there that it rivaled the blue in a baby's eyes.

Maybe. Here, in the mountains, it seemed as if she'd seen nothing except an unrelenting gray that simply turned darker when snowstorms threatened.

From where she stood, she couldn't see the rest of the cabins, but it made her feel less alone to know there were other men, women, and children out there, fighting to stay alive. It had been so many days since she'd gone to see them or she and Raymond and Elizabeth had had visitors.

Had any more died?

She picked up a small handful of snow and placed it in her mouth, breathing shallowly to protect her lungs. As she did, her gaze caught on a massive, white-draped mound. She'd never seen the boulder under its burden of snow, but Mrs. Allsetter had chosen it because there was no other rock this large.

"This way you'll always be able to find it," Mrs. All-setter had said as she and her husband lay together, their flesh slowly sinking inward. "And, when the snow melts, you can find what's buried behind it."

She'd cried when she heard that because it meant that Mr. and Mrs. Allsetter had given up. The money they'd spent a lifetime saving, the money that was going to start them on a new life in California, was no use to them here. They wanted her to have it—if she lived.

Wishing she had the strength to make her way to the Donner or Breen cabins so she'd have someone other than the now distant and frightening Raymond to talk to, she forced herself instead to go back inside. She'd left him alone with Elizabeth long enough.

After standing out in the snow, she found the cabin air to be even more stifling. Half because she couldn't stand the stale smell and clutter, half because she needed something to do, she made an attempt to clean the pots and pans, wash Elizabeth's diapers. She took a few blankets outside so they could air in the weak sun, but by the time she'd done that, her strength was spent.

Raymond sat among his belongings, scribbling in his leather-bound notebook. She'd started a diary the day they left Missouri, but it no longer seemed to matter. Her family was dead; who would care what she thought and saw and experienced? Raymond, a builder of bridges, still talked of working for Captain Sutter, the words often rambling. Maybe he filled his pages with drawings of bridges since his only family was a sister who'd become a Mormon and lived in Utah. How would he ever get letters back to her?

She wanted Raymond to say something; she was glad he remained silent. In truth, conversation had never flowed between them. They wouldn't be together now if they'd known her parents and the Allsetters wouldn't live to chaperon them. She knew Raymond had talked to her dying father about the possibility of a marriage once the party reached Fort Sutter, but he'd never said anything to her.

"If he presses for your hand," Mrs. Allsetter had said, "it's not because he has thoughts of caring for you. He thinks you have money. The man is determined to make a name for himself. It doesn't matter to him how he acquires the funds to accomplish that."

Jessie had told her parents that marrying Raymond was the last thing she'd ever consider. Her father had looked angry enough to strike her—was she ever going to stop being a burden on him? Her mother, eyes sparking a rare defiance, had told her husband that their daughter was going to marry a man for love, not because it wasn't seemly for a single woman to be in California without a man to take care of her.

Besides, as only her mother and Jessie knew, she didn't

need a man to support her. And even if she did, it wouldn't be the brooding man she'd been trapped with.

In the afternoon, Jessie fed Elizabeth again and then went outside to bring in the blankets before they froze. The sky was still clear, but that could change in a matter of minutes. She stood with the blankets clutched to her, wondering how they'd gained weight since morning. The rare gentle breeze smelled clean, so clean that she wanted to cry.

She loved smells, sights, the sounds of a farm at work. Here there was only white snow, gray clouds, screaming wind.

Death.

Did she want to die? She's always loved life, fought to make it hers, held on to her determination not to be buried by a man the way her mother had been. But hunger, the death of those she loved, her own weakness made life seem like a distant mountain peak—out of reach.

If she joined the others in their snow graves, she would no longer watch her hands chap and age. She'd never again smell Raymond's unwashed body or stare helplessly into Elizabeth's eyes.

She'd stop dreaming of a farm, crops growing around her, warm sun on her back.

She'd never again fall asleep asking if there was such a thing as simply being loved by a man.

The blankets nearly slipped from her grasp. She clutched them close to her, shivered, and turned to go back inside. As she did, she thought she caught a movement out of the corner of her eye.

A wolf? Had they become so bold that they would walk right up to the cabin? The movement was repeated, and she realized that what she saw was no four-legged creature. She squinted, trying to see who from the other cabins was coming to visit. But when they came into focus, she realized the two men were strangers. Heavily dressed and carrying large bundles on their backs, they slowly made their way across an open slope. One of the men sank nearly to his belly in the snow, then, with an effort, wrenched himself free and continued on. No one from any of the cabins had the strength for that.

"Raymond." The word clawed at her throat and brought tears to her eyes. She pressed the blankets against her breasts and blinked. "Raymond."

"We're coming." The words, strong, deeply masculine, came from one of the approaching strangers. "We're coming."

Raymond. She'd opened her mouth to call out a warning, a prayer, something, but it hurt too much to speak. Surely this wasn't Mr. Reed and the rescuers he'd promised his wife he'd return with. Mr. Reed carried himself like an aristocrat. These men reminded her of great, determined bears.

She was vaguely aware that Raymond had stepped outside, but she couldn't take her eyes off the newcomers long enough to look his way. One, the man who'd spoken to her, had black hair which tangled around the collar of his heavy fur coat. He walked hunched over because of the weight on his back. Although she could tell the effort it took for him to continue walking, his stride was long, his shoulders broad. She couldn't see enough to tell anything about his eyes, except that they never wavered from her gaze. The other man was an Indian; his tightly woven braids hung down the sides of his neck.

Indians? Attacking?

No. If there were Indians around, surely they would have known that she and Raymond had nothing worth taking. Besides, any Indians who might live in the mountains would have fled for the valley when the first snows fell.

Her vision blurred. When she blinked and strained to focus, she fully expected the men to have disappeared. After all these months, the nights spent praying for rescue, she'd almost stopped believing it would happen. The life would whisper out of her as it had with the others.

But when she stepped toward the two, they didn't become mist.

"Miss Speer. Is that you?"

The man with the rumbling voice knew her name. She tried to answer, but could force nothing through her half-frozen lips. Moisture pooled at the inside corner of her eyes. Knowing how quickly tears could freeze, she blinked them away and took a stumbling step toward Raymond.

He looked as if he'd just met his maker.

"Raymond? Is it—they've come?"

"Rescuers. We've been rescued!"

Rescued. Taken out of hell. Although her feet were little more than frozen lumps inside the boots her father would never again wear, she started toward the men. As before, the larger of the two held her attention.

He was big—big as a grizzly. He needed a shave, but his beard wasn't full grown. With each breath he took, the air in front of him misted; she breathed with him. She couldn't tell his age and wasn't interested in it. Despite his weariness, played out in his slow progress, a deep reserve of strength poured out of him. Enough strength to take her away from here.

They came closer. No one spoke.

She couldn't read anything of the man's thoughts, his emotions. His eyes, black as a night without stars, kept secrets. Stopped her from seeing inside him.

Danger. Although she fought to deny it, needed to believe in him, the thought returned. *Danger.*

Then, when she didn't know whether to run or drop to her knees before him in thanksgiving, he pulled something out from under his great coat and held up a sack.

Food.

"Don't try to move, Miss Speer." His voice carried across the slowly decreasing distance. "Save your strength."

Strength. Suddenly what little she had deserted her. She barely noticed when her knees touched the ground and only instinct caused her to throw out her hands to brace herself.

Daniel Bear saw the young woman pitch forward. If he hadn't noticed her moving about a few minutes before, he would now be frantic to reach her. But in those minutes when he could make out her too-thin form but didn't trust his voice to carry above the wind, he realized there was yet enough life left in her.

Still, he tightened his leg muscles and plowed through the soft snow toward her, ignoring his own need for rest. He heard the man with her say something, but the words didn't carry. He glanced over at Salenack. The Indian was heading toward the bearded man. Miss Speer had straightened slightly by the time he reached her. She now sat half-trapped in the snow, her ragged skirts twisted around her legs. She'd lifted her head so she could stare up at him, white fingers clutching her blankets. He should say something, but what he saw slammed into him with the force of a rifle bullet.

Survivor.

Her lips were pale and cracked. Her mouth looked pinched and determined. Her long, dark hair hung limply around her face and throat. A ragged blanket thrown over her shoulders caught the ends of her hair. The blanket trailed down over her arms but didn't cover her thin, white hands. There was too much color to her cheeks in contrast to the whiteness of the rest of her face. She must have stood out in the wind until her cheeks chapped. Because she was looking for rescue? Because she couldn't stand to be inside the nearly buried cabin? Because her thoughts drove her to seek solitude?

He should drop the burden he'd carried on his back for more days than he could remember and help her to her feet, offer her meat, coarse bread, and acorn-meal mush, but her eyes, her enormous, beaten, and yet fierce eyes held him. When he and the rest of the men who'd undertaken the rescue reached the other cabins, he'd seen too much defeat, too many horrors. But Miss Speer, despite her wasted appearance, hadn't given up fighting.

He wondered what kept the spirit in her and how close she'd come to losing it.

"You—who—"

He stopped her rasping speech, not by trying to lift her out of the snow, but by sinking down beside her. In truth, now that he'd reached this final destination, he was close to exhaustion himself.

She extended her hand toward him. He sat, unmoving, waiting. When her fingers touched the side of his face, he felt the slight pressure against his beard. The touch became firmer. She explored his jawline, up around his eyes, then down to his throat. Her mouth worked, but she said nothing. He saw tears forming in her eyes, watched as she blinked them away.

Finally she brought her fingers to his lips and held them there as if his breath could restore warmth to her.

"My name is Daniel Bear, ma'am," he said. He spoke his name proudly, certain that she would have no idea who he was. Still, not certain whether she might become unbalanced, he kept his tone low and reassuring. "Salenack and I came with a number of men sent up from the valley. After we reached the other cabins and did what we could to provide for the people there, they sent us on ahead to try to find you."

"Mr. Reed?" She licked her lips, wincing as she touched a crack. Her hand dropped to her lap, trembling. "He made it? It took him so long. I was afraid—"

"I don't know about Mr. Reed," Daniel told her. "Captain Kern at Sutter's fort asked for volunteers to try a rescue. I gave my word." She could have sagged against him and thus saved what little strength she had left, but she kept her back straight, her body as fierce and proud and alone as her eyes. "With the help of snowshoes and Indians, a number of your party made it to the Johnson ranch. Mrs. Sinclair who lives with her husband at another ranch appealed to Captain Kern for help. There weren't many who could be—spared to come back with him."

"Spare?"

"From fighting the Mexicans," he said, hoping he'd never have to tell her that most had considered the rescue attempt a fool's mission. "It's a long story, Miss Speer. Later, when you've regained your strength."

She swayed slightly but righted herself before he could decide whether she would want to be touched by him. She stared at her half-buried legs and tried to unravel her skirt while still holding on to her blankets. "You know my name."

"The others told us where to look for you."

"The others?"

"The Donners. The Murphys."

"How—how are they?"

Daniel wasn't ready for the question. In her present

state, he didn't believe Miss Speer needed to be told that the infection in George Donner's wounded arm had left him bedridden and that Elizabeth Donner looked near death. When he and Salenack had left, the decision was still being made as to who had the strength to attempt the long journey down and who would have to remain behind. Instead he mentioned that he'd seen three little girls, all healthy.

"We're going to be rescued?"

She'd barely whispered the words, making him wonder if she really understood that he was here, that he had food for whoever remained alive in her cabin. Because he could think of no better way to reach her, he touched his leather-gloved hand to her cheek. She started slightly, then seemed to lean into him. He heard something that sounded like a half-smothered sob come from deep inside her thin chest, but she didn't cry.

"I have food with me, Miss Speer. We wanted to bring more provisions, coats, blankets, but the mules could only go so far in the snow. We had to turn the animals loose. We couldn't carry anything more."

At the word snow, Miss Speer seemed to pull out of her trance. She dropped the wadded blankets and tried to push herself to her feet, but her hands—why wasn't she wearing mittens—sank out of sight. Although he'd gone almost without sleep for the better part of a week and endured things that turned dreams into nightmares, Daniel stood and held out his gloved hand to help. She placed her icy fingers in his. For a moment he was afraid he'd wrench her arm; she didn't seem capable of doing any of the work herself. Then, grunting, she pulled her legs under her and stood unsteadily beside him. She stared, first at him, then at the blankets she'd left behind. He saw and felt her body shudder.

He wanted to hold her, give her something to cling to. She deserved that, and much, much more. But even though only a Maidu Indian had accompanied him, he'd lived with the disapproval and suspicion of others for so long that he pulled back, not wanting to compromise her reputation in any way.

Salenack bellowed, distracting him. When he looked over, he saw that the Indian was struggling with the bearded man, trying to prevent him from tearing into his pack. Miss Speer turned half toward them, mouth pressed together, nose slightly flared.

"Who's in there?" Daniel indicated the cabin.

She looked at him again. "Elizabeth. Only Elizabeth."

Tamsen Donner, mother of the three little girls, had said that Miss Speer, her mother, Mr. Sage, and a baby were alive the last time anyone had the strength for a visit. There'd once been a total of eight people living in the cabin. According to Mrs. Donner, Miss Speer's father had died not long after the party became trapped. Then the others started dying. "The baby's all right?" he asked.

"You—you have food for her?"

"For all of us. We had to leave much of it for the others, but there's enough—for a little while." After nodding at Salenack, who was trying to restrain the bearded man from gorging on the food he'd been given, Daniel picked up the discarded blankets and gently guided Miss Speer toward the shelter. He had to practically fold himself in half to enter the cramped, low-roofed structure. Because he'd seen the other cabins, he braced himself for what he expected— pitiful conditions, disarray, vermin even. But although the air smelled smoky, the cabin was warm and surprisingly neat and tidy. Still, the careful arrangement of raised bed platforms, a few pieces of furniture, blankets, hid none of the sense of desperation.

How had she survived? What will, what determination kept her going when strong men had died in this hellish place?

He watched Miss Speer walk hunched over toward a small mound. She started to reach for something, then, as she'd done outside, sank to her knees.

She sat with her hair falling over her face, thin shoulders shaking, hands clamped onto her elbows. Her blanket coat had slid off her. He saw that she wore the top to a pair of men's long johns. The hem fit snugly over her hips, holding her bedraggled skirts against her.

He wondered whether one of the men had given her the garment for warmth or if she'd taken it after the owner no longer had a use for it.

When she extended her hand over the small mound, he allowed himself to be distracted from her. He saw something move on the crude bed and came close enough that he could see the baby.

She was a blond. At least she'd once been blond and would be again when there was adequate warm water and soap to wash her hair. He hadn't seen many infants in his life. Babies, to his way of reasoning, were for married folks. He'd never thought of himself as a husband, finding a woman who wasn't afraid of him, settling down.

But the little one with her weakly moving arms and sucking mouth touched him. Pulled something from deep inside him.

He knelt and joined Miss Speer beside the baby. He could hear the sound of an argument outside and wondered why Miss Speer wasn't thinking of her own needs the way her companion obviously was.

Maybe it was as his mother had told him, that nothing is more precious to a woman than her child.

But little Elizabeth wasn't Miss Speer's child.

The woman who should have been barely twenty but looked years older started to lift the baby. She managed to get her a few inches off the ground before her hands began to tremble. Daniel placed his hand under Elizabeth, easing her back down.

"Don't try to lift her, ma'am," he whispered. "You're too weak."

"I can't be. I wasn't this morning."

This morning you were trying to hold on. Now, God willing, we'll all get out of this. "I have food," he said, unsure how much she remembered of what he'd told her before.

At his words, she looked at him. In the dim light, it was as if he'd come across twin pools somewhere deep in the mountains. Whatever secrets the pools held wouldn't be easily revealed. "Hard biscuits and acorn-meal mush that the Indians gave me. Elizabeth can eat that, can't she?"

Miss Speer's mouth worked and something tragic and trapped flashed in her eyes. The emotions were gone before he could learn anything from them. When he realized she wasn't going to speak, he occupied himself by removing the heavy canvas pack that had become part of him during the mind- and body-numbing journey. Her body swaying slightly, she watched as he pulled out dried beef strips and biscuits made from flour ground in stone mortars. He felt half-starved himself and weaker than he'd ever been, but it had to be nothing compared to what she'd endured.

He pulled off his gloves and handed her the half-frozen mush his friend Chief Narcisco insisted he take with him. "Not too much and not too fast," he warned.

She took the cake and placed it in her mouth. He watched her jaws working, appalled by how little flesh remained over her cheekbones. He expected her to take another bite as soon as she'd finished the first. Instead, she began rubbing some between her hands, softening it. When she tried to reach for a pot of water, he understood. He pulled a tin cup out of his pack, dipped a little warm water into it, and dropped the wad of mush into it. He hoped she'd go back to eating, but she seemed to have forgotten everything except what he was doing. After a minute, he ladled out a little of the now softened food with a silver spoon he'd found among her belongings and held it to Elizabeth's lips. The baby immediately sucked what she could of the spoon into her mouth and tried to clutch his fingers.

"Easy, little one," he whispered, surprised by the gentle tone in his voice. Elizabeth didn't seem to have heard him. She swallowed and began coughing.

"She's choking."

Daniel lifted Elizabeth off the bed before Miss Speer could move. Puzzled that he knew how to do something like this, he laid Elizabeth over his shoulder and gently tapped her back.

"Ma'am, please, you have to eat," he said when Elizabeth stopped coughing.

His words seemed to pull her into action. She broke off another piece and began chewing. Her hands still trembled, so much that it alarmed him. He wished he could think of something to say to her, but all he had were questions about why she was still alive and what had happened to the others, and he knew she wasn't up to answering. When he noticed that she was eyeing his coat, he touched it and then balanced Elizabeth in the crook of his arm so he could feed her and keep her head up at the same time. "That's bearskin. It doesn't smell so good when it gets wet, but it's warmer than deer hide. At least I believe it is."

She started to nod, then clamped her eyes shut as if trying to stop herself from being dizzy. "Bear. I saw tracks but I've never— Did you kill it?"

"Yes."

"Yes?" She opened her eyes. "Were you in danger?"

He couldn't understand why she cared about that, but maybe she wasn't able to put her mind to what she'd endured. He thought about telling her of coming across an old bear who'd been wounded in a battle with another of its kind, but he didn't want to distract her from eating. "No danger," he told her. She was still putting food in her mouth as if she'd almost forgotten how that was done. He thought about the small warm weight in his arm, and about what Miss Speer had seen and endured since she'd joined the wagon train.

He'd watched his own mother bleed to death. But her dying had been quick, nothing like what must have happened to Miss Speer's family.

"I have to know," she said in her raspy voice. "The others, how are they?"

"Some good. Some bad. Don't think about that, Miss Speer. Please. As soon as you're strong enough, we'll leave. Go to them."

"Leave?" Desperate hope flooded her eyes. "We don't have to stay—" She looked at her surroundings, shuddered. "We can leave?"

"As soon as you have a little more strength." He indicated her oversized boots. "Do you have anything better than that for walking in?"

She seemed to be considering his question, but when the better part of a minute passed without her saying anything, he decided she must be too far gone to concentrate. By the reaction of those at the other hovels, he'd been prepared to have to restrain her from gorging herself, but she'd finished the acorn-meal cake and wasn't searching for more.

He wanted to put Elizabeth down and replenish the fire, but after days of struggling through first rain and mud and then snow and storms and steep slopes, his legs felt unbelievably heavy. Elizabeth had been staring up at him while she ate. Now her eyes became heavy, and, reminding him of a purring kitten, she started making soft clicking sounds as if lulling herself to sleep. He pressed the limp weight close to him, feeling a small pocket of warmth and life against his ribs.

He looked over at Miss Speer, wondering if she'd understand if he said anything about what he was feeling. She was staring at Elizabeth. Then, without his having said or done anything, her eyes drifted up to him. They still reminded him of night-darkened pools of water.

"Why did you come?" he asked.

"What?"

"With the wagon train. Why were you coming to California?"

"I had— I wanted— He insisted. Papa said there was a new life for him there. And Mama and I—we had no choice."

"Then, this wasn't what you wanted?"

To his surprise, she shook her head. "I have dreams of my own. I believed I would be free in California, free to do what I must."

Her words and the meaning behind them were too much for him to hold on to. Fighting exhaustion, he placed Elizabeth back on her bed. The infant tucked her fist against her mouth, sucked a few times, fell silent and still. Again he looked over at Miss Speer.

Tears, caught by what was left of the firelight, sparked in her eyes.

"Don't cry," he whispered. "It's going to be all right now."

"Is it?" she whispered back. "Can you promise me that, Mr.—Mr.—"

"Bear," he finished for her. "Daniel Bear."

"I don't have anyone. It's just me now. Can you say it's going to be all right for me, Mr. Bear?"

CHAPTER 3

Jessie couldn't put a name to it, but something had changed. She was able to breathe without making a conscious effort. When she looked at her surroundings, they appeared less pitiful. Even the cabin seemed larger. The man, Daniel Bear, had sat beside her for several minutes, sharing meat strips so tough she could barely soften them enough for swallowing. He hadn't spoken. She hadn't been able to think of a word other than a prayer of thanksgiving.

Now he was placing fresh wood on the fire.

His form filled her vision.

He left his task and removed the heavy bearskin coat. He wore, not homespun, but a soft deerskin shirt laced at the throat and caught at the waist by a leather belt. Deer-skin leggings, wet from the snow, clung to his legs. His feet were encased in moccasins instead of the leather boots she and her fellow travelers wore. She didn't think he had on woolen socks underneath like she wore. She'd heard of men like Kit Carson who roamed the mountains free and unafraid. Virginia Reed had loaned her a book on the life of the fearless frontiersman Daniel Boone. Even with weariness etched on Mr. Bear's features, she couldn't imagine him ever being afraid. Ever being anything except free.

Bear. He was aptly named.

Jessie looked down at herself, wondering what he saw and whether he pitied her. How could it be otherwise? Although she hated using what had once belonged to her mother and Mrs. Allsetter, she'd taken to wearing three skirts for warmth. The layers of clothing blanketed her body and hid her thinness, hampered her movements. She wondered what it would feel like to wear trousers, to know the freedom her savior took for granted and her father had always denied her.

Mr. Bear settled himself on the ground, his back to the stove. For a moment he simply watched as she tried to pull her undershirt free from her other garments. Then he met her eyes. She read no pity. What then?

"The others are waiting for us to return to them. Then we will all leave." He spoke softly, firmly. Yet something simmered behind the words, something just out of her reach.

Jessie stopped what she was doing. The thought of walking away from this, of climbing down off this night-marish mountain filled her. "Wh—how?" Her split lip stung every time she spoke. Still, she couldn't remain silent. "How will we get down?"

"Walk."

Such a simple word. "You—they know the way?"

"Oh yes, Miss Speer. That isn't the problem. But everyone is weak. Some so— It isn't going to be an easy thing."

Staying alive hadn't been an easy thing. "We have to do it. There's nothing here, nothing except death."

Her words seemed to have made some kind of an impression on him. Although she didn't fully understand why, he leaned forward slightly and stared into her eyes. She blinked but didn't try to hide from his scrutiny. "Do you think you can?"

"Yes." She didn't know if that was true. "Oh yes."

"And the man outside, will he be able to as well?"

Did Mr. Bear have any idea how Raymond had been able to maintain what he had of his strength? Did he know what had kept Elizabeth alive? She wanted to look to see if Raymond's pot still contained something, but with Mr. Bear holding her with his eyes, she couldn't break free. She wasn't sure she wanted to. "It's all he has talked about. All either of us have."

Mr. Bear looked down at Elizabeth; his features softened and took away a little of his fatigue. "We'll take turns carrying her."

"I made Elizabeth a promise." The words came out a whisper. Jessie swallowed and tried again. She couldn't leach the pain from her voice. "And her mother. That she will grow up in California where the sun can warm her and she will learn how to laugh."

Her hands had been in her lap, worrying her skirts. She sensed and saw the man's large hand start to move toward her and wondered what she'd said to make him want to touch her. But, with his fingers only inches from her, he stopped and then pulled back.

Still, what had changed about her world since he entered it remained.

"It isn't warm in California now," he said. "I can't promise you something that doesn't exist. There's fog in the valley and sometimes freezing rain."

She shuddered, tried to stop when she realized he was aware of what she'd done. "But—Fort Sutter. It's really there?"

"Oh yes." At the sound of movement and voices outside, he spoke more quickly. "With thick walls made of clay and adobe brick, cannons for protection, great wooden doors. Soldiers."

"Cannons?" Again she shuddered. "Why?"

"For protection, ma'am." He swung away from her before the words were fully out of him.

She looked over her shoulder just as Raymond and the Indian entered. Pieces of biscuit clung to Raymond's beard, and there were a couple of red marks on his throat, making her wonder what the Indian had had to do to restrain him.

Raymond staggered over to Mr. Bear and stood weaving over him. Spittle flew from the corner of his mouth. "That Indian—" He pointed. "He says he won't leave until morning. Frankly, I don't care what he does. The rest of us, we're getting out of here right now."

"No."

Daniel Bear's simple yet powerful word caught Jessie's nerves in a vise.

"No?" Raymond echoed.

"It will soon be dark," Mr. Bear explained, his tone both firm and gentle. "We can't travel at night."

"But—" Raymond staggered, spread his legs to support his weight. "You don't know what it's been like." His voice became a whimper. "The hell— What if the others decide to leave without waiting for us?"

"Then we'll follow them."

"What if you can't? What if we get lost?"

Raymond's questions were hard-edged, stripping away the earlier lost-child tone and reminding her of what Raymond had turned into in recent weeks. Although she was looking at Raymond, Jessie sensed Mr. Bear's quick and wary reaction. "We won't. We left marks, burned tree trunks. Mr. Sage, we came near killing ourselves getting here. We tried snowshoes—they didn't work. For days it rained, half drowning us. We spent the nights standing around a fire with only blankets to protect us from the rain because we couldn't lie down in the mud. Three gave up and turned back. The cold, the wet—there isn't a one of us with enough strength to start back tonight."

Raymond flicked a glance Jessie's way. "When then?"

"When we've rested."

For a minute, the silence beat at Jessie. Raymond and Mr. Bear had faced each other, two determined, desperate men fighting for what they believed.

Mr. Bear had won.

"What—" Jessie swallowed and tried again. "How are the others?"

Mr. Bear sighed, his eyes intent on her. "There's some who aren't strong enough to travel, little children. They'll have to wait until others, like Mr. Reed, can come after them."

"Wait?" Jessie whispered. "They might die before then."

"It can't be helped." Mr. Bear hadn't broken eye contact with her. Although his words were matter-of-fact, she saw the agony in him. She'd spoken the truth and they both knew it. "We'll give them what food we can. Mr. Glover and the others are cutting wood, cleaning things up, making the weak as comfortable as possible. They'll— We left food along the way, several caches to sustain us. I'm sorry.

We couldn't do more than that, not after the mules couldn't go on."

"Mr. Reed? He'll be here soon?"

"I pray he will."

Despite what Mr. Bear had just said, Jessie felt clearerheaded than she had for days. Their rescuers were doing what they could; the strong would be brought out now. Like him, she prayed that help for the others would come in time. She couldn't do more than that. She was strong; she had to be! Still, the thought of the effort ahead of them nearly overwhelmed her. She pulled her legs up against her and looked around at her surroundings. They'd have to leave the furniture behind. She couldn't possibly carry the fiddle she'd played to soothe Elizabeth. Mama's pots and dishes and precious silver spoons that she'd hoped to use in her new home would remain. All but the clothing she wore on her back. That and— "Mr. Bear, it will be easier going down than climbing up, won't it?"

He didn't answer. She pulled her attention away from what remained of the Allsetters' belongings—a canvas bag filled with laces and silks for trading with the Indians, a shovel, a silver watch, shaving tools. She'd been able to read Mr. Bear's eyes before. That hadn't changed. He wanted to give her the answer she needed, but he couldn't.

The Indian dropped his burden on the floor near the stove and reached for the simmering water. He tipped the pot up so he could drink from it, then looked over at Elizabeth. He said something to Mr. Bear, the words foreign. Mr. Bear answered in the same way.

"What is this?" Raymond interrupted as his legs gave out and he sprawled on the ground. "You're planning something, aren't you?"

"Salenack asked if the baby was going to live. I told him that she'd eaten and was sleeping."

Raymond looked as if he didn't believe Mr. Bear, but instead of saying anything, he crawled on hands and knees to his bed and picked up the leather-bound book that had been his daily companion. "This is all I care about. This and food and enough clothes to keep me warm." His gaze settled first on the Allsetters' belongings and then on Jessie. "One other thing. You and I will talk about it tomorrow."

When we're alone. She sensed their rescuers' curiosity but because she knew what Raymond was referring to, she said nothing. This was between the two of them.

To put an end to the silence, she told them that her needs were no more than Raymond's. Her concern was that they had enough decent blankets to protect Elizabeth.

Mr. Bear indicated their surroundings. "There's nothing else here? No small thing?"

She couldn't take her mother down to clear streams and rich soil. She didn't even have a picture of her parents because the box holding such treasures had been lost when they forded a river. "My Bible, please. I have some seeds. For corn, wheat, beans."

Raymond swore; Mr. Bear nodded.

"I know what you're thinking, Raymond." If she'd been strong enough to stand, she would have faced Raymond down as she'd done over this before. "That those seeds should have gone into feeding us here. But they're all I have." She turned toward Mr. Bear, knowing she couldn't keep the emotion out of her eyes and voice. "All I have to sustain me on my farm."

"Farm?" Raymond spat. "Dead, what good would that have done you?"

"She isn't dead, Mr. Sage."

Mr. Bear's words stopped her. She'd never before had a man stand up for her. What she'd learned from her father was that if she was going to be listened to, she would have to do it on her own. Her father believed that his only child, a girl, was little more than a mouth to feed. True, she had a gift for coaxing life out of the soil. Begrudging, he'd admitted that. But a man needed sons. And she and her mother had failed him by not giving him what he wanted.

She'd grown up drawing strength and determination from deep inside herself, watching her gentle but weak mother, knowing she could have no pride in herself if she followed in her mother's footsteps.

Today a stranger had understood.

"It doesn't matter anymore, does it?" Raymond sneered. "You didn't have to choose between your precious seeds and keeping yourself alive after all. Of course—" He crawled closer. "If you hadn't been selfish, the others wouldn't have died."

That was a cruel lie. A handful of seeds wouldn't have held back death. But, weak, only half believing that they'd been saved, she had scant defenses against the criticism. In an effort to escape Raymond's words, she turned her back on the men and pulled the undershirt over her head. The effort left her dizzy, but she'd begun to sweat in the now hot cabin. She still wore her linsey-woolsey bodice.

"Morning."

The richly accented word spun Jessie back around.

"At dawn, while the snow is still frozen, we will return to the other cabins."

Mr. Bear nodded to indicate he agreed with what the Indian had said. Jessie saw Raymond glower and guessed that his suspicions had been aroused now that he realized the Indian and Mr. Bear could communicate in a way that excluded them.

She didn't care. "Will we wear snowshoes?" she asked.

"Not if we don't have to." Mr. Bear was staring at her

boots. "Do you have anything else to wear? You won't get a mile in those."

"Yes. My own shoes. I've been trying to save them, letting them dry out."

"Good." He nodded both at her and the Indian. "We can't carry you."

She'd never expected them to. Like standing up for herself, doing her own walking was the way she wanted it to be. "How long—" Her throat constricted. The room seemed to be drawing inward, becoming rapidly darker. "How long will it take us to get out of the snow?"

"I don't know." Mr. Bear loosened the leather at his waist, drawing her attention to the knife hanging from his belt. She was glad he was armed; at the same time it increased his aura of strength and unsettled her. "I can't say if it will take less time to descend than it did to climb," he continued. "But the effort should be less."

"I pray you're right." She thought about taking off her father's cumbersome boots, never having to put them on again. She wondered if she would be able to take her hairbrush with her.

Suddenly the realization that she was truly contemplating leaving this prison alive slammed into her. Feeling short of breath, she lowered her gaze and stared at her hands. Her knuckles were skinned, the nails ragged. There seemed to be only a single layer of flesh over the bones.

But she was alive.

She drew herself as straight as her spent body would allow. "Thank you," she whispered. "Dear God, thank you for saving us."

Mr. Bear walked over to her and knelt in front of her. His heat reached her, feeling different from that of the fire. "We aren't saved yet."

"I know. But I have to believe."

Believe. Her word followed Daniel to bed. Despite the luxury of sleeping with a roof over his head, he couldn't get his mind to shut down. His body ached. His head still pounded from the frigid air. Mindful of the others' needs, he'd barely eaten. On top of what little he'd had during the push up here, he felt weak. Still, that wasn't what kept him awake.

Twice now the young woman had said things he couldn't shake. First, she'd asked him if everything was going to be all right for her. He hadn't been able to answer, hadn't been capable of lying. Despite the desperation in her voice, something about her told him that she didn't need to be lied to, that she was strong enough for the truth. Then, just before she'd drifted off to sleep with her feet still lost in the worn boots, she'd told him she had to have something to believe in.

Not because she was a child who believed in fairy tales.

Not because she couldn't face reality.

But, maybe, because she knew to take dreams and turn them into something she could use to keep herself going.

Did he have dreams? The question was insane, nothing to concern a man whose every act should be aimed at survival. Still, Miss Speer had gone from being a gaunt figure braced against the wind and become flesh and blood—someone who'd lived through the unsurvivable.

There were others like her. He'd seen them today, those who'd hung on through all odds. Tomorrow he and Salenack, John Rhoads, Mr. Glover, and the others would take those they could down to safety, if their fellow rescuers hadn't left already. The rest—

He threw off the thought. Seeds. She'd said she needed seeds for her farm. Was that what held his attention? She wasn't talking about taking shelter at Fort Sutter or living with another family. She hadn't said anything about wanting to go back where she came from. Instead, she wanted to farm.

He had no idea what that was like.

A scant foot away, Salenack groaned in his sleep. Because he'd seen little except the Indian for days now, he had no desire to look at him now. Still, he was glad he hadn't come alone to this cabin. Sage made him uneasy. If the man caused trouble, he would need Salenack's help.

Tamsen Donner had told him that Sage was staying with Miss Speer because when Mr. Speer hurt himself right after the Donner party became trapped, Sage had offered to do what he could to help. At the time, he hadn't cared anything about the relationship between Sage and the young woman he'd gone to rescue. He wouldn't ask questions; it wasn't any of his affair. Still, from what he'd seen of the way they acted around each other, he didn't believe they shared any affection.

If that was true—he stretched out his leg, slowly so he wouldn't risk a cramp—Miss Speer had spoken the truth. She was alone in the world.

Jessie woke slowly. It had been like that for weeks now, as if her mind was loath to leave whatever escape she'd found and return to awful reality. She tried to bury herself back in darkness, but something tugged at her.

A sound.

Opening her eyes, she strained to see in the deep gloom. She could hear Raymond snoring. In truth, she thought she might go through the rest of her life hearing the quick, hard bursts that exploded from his chest. But in between his snorts, her ears detected another sound. She turned toward it.

The Indian was kneeling in front of the stove. He'd

placed a log on the coals and was blowing on it. Salenack. Mr. Bear had called the quiet, strong Indian Salenack.

Mr. Bear. Daniel Bear. Denying that she'd called him by his first name—something she'd done with Raymond only because it seemed easier that way—she moved her head, trying to remember where he'd bedded down.

He was sitting.

He wore nothing from the waist up, revealing shoulders broader than she'd imagined any man having. His chest was lean yet muscled, making her believe what he'd said about having come here to rescue them. He funneled down to a lean waist, flat belly, curling black hair that lightly covered his flesh, strength—such strength.

She'd never seen a man in that state of undress, had always tried not to think about such things. Still, she didn't make herself turn away. Did he know she was watching while he spread some kind of salve on a rubbed area of flesh over his shoulder blade? He remained angled away from her, and she watched firelight dance on the hills and valleys of him, darkening his flesh, making him both wondrous and frightening.

He moved, breaking the spell. He handed Salenack the salve and began shaking out the soft deerskin shirt he'd worn yesterday. After a moment, he slipped it back over his head.

She wished he wouldn't. She wished she understood what she felt.

He and Salenack were saying something to each other. Although she knew only a few words of Spanish, she realized they were speaking that language. Were they afraid she and Raymond might hear? What then were they saying to each other, keeping from her?

She couldn't hold on to the thought. She hadn't had enough to eat last night to keep her brain clear. With her head dizzy and her stomach cramped, she couldn't stay curled around Elizabeth any longer.

As she sat up, she wondered about her sudden, almost overwhelming need to eat. She'd been so hungry when they first became trapped, nearly desperate to make sure there was something nearby at all times. But slowly, conditioned by days when there was nothing, she'd stopped thinking about food. She knew her body craved and needed nourishment. Without it, she'd die.

But there was none and thinking about food changed nothing.

Mr. Bear had brought acorn mush, tasteless biscuits, hard strips of beef that he and Salenack had begun softening in water last night.

"You're awake."

"I'm hungry," she said, not at all shocked by her boldness.

Mr. Bear searched in his pack and handed her a biscuit. "There isn't much. I'm sorry."

"Anything." She bit, fighting to keep from gulping. "Flour. How did you get that?"

"From Captain Sutter's mill."

"Papa said that Captain Sutter opens his doors to everyone who needs shelter. Is that true?"

"He won't turn anyone away. But the problem with the Mexicans has kept him very busy. He doesn't have much time to attend to the needs of those who turn to him."

"What is it like?" She swallowed and took another bite. His voice was so rich, much deeper than her father's or Raymond's.

"What is what like?"

She thought she'd made that clear, but now that she thought about it, she wasn't sure what she'd spoken and what she'd simply thought. Raymond snorted again. "Fort

Sutter. The man who talked to my papa says that he keeps a herd of sheep in there. That he has folks who spin wool and— Will the walls keep out the Indians?"

Salenack grunted. Mr. Bear glanced at him, then looked back at her. "The Indians aren't the problem, ma'am. At least not most of them."

"Only the Walla Wallas," Salenack said.

"All right, only the Walla Wallas." A quick grin touched Mr. Bear's lips and he shook his head at Salenack. "Excuse me, Miss Speer, but my friend insists that I never forget that the Maidu are not warlike."

My friend. "Are there many Walla Wallas?"

"Too many," Salenack answered, then turned back to the simmering meat.

"Miss Speer." Mr. Bear spoke slowly, softly, his voice rumbling like the distant beginning of a thunderclap. "I would like to assure you that once we reach Sutter's fort that all your problems are behind you, and you can put your mind to farming, but I can't. There is the fighting with the Mexicans, the winter, animals. California is a wild place with few white men and even fewer women. Not all of the men can be trusted."

"I understand." She wanted to stand. She wasn't sure her legs would hold her.

"I hope you do." He scooped his cup into the pot and handed it to her. "Drink that. Then we'll wake Mr. Sage and Elizabeth."

Jessie did as she was told. She watched while Mr. Bear refolded his blankets and stuffed them back into his pack. Salenack did the same, chewing on jerky as he worked. The two men's movements seemed slowed even to her. The Indian's left wrist was badly swollen and he stopped working several times to massage it. Mr. Bear favored his left calf but said nothing about what might be wrong with it. As he'd done yesterday, he placed some mush in warm water to soften and then reached for Elizabeth. When she saw what he was doing, she tried to take Elizabeth from him. But her fingers lacked strength, and she had to sit watching while he fed the now ravenous baby.

"Are there pants you can wear?" he asked.

"Pants?" She picked at her skirts.

"It'll make the traveling easier."

"Oh. Of course," she responded, wondering at how easily she'd agreed to his suggestion. "Not my father's—he was a big man. But Mr. Allsetter's—" She broke off, embarrassed.

When Elizabeth cried impatiently, Raymond woke. He started to sit up, grabbed his leg. He pressed, cursing. "A man's muscles can't keep going without food," he said. She didn't know who he was speaking to. "I dreamed—I dreamed that you hadn't come after all. It started snowing and I knew it would never quit."

Jessie had had a similar dream. She'd awakened twice, cold sweat drenching her body until she looked around and saw the two men sleeping nearby. Even now she half expected them to disappear. If they did, would she sob or simply accept? It was a question without an answer, one she prayed she'd never have to face. She'd been flexing her hands and now felt strong enough to take Elizabeth from Mr. Bear. She set about changing the baby's diaper, wondering how she'd keep the little bottom from chafing any more than it already had once they no longer had warm water to wash her with.

Still, all she wanted to do was leave this place.

Night had just begun to fight with day when the five emerged from the cabin. Jessie held Elizabeth close to her, careful to keep a covering over the baby's head. She'd of-

fered to carry something on her back, but Mr. Bear told
her that caring for Elizabeth and taking along a few of her
own belongings would test her strength. He'd twice asked
if she believed she was up to the journey. Although her
legs quivered and she still felt light-headed, she'd said yes.
She had no choice; Mr. Bear knew that.

Raymond looked barely strong enough to hold himself
erect. Still, he insisted on clutching a small bundle, which
held his writing material, a couple of books, and a few
tools that he'd made himself. He'd taken Mr. Allsetter's
silver watch, her father's gold pin, the silver spoons. Although Mr. Bear had given her a sharp look when
Raymond selected the items, she hadn't protested.
Raymond still brooded, still made her uneasy. He wore
three shirts and two sets of trousers. Over that he'd draped
his heavy coat.

Jessie stared down at her feet and wiggled her toes. Her
boots, cracked from having been wet so many times, were
at least easier to manage than what she'd had on yesterday,
and thick wool socks kept the leather from digging into
her flesh. She'd had to tie a rope around her waist to keep
Mr. Allsetter's pants on, but the sense of freedom was incredible. She wore an elkskin coat, a silent gift from
Salenack.

Inside the deep pockets she'd placed the personal items
she would take with her—the seeds in their flour-sack
wrapping, her brush, and the leather pouch she'd dug up
from behind the cabin when she told the men she needed
a moment of privacy. She'd had to leave her Bible behind
after all. It was simply too large. But the money in the
pouch was her legacy, a gift from grandmother to grand-
daughter. Her means for buying the land she needed to
farm.

Her independence.

After explaining that they would break trail and she and Raymond could follow in their footsteps, Mr. Bear and Salenack began retracing their steps of yesterday. Jessie hoped Raymond would simply follow them, but he held back, staring at her. When she tried to step around him, he caught her arm.

"You can't leave it here. You can't!"

She tried to pull free. "It doesn't matter."

"Doesn't matter! It's a fortune. I deserve . . ."

Hardly a fortune. The money Mr. and Mrs. Allsetter had given her was more than what her grandmother had gifted her with, but it wouldn't make her a rich woman. Besides, it lay as deeply buried as those who had died here. "Don't," she warned Raymond. "We've talked about this before."

"Talk? Every time I try to bring it up, you refuse to tell me where they hid it."

Because that was Mrs. Allsetter's wish. Looking into Raymond's angry eyes, she understood why. "It doesn't matter." She tried to move away from him. He blocked her way.

"You're going to leave it here? I can't believe—"

"Raymond, so much snow has fallen." She resolutely refused to look in the direction of the boulder. "I can't dig down through all that."

Mr. Bear joined them. She hadn't heard him returning, but now that he was near, she was aware, very aware, of his presence. He didn't say anything. His eyes asked the question. Before she could decide what to tell him, Raymond broke the silence. "There's gold coins buried somewhere here," he said around clenched teeth. "A lifetime accumulation. The Allsetters gave it to Jessie when they were dying. To her! Not me! I know they told her to hide it—keep it from me." Raymond moved as if to step toward her. Mr. Bear, too, shifted position, offering his body as a shield. Raymond stopped, body trembling.

"I'm entitled. I kept her alive."

Raymond spoke the truth. If he hadn't been an experienced fisherman, there wouldn't have been any fish. His rifle had brought down two wolves. But both the Allsetters and her mother had warned her that if Raymond got his hands on the coins, he would keep it all. And maybe make sure she would never dispute his claim.

"I made a vow, that I would do as they said and use the money for my own needs." She'd told him this before. It hadn't made a difference then. She didn't know if it would now.

"Vow? Are you ever coming back here again?"

Never! "I don't know. When I think of what I have to leave behind—Mama's things, my Bible—"

"Even if you do return, others might come first. Do you want thieving Indians to take the gold?"

She didn't have the strength for this argument. If Mr. Bear hadn't been here, standing between her and Raymond's anger, she might have screamed. But she wanted, she needed to be strong for the man who'd risked death himself to help her and others who were strangers to him. "I want to stay alive, Raymond. If I tried to find the gold now, it would take precious time," she said simply and forced her legs to take her away from the two men. She couldn't look at Raymond anymore, couldn't face his anger.

Her eyes felt hot and dry. Her head pulsed, and she had to remind herself not to clutch Elizabeth too tightly.

Freedom. She was walking to freedom.

But first—despite the effort it took, she crawled up the sloping hill to the tree they'd buried her mother under. She dropped to her knees and laid her hand over the slight mound. "Good-bye," she whispered. "Mama? I love you."

"Miss Speer. We have to leave."

Mr. Bear was right. Besides, she'd already said her final words to her mother, the night she died. She whispered a farewell to the Allsetters and another to Elizabeth's mother, along with a promise to take care of Elizabeth. Finally her attention settled on her father's grave. She felt only a quiet sorrow that they'd never really known each other.

She was alone, except for the bear-pelt-clad man waiting for her.

CHAPTER 4

Nearly a half mile of white broken only by wet, brown bark and glimpses of green pine needles under their pristine burden separated Jessie's cabin from those of the other trapped travelers. In recent weeks she'd made the trip a hundred times in her mind, seeing the clean-running little creek near the cabins, trying not to look at the white barrier of the pass beyond, but to actually do so would have taken strength she needed to check the traps. And, she now admitted, she'd stayed where she was because she didn't want to see what had happened to people who'd become as precious to her as her mother had been, and still was.

With Elizabeth in her arms, keeping her footing on the frozen new snow and hard pack underneath took every bit of energy the welcomed food had given her. Still, her mind worked.

Freedom. Had the word ever meant more? She'd been a prisoner for so long that she'd come close to forgetting what simple liberty felt like, what it tasted and smelled and looked like.

Freedom meant having some place to go to and the means to make it happen. Freedom wouldn't be possible without the determination of the men who'd braved the winter to attempt the impossible. She tried to remember their names as Mr. Bear had told her, but they remained faceless strangers. Her champion was a man named Daniel Bear. She owed him everything.

And wanted to give him nothing.

Desperately needed emotional distance from him.

Jessie changed Elizabeth from one arm to the other and tried to set her mind to placing one foot before another. But the sky was clear; the wind had lost its teeth. She could think.

Freedom went by a name beyond simply following Mr. Bear's lead as they walked between the pine-covered mountains that had hemmed them in for so long. She was even now giving the wonderful word definition by turning her back on what would have become her grave and starting to think of life.

Her life. Carved out by herself. Without the unbelievable wrench of watching yet someone else she loved die.

God willing, she would live, embrace life, nurture it, celebrate it. Only, she would never again leave herself open to the agony of the heart she'd endured in recent weeks. She couldn't stop loving Elizabeth. What she felt for the infant went so deep that it would always be a part of her. But Elizabeth was the only one she'd ever allow to touch, to remain in, her heart.

Any more tears would destroy her.

It was that simple.

Both Mr. Bear and Salenack were struggling to keep their footing. At first she thought it was because the snow gave way beneath them, but after watching them for a while, she realized that like her, they were able to remain on top of the snow most of the time. As she studied their progress, feeling her own weakness gave her the answer. They'd nearly spent themselves crawling their way up the mountain. Resting last night had helped a little, but they would have to call on every ounce of courage and determination to make it back down into the valley.

Why?

Why had they come?

Raymond had been trudging behind her. She sensed him close the ground between them and heard his labored breathing. "I never took you for a fool, Jessie. But this—" He wheezed.

She didn't risk falling by turning to look at him. "It's over with, Raymond. I don't have the strength to try to find where Mr. Allsetter buried his coins."

"I do."

She wasn't sure about that. But even if he did, she'd made a promise, one she intended to keep. Under no circumstances was Raymond to get his hands on what had been the Allsetters' stake in a new life. By taking her parents' things, Mr. Allsetter's watch, he'd gotten his due. "When the snow melts, I'll come back for it," she told him.

"Don't lie to me. You hate that place."

Jessie shuddered. Elizabeth tensed, and her little face contorted as if she was about to cry. Jessie fought to calm herself so the horror of what she'd see without the snow to blanket reality wouldn't be transmitted to the baby.

"Raymond, please. We don't know when there's going to be another storm." She fell silent for a moment, pulling air into her lungs. Mr. Bear had glanced back at her and Raymond. His eyes carried both question and warning. Whether for her or Raymond, or both of them, she didn't know. "If we don't try to get down now—"

"If we don't move as swiftly as possible, this damnable mountain is going to kill all of us."

Mr. Bear's words, thrown over his shoulder at them, chilled Jessie as much as what Raymond said about graves had done. She tried to meet Mr. Bear's eyes to let him know that this thing between her and Raymond had to be brought to its conclusion, but staying alive had been such a battle. Nothing mattered except staying alive, taking care of Elizabeth. And, someday, watching her precious seeds poke through the soil.

Daniel had heard of snow blindness. He'd come close to experiencing it himself the first time he'd climbed over the mountains and into California. What he endured now felt too much like what had happened to him before. Simply, something was wrong with his eyes.

He wanted to sit down in the snow and let it cover him. Protected by his fur coat, he could remain warm for hours. He would sleep, let his aching body rest. Food would slowly restore him.

But there wasn't enough meat and biscuits for that. He would have to hold on, somehow, the way Miss Speer had when by all rights she should have given up. If she could survive—

Strange. He'd taken on this task because, despite the hostility of some of the others, he couldn't turn his back on a desperate plea for help. His mind had been filled first with what they needed to take along and then with the herculean effort of remaining alive.

He never thought any of the trapped travelers would reach out and touch him in a way he didn't understand and couldn't stop.

But she had.

Because he couldn't remember how long they'd been walking, he hadn't been looking for signs of the other cabins. Now Salenack pointed. Ahead, nearly hidden by trees and snow, blurred by his flawed vision, was one of the shelters, half lean-to, half what remained of a covered wagon. Salenack called out a hoarse hello, but no one answered.

"What happened?" Raymond asked when his own call received no response. "Where did they go?"

Daniel didn't bother trying to answer Raymond's question. Until he'd gone inside, there was none. After dropping their packs, he and Salenack pushed aside the canvas door covering and stepped inside. A moment later they rejoined the other two. "They're gone," he said simply.

"Gone? Damn it, if we'd left last night—"

"If we'd done that, Salenack and I would be played out." Daniel held aloft the note that had been left behind. Although his head pounded with the effort of focusing, he read it, wondering if either Raymond or Miss Speer would ask themselves where he'd learned to read. "To the Indian and his companion. The danger of another storm rests heavily on us. We do not dare wait for your return. Those who can't travel have been moved to better shelter where they have what food we can spare. It will do no good to try to take them with you. They must wait for further help. Maybe we will meet where one of the food caches were left and travel together from then on. If the need to move swiftly exists, we will leave food for you."

"What is this?" Raymond snorted. "We've been abandoned."

Daniel exchanged a glance with Salenack. The Indian's gaze said everything; it wasn't Raymond or Miss Speer the others had turned their backs on. If he hadn't already experienced, expected their prejudice, he might have been stung.

Daniel expected an outburst from Raymond. Instead, the disheveled man stared at his boots, his mouth working. Finally he straightened. "So be it. There is nothing we can do about that. You know the way, do you? There is no danger you will miss the food?"

Daniel assured him that wasn't possible, since the supply base at Mule Springs had been carefully marked with a brush tent, as had the smaller ones farther up the mountain. He didn't want to look at Miss Speer. If knowing they would have to descend by themselves had sucked her will from her, he didn't know what he was going to do to make sure she got out alive.

"Mr. Bear?" Her voice touched him, strong, resolute despite its slight tremor. "Do you have an idea when they might have left?"

"They spent the night here. Probably they struck off at or before dawn." He indicated the line of flattened snow leading away from the foul-smelling, listing structure. Another path, less fresh, led to the hovels where those who'd been left behind had been taken. "The tracks were made on a frozen surface."

"Then, if we hurry, we might overtake them?"

Instead of answering immediately, Daniel stepped closer to her. He wanted to cup his hand over her jaw and hold her firmly so she had to look into his eyes the way his mother had done years ago when childish fears overwhelmed him. Her face swam before him. He blinked, tried again. "We might, Miss Speer. But we won't hurry. We don't dare."

He expected her to argue. Instead, she resettled the baby in her arms and met his gaze. He thought she'd swayed slightly but couldn't be sure. He saw, not tears, but an awful acceptance. "I know. I'm sorry I said different."

"There is nothing to be sorry about, ma'am. I want to get away from this place as quickly as you. I understand."

"No. I don't think you do."

He waited, somehow knowing she would tell him the rest when she was ready. It didn't take long.

"Mr. Bear, you didn't watch it snow for days on end. You didn't sit holding your mother while the life left her. And you weren't the one beset with nightmares every night, nightmares about slowly starving—slowly freezing."

"Miss Speer." He took another step, so close now that when she breathed out, she warmed his throat. "You're right. I didn't endure what you did. I hope no one ever has to again. But I held my dying mother." He stopped. Only Chief Narcisco knew that. Why was he telling this woman about the worst moment in his life? If he didn't still his words, he might tell her what had come after. And she would hate him, fear him. "I don't think there is anything in this cabin you might need, but if you want to look—"

She shook her head. He thought her eyes widened. "I-I don't know if I can step inside another building ever again, Mr. Bear. Maybe, maybe I'll spend the rest of my life outside." She shrugged her shoulders as if Elizabeth's weight were too much for her. "I'm sorry about your mother."

"It was a long time ago." He backed away, retrieved his pack, put the burden back on. She still studied him; he felt her eyes penetrating the layers, going deeper. Finding the truth of him.

The thought of what she might find chilled him.

If she was reckoning right by the time, they stopped to rest every half hour. Although the morning had too quickly spent itself, they had no choice. In order to descend, they first had to climb up and through a narrow, snow-choked pass where harsh, jagged peaks hung over them, mocking, challenging. Despite her objections, Mr. Bear insisted on carrying Elizabeth some of the time. When he did, Jessie forged ahead, breaking trail. Once the sun warmed the frozen snow, the task was almost beyond her, would have been except for the powerful forces that pushed her on. Despite the effort, she pulled her legs free time and time again. If Raymond had asked, she would have told him of her need to put distance between herself and their prison. If Mr. Bear had posed the question, she would have pointed to the clouds that threatened to the north, spoken about the way she felt trapped every time she looked up at the knifelike peaks.

But there was another reason. Mr. Bear and Salenack had risked everything for them. She had nothing to give them—not even the money from her grandparents, which she had to keep because without it she would starve, homeless, in the valley below. Maybe, with strength and determination and grit, she could make the men believe that her life had been worth saving.

Every time they halted, it was one of the others who made the decision. Her mind was too full of proving herself, and trying not to think about the children and ill adults left behind, who could do nothing except pray for a miracle. Now, when Mr. Bear called out to her, she let the effort play out of her body. She waited on wide-spread legs half-buried in wet snow, her body trembling, not from cold, but fatigue. She lacked the will to turn and face the men.

"She isn't doing right."

Elizabeth. Despite herself, a sob clogged her throat, then escaped. Wordless, Jessie held out her hands. Mr. Bear turned the baby over to her, his eyes, his proud and determined eyes, asking for help. For an instant she returned his look, wondering if he knew how scared and helpless she felt. Then Elizabeth mewed.

Jessie touched her free hand to Elizabeth's face. It felt icy. "She's freezing. We have to warm her up."

Raymond came to stand beside Mr. Bear. "We can't stop now. How can you even think—"

"She's going to die if we don't get her warm. I won't let her die. I won't!" Jessie turned toward Salenack. "Please. There must be dead wood for burning. If we could heat some water, warm her in it—she needs to have her clothing changed and something in her stomach."

Mr. Bear had begun to remove his pack even before she'd finished speaking. He pulled out a small hand axe. The Indian held up a similar axe of his own. Cursing, Raymond sank to the ground and began rubbing his legs. While the men struggled to hack the lower branches off a nearby tree, the sound of their tools biting into wood, Jessie blew onto Elizabeth's hands and feet. She knew what the problem was. Elizabeth had soiled and wet herself, leaving her vulnerable to the cold. Still, until there was warm water to clean her with, she didn't dare unwrap the baby.

After dragging back a number of branches, the men piled up dead pine needles to start a fire. Soon they added larger pieces of wood to it. The wind swirled the smoke, occasionally stinging their eyes, but Jessie, like the men, huddled around the warmth. Salenack's pack contained a small pot, which he filled with snow. As the snow melted, he added more until there was enough that Jessie could dip a thin flour sack into it. Without saying a word, Mr. Bear stood between her and the wind and spread his coat as protection. Keeping Elizabeth as covered as possible, she washed her again and again until white flesh once again took on a pink tone. Elizabeth seemed more wakeful now. As Jessie dressed her in dry clothing, she turned her head, her eyes wide and curious. When she spied Mr. Bear, she regarded him with grave curiosity, then laughed. He extended his hand and chucked her under the chin, then, after a quick glance at Jessie, returned to the fire.

Then Elizabeth let them know that she was hungry.

Mr. Bear had already anticipated that and had broken off a precious piece of biscuit to soften in clean water. "Come on, little one," he encouraged as he held out his broad, weather-chapped hand with the soggy mass in it. "Eat. It'll keep you alive. Just stay alive." His voice dropped to a whisper that didn't carry to the two men huddled on the other side of the fire. "Just stay alive."

Jessie couldn't go on looking at Elizabeth, pretending she hadn't heard. The effort of caring for Elizabeth while sitting in the snow had left her feeling lethargic, unable to move. But she still thought and listened and reacted. "You mean it, don't you," she whispered. "You don't know her. You might never see her again. But you want her to live."

"Yes."

"Why?" She ran her hand over her eyes, feeling old, so old. "Why should this one life mean so much to you?"

"Maybe because it's a life, Miss Speer."

A life. "Please." She couldn't speak in a normal tone; she was too spent for that. "Please call me Jessie."

He looked as if he didn't quite believe her. "We're strangers. It isn't seemly."

"Strangers? No." She shook her head, then stopped because the movement made her temple throb. "I might be dead now if you hadn't brought me food."

"It isn't enough. You need more."

"I know," she acknowledged. "But without what I had yesterday—Mr. Bear, I place my life in your hands. That isn't something strangers do."

"Daniel."

"What?"

"My name is Daniel."

It wasn't until Salenack tried to stand that Jessie fully understood that they wouldn't be going on today. She'd put off trying to move, hoping that by will or the example of the others or both, she'd find the reserve she needed to continue. But when the Indian all but pitched forward, she took a deep, shuddering breath. Raymond had been watching Salenack, the flesh under his eyes sagging. Now it seemed as if his entire body had begun to sink in upon itself. "I can't do it." His voice barely made it across the fire. "Tomorrow—after we've— One more day, it isn't going to matter."

"Daniel?" Jessie tried her voice. Why she looked to him as the leader she couldn't say. Maybe it was his size alone, and maybe there was another reason—one just out of her grasp.

"I can't."

Although he'd spoken the words calmly enough, whatever simmered beneath them alarmed her. She stared at him. He wasn't looking at her. She couldn't tell what held his interest, what—

Couldn't he see?

The question slammed into her and robbed her of breath. She clenched her fingers so tightly that what remained of her nails dug into her flesh. She went on staring.

"Daniel? Something's wrong, isn't it?"

He remained silent. Still sitting half-sprawled in the snow, Salenack reached out as if to touch his friend. "Snow blindness."

"Not total." Daniel's voice held no emotion. "When I fight, I can see. But my eyes tire quickly."

"Damnation!"

Jessie ignored Raymond's outburst. She hadn't taken note of her surroundings. In truth, she didn't want to see the world. But now she knew she had no choice. Although they were nestled between two peaks that shielded them from much of the wind, the granite masses seemed to loom over her, to mock the blood flowing through her veins. The gray clouds she hated had dipped to touch the mountain above and behind her and were beginning to crawl down its length like some massive, formless snake. It stretched forever, trapping their legs when they tried to walk, an endless white blanket. A beautiful prison.

How much of that could Daniel see? What would happen to him if his eyes continued to fail? "Is there anything we can do?"

"Only a little," Salenack answered, his voice thick from the effort of forming new sounds, new words. "With care, it will pass. Sometimes it takes days. Sometimes weeks. As long as he continues to look at the snow—"

"I won't let it stop me," Daniel interrupted. "I can see well enough."

"Today, maybe," Salenack challenged. "But if you don't rest them, tomorrow you will need to be led around."

Led around? The very thought made Jessie want to scream. Daniel Bear was an aptly named man. If he'd been leading the wagon train, there wouldn't have been any of the delays that had brought the Donner party too late to the passes. He would have driven the others, driven them the way he'd pushed himself to reach her and Raymond and Elizabeth. He looked like a man of the mountains, dressed like one, sounded like one, faced the monster with a courage she wanted herself.

He couldn't be made helpless. He couldn't.

"You say he needs to rest his eyes?" she asked Salenack. "How?"

"By protecting them from so much white until they've had time to heal."

She wanted Salenack to be able to tell her how long Daniel's eyes needed to be shielded, but the Indian didn't know that. "If we travel at night, would that make a difference?" she asked. "We could rest during the day."

"What are you saying, Jessie?" Raymond demanded. "We're never going to overtake the others that way."

"Don't." Daniel's voice sliced through Raymond's words. "I won't have anyone's life risked because of me. We'll leave in the morning. I'll—"

"Daniel," Salenack warned. "If you don't give your eyes a little time now, you may never see again."

That was all Jessie needed to hear. Although Elizabeth was warmly bundled, she spent a moment tucking the blanket around her. Then: "We won't move tomorrow. Daniel will sit in the shadows or keep his eyes closed. Maybe warm water— Tomorrow night we'll move again."

"No!" Raymond bellowed, anger and desperation contorting his features. "We can't spare that much time. Jessie, there isn't enough food."

"There has to be."

"There isn't," Daniel told her. "I'll stay here. When my eyes are better, I'll follow the rest of you."

She couldn't, wouldn't leave him. Warmth and rest,

safety and salvation lay ahead, maybe, but she couldn't leave the man who'd saved her life alone and defenseless. "I'll stay with you. I can be your eyes."

"No."

"Yes." Her throat constricted at the word. Mindful of her need to husband her strength, she went on in a softer tone. "You can't make me go. I'll take care of Elizabeth. And you. Raymond and Salenack, they can reach the food cache and bring some back to us." She turned her eyes, not on Raymond, but Salenack, asking for verification. The Indian nodded. "Daniel—I need to rest, too."

"Resting could kill you."

"Trying to go on now might kill me as well."

He groaned. She heard the sound, saw it almost, believed she could reach out and touch it. "I can't force you," he said. He looked as haggard as she felt.

"No. No, you can't."

Daniel lay with his back to the fire. He could hear Salenack moving about and more occasionally another sound which he took to be Raymond. He could have opened his eyes and looked at them. In the predawn and with the fire to help, he would watch their silhouettes, feeling helpless. Angry. But he'd rather stay in the dark, where yesterday afternoon played itself out over and over again inside him.

He should have told her no, ordered her, demanded that Salenack and Raymond make her go with them. For Elizabeth's sake, he would tell her. For Elizabeth's sake, you have to try to overtake the others.

But, even though he had to struggle to make anything come into focus, he'd seen the tight, hard lines that bracketed her mouth and knew she wasn't lying about being exhausted.

He'd given up trying to convince her to leave him because her body needed rest as much as his eyes did.

At least that's what he told himself.

His leg muscles threatened to cramp. To prevent that from happening, he shifted position and opened his eyes. Now he was staring upward, seeing nothing except the haze of a reddish glow from the fire Salenack had built. That didn't bother him; it was all the others could see.

"Daniel." Salenack spoke in the Maidu language this time. "I am leaving you a little smoked meat. And acorn mush for the baby. I will be back. As soon as we find food, I will return."

"No." Daniel sat up, not caring that both Jessie and Raymond must be trying to understand what he and Salenack were saying. "I will see you at Sutter's fort, my friend."

"Daniel—"

"Listen to me, friend. Tomorrow, even if I must be led around, Jessie and I will start walking again. If you come back for us, it will rob you of strength you need."

Salenack said nothing.

"Leave some food for us there. That's all I ask."

"I want to see you again, Daniel."

"You will." He made himself smile. "This summer we will race on our horses again. Maybe this time you will be lucky enough to beat me."

"Lucky! Who taught you how to ride, white man?"

"Not you. I learned that skill from the finest horsewoman in Texas."

"I believe what you say about how your mother could tame the wildest stallion. But you—stubborn as a mule and slow as an ox." Salenack cackled, then fell silent.

Daniel saw a shadow moving toward him, recognized it as Salenack's hand, and clasped it. Sometimes they showed respect for each other in the white man's method, sometimes in the way of the Maidu. It didn't matter. "Maybe your legs will have healed by then and you won't walk like an old woman," he teased.

"And maybe you will no longer boast about things you can never make come to pass. I look forward to that race. I'll give you an old mare to ride so you won't hurt yourself."

"That's all you have in your herd, old man. Broken-down mares."

"At least I have a herd."

Still feeling the warmth from Salenack's hand, Daniel turned away. His clouded vision chafed at him, limited his world, but he didn't want to burden anyone with that. Raymond was talking to Salenack about what they would take and what should be left behind as if he and Jessie were beneath consideration. He opened his mouth to remind Raymond that he could speak for himself, make decisions.

Jessie.

Her name had a lilt to it, a quick, simple sound. He wanted to whisper it aloud and see what the wind would do to it.

He wanted her to tell him about planting vegetables and what she did to make them grow, why she seldom spoke of her father.

Once they were alone, he should ask her what she and Raymond had argued about. He might even tell her why the letter the others had left had barely mentioned him, but when he tried to put words to the thought, they slipped away.

Jessie.

The wind would love to play with her name.

* * *

For a long time after they moved out of sight, Jessie continued to stare after Raymond and Salenack. She'd been struck by their labored progress and could only pray they'd reach the food that had been left for the return. Salenack had taken more with him than had been wise, burdening himself with some of Daniel's load. Daniel had argued and even sworn, but Salenack had said something in that language only he and Daniel understood and Daniel's voice had lost its punch.

She could tell Daniel was watching their progress as well. He leaned forward slightly, eyes squinting, body tense and uneasy. She wanted to tell him to save what sight he had, but knew he wouldn't listen. He didn't want Salenack to leave.

Was it because he was afraid of staying here alone? She didn't think so; Daniel wasn't a man to turn fear in on himself. But there was something between the two men, a bond, an understanding, something she wished she understood better.

Daniel.

He'd told her to call him by his common name, and she had. There was a force to the name Daniel. It rolled easily off her tongue and yet echoed after she was done saying it. She wondered who had named him. Maybe his father had been called Daniel, and the son was carrying on the tradition, but Daniel hadn't mentioned his father.

She knew his mother was dead, had died in his arms.

She hoped his mother had put the name to him.

"Daniel? What did Salenack give you?" she asked, to put an end to what was going on inside her.

"A poultice. Some herbs. He said it might help my eyes."

Leaving Elizabeth, Jessie half walked, half stumbled over to Daniel and squatted beside him. From her mother, grandmother, and other farm women she'd learned how to use herbs as medicine. She took the small leaf-wrapped package out of Daniel's hand and dipped it in warm water. After a minute, she handed the soggy poultice back to him. "Put it on your eyes. We'll see if your friend is right."

Daniel seemed hesitant to do as she said, but after a minute he covered his eyes, holding the leaf wrapping in place. He took a long breath, then sighed. "It cools them."

"Good." She wished he could see her smile. Maybe he didn't care, but she wanted him to know that she was capable of doing that. That he could make her smile. She thought about returning to Elizabeth, who was lying on a pine-branch-and-blanket bed, examining her hands as if they were the most fascinating things in the world. But what little she'd done this morning had left her trembling. It seemed easier to stay where she was. "Daniel? What made you come here?"

"What?"

"What was it?" she pressed. She ran her hands down her pants legs. In only a couple of days, she'd gotten used to the strange feel of fabric surrounding her legs. "You didn't know any of us. You knew what trying to climb up there was going to be like. You didn't have to come."

"The money."

"Money?" The word stung her.

"Captain Sutter and John Sinclair, who has a ranch near Sutter, both offered to pay the wages of those who volunteered."

"Oh." What had she expected? For Daniel to risk his life simply because there were other lives at stake? Would she have? "How much?"

"I don't know."

"You don't—" He started to twist his head toward her,

and she was afraid he'd remove his bandage. "What do you do? I mean, do you have a ranch?"

"A ranch." He clipped the words. "A man needs money for that, Jessie. And if he has the money, he has to want to be tied down."

"Tied down. That's how you see it?" She tried to focus on the tall, thin white tree pyramids that surrounded them. But she couldn't take her eyes off Daniel. He wore his bearskin coat this morning. It covered him from neck to legs. Maybe she hadn't seen him without a shirt after all.

"It's not something I want, Jessie. Maybe wanting to plant and nurture things has to be something a body grows up with. Like you did. Missouri. Is that a good place to farm?"

She didn't want to talk about what she'd left behind. It hurt too much. As long as Elizabeth played with her hands, she wanted to sit beside Daniel and listen to him— not so much to what he was saying but the sounds that came from his chest.

"Jessie?"

With a start, she remembered they'd been talking about something. "What?"

"What is Missouri like?"

"It's beautiful, especially in the spring. I loved it there. Daniel, you said your mother died."

"She was killed."

"Killed. I'm sorry."

He didn't say anything, his silence telling her that the wound was still raw. She thought of telling him something about her own mother's death, because if she did, maybe he would share more of himself with her. But he was here because someone had offered him money. Nothing else.

Besides, she didn't want to cry.

CHAPTER 5

It seemed as if every time she woke during that afternoon of fitful sleep, the fire needed replenishing. Although Daniel offered to do that, Jessie all but ordered him to keep the herbs over his eyes. To her surprise, he complied.

As it was getting dark, however, she was forced to tell him that the wood he and Salenack had cut needed replenishing. He sat up, uncovered his eyes, and looked around, not blinking. Her attention was drawn to long black lashes caught into thick, wet spikes. Except for Indians', she'd never seen eyes that dark, that deep. She thought about asking him if he carried Indian blood; it would explain his midnight hair and the equally dark beard that made her think of his namesake. But although they now called each other by their first names, she barely knew him. They were alone together; she couldn't forget that. Along with her competence on the farm, she'd been raised to think of herself as a woman worthy of respect. And women who cared for their reputations didn't willingly remain in the presence of strange men.

Only, none of that mattered now. "I slept," he told her. "Did you?"

"I couldn't stay awake."

"What about Elizabeth?"

"She's all right now. Weak."

"I know." He groaned and got to his feet. She watched for signs of weakness, but if they were there, he hid them from her. Grasping the axe in his right hand, he headed toward the nearest trees. He hadn't said anything about his eyesight; she didn't ask.

The moment he stepped out of sight, she felt lost. It was almost impossible to tell where the snow ended and the sky began. The mountains' vastness had preyed on her mind from the day she knew they were trapped. Now, utterly alone, she wondered if she existed at all. Maybe she was no longer flesh and blood, only a wisping, fading thought.

Then Elizabeth whimpered and she pulled herself free. Speaking of nothing and everything, anything so she would have her voice to listen to, she changed Elizabeth again and parceled out a little of the precious food. The baby gulped down her biscuit, then squalled for more.

"Give it to her."

Jessie looked up. Had she been so lost in thought that she hadn't heard him approaching? His arms were filled with wood, several long branches dragging behind him. Hues of red from the fire danced in his eyes. Light and shadow, constantly moving, muted his features. She didn't recognize the man standing over her. He'd become larger somehow, a blending of dark and red, backlit by the relentless white that slowly folded into night. He was a voice, a presence, power.

"Jessie, she needs the food."

She rode the words until they made sense to her. "So do you."

"We all do. But she's growing. And when she cries—"

As in response to his comment, Elizabeth sucked in air and let out an indignant squall. Jessie wanted to tell Daniel that there might be no satisfying Elizabeth's appetite, but she couldn't make herself heard over the sound. She smiled up at Daniel, holding the gesture, wondering if he cared what she was capable of. Then, feeling surrounded by Elizabeth's crying, she set about softening yet another biscuit.

As soon as she placed a little on Elizabeth's tongue, silence cut through sound, and she could think again.

"She's still strong," Daniel observed.

"That she is. How are your eyes?"

"Not as hot as they felt before. And I think I can see better." He knelt beside the longest branch and began hacking it into manageable pieces. Jessie concentrated on the rhythmic thunk, thunk, thunk. Her eyes, her emotions even, took in the way his arm rose and fell, the bunching of his shoulder muscles as he readied himself for each blow. He'd removed his coat. In the firelight, she could see that his throat was sweat-slicked.

"Be careful," she said. She needed to say something, anything. "Don't exhaust yourself."

"We have to have enough wood for the night, Jessie."

Jessie. She loved the way he made her name sound. "How did you think to bring an axe?" she asked.

"We almost didn't, because of the weight. We talked

about how the folks we were coming after would have tools and weapons, and we could use those. But we needed to keep ourselves warm while we were trying to reach you."

"Oh." Once again she felt the impact of what he'd risked for her—for the others as well. "Of course. The way you talked about it, it must have been horrible. Daniel, I have to ask you something. Did anyone—did anyone with you die?"

He let the axe slide slowly out of his fingers and stepped around the pile of wood. He sat down near her. "No."

"Thank God. I don't think I could have stood it if they had. Then—everyone is all right?" *Except for you. You almost went blind.*

"Three turned back. I told you that."

She couldn't tell whether there was condemnation in Daniel's voice for those who'd given up. Mindful of how deeply she was digging, she nevertheless asked, "Did you ever think of joining them?"

He sat, head up, eyes steady on her. She felt their depth reaching out to her, maybe to suck her in, maybe to probe. "Not really, Jessie. Not even when we had to ford the hundred-foot-wide torrent which filled the canyon at Steep Hollow."

Thank you. "Why?"

"Why? I don't know."

She opened her mouth to question what he'd said, but stopped herself. Maybe he didn't fully understand his reasons. And maybe he'd chosen to keep them to himself.

"Don't probe too much, Jessie," he said after a minute. "Reasons, questions, thinking how things might have turned out different, how you might not have spent so long trapped up there—that isn't going to change what happened."

"I know that."

"Do you?" He pressed the heel of his hand against his eye, shook his head, blinked. "I hope so."

She believed him. She also sensed that he was speaking not just to calm her but out of his own experience. "Please eat something," she said when she became aware of the silence. "You'll need your strength for morning."

"So will you."

Jessie was afraid Elizabeth would continue to cry for food, but the infant soon fell asleep. She and Daniel shared a little of what meat was left, agreeing that they should save as much of the biscuits and mush as possible for Elizabeth. Jessie wanted to remain awake and make sure that Daniel placed the poultice back over his eyes, but her head had become so heavy. Her stomach still felt as if she'd put nothing in it. Maybe the only way she could stop thinking about that was by sleeping.

Without trying to remove any of her clothes, she stretched out on the blanket she'd spread over the branches Daniel had laid over the snow. She placed Elizabeth next to her, curling her body around the smaller one. Her feet felt cramped from having to wear her boots all the time, but Salenack had warned her that if she took them off, her feet might swell.

Daniel sat hunched over the fire, eyes closed. She studied him, watched his beard absorb the red and orange lights, smelling smoke, feeling comforted by it. She'd gone to a couple of barn dances in Missouri. Although she hadn't been sure what was expected of her, when the young men from the neighboring farms asked her to dance she did her best to follow their lead. Her mother had always wanted to teach her to dance; her father had said he needed her to help him work the land. Still, she'd managed to keep up with the boys without embarrassing herself or breaking her partners' toes. When her mother asked if she'd enjoyed herself, she'd been forced to admit that she'd been too nervous to think about enjoyment. And, no, she couldn't remember anything about her partners.

Did Daniel Bear know how to dance? She doubted it. From what little he'd said about himself, she couldn't imagine him putting on a starched new shirt and moving about with tight, precise steps. Daniel—

Her thoughts dead-ended, then started again. What did he do when he wasn't risking his life to climb a mountain? He didn't farm. He'd told her he had no interest in such things. But he must support himself somehow. Maybe he hunted to feed those in Captain Sutter's employ. She could imagine him stalking a deer through the forest, endlessly silent, forever patient, aware of everything in the world of trees and animals. Maybe, like Raymond, he had a skill. He might be a blacksmith, a builder, a— Again she ran out of thought. She'd never considered the other things a person would do in California if they didn't till the land.

He'd been right. She didn't want to put her mind to make believe. Telling herself that the wagon train had reached California before the snows fell and trapped the travelers near the summit wouldn't change what had happened. She couldn't bring anyone back to life.

And she couldn't take herself, Daniel, and Elizabeth down off this god-awful mountain.

"Daniel?" she said, watching to see if he would open his eyes. He didn't. She could sense him waiting for her to continue. "Do you have a family?"

"A family?" His body, she thought, tensed slightly. "Why do you ask?"

"I was just thinking about it, that's all." She was being too bold; she should know better. But he now waited for her to continue. "I don't know anything about you. Where you came from, what your life here is like."

"No. You don't know that." His eyes remained closed.

She felt the wall being set in place. Having it there both hurt and made her angry. What wasn't he willing to share about himself? Why? Without him she'd be dead. If he could help her this much, risk his own life, why wouldn't he do away with the barriers? "Anything you want to know about me, I'll tell you," she said.

"I don't, Jessie."

She couldn't speak now that he'd said her name. He pushed himself away from the fire and walked over to her. Silent, he spread a blanket near Elizabeth and lowered himself onto it. He pulled his heavy coat up around his neck and settled himself so that Elizabeth was between them. He tucked one hand under his head for a pillow. The other went over Elizabeth, shielding her from the night. Jessie closed her eyes; they were wet.

Liar.

Daniel felt something digging into his back, probably a chunk of ice. He should pull it out from under him, but if he moved, Jessie might say something. He wanted her to get the rest he knew she desperately needed. If Elizabeth woke during the night, he'd take care of her, do that one little thing for Jessie.

Liar.

He'd told her he wasn't interested in hearing about her life, but that wasn't the truth. In reality, he wanted to know everything about her—how she felt about having to leave her Bible behind, whether she considered herself a horse-woman, if she could handle a weapon, what her room back in Missouri looked like, whether she felt lost in the nothing that surrounded them. If she'd left anyone she loved behind.

But she'd want and deserve to know something about him, and he couldn't do that.

He wished now that he'd insisted on traveling with Salenack and Raymond. The effort might have left him totally blind, but at least he wouldn't be here alone with Jessie—his presence risking her reputation. They wouldn't be forced to talk to each other. And silence wouldn't weigh so heavily on him.

Knowing she had no family waiting for her in the valley made him uneasy. She wasn't that old, maybe twenty. If she was as innocent as he believed, she had no idea of the world she'd soon—God willing—enter. California Territory wasn't a sweep of rich farms and clean-flowing rivers. The land around Sutter's fort was filled with Indians—not all of them peaceful. The settlers who'd come before her, most of them single men, were a rough and hard lot who, like him, had pasts no true woman could condone. The few soldiers not off fighting the Mexicans were little better. If they knew there was an unattached woman around, she would need a benefactor to keep her safe.

That benefactor couldn't, wouldn't be him.

That was what kept him awake, that and the way her voice kept reverberating through him.

By morning Daniel knew Salenack's herbs had done their job. He could see Jessie clearly as she went about washing her face and combing her hair. Something about her hair wasn't right. He studied it. "There's some missing." He indicated the right side near her ear. "What happened?"

Jessie ran her fingers down her hair and pulled the

shortened lock away from the rest. "He cut it. He would have cut it all off if I hadn't run away from him."

"Who? Your father?"

She nodded. "I was handling the team, walking beside them. We were trying to get the wagon up a steep hill. Papa didn't like the way I was doing it and tried to take over. But when he yelled at the horses, they shied and knocked him down. I hadn't done up my hair that day. He said the horses got scared because it was flying all over."

"Do you believe that?"

"No. He'd shoved me away. I wasn't anywhere near the team."

Daniel hated Jessie's father. Just like that, without ever having met the man, he wished he'd been there so he could tell him that he couldn't treat his daughter that way. "It'll grow out."

"I know. Right now—" She tucked her brush back into the small bundle she carried. "All I care about is being able to clean it. It's been so long since it's felt decent. Mama always said that a woman's hair was her crowning glory."

Daniel's thoughts went to a long, lean, dark woman with ink-colored braids flying behind her as she mastered one wild horse after another. He didn't say anything.

Jessie captured her hair with a thin leather thong, then released it so it hung down her back. "We can't stay here much longer. The food—"

"I know," he interrupted, saving her from having to say the rest. Then he told her he believed he could look at the snow without risking his vision. She nodded but said nothing. When she got to her feet, he knew why.

She was weak, so weak she barely had the strength to carry her own weight, let alone Elizabeth. With his belly knotted in concern, he gathered up their belongings, kicked snow over the fire, and prepared to leave. Once again they'd eaten only a few ounces so Elizabeth would have enough. He felt the effect in the way his legs threatened to buckle under him; he was light-headed from lack of food.

But if Jessie thought he couldn't go on, maybe she'd give up. He insisted on carrying Elizabeth, and after a short argument, she gave in. Still, she refused to let him lead the way, saying that with her lighter weight, she would be less likely to founder.

He walked behind her, concentrating on conserving his strength as much as possible, trying not to watch the way her legs worked under the baggy pants as she carefully picked her way up over the frozen surface, following the tracks of those who'd gone ahead of them. He found himself wondering whether there was a dress at the dry goods store that would fit her. Maybe she'd allow him to buy one for her.

He'd never done that for a woman.

She broke the silence, speaking without turning to look at him. Her voice sounded hollow, weak. "Where you live, what is it like? I keep trying, but I can't imagine what Sutter's Fort looks like."

"I don't live at the fort, Jessie. I try not to go there any more than I have to."

"Why not?"

He'd known she was going to ask the question. Still, it took him the better part of a minute to come up with an answer. "Maybe I'm like you. I don't like walls around me."

"But you said you don't have a farm." Her breath sounded labored. He wished she'd stop talking; he was glad she still wanted to know something about him—even if he couldn't tell her everything. "What else is there? Where else do people live?"

"I don't live anywhere, not really. These days I'm in charge of Captain Sutter's cattle. We, the Indians he hired and I, we travel with the herds. Bed is wherever the cattle stop for the night."

"You work for Captain Sutter? I—that isn't what I thought you'd be doing. Oh. Oh my—"

"Jessie?" He tried to catch up with her, but Elizabeth and his pack held him back. "What's wrong?"

"Nothing." She stopped and swiveled, a hand pressed against her midriff as if holding back a pain. Her face had paled, but she held her head up. "I was just trying to think what that's like. You have a bedroll, do you? What about food? Water. Don't you ever want to stay in one place?"

He hadn't. Raised by a woman with gypsy in her soul, he'd spent his childhood constantly exploring, always on the move. "What I want isn't what matters." He wished she'd stop pressing against herself. It scared him because he didn't know what might be wrong with her. "Cattle need a lot of grass, and if we're going to keep bears, wolves, certain Indians away from them, we have to stay with them at all times."

"Bears?" She kneaded her middle. "They're dangerous."

"They can be. Jessie? Are you all right?"

She looked down at herself, following the line of his gaze. A quick smile, so fleeting that he couldn't get a grasp on it, touched her lips. "I thought that maybe if I pressed on my stomach I wouldn't be so hungry."

"Does it work?"

"No."

I'm sorry. I wish there were something, anything I could do about that. He asked if she wanted him to lead, but she turned him down. After a minute, she pulled her elkskin coat up around her neck, trapping her hair beneath the collar, and set the pace.

She kept stumbling. She never said a word when her legs failed her, and he didn't think she expected him to help her to her feet. He hoped not because in truth, it was beyond him. As the long, hungry, cold day stretched out around them, he asked himself impossible questions and faced the hardest of answers.

They might not get out of here alive. Even if the others had left some food for them, it might not be enough to replenish their rapidly decreasing strength. He cursed himself for allowing himself to be talked into stopping to rest his eyes. At the same time, he knew Jessie wouldn't have been able to keep up with Raymond and Salenack.

She was much weaker than Raymond. Although they hadn't said anything about that, he believed he knew why. He'd seen proof of how some at the other cabins had held on. He didn't think Jessie had resorted to that desperate act; that's why she had no reserve, why nothing but will kept her going.

The wind that had come up since dawn slammed into the back of his head, rocking him. Still, he wasn't distracted from his thoughts. He'd come so far, and yet his mission wasn't over. They weren't yet safe. Jessie hadn't cast her eye on the land she was so determined to have for her own. Right now, he couldn't do anything about the others they'd had to leave behind. Jessie and Elizabeth were his responsibility.

Jessie had touched him, somehow, some way.

He made a silent vow to her. He would keep her alive, no matter what it took.

Now that he'd thought about it and given it form, he felt no desire to shrink from the responsibility. Except for his mother—and he'd failed her—he'd never had anyone's life placed in his hands.

With Jessie, that had changed.

He didn't tell her what he was thinking. The truth was, he didn't know what her reaction might be. Raw will kept her going. From what she'd told him about herself, he knew she wasn't a woman to turn her safekeeping over to another human being, a stranger, an outlaw.

Because he believed he understood the forces that ruled her, he would carry his vow deep inside him, a promise of the heart. She'd risked her own death to keep Elizabeth alive. He would do the same for her.

Ahead of him, she swayed, then pitched forward onto her knees. She'd done that before, and each time she'd managed to right herself before he could reach her. But now she sat hunched over, her hair hanging over her shoulder so it almost brushed the snow that trapped her.

He touched her on the back, shocked again at how thin she was through the layers of clothing. "Jessie. It's all right. You can rest."

"No." Her head came up a few inches. "No. We have to find food."

"Stay here. It isn't much further. I'll bring some back to you."

"Not much further?" She turned toward him, and he saw that she had bitten into her lower lip. Her eyes seemed to have sunken inward and the flesh around them had a gray cast.

"Only about a half hour." He wasn't sure that was true, but he had to tell her something. "Stay. Rest. Keep Elizabeth with you and I'll be back before dark."

"No."

She'd cried more than spoken the word. It wasn't until he saw his dark and hardened fingers on her white cheek

that he realized he'd touched her. She didn't flinch or try
to move away. Maybe she needed what little warmth he
could give her. "Jessie," he whispered. "It's all right.
Please believe me. You've done everything you possibly
can." Although he had no right being so familiar, he didn't
step away. At the base of his hand where it rested against
the side of her neck, he felt her blood pulsing in the vein
there.

"No. You said—not much further."

If she'd been a child, he would have ordered her to listen to him, but she'd survived the unsurvivable. Who was
he to tell her what to do now? "No. Not much further." He
pulled his hand away, slowly. It continued to feel warm,
softened somehow. "We'll rest, then we'll go again."

"All right. But for only a few minutes."

How much time passed before she forced herself to
stand up, Jessie couldn't say. She might have fallen asleep;
she couldn't be sure. What she remembered was closing
her eyes, opening them to find Daniel sitting beside her,
closing them again, sensing that he was still there.

He helped her to her feet, and for a moment held on to
her, offering her his side to lean against. She couldn't remember if standing next to someone had ever felt like
this—unsettling, too warm, as if she never wanted it to
end.

"Are you sure?" he asked. The words expanded his
chest, brought them even closer together.

"Yes. Yes."

He tucked Elizabeth in the crook of his arm and then
took Jessie's hand. Without asking what he had in mind,
she let him wrap his fingers firmly around hers. They were
able to walk side by side because they were on a shaded,

treeless slope with thick-packed snow underneath. With each step, they touched.

It shouldn't be. Hadn't her mother told her that if she was to be considered a lady, she should never allow a man to be too familiar with her? Certainly the few men she'd danced with hadn't gone on touching her once the dance was over. But without Daniel there to pass his energy on to her, she knew she wouldn't be able to continue.

Each step took such effort, such time. She thought they'd been traveling longer than he'd told her they'd have to, but she didn't say anything because she needed every ounce of air in her lungs just to keep going. After a while, Daniel led her away from the slope and toward a thicket of trees. She wanted to cry out for him not to leave her side, but even her muddled mind knew that wasn't possible.

Now he led the way, explaining that the snow was uneven here because some had fallen off the trees. He didn't want her to become buried in the drifts. How he kept going, she didn't know. She started counting to herself, measuring off every labored step, telling herself that once she'd reached one hundred she would stop and rest.

She remembered saying fifty-seven. Then, somehow, there was snow in her mouth and more was pressing against her throat.

"Jessie. Jessie. Are you all right?"

She didn't know how to answer his question. Maybe, if he'd tell her what had happened, she could. She tried to get her hands under her so she would have something to lever herself with, but they sank down in the snow, leaving her trapped.

"Don't," he warned when she started to struggle. "Save your strength." She watched as he lowered Elizabeth, warmly bundled, onto the snow and began digging at the white that surrounded her. A minute later he pulled her hands free and rolled her off her stomach and onto her side. She couldn't do a thing to help herself.

"I'm sorry." His thigh was only a few inches from her face. If she moved her head that much, she would be able to rest her head on him. "I'm so sorry."

"Don't be, Jessie." He brushed his hand over the top of her head, soothing her. "Don't apologize."

"Just—" Why was it so hard to think when he touched her? It must have something to do with hunger, weakness, the fear that she'd never leave this place alive. "Just let me rest a few minutes. I promise—"

"No more promises," he whispered, cutting off whatever it was she was trying to say. "You're spent."

He was right. Tears stung her eyes, but she was too tired to even cry. "Go on," she managed. "Take Elizabeth."

"No. Never. Listen to me. We're going to rest a little while." He looked up, his attention drawn to the heavily laden clouds. "Then I want you to hold Elizabeth. I'll carry you."

"What?" She grasped his coat sleeve with all the strength that remained in her. "You can't. It'll kill you."

She might be right, Daniel thought as he struggled to keep his balance with Jessie in his arms. That she managed to hold on to Elizabeth in her half-conscious state amazed him. If she could do that, then surely he could keep his promise. Only, the cost—

His legs trembled—not from the effort of carrying her, because she didn't weigh that much. But with every step, he sank nearly thigh deep in the snow, and the wrench of freeing his legs left him panting.

He didn't think she knew. She had her arms around Elizabeth, her body nestled against his chest. Even when he nearly pitched her into the snow, she didn't lift her head. Twice he tried to speak to her, but it cost him too much and he gave up. Besides, she didn't seem to hear.

She'd nearly cried when she realized how far gone she was. Now he felt like punching something, anything, in frustration. He would have if he had had an ounce of reserve left.

The day was nearly gone. Without daylight he wouldn't be able to find the first precious food cache. They'd have to spend the night without food, since there was nothing left except a little bit for Elizabeth. He hadn't told Jessie that, hoping to spare her as long as possible. But knowing he had nothing to offer her grated at him and kept him going.

Elizabeth began to stir in Jessie's arms and would have fallen if Jessie hadn't grabbed her. Jessie shifted slowly, then stared up at him. "Let me down," she whispered.

"No. You can't—"

"I have to. It's killing you." She glanced down at Elizabeth, then looked at him again. "Daniel, please."

If she'd ordered him, he might have refused her request. But her gentle plea nearly did him in. He stopped, only slightly surprised to discover that his body still swayed. Then he lowered her to the ground. She stumbled, then righted herself. Without saying a word, she touched his cheek as he'd touched her earlier. Her eyes seemed to glitter, but in the dying day, he couldn't be sure. He could hear her breathing. His own breath was labored and painful as the night air slapped at his lungs.

He shook off the discomfort. She'd touched him.

"It wasn't a half hour, Daniel."

"I know." He waited until she'd removed her hand from him, then went on. "But it isn't much further." He pointed. "There, at the Yuba."

She turned from him, straining to see. "Surely? You aren't saying that to keep me going?"

"I promise you." His arms throbbed from the effort of having carried her.

If it hadn't been for the moon, they wouldn't have been able to continue to follow the tracks they'd pursued all day. As it was, Jessie could see only a few feet in front of her. Elizabeth had begun crying, but the baby would have to wait. If they stopped now, she wasn't sure either she or Daniel could move again.

Food. The thought filled her legs with unexpected strength. Still, she knew that if Daniel hadn't carried her while she recovered a little, not even the promise of sweet cakes and honey could have kept her going now. She remembered little of that time in his arms, wished she could hold on to more.

Honey? Would there be a hive on her farm? If so, she could use it to sweeten the breads she planned to bake. Bread, and pies. Her mouth watered; she thought of picking ripe berries and then cooking them.

An oven. She'd started her journey with her precious Dutch oven, but it, like so much, had been swept away when they tried to ford some nameless river before the fateful climb into the mountains. Others had told her she'd be able to purchase another from Captain Sutter, but since none of them had laid eyes on the man, who was to know whether they were right?

She wanted to believe. With an oven, she could bake pies and present them to Daniel.

Daniel. She felt him behind her, his bulk seeming to block a little of the wind that had dogged them for hours. She might never be able to tell him how much she owed him, but she could give him a pie, vegetables, bread.

Would she even see him in California?

Unable to deal with the question, she turned her attention to breathing onto Elizabeth's face to keep her warm.

Elizabeth had family, an aunt and uncle. Surely they would want to raise the little orphan. But without Elizabeth—without Elizabeth she'd be alone, truly alone.

It was what she wanted, wasn't it?

The way it had to be for her heart to go on beating.

Would Daniel ever want to come see her farm?

Or would his work take him far from her?

She heard him breathing but was unable to tell how much strength remained in him. One moment he plodded behind her; the next, he'd pulled alongside, sinking into the soft snow surrounding the tracks. "There." He pointed toward a thicket of pine trees in a narrow valley ahead of them. "That's it."

It. The precious food that would keep them alive. Despite her urgency, Jessie allowed Daniel to step around her and plunge ahead. She clutched Elizabeth to her. "It's all right now, sweet baby. Everything's going to be all right."

Daniel ducked under a low branch, momentarily out of view. Still, Jessie half plodded, half ran after him. She'd pushed the branch out of the way and was casting around for him when she heard him curse.

Her heart thudded against her chest; she couldn't breathe.

"Daniel? What is it?"

"Wild animals. They've taken everything."

CHAPTER 6

Daniel! Where are you?

The thought shook her, pulled her out of that nothing place where she'd been. Jessie turned her head slowly, amazed that she could do even that. She saw light, a small pocket of brilliance in a shadowy world.

It seemed as if she'd been in that world for days now, but that couldn't be right, could it? Maybe.

Her body felt hot, then cold, then both. *Daniel. Something—something about Daniel.* After a minute, she reached out her hand, fully expecting to touch snow. Instead, her fingers rested on rough and tightly woven fibers. Fascinated now, she traced the design. The mat under her consisted of a large number of connecting squares.

She blinked and concentrated on the light. Like whatever she'd touched, the light source too was square.

A window?

She tried to sit up. There were a number of blankets over her; they felt so heavy. But more than just the presence of blankets surprised and confused her. She was warm. Whatever she lay on felt wonderfully soft, not at all like icy snow.

Daniel.

As more and more of her surroundings came to her, Jessie again tried to reach a sitting position. This time, after pushing the blankets off her chest, she accomplished the simple and yet massive task.

The room—yes, a room—felt cold. Still, because of the wool that had been draped over her, her entire body still felt toasty.

She ran her hand through her hair, the movement hampered by a mass of tangles. Her hair hadn't been washed.

How could it? She'd had precious little soap or warm water while in the mountains and she knew she hadn't even thought of her hair in the last few days.

She wasn't hungry.

Snatches of the past few days surfaced. She remembered crying from exhaustion, forcing herself to stop because tears solved nothing, changed nothing. Daniel telling her they had no choice but to go on. Then—then they walked until she couldn't possibly take another step and still they kept moving. Elizabeth cried, then fell silent.

Elizabeth! Was she alive?

Jessie forced her legs under her and tried to stand. She stumbled forward and stopped only when she braced her hands against a cold, stonelike wall. She tried to make sense of it all, but the memories continued.

Daniel had seldom said anything, but when he did, it

was to encourage her with gentle, understanding, yet firm words. They had to keep going. They had to.

How long had they walked, their stomachs empty? She thought another night had passed, but it might have been more than that. Her feet had felt swollen in the wet boots, and her arms were on fire from Elizabeth's weight.

And then—had it been night or day when the others came?

Jessie's hands felt cold. She pulled them off the wall, tested her legs for a moment, then slumped back onto her bed. She saw now that she'd been lying on a thick ticking of some kind and that the floor was carpeted with tightly woven fibers in an intricate, square design. The blankets had been spun from wool so new that they still smelled of sheep.

She buried her nose in the wool, breathing in scents from home, thinking of newborn lambs in love with life and energy and freedom. Alive! She was alive!

She was in some kind of room. It was at least twice as long as it was wide, the width not much more than what she could span with her outstretched arms. There were panes of glass in the single window.

Glass?

How wonderful.

Whatever she was wearing threatened to slip off her shoulder. She shoved it back up around her neck before examining it. The neckline was too wide for her narrow frame, but as best she could tell, it wasn't overly long. Except for the loose-fitting sleeves, it hung in a single sweep from her armpits down to her feet. She touched the hem. Calico, clean, soft, wonderful.

Who had dressed her in this? What had happened to her own clothes? What miracle had brought her here, and who did she need to thank for the incredible kindnesses she'd been shown?

After resting a minute, Jessie stood again. This time, although she had to shake her head at how wobbly she felt, she believed her legs would hold her. The room felt cold, a deep, dark cold. When she glanced around, she understood why. There was no stove. In truth, there was barely enough space for one. After wrapping one of the blankets over her shoulders, she walked in stockinged feet over to the heavy wooden door and tested the metal latch. It lifted, but she didn't try to step outside. Dressed the way she was, barefoot, it wasn't seemly.

Breathing deeply, she focused again on the room in an effort to pull even more together. She might have been dreaming or delirious, but she thought she remembered a woman kneeling over her, washing her face, encouraging her to eat.

The woman had helped her pull off her ruined clothes and then guided her into the muslin nightdress. Her hands had been so gentle, her voice reassuring. "You're all right," she'd said again and again. "You're all right."

Daniel.

Why, if she could remember a woman's kindness, couldn't she piece together what had happened to Daniel since those strange and burdened men, their faces drawn and determined, found them half-dead?

Had Daniel died? Had help come too late for him?

The horrible question came close to overwhelming her. Still, she didn't try to hide from it. Someone, somewhere would give her the answers she needed. And if—if Daniel was dead, she would cope.

Feeling a sense of urgency now along with another emotion that had begun building inside her, unsettling her and making her restless, she left the door and walked over to a wooden shelf that had been fastened to the wall with metal pegs. The shelf held a couple of empty whiskey jugs, three worn cast-iron pots, a cracked butter churn, and several intricately woven baskets stacked one inside another. The room, she now noticed, also held a small wooden table and a well-crafted wooden chair. She marveled at the workmanship of whoever had made them.

"There's been so many people staying here. These things belong to them."

Remembering the high-pitched voice of the woman who'd helped her, Jessie felt less uneasy. If she could remember her saying that, surely she would remember if Daniel and Elizabeth were dead. She searched her heart and found pain and loss, sad memories of those who'd died in that place high in the mountains, but of Daniel and Elizabeth she felt nothing.

Where were they? She remembered—being given something to eat by the men who'd found them, being told she must continue to follow the trail made by those who'd gone ahead of them, that she'd have to do it on her own because—because why?

Why hadn't Daniel stayed with her and Elizabeth?

Jessie had been standing with her back to the room as she studied the shelf's contents. In that short amount of time, it seemed as if the room had started to move inward, squeezing in on her. She whirled, nearly losing her footing. The walls, stark and cold, fortresslike, made her shiver. The door looked so heavy that if it had been locked there would have been no way she could break free. The window wasn't large enough. The air in the room smelled stale and trapped. Hurrying now, Jessie reached the window and pressed her face against the glass. No snow. Praise be, no snow!

She blinked and looked again, marveling at what

seemed a miracle. Beyond her room, she saw a large, winter-grayed courtyard ringed by walls and rooms made from the same stone that her walls had been constructed from.

There were people and activity everywhere, Indians in deerskin laying planks on the ground near these walls, a number of ill-dressed soldiers, two mud-coated boys walking hand in hand. The boys looked so healthy, so strong. One of them turned toward the other and punched him on the shoulder. The other punched back, causing the first to land on his knees in the mud. They both laughed. Laughing!

A short, solidly built man came into view driving a number of mud-browned sheep ahead of him. One obviously pregnant ewe kept trying to head toward a lean-to piled high with hay. There seemed to be as many horses as people. They were shaggy-looking beasts, some with saddles, some without, most apparently free to roam wherever they wanted. At one end of the great yard she spotted a large, raised, cone-shaped object. A thin spiral of smoke drifted up from the top of the cone. As she watched, a man approached the structure and reached deep into it. He removed something—bread, loaves of bread. Her mouth watered; if it hadn't been for her attire and the human and animal gauntlet she'd have to traverse to reach him, she would have asked for a piece. As the man passed out of view, a huge, smoldering campfire near the oven caught her attention. A black pot of some kind, nearly large enough for a person to bathe in, sat to one side of the coals. A heavily bearded man who'd been standing nearby looked into the pot, then walked away.

Fort Sutter?

She was at Fort Sutter?

If this wasn't a dream, then it was a miracle, and she'd been given another chance at life.

Although she continued to stare out, now aware of a slight yet growing tension inside her, the courtyard became less distinct in her mind. Maybe standing on the hard ground with its thin woven covering was making her too cold to think properly of salvation and who she wanted to thank. After a moment, her head stopped pounding, and she knew this new emotion went beyond reacting to the chill.

Something was pulling her away, back up the mountain.

Memories. Daniel telling her to do as the newcomers ordered, that he had to go with them, that if she remained strong, she and Elizabeth would reach Raymond and Salenack and the others who'd gone ahead of them. She would be safe. He couldn't help her anymore; he'd done all he could. There were others still trapped, and strong men willing and ready to help.

He had to go with them.

At the sound of the door latch lifting, Jessie spun away from the window, away from the scene inside her head.

"Miss Speer. How wonderful to see you on your feet."

"Mrs. Buckhalter." The woman's name came easily to Jessie's lips. She remembered her holding Elizabeth, giving her her breast. Thank God Elizabeth was alive.

The buxom woman, who looked to be around thirty, closed the door behind her and presented Jessie with a cloth-covered basket. The aroma of freshly baked bread filled the room. Instantly, Jessie's head cleared. She felt like laughing, crying, hugging anyone who came close.

"There are a number of benefits to be gained from being married to Captain Sutter's personal cook," Mrs. Buckhalter explained. "I told my husband that I wanted his finest loaf for you."

Jessie placed her hand over the loaf; her fingers became warm and moist. "This is wonderful. You didn't have to—"

"I wanted to, my dear. You must know that. Are you sure you feel up to standing?"

Now that Mrs. Buckhalter mentioned it, her legs did feel as if she'd been walking for days.

Walking. That's where she'd last seen Daniel, walking away from her.

He'd been alive when they parted; she was certain of that now. Only, why had he left her and Elizabeth? Why was it more important for him to do as those men ordered than remain with her? Struggling with questions, Jessie sat down and watched as Mrs. Buckhalter removed the cloth covering. The round loaf was a golden brown, shiny from having been basted with butter. Her mouth again watered. She wanted to cry and laugh from the pure joy of smelling something so wonderful. "Oh. This is— It's been so long. Won't you join me?" she asked.

"I believe I will." Mrs. Buckhalter plopped down next to Jessie on the ticking and crossed her legs like a carefree child. "I told my husband I wanted fresh butter on the loaf he made for you. He's a good man, tries so hard to please me since I did *not* want to come here. It's a hard land, not for the weak. But he was determined. What choice did I have?"

Jessie wanted to know more about Mrs. Buckhalter, more about everything that had happened since Daniel led her away from what might have become her grave and toward freedom. But she was afraid she might ask questions that Mrs. Buckhalter had already supplied the answers for and the woman would think she was unhinged.

Maybe she was.

What did she care? The Heavenly Father had taken her

under his care, answered her prayers. Soon—soon she would stand on her own land and nourish life into the soil.

"This is wonderful," Jessie exclaimed, her mouth full. "I haven't tasted anything like this for so long."

"But you have, my dear." Mrs. Buckhalter grinned at her and yanked impatiently at her mud-splotched skirt. "This everlasting rain. How hungry I am for spring. You and I went through most of a loaf fully this large yesterday."

"We did? I'm sorry, I don't remember."

"That's all right. I think it's to be expected. Yesterday I had to keep reminding you to eat. It was as if your mind was asleep while your body fought to live. If I'd endured what you did— I'm just so glad Mr. Reed and the men he'd brought with him had enough food to share to keep you going. When I think of what might have happened if you'd gone without for much longer—" She shuddered.

Mr. Reed. He was part of the rapidly snowballing memories. Suppressing a shudder of her own, Jessie pulled up an image of Mr. Reed and a number of men, all strangers, all strong and healthy, coming up the trail toward her, Elizabeth, and Daniel. Bringing them back from the brink of starvation.

"Miss Speer? Are you all right?"

Jessie blinked back the uncertain image and turned to another, clearer, fresher in her mind. "Oh yes. You've done so much for me—" She remembered a soft voice encouraging her to drink warm milk, hardworking hands tucking blankets around her. "I don't know how to thank you."

"By putting on some decent clothes and walking about. You'd like that, wouldn't you?"

More than she dared to say. "My clothes? I didn't see

them. Where are they?" She broke off another piece of bread.

"Those things. I threw them away. Except for your coat, nothing was fit for rags even."

Suddenly Jessie felt cold. "I had some things in my coat pocket. Personal things."

"I know." Mrs. Buckhalter squeezed her hand. "Your brush. All those seeds. And the bag with your coins. I have them safely with me. You never know—" She nodded to indicate the compound beyond the window. "So many strangers come through here, so many rough men without conscience or compassion. I couldn't watch you every minute. Elizabeth and my own children needed me. I thought your belongings would be safer with Mr. Buckhalter and me."

"Thank you. The money, the seeds, they're everything I have."

"Almost everything," Mrs. Buckhalter said with a gentle smile. Then she handed her the tightly wrapped bundle that had been tucked under her arm. "These are some of my things. I wish I could give you new, but that's nearly impossible here. The dress fit before I had my first child. Since then—" She sighed. "Having a baby changes a woman's figure, you know." She pressed a hand to her ample bosom. "Thank the Lord I have a plentiful supply of milk."

"Yes, thank the Lord," Jessie echoed. "How is Elizabeth?"

"A delightful creature. Good heavens, can she kick. And cry."

"I know. I think she frightened off the wolves."

Mrs. Buckhalter tapped the bundle that now rested beside Jessie. "Why don't you get dressed? I'll wait outside so no one will surprise you. Then, if you're strong enough, I'll show you Sutter's fort."

Jessie felt weaker than she wanted to admit by the time she'd put on the simple too-large dress and run-down moccasins Mrs. Buckhalter had supplied. If she had cared about husbanding her strength, she would have put off going outside a little longer. But the walls now felt as if they were closing in on her. She could hardly wait to breathe fresh air, to lift her hands toward the sky.

Only, when she stepped outside, what she pulled into her lungs wasn't what she could call fresh. The air smelled of damp winter, livestock, wood smoke, ill-tanned leather, unwashed bodies. Sounds—they surrounded her, making it impossible for her to sort one from another. After so many weeks, months, of silence, the din of dozens of voices beat upon her ears. Because Mrs. Buckhalter was waiting for her just beyond the heavy door, at least she didn't feel lost.

"Thank you." She indicated the dress. "It's wonderful. To be able to wear something so clean—"

"Not wonderful, I'm afraid, but I'm delighted to be able to do anything for you. Well, is it what you expected?"

The day was cold, gray, foggy, just as Daniel had told her it would be. Despite the joy of being alive, she felt hemmed in by the fog, by the masses of people after seeing so few for so long now. She didn't want to tell Mrs. Buckhalter that. "Where I'm staying, what is it?"

"One of the rooms Captain Sutter had built for his visitors, settlers, men he does business with. There are nine rooms, at the moment all filled with the people you were with."

"They're all right?" She thought of Raymond, Salenack, little Naomi Pike, Mrs. Reed and her two oldest children, young William Murphy with his frostbitten feet, the rest.

Mrs. Buckhalter didn't quite meet her gaze. "Most of them."

"And—what about those we had to leave behind? Is there any word of their rescue?"

"None yet. But we are all praying."

Jessie lifted her head, searching the gray sky for a glimpse of sunlight. If she had her Bible with her, she would have turned to it for comfort. Daniel, and other men, had gone back for them. He hadn't failed her; he wouldn't fail now. "I pray we won't have to wait much longer."

"Amen. There's nothing you can do for them now, though. Getting your strength back, that's the most important thing."

That and being able to move around, to eat what I want, to wait for spring. To feel safe. "It feels so good to be outside," she admitted. She meant it, with every fiber in her. Still, she felt as if the people and livestock all around them might at any moment overwhelm her. She breathed deeply, hoping to clear her head.

"I thought it might. You seemed so restless; I could barely keep covering on you. Watch your footing," Mrs. Buckhalter warned. "The water simply can't sink into the ground fast enough. The Indians have put down planks for folks to walk on, but they're scant protection. Everything is so terribly muddy what with everyone churning things up. Would you like to see where my husband spends his time? I promise we'll go slow. If you feel faint, we'll stop."

Although her need to ask about Daniel pressed like a weight on her heart, she agreed with Mrs. Buckhalter's suggestion that exercise would do her good. Daniel hadn't come with her; he'd gone instead back up the mountain with Mr. Reed and the others, a silent prisoner to—to what?

Why couldn't she remember why she thought of him as a prisoner?

Had he tried to hide things from her, leaving her with nothing except his tension, his anger?

When Mrs. Buckhalter touched her elbow, Jessie fought to let go of her final sight of Daniel—tight-lipped, looking trapped. "This is the flour mill." Mrs. Buckhalter pointed at an open room to their right. Inside something that resembled a stable was a massive, round white stone with a long wooden pole lashed to the top. Below it was an identical stone. The two had been secured in a wood-and-brick-bottomed box. An Indian, his buckskin shirt white-dusted, leaned into the pole, slowly turning the stone wheel. "Without wheat for bread, the captain's cavalry and foot soldiers would probably desert."

Jessie sensed eyes on her. She glanced over her shoulder. Instantly, she realized she was the object of more than casual interest from a number of folks, the great majority of them men. Did they know who she was, what she'd endured? "I—was told Captain Sutter has an army. It's really necessary?"

"I'm afraid it is," Mrs. Buckhalter said as an Indian boy, half-naked, sprinted past in pursuit of a scrawny dog. She indicated a massive wooden gate fully eighteen feet high with a double arch of spikes overhead. The equally high fort walls had the look of stone. The two longest sides Jessie guessed to be over three hundred feet in length. If she needed to run, to feel free—

"What is that?" She indicated the great walls. "Those aren't rocks. They're so perfectly formed."

"Rocks? No. The Indians Captain Sutter hired made bricks for the walls from clay and straw. It took years. But now—now no one except those Captain Sutter approves of can enter." Mrs. Buckhalter inclined her head, coolly acknowledging a huge, heavily bearded man a few feet away. She said nothing to him. Jessie became aware of a sudden tension in the other woman.

"Indians?" Jessie pressed. The man was looking at her, his eyes bold, not on her face, but her breasts. She turned away, determined to continue her conversation with Mrs. Buckhalter. "Then—Captain Sutter has made friends with them?"

"Not all of the Indians can be trusted. Or the Mexicans." Mrs. Buckhalter leaned close to Jessie, whispering into her ear. "Or any of these rough men. I should have warned you; no decent woman is safe from their attention."

Before Jessie could think of what to say, Mrs. Buckhalter grabbed her arm and pointed excitedly. "There he is."

Daniel?

The straight-backed horseman who'd just passed through the open gate wore a cape and plain blue frock coat. His forehead was high and his mustache neatly trimmed. He seemed to be around forty years of age, a little soft around the middle. Still, from the way he carried himself, it was plain that he held a sense of responsibility and pride for what surrounded him.

"Captain Sutter?" Jessie guessed.

"He left early this morning. My husband wasn't sure he'd be back before nightfall, but the captain has enemies. He prefers to spend the night in his own quarters, next to the guardroom."

"He owns all of this. And the land beyond?" The words came out soft, disbelieving.

"If he is to be believed, he does."

Jessie turned toward Mrs. Buckhalter. "But I thought—"

"I know. Everyone who comes here believes he is nearly a king. And he does own a great deal, has accomplished a great many things, but he is not a man without debts."

"Still—" Jessie couldn't take her eyes off the captain and his entourage of Indian soldiers. "Without his help, those brave men who came up after us wouldn't have had the means to attempt a rescue. Mr. Reed told me that."

"True. True." Mrs. Buckhalter's eyes remained sober. Without asking Jessie whether she minded, she led her to a low-roofed shelter half-filled with firewood. Mrs. Buckhalter sat on one stack and indicated that Jessie should sit down beside her. As she did, Jessie felt her legs quiver. She might be a hundred times stronger than she'd been when Daniel had to carry her, but she still had a long way to go. Her weakness made it impossible for her to concentrate fully on her surroundings, or how she should react to the curious looks being cast her way.

"You called out a name last night."

Jessie didn't quite know how to respond to Mrs. Buckhalter's quick, whispered words. "I—did."

"The name of the man you were with when Mr. Reed and the others found you."

Daniel. "Yes." Jessie's breath caught. Warned by the tone in Mrs. Buckhalter's voice, she chose her words carefully. "I suppose I did. He saved my life, after all."

"And forced you to remain alone with him."

Jessie shook her head vigorously, ignoring a sharp pain in her temple. "It wasn't like that. He'd become snow-blind. Carrying Elizabeth, I was too weak to keep up with the others. We had no choice but to go at our own pace."

"I saw how exhausted you were. But there was no other way? You couldn't have asked anyone else to remain with you?"

At that time, there'd only been Salenack and Raymond, but she didn't try to tell Mrs. Buckhalter that. The woman wanted to discuss something but didn't quite know how to bring it up. Until she better understood, she would be careful with her own words. "Mrs. Buckhalter, when Mr. Reed and his men found us, Daniel and I were half-dead. I—"

"Daniel?"

Was that it? Mrs. Buckhalter was suspecting the worst? "He was a gentleman."

Mrs. Buckhalter stared at her feet as she traced a circle in the wood chips that littered the ground. "I'm simply thinking of your reputation, Miss Speer. It won't be easy for you here."

"I know that."

"Yes." She indicated the big, bearded man, who hadn't moved from his post near the huge cooking pot. "I'm sure you already do. I just wish it had been anyone else up there with you."

"Anyone except Daniel Bear? Why?"

The circle became larger. "Maybe you'll never see him again."

"Maybe." What was this about?

"I hope so." Mrs. Buckhalter patted her hand. From somewhere in the middle of the courtyard came an angry shout, loud enough that it overrode the other sounds. "Oh, I hope so."

After she felt a little stronger, Jessie accompanied Mrs. Buckhalter to the kitchen with its large work space and long bench where people ate during bad weather.

Mr. Buckhalter loved to talk. His continual chatter about everything, from how glad he was that his employer had moved the evil-smelling tannery several miles from the fort to his opinions on what the Donner party could have done to prevent tragedy, gave Jessie little time to wonder about Mrs. Buckhalter's comment that she hoped Daniel was out of her life.

Despite her sense of wonder about where she was and what she'd seen today, she was beginning to feel a little light-headed when fourteen-year-old Virginia Reed came in with a bearded, buckskin-clad man close behind her. The moment Jessie recognized the eldest Reed child, she scrambled to her feet and clasped the girl to her breast. The last time she'd seen Virginia, she'd been one of the brave, tight-lipped survivors she and Elizabeth had caught up with after leaving Daniel. Although thin and pale, Virginia looked healthy—and confused by the attention from the young man beside her.

"I've been looking for you," Virginia exclaimed. "Praying you were all right."

"I am," Jessie assured her. "And your mother?"

"She's fine." Virginia's face sobered. "Praying that Papa finds the little ones before it's too late for them."

"We're all praying," Mr. Buckhalter cut in. "You've come for something to eat, have you?"

Virginia nodded shyly. "For me and my brother and mother, if you don't mind."

"Not at all." Mr. Buckhalter ladeled meat and onions from a large pot into three tin cups, then handed one to Virginia and the other two to the young man. "It does my heart good to see you up and about." He indicated Virginia's companion. "And I don't believe I'm the only one."

Virginia blushed and muttered something Jessie didn't

catch before leaving with the attentive young man. "Isn't she attractive?" Mrs. Buckhalter said. "Believe me, she has turned the heads of half the men here."

Jessie frowned. "She's only fourteen. Still a girl."

"True. But it's different in California than back home. Under normal circumstances, I would want Miss Virginia to wait until she's older. But she needs protection from the rough sorts. Her beau is an educated man. He'll do well by her. He won't let anything happen to her."

Jessie didn't know whether anything was expected of her by way of response. She hoped not. Although she hated being so weak, she knew she needed to lie down. She barely made it back to her feet and wasn't sure her legs would hold her during the long walk to a bed.

"You've overdone." Mrs. Buckhalter took her arm and gave her something to lean on. "I should have thought— You aren't going to faint on me, are you?"

"No," Jessie said, although she wasn't sure. "I just wish I had more strength."

"You will. Give yourself a little more time. Come now. We'll get you right back." Before Jessie could say a word, if she was going to, Mrs. Buckhalter had her through the door and was forging a path through those who'd chosen the planks to stand on. Jessie saw a blur of faces, heard sounds without meaning. If she hadn't had Mrs. Buckhalter's arm to lean on, she wasn't sure she'd have been able to keep her feet under her.

Still, when she spotted the dark, heavy door that led to her room, she couldn't make herself take that final step. Instead, she stood before it, breathing deeply, trying to clear her head. What was wrong with her? Maybe—maybe she could buy a horse and ride out someplace where there were no walls, no doors.

"Miss Speer?" Mrs. Buckhalter asked. "What is it?"

"I—don't know. I'm afraid to go inside."

"Afraid? Whatever are you talking about? You need to rest, where prying and overly bold men can't stare at you."

Mrs. Buckhalter was right. Certainly she and the other survivors must be objects of great curiosity.

She turned, slowly, carefully. She thought she felt even more eyes on her than she had before, but it might just be her overworked imagination. If she stepped inside the small, cold room and closed the door behind her, she would have privacy.

"Jessie."

At the sound of Raymond's voice, she half staggered. Before Mrs. Buckhalter could catch her, she straightened. Raymond waited for a man on horseback to pass, then carefully made his way along the half-buried planks toward her. He wore clothes she'd never seen on him before: blue trousers, a loose buckskin tunic much like the one Salenack had worn. She thought he'd trimmed his beard. Although flyaway, his hair was clean. His arms were too thin and his dull eyes had a sunken look. Still, he no longer walked hunched over.

"Raymond." No matter that they'd argued over the Allsetters' money, that she'd had moments when she didn't believe she dared leave him alone with Elizabeth, she was relieved to see him looking much recovered. "I asked about you. Mrs. Buckhalter said you were rapidly regaining your strength."

He nodded, his hair seeming to float in the air. His eyes remained riveted on her, taking her back—to the nightmare. "I wanted to see you yesterday and the day before, but they said you needed to be left alone."

Wondering if Raymond had tried to assert himself to Mrs. Buckhalter as he'd done with her, she turned her attention to the other woman. Mrs. Buckhalter was smiling at Raymond. "Simply because I knew how weak she was, Mr. Sage. I trust you'll agree that I've done well by her."

"I do indeed." Raymond's eyes traveled from Jessie's hair to her moccasins. "You need decent shoes, Jessie. Surely there must be some for sale."

"I don't know." Her light-headedness hadn't gone away. If anything, it was becoming even harder to ignore. "I'm grateful for anything I have. Just being alive is so wonderful. Your things?" She indicated Raymond's leather belt. "Were you able to purchase them?"

Raymond's features clouded, so quick, so furtively, that Jessie didn't think Mrs. Buckhalter had seen. "Until I've secured a position for myself, I must make due with charity. But it won't be much longer."

How did he know that? Before Jessie could voice her question, Raymond smiled, the gesture as fleeting as the earlier, unsettling one had been. She felt chilled by it. "I have already spoken to Captain Sutter. He's most impressed with my skills, as are others. I plan on eating with the captain tonight, and showing him my sketches. It won't be long, Jessie, before I'm able to offer you proper protection."

Mrs. Buckhalter's breath escaped in a sharp burst. She looked from Jessie to Raymond, then back to Jessie. "Thank heavens," she whispered when Jessie couldn't form a sound. "I was so worried, thinking about you alone, without a man to care for you."

"I don't need—" Had it suddenly gotten foggier? Jessie blinked, unable to wipe the gray curtain from her vision.

"You don't know," Mrs. Buckhalter said. "This isn't your farm, your nice, safe farm. A woman without a decent man to look after her here, oh my, you just don't know."

"I want . . ." Why couldn't she remember the rest of what

she'd been going to say? She felt Mrs. Buckhalter's grip on her arm tighten and didn't protest when she was led inside. She half sat, half collapsed on the bed and let her head fall back. She stared up, seeing Mrs. Buckhalter's worried face. Raymond crouched nearby, his features blurred.

It wasn't Raymond she wanted to see.

CHAPTER 7

"**D**o you want to risk your life?"

"If I was going to die, it would have happened up there."

"That is not what I am talking about, Daniel. Surely she has people caring for her. Your reputation ... They will not allow you around her."

Daniel cut off Chief Narcisco's words with an angry jerk of his shoulder. The quick movement jarred his still weak body. What did he expect? Because Mr. Reed had both begged and coerced him, he'd given that damn mountain another month of his life. "I'm not the only man in the Sacramento Valley with a price on his head."

"No." Chief Narcisco drew out the word. He stepped

away from where he'd been standing beside Daniel's raised pole-frame bed and picked up a tightly woven cone-shaped basket. He drank from the basket, then handed it to Daniel. "But I have seen the look on men's faces when you approach them. I hear what they say about you, their distrust. Their fear even. Captain Sutter will not want you near a woman under his care."

Daniel propped himself up on his elbow and swallowed warm water. Sitting in his friend's dark, underground home, he could almost believe he'd spent the winter here, almost. "I have to see for myself that she's all right." Narcisco stared at him, features immobile, grave. "She is all right, isn't she?" The instant the words were out, he regretted them. A few days ago, he'd begged his friend to go to Fort Sutter, to ask about her, to watch. At that time, Daniel had been so weak and bone-cold that all he could do was sleep, half-dead. Now, strengthened by dried salmon and acorn meal and the end to wind and snow tearing at him, he only wanted to forget what he'd endured and seen and done since he last saw Jessie.

Jessie. Had her eyes and hair and flesh been touched by sunlight?

"She is stronger than you, my friend. She cares for the baby girl and, they tell me, has already spoken with Captain Sutter about what he should do so his garden will produce more."

"I hope he listens to her." Daniel slid off the bed. His feet landed on warm earth. He ran his hands down his bare chest, feeling sweat. He barely glanced at the elaborate arrangement of long, sturdy poles that acted as the hut's frame. The first time Narcisco invited him in, he'd been filled with questions about his friend's home. Now he took the combination smoke hole and entry overhead for granted and no longer stared in wonder at the array of baskets used for everything from storing acorns to gambling trays. "Did she say anything about me?"

"I did not talk to her, Daniel. I told you that."

Had he? As late as yesterday, little had mattered except sleeping. "But you saw her? She looks all right?"

"Daniel. Think what you are saying. This woman has touched you. It is not wise."

Not wise? Maybe. No, he thought, gritting his teeth. Narciso, a chief of the Maidu tribe, a man trusted by Captain Sutter, didn't speak his mind unless he held a firm belief. "I worry about her. That's all, worry," he said, hoping the explanation would satisfy his friend. "The last time I saw her, she looked half-dead."

"The way you looked when I brought you here." Narciso handed Daniel his buckskin pants. "A wise man would not have climbed that mountain another time. Maybe you left your wisdom up there."

"I couldn't take the chance of refusing."

Narciso grunted. "I think that would be a terrible thing, always wondering when my freedom might be taken away."

It was. If it hadn't been for the price on his head, Daniel would never have allowed himself to be forced into returning to the mountain pass. It wasn't that he didn't care about those still up there. He did, deeply. But Mr. Reed needed strong men with him, not someone in his condition. In the end, though, strengthened by a little food, he'd done as he was ordered, tight-lipped, tense, and angry.

The bargain had been simple and unspoken. His freedom in exchange for guiding Mr. Reed's party.

He wondered if Jessie remembered any of that.

Narciso squatted before the fire and dipped a spoon carved from an elk antler into his acorn gruel. He ate slowly, brown eyes flashing in a broad, heavy face. Firelight glinted off his bare torso and short, sleek hair. "I will never understand white men. They fight among themselves. They spend much time arguing over who should have rule over another. They want what belongs to someone else."

Daniel had heard Narcisco's opinions of whites before. He suspected that most of what the chief said came because he wanted to see his reaction. Any other time he would have argued with him, as Narcisco obviously wanted. But he couldn't concentrate today.

It had only a little to do with the weakness that was slowly seeping out of his body.

"I have to go there. See—"

"Daniel, it is over. You have done enough."

He shook his head. "She doesn't have any family."

"It isn't you she needs, my friend. Think. Did any white man offer you shelter when you returned? No. They turned their backs on you. You might be dead if I had not been waiting for you."

"I appreciate that. More than—"

"You have said thank you, Daniel. I do not need to hear it again." Narcisco, if he had counted right, was not yet thirty. Today, when he frowned, he looked much older. "I see you as a friend. A man who tames wild horses and rides bulls, who listens when I tell him of Coyote and the healer of the sick. Sometimes I think you should have been born a Maidu. Surely you are not one of them, the white men."

"I used to be."

"I did not know you then. I see a man without a place to sleep among what should be his people. Now he wants to reach out to one of them. It is not wise. It could bring you grief."

"That has to be my decision."

"Does it? What if you bring her grief, Daniel? Do you want that?"

A sense of energy, of things happening, filled Fort Sutter. It was as if the time for hibernation had ended along with the rains. Daniel, intent on what had brought him here, ignored the knots of people. Few paid any attention to him. For now, he was invisible, free to move about. He'd been given access by the Ochecamnes gate guards who recognized him. Leaving his horse tied just inside, he struck off on foot, taking little note of the drying mud. Narcisco had told him which room he'd watched Jessie enter. Daniel had only one thought—to see her, ask her how she was.

And then to tell her he wouldn't be seeing her again.

The door was open. For a moment he stared at it, feeling as trapped as he had when Mr. Reed's party asked him to guide them through the pass. He'd complied because he couldn't turn his back on what they were asking. Not that much had changed today. He couldn't walk away from Jessie, not yet.

He stepped inside, looked around. Except for a few pieces of furniture, the small, cool, rectangular room was empty. For a moment he simply stood, trying to find Jessie in it. Someone had placed a mattress on the floor and covered it with woolen blankets. On the small, battered dresser was a woman's dress, faded and worn but clean. A water pitcher, half-full, shared the same space. He stepped closer and pulled the top dresser drawer open. It was empty.

Frowning now, he turned his attention to the rest of the room. He'd been in here once when he'd had to wait out a storm and Captain Sutter had offered him his hospitality. The wall shelf's contents hadn't changed—castoffs left behind by previous visitors. If Jessie was still staying here, she hadn't done anything to make it hers.

Wouldn't she want to do that?

After closing the outside door, he held up the dress. It looked too large for Jessie. Maybe she'd gone to live with Elizabeth's aunt and uncle, waiting for spring to settle in before placing her mark on the land. If so, he'd ride out to see how she was. He'd tell her a little of what he'd done after they parted, keeping the words as simple as possible. She'd show him where she was living now and introduce him to the people who'd taken her in. They'd talk some about her plans and then—and then he'd wish her well and go back to his life.

The thought pushed through him like a strong, wet wind. He laid the dress back on the dresser and tasted the water in the pitcher. It was fresh and cold. Only half-aware of what he was doing, he opened the second drawer. In it, he found Jessie's brush. After a moment of indecision, he touched it, caught a dark hair between his fingers, lifted the long strand, let it flutter to the floor.

Then he opened the door and stepped back outside. He stood, slowly scanning his surroundings. It had rained for days on end since he'd last been here, rain when he'd endured what seemed like an endless snowstorm. There didn't seem to be an inch of ground that hadn't been touched by the downpour, and yet, because winter had lost its teeth and there was a little warmth in the constant wind, the mud underneath his feet was drying.

What did Jessie wear on her feet these days? Her boots had been all but ruined. Had someone given her something decent? That might explain the dress; she'd had to rely on charity for the clothes on her back. He had a few coins of his own and no desire to purchase land the way she did.

Maybe he'd buy her a bolt of calico. No one else had to know; her reputation wouldn't be tarnished.

His attention was drawn to the big-bellied man picking his way through a half-dozen sheep to the outdoor oven. Daniel studied his slow, measured movements, wondering how Mr. Buckhalter managed to move at such a pace and still feed the number of people he did.

The fort cook might know where Jessie was. He could walk over to him, remind him that he was in Captain Sutter's employ and had been one of those who'd gone up after the Donner party. He'd mention that there'd been a woman with a child, that he wanted to know what had become of them. It was an honest, expected question.

But Mr. Buckhalter came from Texas. He knew why Daniel had fled the state.

Still—

Despite a bellow from one of the milk cows stabled nearby, Daniel heard the massive oven door open. He almost imagined he could smell the bread being pulled from its interior. Jessie needed to eat. She had no means of preparing her own food. She would have talked to Mr. Buckhalter, maybe told him of her plans. Would the cook share that information with him?

After drawing in a deep breath, Daniel left the doorway and started across the open yard. His mind ticked with the need to find out where Captain Sutter's cattle were so he could return to the Indian wranglers and his job, but until he knew for himself how Jessie was, he couldn't ride away.

Mr. Buckhalter had stopped. He stood, holding a flat board filled with steaming bread as he waited for whoever he was looking at to join him. Daniel recognized his ample wife. It was a heartbeat before he realized who was with her.

Jessie.

She wore a dress that hung on her thin frame. The garment had been caught at the waist with a blue sash of some kind. She had a shawl around her shoulders and was holding it in place with her right hand. Because of the dress's length, he couldn't tell what she wore on her feet.

Her hair fairly glinted in the rare sunlight. Even with the distance between them, he could tell that it had been neatly done in a loose bun at the back of her head. She was saying something to the Buckhalters, but he couldn't make out the words. For now he was content to watch.

She moved easily, putting a lie to the struggle she'd endured. Only one sign remained; she was too thin. When Mr. Buckhalter tried to reach for something in his pocket, Jessie took the laden board from him and held it, balancing the weight by leaning back slightly. The gesture caused her to carry herself more on one hip than the other. He remembered her crawling on hands and knees, dragging herself over one snow-covered boulder after another, clutching Elizabeth to her with fingers that had turned blue from cold.

Today she stood straight and tall.

She handed the board back to Mr. Buckhalter, inclined her head toward the couple, turned away from them.

She was heading toward him.

He watched, knowing nothing except that she kept her steps slow and measured. She'd lifted her dress a few inches and had her attention focused on the uncertain ground. She came closer. She wore moccasins, soft and new-looking, nearly mud-free.

"Jessie."

For a heartbeat he wasn't sure she'd heard him. Then,

slowly, so slowly that he felt the movement being pulled out of him, she raised her head and looked at him. Something wondrously alive flashed into her eyes and stayed there.

"Daniel. Oh, Daniel."

He wanted to clutch her to him, to have her tell him everything that had happened to her. He wanted to ask questions and fall silent as he told her as best he could what his days and nights had been like. But when he searched inside himself, he couldn't think of a word beyond her name.

"Jessie."

"You came. You—you're alive."

She thought he might be dead? "Alive. And well. Like you."

"Alive, yes," she mouthed. The skirt slid from her fingers, landing scant inches from the mud. "Well? Oh, Daniel, I don't know."

What? What's wrong? Instead of voicing his hard-beating question, he held out his hand, palm down. After a moment, she placed her fingers over his and he led her away from the dirt and humanity. Now, feeling surrounded by her, he didn't give a damn who saw them together.

Silent, they stepped inside her room. She came with him easily. He didn't belong here; he needed to tell her that. Soon.

She pulled back a half step and he stared down at her. Through the light that came from the window, he saw moisture glittering in her dark eyes. Had seeing him done this to her?

Because he didn't trust himself, he backed away until he was leaning against the wall. Cold seeped into his back; he ignored it. "You look good," he said because he needed to put an end to the silence. "So much has changed about you."

"Has it?" She lifted her hands, then quickly dropped them. Still, he could see they were trembling. "I didn't know whether you were alive. No one would tell me anything." She blinked, blinked again. "I asked. Everyone I talked to said you weren't with those at Johnson's farm."

"No." *I wasn't welcome there.* "I have friends, Jessie. Chief Narcisco of the Maidu. He took me to his place."

"Took you? You needed help?"

He felt no need to keep that from her. In truth, he wanted to tell her everything about himself, would have if he could be sure she wouldn't run from him when he was done. "Going after the others took so long. I was spent."

She shuddered. "The storms. We—I—watched it rain and knew it was snowing up there. I hated the rain. But every day now it gets warmer. The sun feels wonderful. Sometimes I want to sing with the miracle of it all. They said—folks said it was horrible up there for you and the others."

"It's over now."

"Is it, Daniel?" she whispered. She folded her hands over her middle and briefly rocked herself. "I keep telling myself that. Most of the time it's all right, but—"

"You have nightmares?"

"Sometimes. You don't?"

He did. "I don't think there's a man alive who wouldn't after what happened."

She drew her lower lip into her mouth and held it between her teeth. Her eyes still danced with that light he didn't understand. If he had been a sane man, he would have walked away from her and the danger in her eyes.

But he'd spent too many nights, and days, thinking of her. His fingers and arms and body ached with the need to clutch her to him, to tell her everything.

"There's been so much talk. So much—" She released her waist and raked her hands through her hair. When her neatly done bun started unraveling, she yanked again. "All I could do was pray you were safe. And now, to see you here, to have you call my name and know—"

"I meant that much to you?"

When she didn't answer but only stared, now open-mouthed, he didn't know what to say or do. Mr. Reed and the others had talked endlessly about what they were going to do once they were safe. Knowing none of them cared what he thought or did or how he lived, and that none of them would have had him there if they'd had a choice, he hadn't said anything. He hated knowing that. That's what had prompted his insane question.

"I'm sorry." He made a show of being interested in what was going on beyond her window. "I had no right asking."

"No. No." She waved her hand in the air, glanced out the window herself, returned her attention to him. "Daniel, I can't think. Seeing you— Please, give me a minute. I—" Her hand inched toward him, stopped. She looked at her extended fingers. "Why did you go with them? You were spent, as far gone as I was. But—you didn't stay with me."

Because your reputation would have been ruined if I had. "There was a greater need."

"I know." She groaned. "Those who couldn't—will you tell me about it?"

He wanted to tell her that he wouldn't leave her until all her questions had been answered, until he knew everything she'd done and experienced since they parted. But she hadn't touched him. Her hand, reaching for him a moment ago, was now buried in her skirt. She knew he was alive. Maybe that's all she needed.

It was better that way—for both of them.

"You're still here," he said. "Your farm—"

"I'm still getting my strength back. And with the rain—worrying about you and the others—I-I have to approach Captain Sutter."

"Are you afraid to?"

Her shoulders stiffened, and he sensed he'd asked a question she didn't want to answer. "The time hasn't been right. He's been so busy doing . . ."

"At least you can stay here," he said when she let the words trail off. "You have a roof over your head."

She glanced at her surroundings. "I come here only to sleep."

"Only—and the rest of the time?"

Instead of answering, she stuck out her foot, showing him her moccasins. "These were a gift, from Salenack's wife."

"I'm glad you have them."

"And my dresses, they're gifts, too."

"Good. Good."

"You—" She took a deep breath. He watched, breathing with her. "You really are all right?"

"I will be, now." He froze, wondering whether simply seeing her had pushed the words from him. Maybe. He looked around, needing to find something, anything, to build a conversation on. He thought to ask about Elizabeth and opened his mouth, forming the words.

The door swung open. Raymond, looking healthy and well dressed in a linen shirt and wool pants, led the way, followed closely by a man with heavy shoulders and an unkempt beard tinged both red and gray. The other man,

George McKinstry, sheriff of the Sacramento District, said nothing.

"Get out of here, Bear. Now," Raymond hissed. "Before I have you arrested."

"Arrested? Raymond—"

Feeling as if he'd been struck, Daniel forced himself to block out Jessie's cry. He faced not Raymond but the sheriff. Although he fought not to, his hands clamped into fists. "You have no business," he warned. "This is a private conversation."

"I have every business, Bear. Miss Speer is a decent woman. I will not have the likes of you bothering her."

"The likes—" Jessie started. She sucked in a breath, then continued. "What are you talking about?"

"Go on, Bear," Raymond challenged. He thrust out his chin, sporting a neatly trimmed beard. "Tell her."

"That's not what we're here for." The sheriff narrowed his eyes at Daniel. "Mr. Sage, you asked me to step in for Miss Speer's sake. To get *him* out of here. Anything beyond that is between you and her. I've never trusted you, Bear. You know that."

"Yeah. I know."

"If there was any way I could get you back to Texas, that's where you'd be. Locked up."

"But you can't. And there aren't any charges against me here." Daniel didn't look at Jessie. He didn't want to see.

"This is my territory. I'm the law here. And I'm telling you to quit bothering her."

"He's not bothering. Raymond, Daniel, what is this about?"

The pain and confusion in Jessie's voice nearly undid Daniel. Maybe she deserved to know everything, now; he couldn't say. But the sheriff carried a rifle in the crook of his arm. A rifle against a Maidu hunting knife was no match. "Sheriff—"

"Listen to me, Bear. Whatever business you have with Captain Sutter, you can conduct it somewhere else. You have no other reason for being here."

None, except for taking the hurt and confusion out of Jessie's eyes. But Sheriff McKinstry and Raymond were right. She was a woman, a gentle, God-fearing woman. If Raymond and McKinstry had seen him come in here with her, how many others had?

Silent, he stepped toward the door. Silent, he lifted the latch. Still silent, he looked over his shoulder at Jessie. Her eyes, bright as moonlight, large as twin mountain lakes, stared back at him. For several long seconds he simply regarded her, feeling an unspoken communication.

Jessie waited until the door closed behind Daniel. Daniel, whom she'd desperately wanted to see, had just been ordered from her.

"Tell me." She stepped toward Raymond. After trying to avoid him for too long now, she found that so much hung on what the man might say. "What is this about?"

Raymond met her stare. "You don't know?"

"I wouldn't be asking if I did. Daniel and I were having a conversation. Simply a conversation." *Was that it?* "You have no right—"

"I have more than a right, Jessie. It's my responsibility."

"It's your responsibility to order the man who saved our lives away from me? I'm not your servant, your wife." She nearly gagged on the word. "I'm free to do what I want, talk to who I want." She wanted to run to the window and look for Daniel, but if she did, she'd give herself away to Raymond and the sheriff.

"It's not that simple, Miss Speer."

Jessie had only seen the sheriff twice, both times in the company of Captain Sutter. From what the Buckhalters told her, the relationship between the two men was strained at best. If she told Captain Sutter what had happened, would he order the sheriff to leave Daniel alone?

What was she thinking! She had no idea what this was about. "All right." Determined to face them on level footing, she kept all emotion out of her voice. "You say it isn't that simple. Don't you believe I deserve to know everything?"

Sheriff McKinstry exchanged a quick look with Raymond. It was clear to Jessie that he felt uncomfortable with the whole situation and was only waiting for Raymond to say his piece. "Tell me, Raymond," she ordered. "Now. Before I go after him and bring him back."

"He won't come."

Maybe he won't. "Why not?"

"Because he's a wanted man."

"Wanted?"

"In Texas. If certain men could take him back, he'd spend the rest of his life behind bars. Or at the end of a rope."

Jessie could only gape at Raymond. She raked her hand through her hair, vaguely aware that she'd already done that today—when she was trying to make herself believe Daniel was real and standing before her. "Tell me." Her voice didn't quaver.

"For murder."

"Murder?"

"He killed a man, Jessie. Gunned him down in cold

blood. Then, like the coward he is, he fled. That's why he's here, so the man's family can't reach him."

Daniel, a killer? Feeling frantic, Jessie tried to make sense of the words. She thought of his gentle strength as he fed Elizabeth, the way he'd kept her going when without him she would have died.

He'd killed a man. "You—you said he gunned him down. How do you know that?"

The sheriff jerked his head toward the window. "Mr. and Mrs. Buckhalter hail from west Texas. They were living there when it happened."

"When what happened?" she demanded.

"When he put a bullet in the back of an innocent, God-fearing man."

"In the back? I don't believe—"

"Don't," Raymond warned. "Face it, Jessie. The man I just ran out of here deserves to hang."

"He saved my life. And yours."

Raymond's eyes flickered away. "Maybe he came after something else. Money. Gold. Rings off the fingers of dead women."

She couldn't listen to this! "I'll never believe that of him."

"Then you're a fool, Jessie." He tried to touch her arm. She jerked away. "It doesn't matter what you think of me. It's my duty to protect you from him."

"I don't want your protection. I don't need it." The room had begun to cave in on her. If she didn't get outside, she might start screaming.

"You're wrong, Miss Speer." The sheriff shifted his rifle from one arm to the other. "Daniel Bear is a dangerous man, given to quick violence. A decent woman doesn't dare be seen with him."

She couldn't listen to this. She had to breathe in clean air, to stand in the open. Ignoring both men, she pushed past them and yanked open the door. After a half-dozen aimless steps, she stopped. Her arms and legs trembled; she didn't care enough to try to still them.

Daniel had murdered a man, shot him in the back.

CHAPTER 8

Elizabeth grinned up at Jessie, the nub of a brand-new tooth proudly in place. "Aren't you the sly one?" Jessie teased. "Hiding that from me until today. Just please don't start walking tomorrow. I need you to remain a baby a little longer." Her voice caught. She tried again. "Don't ever forget how to laugh. You laugh so wonderfully. Promise me you'll always be as excited about life as you are today, won't you?"

Elizabeth continued to grin, now with a thumb securely over the tooth.

"You're a miracle. You know that, don't you?" Jessie's vision blurred. "Two miracles. You stayed alive, and you gave me a reason to go on living."

"Jessie?"

She'd been expecting to hear her name spoken. Still, the sound jarred her. "I know. I'm ready. It's just that it's so hard to—"

"It isn't really good-bye. You can come and visit whenever you want. I mean that."

"Thank you." Jessie touched her lips to Elizabeth's forehead, smiling despite herself when the baby doubled up her little hand and punched her on the cheek. "I'll be making a pest of myself."

"You'll never be a pest, Jessie. When I think of what you did, well—"

When Annie Larkin didn't continue, Jessie faced the slim young woman. Annie had brought a new, soft wool blanket to carry Elizabeth home in. It hung over her arm, leaving her hands free to take her orphaned niece. "I did it for me, Annie," Jessie told her. "She gave me something to cling to. A reason to go on. I-I thought you might bring the boys with you."

Annie rolled her head skyward. "Those wild ones are more of a handful than I want to be burdened with today." She ran the tip of her forefinger over Elizabeth's nose. Elizabeth jabbed her fist at the elusive hand. "They're waiting at home for their new baby sister. Isn't that wonderful? They've only seen her once, and yet they already think of her as their sister."

"It is indeed." Jessie had taken Elizabeth out to visit her aunt and uncle and boy cousins two days ago. The Larkin cabin, built along a creek that fed into the Sacramento River, had been in place for over a year now and had weathered the winter well. It had two rooms, one for sleeping, the other for the family to do the rest of its living in. Mr. Larkin was a giant of a man, a little in awe of his diminutive wife and the infant girl he could nearly hold in one hand. But when Jessie saw how comfortable the strapping boys were around their father, she relaxed. If he could teach his sons to clear land, build a cabin, and farm, surely he would give his heart to a daughter—especially one who looked as if she was determined to grow up to be a boxer.

"I don't want to rush this moment," Annie said. "I know it isn't easy for you."

"No," Jessie admitted. "It isn't. But I made her mother a promise."

Annie nodded; her bright blue eyes clouded. "How I wish Elie had lived. She so wanted to come to California. More than her husband. When I left Fort Bridger, we hugged and promised each other that we'd soon be together again." She wiped away a tear. "I can't have my sister, but I'll raise her daughter as best I can."

"You'll do a wonderful job." Jessie meant it. Annie had come to Fort Sutter a half-dozen times since she'd received word that her niece was alive, getting to know her, rejoicing in Elizabeth's growing strength. Jessie, Annie, and Margaret Buckhalter had all agreed that Elizabeth should be breast-fed for a while before being introduced to cow's milk. Jessie and Margaret had shared responsibility for Elizabeth, spoiling her. Now that time was over.

Jessie didn't try to hide her tears. "I love it when she pulls my hair into her mouth. She gets this funny little look on her face, like she's done something so mischievous."

Annie tentatively stretched out her hands. "Jessie?"

"Yes. Yes." For the second time, she kissed Elizabeth's forehead. Elizabeth kicked out, hard enough that Jessie knew she would feel the punch in her ribs for several minutes. "You're a fighter, aren't you? Good. That way you can hold your own with those boys."

Elizabeth laughed in delight, displaying her new tooth again. Jessie stared upward, focusing on a dozen wisping clouds in the first truly blue sky she'd seen in months.

Think spring. Put your mind to a warm afternoon, the sound of birds. Being surrounded by your own land.

After she'd waved off Annie and Elizabeth, Jessie started toward Captain Sutter's quarters. But before she could reach them, she spied the man standing outside his room talking to a couple of uniformed men. She couldn't approach him when he had important matters on his mind. Maybe tomorrow.

She gathered up her skirts, wishing she could run— anywhere. The days had all floated together until she couldn't remember how long she'd been here, or how long she'd been fighting the press of walls against her. At first she'd been too weak to care about anything except regaining her strength and watching Elizabeth—and praying for Daniel's safe return. Along with the others at the fort, she'd rejoiced when she heard that more members of the Donner party had been brought down. Her relief had turned into a hard knot inside her when she heard what those brave souls had endured and how many more had died.

No one had said a word about Daniel. Her questions had gone unanswered. It seemed that no one cared about a lone man when the lives of dozens were at stake. Then he came to see her and she thought she might fall apart just looking at him. Before she could tell him how she'd prayed for him, how much she owed him, anything of what had been trapped inside her, before she risked everything, he'd been ordered from her.

Since that day last week, she'd lived in an agony of un-answered questions. Twice she'd tried to approach the

Buckhalters, but Mr. Buckhalter refused to say anything, and Margaret called Daniel a dangerous man.

Dangerous.

The fort beat like a wild animal's heart. Men, many of them wearing military uniforms, came to see Captain Sutter daily. Most of the settlers who'd traveled over the mountains before winter now lived on their own land, but came to the fort for supplies. Livestock was always being brought in, and Jessie never looked around without seeing a number of the Indians Sutter had hired to provide protection. The rooms Sutter had had built were full. Other members of the Donner party, like her, were waiting for spring to take hold before striking out. Most of the last group of survivors were staying at the nearby Johnson ranch. If it hadn't been for Elizabeth, she would have gone to see them.

Raymond had been given shelter in the barracks and already was eating with Sutter, riding out with him, receiving audience with him. Sutter wasn't the only one who seemed taken with Raymond. She often saw him in the company of a half-dozen soldiers, dirty, ill-dressed men who made her uneasy. She tried to avoid Raymond, but it was difficult. Whenever he spoke to her, she answered in a civil tone, but refused to be drawn into a personal conversation. Raymond wanted things different between them; she didn't.

The sky, a newborn blue, called to her today. Although she very much wanted to, she'd only left the fort twice since her arrival. But she no longer had responsibility for Elizabeth, and the weather was glorious. The Buckhalters, the Larkins, Raymond, and the single men bent on courting her no matter how strongly she discouraged them, all admonished her not to venture out by herself.

But they didn't know what it was like for her. Surely

none of them had to wrench their hands into fists before they could enter a building. They had horses to ride, freedom. How could they possibly understand how desperately she wanted those things?

She could have a little of that today. She needed it—otherwise her empty arms and the memory of Elizabeth's toothy grin would reduce her to tears. Because she'd prevailed on his good nature when she went out to the Larkin farm and earlier for a short ride, she went to the blacksmith and hinted that if he had a horse in need of exercise, she would love to be given the responsibility. He seemed surprised, but when she reassured him that she only meant to travel a mile or two, he agreed. He looked even more surprised when she told him she didn't need a saddle.

She mounted, straightened, and, barely able to keep herself from kicking the mare into a gallop, passed through the open gate. As soon as she was no longer on the slight rise where Fort Sutter had been built, she dug her heels into the mare's side and leaned low over the arched neck. The mare ran, hooves beating against the hardening earth. In all directions, Jessie saw nothing but open valley covered by greening grass.

Green. Life. And above, a sky as blue as Elizabeth's eyes.

After a few seconds of indecision, she headed toward the wide, rain-swollen river where she'd been told the Maidu had their village. The land was so flat that for the first mile she felt lost in it.

The grasses were streaked with trails, some widened by passing cattle, others twin strips forged by wagon wheels. Everything smelled wonderful—rich, damp earth, new grass, the wind coming in from the mountains. Her heart and lungs felt as if they might never stop expanding. She wondered if she might burst with whatever she held inside her, then decided she didn't care. She wanted to shout, to yell, to sing, to thank her maker for this day.

Spring had come, and she was part of it.

Alive with it.

Soon—soon she'd show Captain Sutter the money she kept on her at all times and ask to buy several acres from him. She'd place her seeds in the ground, and when they sprang to life, she'd have the means to support herself.

The land remained flat, but in the distance she could see a number of trees. As she came closer, she realized that they were oaks just losing their winter-gray coloring. The river, swift and clean, had cut deep into the earth at this point. The trees growing closest to the riverbanks were larger, more spreading than their slim, mistletoe-laden neighbors.

Everyone she spoke to said the Maidu were a peaceful tribe. Many of them worked for Captain Sutter. Some tended his cattle. Daniel had told her he spent his days caring for the livestock. If she approached one of the Maidu, would they tell her where she might find him?

Daniel. Don't have anything to do with him, Margaret had warned. He's a killer, Raymond and the sheriff had told her. But they didn't know him, not the way she did.

Daniel Bear hadn't touched them, hadn't disturbed their sleep.

She was strong, free, with a horse under her. If she wanted to go looking for the man who'd saved her life, she would.

As she drew closer to the oaks, she sensed that she was being watched. Drawing on the reins, she slowed the mare's trot to a walk. She straightened, straining to see if anything moved in the shadows cast by the trees. As if it had been borne by nothing more than a breeze, a tinkling laugh reached her ears. After a moment's hesitation, she headed toward the sound.

When her mare shied and threw back her head, Jessie stopped her. Had she made a mistake by coming here?

But she'd been surrounded by people for weeks now, wanting to scream with the need for a warm, spring-scented wind on her flesh and silence instead of the never-ending sound of man and animals. Her heart and head had always embraced the land. She had to have that back.

The high-pitched laugh was repeated. Recognizing that it was a child's voice, Jessie relaxed a little. "Hello," she called. "Where are you?"

No one answered, but a moment later a young Indian boy, naked except for a diaperlike garment, emerged from behind one of the larger oaks. He regarded her not with fear or hostility but open curiosity. She tried to tell him she'd come for a visit—if that was the word—but he continued to look at her as if she'd sprung full-grown from the grass. Finally he gave an impatient shake of his head, indicating she was to follow him. Feeling more like a child than an adult, she did as she was ordered.

Five minutes later she spotted a large mound rising from the ground ahead of her. She judged it to be some thirty feet in diameter, covered with what looked like matted grass. Smoke drifted up from a hole in the center. She'd heard enough to realize that she was looking at the roof of a Maidu underground home.

When the boy stopped, she did the same. He looked around, then called out something she couldn't understand. After a moment, a dark head appeared in the hole; then a broad-shouldered man emerged, wearing no more than the boy did. The brave stood with his arms hanging from his sides, regarding her. Then he stepped off the mound and approached. His dark chest glistened with sweat. He didn't seem at all surprised to see her.

"I—" She stopped, feeling foolish. Should she dismount? Maybe it wasn't polite to expect him to go on staring up at her. "I'm trying to find someone. Ah, do you understand English? I'm sorry, I—"

"Daniel Bear."

"What?"

"I ask if you are looking for Daniel Bear," the brave said in precise, accented English. "Are you Jessie Speer?"

She felt both hot and cold. "Y-yes. How did you— You know him?"

"He is my friend. You came to find him? I told him you would not."

Distracted only slightly by her mare's attempts to graze, Jessie stared. The warrior hadn't taken his eyes off her, either. She needed to understand him better; she realized that. But he knew Daniel, and Daniel had spoken of her to him. Until she'd made sense of that, she couldn't put her mind on anything else. "I wasn't—" No. She couldn't tell this brave that she'd simply gone out for a ride and nothing more than curiosity had brought her here. "I only saw him for a few minutes the other day. I still haven't thanked him properly."

"And you want to do that today?" The brave glanced over at the boy, then shooed him away with a wave of his hand. "Seshun would like to be a chief when he becomes a man, but for now he is simply a little boy who wants to know too much. He called me because I speak your language. He should have asked for my guest."

"Your guest?"

"He is here."

The quick mix of hot and cold she'd experienced a few

minutes ago returned. "He? I—didn't know. I thought he would be with the cattle."

"He was. He is with us because my daughter has become a woman. It is a time I want to share with my friend."

A lump formed in her throat at the thought that this savage-looking man considered Daniel his friend. "Then he's inside?"

The brave nodded. "You would like to join him?"

She only had to think about crawling into that dark, underground place to know she'd never be able to force herself to do it. "Maybe he could come out here?"

"Maybe." The corner of the brave's mouth lifted. Before she could wonder what she'd said to make him smile, he walked away from her and back up the smooth mound. He knelt before the opening and lowered his head through it. Jessie clenched her teeth. How could anyone possibly live underground?

The thought faded. The Indian had backed up and was obviously waiting for someone to join him. Jessie started to touch her hair; then, remembering what she'd done to it the last time she saw Daniel, she picked up the reins, worrying them between her fingers. She wished she had more than two dresses to her name, that she'd thought to clean her moccasins before coming here.

Maybe nothing about her mattered to him.

When Daniel braced his arms on the outside of the hole and easily lifted himself out, she realized she had no idea what she would say to him. She should turn the mare and race back the way she'd come from.

Only, she didn't want to.

"I wonder what the captain would say if he knew you weren't with the cattle," she said in what she hoped was a teasing tone. He wore nothing from the waist up, and she remembered how he'd looked that first night while he tended to his injury. Nothing of his beard remained. He seemed less remote without it.

His chest—if she touched him, how would it feel?

"I don't think you're going to tell him anything." Daniel stood beside the Indian now. His flesh wasn't as dark, but he was leaner, taller, hard-muscled. He wore no shoes. His doeskin pants hung at his hips, dipping low enough that she saw too much of his flat belly.

What did he look like naked?

That she'd had such a thought so unsettled her that she couldn't think of a single word, let alone anything that would keep up the teasing tone she'd begun. She wanted to order her question away, to tell herself she couldn't possibly want to see him without clothes.

But she did.

"Where did you get the horse?"

"Where?" she echoed his question. Dimly she realized that the Indian was watching her as well. "From the blacksmith. He let me borrow it."

"Why?"

"Why?"

"Why did you need a horse, Jessie?"

Her name coming from him broke through the fog that had surrounded her. She shut her eyes, hoping that when she opened them again he would be wearing a shirt. He wasn't. She would have to deal with that. "I couldn't stand to stay there any longer." The words rushed out of her. "I feel trapped in that place, like there isn't enough air. There's nowhere I can go for privacy."

"And you need privacy?"

She couldn't say whether answering him was wise or not. All she knew was that she had to tell him as best she could. "Up there, I never had a moment away from other people. Only when I went to the traps. But I was so scared. I—" She'd dropped the reins. Now she picked them up and started worrying them again. "I didn't like being with the wagon train because I could never be alone there. It only got worse once we knew we couldn't go on. And the last few weeks—" She caught a clump of the mare's mane between her fingers. Daniel hadn't moved, had barely breathed. How could she possibly think? "I grew up on a farm, Daniel. We could only see one neighbor and just when we were on the hill between the two places. I spent my childhood with space around me. You don't know what losing that is like."

"Maybe I do."

Did he want her to tell him more? She wished she knew him better, or maybe it was her reaction to him she needed to understand before she could go further. In an attempt to put an end to the questions inside her head, she indicated the Indian. "He said he's your friend. That you're here for his daughter's birthday."

"Not a birthday. She has become a woman."

As what the Indian said sunk in, Jessie blushed. Fortunately, before the silence could stretch out, Daniel placed his hand on the other man's shoulder. "Chief Narcisco, I'd like you to meet Jessie Speer. Jessie, the chief and I met, what, two winters ago?"

Narcisco nodded.

"He'd gotten himself into a little trouble with a bear. You would think that a man who has lived as long as he has would know not to be around blackberrries the same time a bear and her cubs decide it's time to eat."

"You were attacked?" Jessie asked.

"I did not know she was there." Narcisco shook his head at Daniel as if he wished this conversation wasn't taking place. "I was trying to find a tree to climb when Daniel came. He shot the bear."

"Just like that?" Daniel teased. "I shot the bear? Aren't you going to tell her how you all but dug a hole in the ground trying to get away from that old sow?"

Narciso grunted. Then, eyes glaring, he jabbed at Daniel's shoulder. "Maybe, if you tell her what happened when you tried to capture one of the cubs."

Instead of saying anything, Daniel rubbed his side. Despite the distance between them, Jessie could make out three faint white scars. He didn't seem to care that she saw him half-naked. Maybe he'd lived around the Indians for so long that he'd come to think of himself as one of them. "You had to kill the bear?" she asked. "She was just trying to feed herself and her cubs."

"I had no choice, Jessie. It was either her or Narciso. I don't know what I was thinking when I tried to pick up the cub, maybe that I was going to raise it. He didn't want anything to do with me."

"What happened to the cubs?"

"They ran away."

Because she'd grown up on a farm, Jessie filled in what hadn't been said. Without their mother's milk and protection, the cubs would be easy prey for wolves or the cougars she'd been told lived in the hills. She wondered if Daniel had had any thought to spare her, then hoped it hadn't occurred to him. She wasn't a child to be protected from life.

"And you two have been friends since that day?"

"I tolerate him."

"And I have not yet had reason to scalp him."

"Scalp?" Daniel laughed. "If I hadn't told you about the Plains Indians, you wouldn't know the meaning of the word."

"Be glad, white man. If I was an Apache, your scalp would be hanging from my belt."

Daniel said something about Narcisco needing to rely on help from the rest of the men in the village for that to happen. Jessie didn't try to hold on to the words, just the relationship between the two. She'd sensed that Daniel and Salenack were more than strangers thrown together by circumstances. Obviously what Daniel felt for Narcisco went even deeper. Daniel was considered part of Narcisco's family; he shared in their celebrations.

And yet the district sheriff had ordered him away from her at gunpoint.

Daniel, if everyone was to be believed, had murdered a defenseless man. How could she possibly ask him about that?

Shaking herself free of her inner turmoil, she tried to concentrate on what the men were saying, but the words made no sense. All she knew was that the sounds were the same as those she'd heard between Daniel and Salenack. After saluting, obviously something he'd seen the army men do, Narcisco turned and walked up the slight rise to his home. He dropped to his knees on the domed roof, then disappeared.

"He said we need to be alone."

"Did he?" Daniel hadn't moved. She didn't feel right sitting on her horse while he had to stand. Without asking him whether he wanted to talk to her, she dismounted and gave the mare her head so she could graze. She looked around for some place to sit. Daniel pointed, indicating an oak with a double trunk not far away. She followed him to it, then stood feeling awkward when he sat down next to the tree and looked up at her. She didn't want to be so close to him that she might risk touching his bare flesh.

Still, she'd come this far and she didn't know when she might see him again.

"I thought, after what happened the other day, that you might not want to see me."

Someday she would tell him what she thought of his directness, but not today. "I don't know enough. What they said—"

"What did they say?" he asked as she sat down.

She gathered her skirts around her legs and leaned forward. As long as she held this position, she couldn't look into his eyes, or at his chest. "That you killed a man."

"And you still came looking for me?"

He wasn't going to say anything more about what he'd been accused of. She had to accept that. "We didn't have enough time the other day." Near the toe of her moccasin an ant wrestled with a leaf. "I have so many questions. I want to know what happened when you went back up there."

"No. I don't think you do."

Because it had been too horrible? "Isaac Donner died. Mary burned her foot in the fire after it was frostbitten. The storms—you had to struggle through the storms."

"That was part of it."

What else? What else? "Don't you want to think about it?"

"It's in the past."

Just as what had happened in Texas was in the past? "It's going to be spring soon," she said. "Really spring. There's already new grass."

"Yes. There is."

She leaned back, remembering too late how close he was. If she didn't keep her hands in her lap, their shoulders might touch. She'd been right. Her dress wasn't heavy enough to guard her against his heat.

His heat. She remembered burying herself in it as he carried her.

She breathed deeply, caught on a thought. "The Larkins, they're Elizabeth's aunt and uncle, they bought their land from Captain Sutter."

"Don't do it, Jessie."

"Don't do what?"

"Try to make it on your own. You have no idea how hard, how dangerous it will be."

She stared at her mare, fascinated by the strength in the long teeth tearing at grass. "Don't I?" she flared. "What would you have me do? Bake bread with Mr. Buckhalter? He is so formal around me these days—because he knows you and I were together, alone, and that you came to see me the other day. He isn't the only one."

"I'm sorry. I shouldn't have."

No. "I don't care what anyone thinks. Nothing happened."

"I'm not sure they believe that."

The mare no longer interested her. Her mother would have been scandalized if she'd seen her now. Her father would have taken his belt to her. But she didn't have her parents anymore, or anyone. When she left the fort this morning, she'd thought she needed solitude.

But she'd come here. She was sitting next to Daniel Bear, a man who, everyone said, had gunned down another. "That's the only thing I think about," she told him, although right now that wasn't the truth. "Having land to call my own, that's all I want."

"Despite the danger, and the odds against you?"

"Despite everything." She breathed in deeply, gaining strength from the air. "That's my life, Daniel. It's what I want it to be."

"I wish I understood."

"I wish you did, too." She looked at him, nearly lost herself in his Indian eyes. "Back home Mama and I planted enough of a garden to feed a half-dozen families. Papa said it was a waste of time, that I should be with him taking care of the animals. But I hated that. I wanted to watch things grow, to take pleasure from my garden."

"You hated caring for livestock?"

"Not them." She should stop looking at him; he'd see too deep inside her. "Being with Papa."

"Why?"

"You know." She touched her hair where her father had hacked at it. "I wasn't what he wanted. It made him angry, and he never lost hold of his anger. He wasn't good to Mama either. That's what hurt the most, the way he treated Mama."

"Why'd she stay with him?"

Jessie didn't expect the question. True, she and her mother had often talked about how difficult life with a hard man was, but leaving . . . "What would she have done, Daniel? She had no money, not a single coin to call her own. The horses were his, and the wagon. Even the roof over our heads was his."

"Why?"

"Why?" she echoed.

"Why were all those things his?"

"Because he was the man."

Daniel, who'd been probing at her with his eyes, now looked as if she was speaking in a foreign language. "That's not right."

"Not right?"

"You and your mother, the two of you grew the food that fed all of you, didn't you?"

"Yes."

"And, even if you didn't want to, you took care of the cattle and horses, didn't you?"

"Oh yes. One time we had a storm while Papa was off arranging to sell some of the cattle. The barn was struck by lightning. I got the animals out. I was so scared, but I knew what I had to do. I couldn't let them die. And all those nights when I helped a cow give birth—the seasons mean so much on a farm. I love that part of it."

He picked a leaf off her shoulder and examined it. He seemed lost in something, maybe what she'd told her. "Have you talked to Captain Sutter about how you feel and what you want to do?"

The rest of her life was tied up in the captain's answer; surely he knew that. "Not yet."

"Why not?"

Without thinking through what she was doing, she sighed. The gesture brought her shoulders against Daniel's. The touch was so light, barely a feather's caress. "He's always so busy. And I was taking care of Elizabeth, getting stronger. I need to look at the land, decide what I want, before I approach him."

"You could have gone looking today."

Was he trying to get her to tell him why she'd come here instead? No matter. "I haven't thanked you."

"Thanked?"

"For saving my life." She should do something to end the feather touch. Only, she couldn't think how or what.

"You already did, Jessie."

"No." She turned toward him. Her movement freed her shoulder. Now he held her with his eyes. "Not the way I should; the way I want to."

"And how is that?"

She didn't know what to make of his question, which way to turn it in her mind so she would understand. People called him dangerous. She sensed danger in his eyes and strong body. He might want something from her—something her mother had hinted at but never spoken about. Was he a man she could, should trust?

It didn't matter. He'd kept her alive.

"I want to bake you a pie."

"A pie?" He looked as if he might laugh.

She blushed. If he kept on staring at her, she might never control the flush in her cheeks. "When we were walking, cold, hungry, I kept thinking about picking berries and baking pies."

"I'd like that."

"Would you?" She held his words in her mind, needing to see if he meant them. She sensed honesty. "I wish I could give you more."

"You're the one with needs, not me."

Still aware of how near he was and how hard it was for her to think, she nevertheless concentrated as best she could on what he'd said. "I don't have many needs. Margaret Buckhalter gave me two dresses. I do what I can to help Mr. Buckhalter. In turn, I have as much as I need to eat. My money—that's for the farm."

He nodded, making her think that he'd expected that to be her answer. "Don't put it off. Go to Sutter. All he can say is no."

"No?" The day was warm. Why did she feel suddenly chilled. "Why would he do that?"

"Maybe he needs the land himself. Maybe it's promised to someone else."

She'd already thought those things. She didn't want or need Daniel to remind her of that. "Then I'll go to Mr. Johnson, Mr. Sinclair. Someone will help me."

He looked toward the river, freeing her from his gaze.

He seemed content to sit beside her. If he had other things to do, surely he would have told her that.

"Where are the cattle?" She studied the ant, which was now trying to drag the leaf over a half-buried rock.

"North." He pointed. "I'll be going back in a little while. I want to get there before dark. You said Elizabeth's aunt and uncle have a farm. Do they feel safe out there?"

Mr. Larkin had mentioned that the farm used to fascinate the Indians, but they no longer sat on their horses, watching. She explained that the two boys were now free to roam as far as their energy would allow. "Folks keep talking about the problems with Mexico, but the war seems so far away."

"Maybe. If you do farm, I'll ask Narcisco and the other braves to keep an eye on you."

If. "If others can till the land, so can I."

"You're alone, Jessie. A woman alone."

She was so weary of hearing that. "And stubborn. I'll make it. Believe me, I will make it."

She felt his eyes on her. When she turned to look at him, she read respect in his expression. "I think maybe you will." Before she had time to fully understand what he was doing, he stood and held out his hand. Had he leaned over a little, come closer to her? "Go home, Jessie. Make that farm what you need it to be."

"Go home?" She placed her hand in his. The instant their fingers touched, she knew. She'd never forget today.

"You can't be seen with me."

"Don't say that."

He pulled her to her feet; she felt weightless. "I have to. You're a lady, Jessie. I'm not good for you."

Not good for me? I feel alive around you. "I don't believe that. Every time I think of what you did for me, your sacrifices—"

"I don't want you to become an outcast. Shunned."

Like you? No. He wasn't shunned. Captain Sutter held great store by him or he wouldn't have put him in charge of the cattle. Chief Narcisco and Salenack called him their friend. But the sheriff had ordered him away from her. "When I have my own place, it won't matter what people say or think."

"Yes it will."

He hadn't released her hand. Sensing that she might lose herself in thoughts of him, she pulled gently. He held on, his strong, work-able hand wrapped around hers. She wanted him to know that her hands were made for work as well.

But he'd pulled her close.

Close.

The sun and wind had touched his flesh all his life. He seemed to have been embedded with heat and a restless breeze. Standing with little more than an inch between them, she wondered if she could press her hand against his naked chest and feel his heart.

He was looking down at her. Although she trembled, she lifted her eyes and met his gaze. His mouth had softened—softened and challenged. He wanted—what did he want from her?

If she pulled free, if she ran for the pinto and fled for safety, she would never know what he wanted. Never understand the challenge.

She stayed.

"I'm not good for you, Jessie."

She thought to argue away his words, but she didn't know how to turn what she felt into speech. He released her hand. Then, quickly, surely, he slipped his hand over her back and drew her against him. She couldn't tell which of them was trembling—maybe both. A terrible battle was taking place inside him. When she breathed, when her heart beat, she felt his struggle.

Tell me. Please let me understand.

He lowered his head and surrounded her with himself. She felt like a captured animal, a bird held in a massive hand. Then, a heartbeat later, she no longer felt trapped.

She wanted to be here. Wanted him to be asking with his eyes and body and the mouth she longed to cover with her own.

As she rose onto her toes, she spread her hands over his shoulders. Next to him the mountain was nothing. There was nothing but him.

And her mouth seeking his.

CHAPTER 9

"**K**eseberg."

Jessie frowned and turned from the lame sheep she'd been feeding. She leaned against the low wooden railing, facing Raymond. "I barely ever spoke to him. Why does it matter?"

"You haven't heard the things they've been saying about him?"

In the two days since she'd seen Daniel, she'd spent most of her time riding the borrowed pinto and scouting the rich land along the river, looking for what she needed to put her life on course. She'd been careful to keep her thoughts not on what had happened between her and Daniel, but on whether anyone had a plow to sell so she could dig a deep farrow in the earth. She filled her nights with images of herself crawling on hands and knees as she dropped corn and bean seeds into the ground. And if thoughts of Daniel fought their way through the barriers she'd built around herself, she clenched her fists until the pain of her nails digging into her flesh distracted her. She told Raymond that she'd done little more than sleep at the fort.

"I don't understand you, Jessie." He hooked his thumbs over his waistband and stared at her. "Why you insist on this insane dream of yours despite all the warnings— You haven't been going out to see *him*, have you?"

That was none of Raymond's affair. Daniel—what she thought and felt and dreamed of him would remain inside her. "You aren't my husband. You have no right asking such questions."

"I have every responsibility. Why do you think I brought the sheriff when Bear insisted on seeing you? My business associates—they are willing to do whatever it takes to keep him from you."

Business associates? Riffraff was more like it. The sometime soldiers made her flesh crawl. "You said we needed to talk about something. What is it?"

"What? Mr. Keseberg has done some horrible things."

"Tell me."

"I can't. Some of it—when they came to rescue him, they saw proof—proof not fit for decent conversation. They say he is a murderer."

"Murder? I don't understand."

"Maybe no God-fearing man or woman can. I can't make myself repeat what I was told." Raymond pulled his hands free. Slipping closer to Jessie, he reached over the railing and rubbed the sheep between its ears. "All I want is for what happened to be behind us. I can't stop the nightmares. Maybe they'll follow me to my grave. But I never thought I'd have to talk about it. Answer questions."

Only half comprehending what he was saying, Jessie waited him out. But Raymond, who'd always been quick to speak his mind, seemed more interested in tending to the sheep than speaking. Finally his chest heaved. "Folks know."

"Know?"

"What we had to do to keep from dying."

Jessie's legs felt weak. She gripped the railing, staring not at him but up at the sky. It was as richly blue as it had been the day she rode out to see Daniel. A few minutes ago her heart had ached with the need to stand on her own land while spring painted the valley in gentle colors. Why couldn't she concentrate on that instead of— "You're sure?"

Raymond looked at her as if she was a child. "There's been talk ever since Reed and the others returned. If Keseberg hadn't boasted, not so much would be made of it. People understand. They aren't judging."

"Boasted? Raymond, what is he saying? I have to know."

"That he ate human flesh."

He must have said more than that. Boasting. What details . . . Jessie wrapped her arms around her waist to keep from shuddering and waited. After a minute, Raymond left off scratching the sheep. Staring out at nothing, he told her what he knew. When the rescue party had come across Keseberg, he'd been surrounded by proof of what he'd done. He wasn't the only one, but the others had been so ashamed, so desperately heartbroken that there'd been no other way of staying alive. As if he was proud, Keseberg had relayed in great detail what he'd done.

"It's worse than that, Jessie. Some are saying he murdered a boy so he could live. And that he killed Tamsen Donner for her money. Mr. Fallon put a rope around Keseberg's neck to try to make him say where the money for the little Donner children was. The next day Mr. Tucker and Mr. Rhoads found the coins. Keseberg had hidden them."

"No."

"Do you think I want to tell you this?"

Jessie pulled in air. What had he told her? That he only wanted to put what they'd endured behind him. She wanted the same. "Is the talk just about Keseberg?"

When he shook his head, she understood. "What—have folks been asking you?"

"What do you think?"

"What are you telling them?"

"That we did what we had to to stay alive. I have never done anything in my life for which I am ashamed."

Suddenly Jessie was angry. "We? I didn't. You know that. Have you told folks that?"

"What kind of a man do you take me for, Jessie? The truth is the only thing I know."

Was that true? Memories assaulted her. She remembered being so hungry that she nearly wept. She would die if she didn't eat; she knew that. But when Raymond told her what he'd decided to do, she couldn't force herself to join him.

"Don't thank me, Jessie."

"What?" How long had she been staring at him?

"You were thinking to thank me for sparing your repu- tation with folks, but you aren't innocent."

"What are you saying?"

"Tell me something." He leaned toward her, making it impossible for her to see or concentrate on anything except him. "Why did you let me do it?"

"You did what you had to. I didn't judge."

"No. You didn't. Because you couldn't." His eyes glittered, for an instant reminding her of the strange, almost frightening man he'd become on the mountain.

"I couldn't let her die, Raymond. She's only a baby. I pray she never knows what we did."

"And if she does?"

"Then I pray she'll understand that I did what I had to to keep her alive."

"It's more than that."

"More?"

"Don't make me say it."

As uneasy as she was in his presence, he was right. It wasn't fair for him to have to pull everything out of her. And she didn't want to lie to herself. "Given a little more time, I don't know what I would have done."

"You would have rather died, and left Elizabeth without anyone to take care of her?" he challenged.

"No. You know I couldn't do that to her."

Jessie wasn't sure whether she'd slept at all. The day had barely begun when she left her room and walked to the livery stable. The blacksmith wasn't there, but the pinto was sleeping in its stall. Jessie bridled the horse and left a message saying that she and the mare might be gone until night. She swung onto the broad back, rode over to the high wooden gate, and waved at the two sleepy-eyed guards. The Indians looked at her as if she'd taken leave of her senses. She kept her explanation as short as possible. She was going to visit someone; she didn't know when she would be back.

Dew painted the valley grasses with a cool, glossy sheen that caught the rays of the rising sun. Because she'd thought to bring along a shawl, Jessie felt warm enough.

Leaving the fort behind, she turned the mare north and then gave her her head.

The day she'd gone to the Indian camp and found Daniel, the ground had still been wet from the rain. Now the soil had begun to dry out. If the weather held, soon she would be able to bury a shovel in the earth without mud sticking to everything.

Daniel had told her where the cattle were. When she was out yesterday, she'd seen where the herd had passed by several days before. Yesterday she hadn't allowed herself to think about that—to wonder where she might find Daniel.

But she had to talk to him.

Him. No one else.

The sweet-smelling morning slipped away. She soon removed her shawl. When the sun was high overhead, she stopped under an ancient oak to let the mare rest. She ate a couple of sweet cakes and a beef strip, still in awe of how easily food came to her these days. A squirrel scolded from somewhere high in the sheltering oak. She placed a little of the sweet cake some distance from her and watched as the lively creature slowly descended, nose twitching, and sat with its bushy tail arching over its back as it ate. Once the squirrel scampered back up the tree, she mounted and headed north again.

After traveling little more than a mile, the mare perked her ears and held her head high, prancing. Mindful of what Daniel had said about the possibility of thieving Indians, Jessie fingered the knife at her waist. She glanced down at the weapon, which one of the Indians had given her. What good would it do if Indians, or outlaws, surrounded her?

Then she heard a distant, sharp bellow and realized what the mare had heard. "We're almost there," she reassured the nervous animal. "I'll let you rest and eat a little. I'll talk to Daniel and then we'll go back."

It wasn't until she spotted the moving mass in the distance that she set her mind to trying to form what she needed to say to Daniel, the questions she would ask. No matter how hard it might be, she needed to tell him everything she'd learned from Raymond. And then—then she'd wait for his response.

Was that why she'd spent hours looking for him?

An angry bellow rent the air. The sharp, powerful sound jerked her free of the question. From what she could tell, most of the cattle were off to the right, grazing. But the men on horseback she'd just spotted were clustered near a couple of oaks, intently watching something. She pressed her knees against the pinto's belly, not to force the animal into a run, but to keep her from shying away from the earthshaking sound.

A few minutes later she'd drawn close enough that she could make out a massive bull whirling about as if trying to free himself of the devil. Sometimes he flung his hind legs skyward; other times he tossed his great head into the air, striving to gore the burden on his back.

A man rode him. Whoever he was, he fought to remain seated by keeping his hands wrapped in the strap tied around the bull's girth. Every time the bull kicked, the man's head snapped back. The earth vibrated with the sound of heavy, pounding hoofs. The man shouted; his yells were nearly lost in the encouraging cries that came from the Indian wranglers.

As she drew nearer, the rider closest to her turned in her direction. She was both surprised and relieved when she recognized Chief Narcisco. He nodded. "Watch. Watch him."

Jessie leaned forward, already guessing what she would

see. Although it was impossible to make out the face of the man riding the bucking bull, she'd seen the large, lean frame enough times that she recognized him.

"What's he doing?"

"Proving himself."

Jessie wasn't sure she understood Narcisco's meaning, but she couldn't take her eyes off Daniel long enough to ask for more of an explanation. His hair flew about wildly, telling her more than she wanted to know about the punishment he was enduring. The bull had stopped trying to hook his horns into Daniel and now bucked stiff-legged, throwing his head from side to side, spinning, packing the earth beneath his hoofs. With every jump, Daniel lost contact with the bull, but, held in place by the strap gripped in his fingers, he kept being jerked down again onto the broad, sweating back.

She didn't want to watch. Why would he willingly punish himself this way? If he lost his grip and hit the ground, would he be able to scramble away from those deadly hooves in time? He could be killed! That's what robbed the breath from her lungs. He could be killed!

She brought her mare closer to Narcisco. "Why?"

"To prove himself."

"I don't understand." Much as she wanted to turn and ride away, she couldn't take her eyes off Daniel. "Prove what?"

"Ask him."

She hadn't come here for that. But, with hard, sharp bellows rending the air and Daniel fighting to stay on the beast under him, she couldn't think of anything except him. She'd grown up around bulls and knew that their strength could be almost endless. This creature was battling with every ounce of power in him. He was a long time from giving out.

What about Daniel? Could his arms keep up the punishment, or would the strap be torn from his grip? Would he make the deadly mistake of letting his head fall forward where the bull's horn would find him?

The questions were still hammering through her when three of the mounted Indians pressed forward, cutting off the bull's movement. The beast whirled, changing direction so swiftly that the horses couldn't keep up with him. Still, his momentum had been broken. He whipped his massive rear end around; his head followed more slowly. Then he lowered his horns as if to charge one of the horses.

At that moment Daniel flung himself outward. The bull took off after him, but Daniel was already running. As he raced away, the three Indians pressed in again, coming between Daniel and the bull. The beast charged first one and then another horse, but the frantic animals were able to keep out of his reach.

Finally, bellowing, the bull raced toward the rest of the herd.

Jessie had eyes only for Daniel. Despite the curious Indians, she headed toward where she'd last seen Daniel. He hadn't gone far. He stood beside a boulder, bracing himself with his hands as he sucked in air. After a moment, he straightened. His eyes caught hers, but she couldn't say a word. Magnificent! Wherever the thought had come from, it was utterly, totally right.

"W-what are you doing—here?"

Because she knew he needed time to catch his breath before he could truly talk, Jessie dismounted and waited him out. Finally he took a long, slow breath and faced her. His chest no longer heaved. "What are you doing here?" he repeated.

"I came to see you."

"Did you?" he asked softly. "Jessie, you might not be safe."

If I hadn't come, I would have never seen what just happened. "I have to be the one to decide that." She felt stronger somehow, as if his courage and daring had touched her. She might never ride a rogue bull, but neither would she hide behind fort walls, denying that Daniel had kissed her—that she'd kissed him back. "I asked Narcisco why you were risking your life. He said you were the only one who could tell me that."

Daniel wiped the back of his hand over his forehead. Enough sweat remained that Jessie couldn't dismiss what he'd just done. He wore a buckskin shirt. Although it was slit at the neck and a length of leather had been laced through it to hold the opening in place, the strip had pulled free. She could see his glistening throat. Dark hairs stuck to his flesh.

"Did he? It's hardly the first time I've ridden a bull."

"No. I didn't think it was. Who taught you how?"

"My mother."

"Your mother?"

"She rode as if she'd been born on an animal's back." He ran his hands along his temple and pulled at his hair, allowing the breeze to touch his flesh there. "I had to know if I could still do it."

"Because of what you went through saving my life, and the lives of others? You had to find out whether you were still as strong as you'd been before?"

Although he didn't move, his eyes told her that she'd guessed right. "I watched," she said softly. "I know the answer."

He rolled his shoulders backward. Smiling wryly, he ran his hand over his rib cage. "What I know is, I'm going to be sore tomorrow."

But he'd done it; he'd gotten the proof he needed, met his private goals. Although they stood several feet apart, she could smell his hot sweat. His hair looked as if it had been whipped by an angry wind. Pride held steady in his eyes. For an unbidden second she fought the need to press herself against him. "You were wonderful."

"Wonderful? I'm glad to see you, but how did you find me?"

She told him. Before she was finished, his features sobered. When he spoke, the words seemed reluctant. "We don't belong together, Jessie."

"That's what Raymond said. And Mr. and Mrs. Buckhalter and the sheriff."

"But you aren't listening to them, are you?"

"No," she told him. "Raymond uses the truth as it benefits him, and the Buckhalters don't know you." Then, while he stood before her, silhouetted against the sky with the sun glinting off his hair and sweat-slickened flesh, she relayed what Raymond told her yesterday. Saying the words made her throat raw. "I couldn't sleep last night. I—I'm not sure what I felt. Horrified. Terribly sad. Filled with questions."

"Questions?"

"Ones I need you to answer for me." She kept her eyes trained on the ground. Was that why she'd come out here? Because she believed only Daniel would be truthful, that he'd give her answers she needed? "Keseberg might be brought to trial for some of the things folks say he did. If they ask me, what will I tell them?"

"You weren't with him, were you?"

"No. You know that."

"And you didn't see him do anything, did you?"

"No."

"Jessie. What are you thinking?" Earlier, his voice had

been hoarse, as if reaching for air while he rode the bull had bruised his lungs. It no longer sounded that way. Now he was the gentle and compassionate man who'd encouraged her and Elizabeth to eat, who'd risked his own life for them.

"Thinking? I don't know. It's all mixed up inside me."

"Tell me about those things."

She hadn't looked at him. Still, she knew he was going to touch her before he did. He settled his hands on her shoulders, pressing down slightly, reaching through layers. "You never said anything." She couldn't plan her words. They'd simply come out of her, and he would have to make sense of them. "Raymond went to one of the frozen graves. I don't know which one. He—"

"I know."

Of course he did. "Why didn't you say anything?"

"I didn't care, Jessie. I still don't. You did what you had to to stay alive."

"I didn't!" she cried. "I didn't."

"I know."

Finally she found the strength to look at him. She saw it in his eyes; he'd said what he had because he wanted to make the telling as easy as possible for her. "I wouldn't even talk about it with Raymond. I would have rather died than—but that doesn't make me innocent. I did something."

"You kept her alive, Jessie."

Was there anything he didn't know? "Will she hate me for it?" She moaned. Still, she went on looking at him. Feeling something of him inside her. "That's why I couldn't sleep last night. Asking myself questions."

"I don't think that's the whole of it."

He was still sweating. She could smell, could feel his heat. "What do you mean?"

"Jessie, she's only a baby. It'll be a long time before she'll understand anything of what happened. You shouldn't be in this state over something you won't have to deal with for years, if at all."

He was right; she wanted to slap him for that. She also wanted to thank him for understanding her as well as he did.

"It's you you're thinking about, isn't it?"

When he said that, she could only nod in mute agreement. He could have pulled her closer to him, offered his chest as comfort and strength. But, although he still had his hands on her shoulders, he was making her stand alone. "I didn't want to die, Daniel," she made herself say. "I watched it happen to my mother. After she was gone, I was angry at her for leaving me."

"I know."

He knew. She wanted more from him, a better understanding of who and what he was, but that would have to wait until she'd worked through what she was trying to say. "I love my mother. She meant everything to me. But she died and left me behind to bury her."

"And that's why you were angry at her."

"I swore I'd never let that happen to Elizabeth."

He didn't speak. He still held her before him. She waited, needing him to break the silence. Finally, though, she understood that he was waiting for her to say something. "When I gave Elizabeth what I did—I knew it was only a matter of time before I took some for myself."

"Because you wanted to stay alive."

"Because Elizabeth needed me."

"Jessie." He whispered her name, almost gave it up to the wind. "That's the only thing that matters. You had a right and a reason to go on living. Don't make yourself sick thinking about what someone might say."

"But you don't know what they're saying."

"Yes I do."

Of course he did. He'd been there. "And you don't judge," she whispered. It wasn't a question. She knew what his answer would be. "Thank you."

Inches away, she watched his mouth lose its hard line and soften. The last time she'd seen that, he'd kissed her. And she'd kissed him in return. Did he want that now? Did she?

"Daniel."

At the masculine sound, she started and pulled away from him. Whirling, she watched as Narcisco walked toward them. "You play a dangerous game, my friend," the Indian said.

"What do you want?"

Narcisco stepped closer to Daniel. "To tell you I got your bull rope back for you. When she left the other day, you said you would not see her again."

"She came to me."

Narcisco grunted. "And she placed your hands on her shoulders. Miss Speer, it is good to see you."

Jessie didn't know whether Narcisco meant that or not. "I wish you'd call me Jessie. I, ah, I did what you suggested. I asked him why he rode that bull."

"Because that is something a man must do."

Daniel hadn't used quite those words, but the meaning was the same. "Not just men," she said softly. "Women have to prove themselves, too. And, sometimes, they have to ask themselves why they do certain things."

"I know. I heard what you said to Daniel."

"The conversation wasn't your concern," Daniel told Narcisco. Still, there weren't any hard edges to his words.

"You come to me when you want a roof over your head,

white man. You accept my hospitality. Your life is my concern."

Daniel grunted; then, so quickly that she almost missed it, he winked at her. Jessie wanted to know more about the relationship between the two men. There was something there that went deeper than anything she'd ever experienced. But exploring the depth of a friendship wasn't why she'd come here. Denying that seeing Daniel, being near him, had been part of the reason, she asked Narcisco how much he'd heard of what she'd said.

"Enough to know you have been questioning yourself."

She felt her jaws clench. "I have to. Others are going to. They already do."

"It is not their concern. They have not walked in your moccasins, Jessie Speer. Listen to me. The Maidu believe that spirits live in all things. Still, the spirit of the mountains does not hear everyone who prays to him. Maybe he only heard you."

Jessie didn't know what to make of Narcisco's explanation. Still, there was something in the simple words for her to take comfort in. Could the fact that she'd lived when others died be no more complex than that the mountain spirit had heard her?

"Do not question it, Jessie," Narcisco went on. "You are alive. It is a gift. Give thanks and then do what you can to be worthy of that gift."

"Worthy? Oh, Narcisco."

"You are listening? You hear what I am saying?"

She did. She'd come looking for Daniel because she wanted him to tell her she'd done what was right, what she had to, when she didn't know whether she'd ever be warm again and was terrified that Elizabeth would die. He'd given her what she needed to hear. But Narcisco had done more than that; he'd shared his belief and the belief of his people with her. She felt stronger for it, and ready to face whatever lay ahead of her.

"I hear," she told Narciso. "I think, maybe the Maidu are wiser than us." She should leave. She had what she'd come here for.

But both men were still looking at her. Daniel stood so close that she felt encompassed by him. Narciso, dark, intelligent, and compassionate, had known what she needed to hear, but it was Daniel she had to say good-bye to.

"After what I heard yesterday," she told him, "all I could think about was talking to you. Asking you—"

"Go back, Jessie. You belong with people like the Buckhalters."

"Do I? I'm not so sure. Maybe I'll stay here. I can't ride bulls, but I know how to help cows give birth. I've raised orphan calves. I know what to do when they eat too much new clover. Daniel, I can calm a steer caught in a fence."

"There aren't any fences here."

He didn't want her around. If he'd been going to kiss her—if—it was only because he was a man and men had certain needs. Why couldn't she face that he'd been ordered away from her at gunpoint? Maybe he was a murderer; they said he was, and he hadn't denied it. He hadn't come looking for her since the sheriff confronted him. Twice now she'd searched him out.

She. Not him.

"No. There aren't." Turning from him, she retraced her steps until she caught up with her mare. She mounted and yanked on the reins, causing the mare to toss her head. Still, she couldn't order the tension out of her arms. Daniel Bear was done with her.

She had to remember that. She would.

"Narcisco?" She spoke around what was closing down

in her throat. "Thank you. What you said means a great deal to me. It'll get me through whatever happens now."

She rode away without looking back. Until she could no longer hear the cattle, she kept hoping she'd hear her name being called. But when the sound didn't come, she turned her attention to the sky.

There hadn't been a cloud up there all the time she'd been looking for Daniel. Now two puffs of white slid over the horizon and merged together.

He'd looked so magnificent riding that bull.

Magnificent.

CHAPTER 10

The moon was full, making it possible for Jessie to find her way back to the fort. Still, because she'd spent too much time riding aimlessly, looking—she told herself—for the land she wanted to purchase, it was late enough that most folks had settled in for the night by the time she finished feeding and brushing the mare. Although she was hungry, she stayed at the livery stable long enough to ask the blacksmith if he might consider selling her the horse. To her delight, they arrived at a fair price.

Except for the Buckhalters, no one was in the fort kitchen. As she entered, Mr. Buckhalter gave her a long, silent look. Margaret leaned on the broom she'd been using around the oven. "I was beginning to worry about you."

"I'm sorry." Did they know where she'd been? If so, maybe she wouldn't be welcome in their company anymore. "I had a lot on my mind."

"Did you?"

Jessie took the crust of bread Margaret handed her. "I've seen so much productive land. I know it won't take long to ready the soil for planting. As soon as I buy a few acres—"

"That's not what we're talking about, Jessie."

Wasn't it? "I don't want to be beholden to you any longer than necessary. You've done so much for me. And for Elizabeth."

"It was the Christian thing to do." Margaret went back to work. Still, she kept glancing at Jessie over her shoulder. Then she sighed. "Mr. Buckhalter and I were talking to the military governor and Consul Larkin today. Both men are quite concerned about the future of the California Territory. The lawlessness, the fighting with Mexico, thieving Indians, they agree with us that life for decent, God-fearing men and women is not what it should be. We spoke of you."

"Me?"

Walter Buckhalter cleared his throat, glanced at his wife, then cleared his throat again. "You are free to do as you wish, of course. We know that. And, because of what you have been through, we all want the best for you. But, except for you, every other woman here has someone. Family, a husband, someone to protect her in this hard land. I've watched any number of eligible men try to catch your eye. You ignore all of them."

Jessie waited.

"Governor Kearny and Consul Larkin are concerned for your safety. They have spoken to Captain Sutter about you."

The thought that she was being discussed without her being there and that those powerful men felt responsible for her filled her not with gratitude but with confusion. Certainly her father would never have concerned himself with her welfare. He'd always expected her to take care of herself and to work side by side with him. Despite their strained relationship, she knew that when it came to self-confidence, she was more like him than like her gentle, unsure mother. "Have they?" she asked, keeping her voice as level as possible.

"They asked if I had assumed responsibility for you," Walter said.

"What did you tell them?"

"That while you were recovering from your ordeal, you were most grateful for the care we gave you. But—" He glanced at his wife, then ran his hands down his legs as if his palms had grown sweaty. "I told them you are a most independent woman. And that your choice of who you speak to is not always wise."

That's all they'd said about Daniel? Jessie couldn't believe that. "I see," she said, then waited him out.

"Men like Captain Sutter, Governor Kearny, and Consul Larkin take seriously the responsibilities that have been thrust on them. They can't, in good conscience, ignore your plight."

What plight, Jessie nearly asked. No matter what she said, the Buckhalters and Sutter, Kearny, and Larkin refused to believe that she wasn't terrified of being alone in the world. Maybe, if her grandmother hadn't given her the precious gift of financial independence, she would be facing a life fraught with unknowns and no way of changing that except by marrying some man. But she wasn't a homeless charity case. She had the means to support herself. And the skill.

"I wish they wouldn't concern themselves with me. I don't need their help."

The Buckhalters exchanged the look she knew they would. "You don't know, Jessie," Margaret said. "Life is hardly the same here as it was back on your farm. Daniel Bear concerns us the most. You have no idea what he's capable of, or what might happen if he comes around while you're out there on your farm."

"He won't. Margaret, I just want to be responsible for myself."

"It isn't done, Jessie. It simply isn't done. Nothing but grief can come to a woman alone here."

Margaret's words followed Jessie to bed, and she spent the better part of an hour in a silent argument with the well-meaning woman. The thought that three of the most influential men in California had been talking about her still made her uncomfortable. Unlike some of the Indian girls she'd seen, she wasn't anyone's slave. The money her grandmother had given her was hers; no one could take that away.

But men like Sutter, Kearny, and Larkin had influence she could only guess at. Could they, somehow, direct the course of her life?

No.

Only Daniel with his dark eyes and the incredible things they'd shared touched her these days. And what she felt around him she didn't understand, and couldn't begin to put words to.

When she slipped out of bed a little after dawn, she felt heartened by her decision, or rather, by the reaffirmation of the decision she'd made years ago. She would succeed in the life she'd planned for herself. And the sooner she put that plan into action, the sooner she would stop being aware of the great adobe walls and constant sound, so many people in a small space. She'd stop being the object of conversation.

Yesterday she'd finally found what she'd been looking for, a rich, level sweep of black earth covered by low-growing grasses and dotted with massive oaks. The land was cut in half by one of the many streams that fed the Sacramento River. All she had to do was approach Captain Sutter.

And if he refused her—

Jessie yanked her dress over her head and concentrated on the small buttons. Why should she worry herself half-sick looking trouble in the eye? Captain Sutter had already agreed to the purchase of land by other pioneers. She wasn't any different.

She was arranging her hair into a neat coil when she heard a knock at her door. Raymond stood just outside. She came within a breath of telling him to go away, that she didn't want to see or talk to him. But he looked as if he'd been kicked by something or someone.

"They want us to talk to them this afternoon."

"Who?" Although she wanted to keep their conversation as private as possible, she knew better than to invite him inside. He might take her gesture as encouragement when lately she'd been doing all she could to absent herself from him. "Raymond, what are you talking about?"

"Sutter's lieutenant, John Sinclair. He wants to question everyone who might know of Lewis Keseberg's character."

"What? I don't understand."

"You must. We spoke of it the other day."

Raymond was right. What he'd said about Keseberg had sent her to Daniel. "We were talking about rumors then. But this business with Lieutenant Sinclair. I don't understand."

Raymond glanced around as if reassuring himself that no one could overhear. He leaned forward, his voice low. "Mr. Coffymere and Mr. Fallon, as well as other rescuers, have been telling everyone who will listen that they hold Keseberg responsible for Tamsen Donner's murder. Now Keseberg is bringing suit against those gentlemen, saying they defamed his character."

Jessie could only shake her head at this turn of events. After everything Keseberg had been through, she would have thought he'd simply want to put the past behind him. "You and I weren't with him. Doesn't Lieutenant Sinclair understand that?"

Raymond shook his head. "Keseberg approached me last night. He wants me to testify in his behalf, to tell the lieutenant of his character from the time we began traveling together. He said he has already told Sinclair that you will do the same."

"I don't want anything to do with this."

"Neither do I."

Jessie blinked, confused. "You said he admitted what he did. Why is he bringing suit against them?"

"Because he now says his life was threatened, and they had no right to treat him like a criminal. He was crying when he approached me, saying that those men have made his life unbearable. He is only doing what he believes he must."

Jessie pressed the back of her hand to her forehead in an attempt to slow her head's pounding. "He hasn't said anything to me."

"He couldn't because you were gone yesterday. He gave your name to the lieutenant." Raymond glared down at her. "You saw him, didn't you?"

Him. Daniel. Yesterday seemed a lifetime away now. "I had to talk to someone. I couldn't stop thinking about

what we'd endured. Daniel was there. He saw how desperate things were. I prayed he would show me the way
through my thoughts."

"And what did he say?"

It hadn't been anything Daniel said. Yes, she'd been
heartened by his nonjudging acceptance of her actions, but
the words she'd needed to hear had come from an Indian
chief. Raymond wanted nothing to do with the Indians,
saying they were savages incapable of intelligent thought.
"Daniel doesn't live in the past. Only today concerns
him."

"Today. And you? Do you concern him?"

No. She wasn't going to let the conversation take that
turn. "He's tending cattle, Raymond. I'm looking to farm.
We don't have anything in common."

"How can you even say that? He's a murderer. How you
can want to see him, talk to him— Don't ever turn your
back on him, Jessie. If he believes you have something he
wants, something—" His eyes narrowed. "Nothing will
stop him from placing a bullet in your back. Think of all
that money left up there, never to be used. There's so
much—"

"Stop it!" She no longer cared whether anyone might
overhear. "I don't want to hear this." She reached behind
her, thinking to close the door between them. But before
she could move, Raymond grabbed her shoulder.

"If anyone's entitled to what's up there, I am. Me. Not
him. I won't stop warning you about him. You don't know
what he did."

"I don't care." That wasn't the truth. "He saved my life.
And now you're warning me about him—" She tried to
yank free.

"Jessie." Raymond clamped down, holding her before
him. "We can't fight among ourselves. We don't dare."

Made wary by the look in Raymond's eyes, she waited, suffering the feel of his fingers on her.

"I don't want to."

He cocked his head, looking for all the world like a man who didn't understand either himself or the world around him. "I simply want you to be forewarned. Keseberg has given your name to the lieutenant. He will ask you questions."

Jessie was carrying a sack full of flour to the kitchen an hour later when Keseberg approached her. The tall, blond, still handsome man had lost a great deal of weight since they met at Little Sandy. He limped badly, and his eyes had taken on a haunted look. In the past he had always treated her with respect. He still inclined his head toward her, but this time he asked nothing about her well-being. "I've just left Raymond," he said without asking whether she had time for him. "He's on his way to speak with Mr. Sinclair. He told me he has informed you about my suit."

"I don't know anything about the charges." Maybe, if she shifted the flour sack from one shoulder to the other, he wouldn't keep her long. "I stay to myself as much as possible. I don't concern myself with gossip."

"Don't you? I wish it was that easy for me. The things that have been said about me— My children are dead. From the moment my family and I signed on to travel with the Donners, life has been nothing but a nightmare. Miss Speer, I speak four languages. I am an educated, refined man. I was."

Jessie felt almost sorry for the man, who looked nearly broken. But whatever he'd done, the accusations he was defending himself against, weren't her affair. She tried to tell him that.

He shook his head, nearly losing his balance. Resting heavily on his cane, he repeated what she already knew, that he was determined to put an end to what was being said against him. "I've already given your name to Lieutenant Sinclair. You can either go to him of your own will, which I hope you will do today, or you will be required to testify during the trial itself."

"Trial? When will that be?"

"As soon as possible. Certainly within the next week or so."

Jessie hoped to be on her own land in a week. She didn't want to be forced to answer Lieutenant Sinclair's questions while the entire fort population listened. Couldn't they all put the past behind them? "I don't know what I should say."

"I'm attempting to rescue my reputation, Miss Speer. I want you to tell him of the role I played when Mr. Reed killed Mr. Snyder. When he understands how I took charge, and that I would not allow a murderer to go unpunished, he will see what kind of a man I am."

The flour sack nearly slipped from Jessie's fingers. Take charge? Keseberg had tried to hang Mr. Reed when he'd only tried to stop Mr. Snyder from beating his oxen. Mr. Snyder's death had been an accident. If Keseberg wanted her to tell the truth, she would be forced to tell the lieutenant about the bruises she'd seen on Mrs. Keseberg's face.

"I think you should ask someone else," she told him.

Keseberg shifted his weight, then smiled down at her. He'd looked so haunted a moment ago. Now she felt like a deer and Keseberg the hunter. "Once this unpleasantness is behind me, Miss Speer, I will be in a position to defend you. You need a protector. I am offering myself."

Protector? Jessie almost gagged on the word.

Raymond had asked her to marry him; she'd turned him down. And she'd made a vow to herself that she wouldn't lean on Daniel. What made Keseberg believe she wanted anything from him? "If I testify, it will be the truth."

"I—wouldn't want it any other way."

He was no longer looking her in the eye. As she stood helpless to stop him, Keseberg quickly ran his eyes down her body. She seethed under his unwanted advances, wanting to throw the flour sack at him. Crippled as he was, he wouldn't be able to get out of the way.

"You're a brave, strong woman, Jessie. Can I call you Jessie? I know you kept an orphaned child alive. Even before we were trapped, you never hesitated from doing what had to be done. That wouldn't change."

He thought she'd helped Raymond! Maybe he even believed she didn't condemn what he'd been accused of. Suddenly, she no longer wanted to avoid talking to Lieutenant Sinclair. Tight-lipped, she asked Keseberg where the lieutenant could be found; then, without telling him what she intended to say, she stepped around him. Her shoulder ached with the weight of the heavy flour. She wanted to heave it from her, to release her anger through action.

In midafternoon, one of the Indians told Jessie that Lieutenant Sinclair had received her message and wanted to speak to her now. She went up the steps that lead to the room used for meetings between Sutter and his most important visitors. Beneath her, she could hear the soldiers moving about in their barracks. She'd never been here before, never thought she'd have a reason. As she waited at the top of the stairs, she looked down at Fort Sutter. Was there ever a time when people weren't walking about, when horses weren't tied to the hitching posts, when meat wasn't being smoked on racks set over a bed of coals?

Daniel had spent the night with only the stars and moon to light his world. Surrounded by his Indian friends, had he thought of her or had talk of cattle been more important? Could he possibly imagine what she was about to do?

Would he care?

Except for the lieutenant and the two somber-faced army men who flanked him, the dark room she entered was empty. At the lieutenant's prompting, Jessie sat in a rough-finished chair near a table made from a wide plank set on two sawhorses. Sinclair, looking stiff and uncomfortable in his gray military uniform with its high collar, stared at her over a thick pair of spectacles. "You understand the gravity of this charge, do you, Miss Speer?" he asked after inquiring about her health. "Mr. Keseberg was concerned that you might not be the most sympathetic of witnesses. Let me assure you, it is my every intention to make sure there is no miscarriage of justice. A man's reputation is at stake."

Jessie thought that Lieutenant Sinclair seemed overfilled with himself. From what she understood, Sinclair had come to California with Sutter, as his aide. Obviously, he was taking his new position as court officer most seriously. She told him that she understood what Keseberg was hoping to accomplish with his suit, but that she couldn't shed light on the truth or untruth of what Mr. Coffymere and Mr. Fallon had accused Keseberg of. However, she had spent several months traveling with Keseberg and knew something of his nature.

"That is not the issue which concerns me, Miss Speer. I have tried to tell Mr. Keseberg that. He has not been charged with a crime. Still, the gentlemen in question persist in spreading stories about him and that is what concerns him. You have heard these stories, haven't you?"

"Only a little. I keep to myself, Lieutenant. Most days I work for Mr. Buckhalter. When I'm not doing that, I'm making plans to buy my own farm."

"A farm? You and Mr. Sage are planning to marry? He indicated to me that the matter was not yet settled."

The thought that the lieutenant had joined her name with Raymond's made her want to laugh. "I have no plans to marry anyone."

"You can't be thinking of going out on your own. Miss Speer, I don't want to be the one to bring up a delicate and painful matter, but I understand you lost your family, and that you are alone in the world."

She was so weary of hearing this. "Not truly alone," she said, and went on to tell him about the Buckhalters and Larkins. She nearly told him she'd begun a friendship with a Maidu chief and owed her life to a man others called a killer. Instead, hoping to bring the conversation back to her reason for being here, she explained that she hadn't been close to the Keseberg family and had barely spoken to Mrs. Keseberg. However, she had observed enough that she felt she could speak about Keseberg's character.

The lieutenant still wasn't interested in that. Instead, he asked for a detailed explanation of her experience once it became clear that she and her family were trapped. "I need to know what you did. That way I will have a better understanding of what everyone endured."

"What *I* did? Lieutenant, I wasn't near Keseberg. I can't say whether he did what he is being accused of. That's the matter at hand, not how I survived."

"Miss Speer, trying times call for people to do things they wouldn't otherwise. If you acted in a manner different from your usual behavior, then it might be easier for folks to understand the strain Mr. Keseberg was under."

What direction was this questioning headed? Certain now that she wouldn't like the answer, Jessie straightened and folded her hands in her lap. Despite the churning in her stomach, she refused to let her anger show. "It seems to me, Lieutenant, that you are asking me to reveal details of my life that I am determined to put behind me. I came here because I didn't want someone else speaking for me. Those were inhuman times. If we all acted a little inhuman, I can only pray that those who didn't experience what we did will understand how strong the will to live is."

"What inhuman acts?"

Jessie froze. She had no doubt that what was said here would be spread throughout the fort. "Why do you feel you need to know that?"

"Because—" The lieutenant leaned forward. As he rested his elbow on the table, the two other men did the same. "Because if Mr. Keseberg is being scorned for something that was a common practice, then that must stop."

That wasn't the issue. If Keseberg was bragging, how horrible that must be for those who'd lost loved ones. He *must* be held accountable for his words. "Lieutenant, I came here to talk about Mr. Keseberg, not me."

"Why? Have you done something you're ashamed of?"

This was insane! True, she'd never before been involved in a legal proceeding, but certainly the questions asked at such things dealt with the charges that had been leveled, not—was that it? The lieutenant was indulging his own curiosity about what the Donner party had endured? If so, she refused to cooperate. "I've changed my mind." She stood, taking a small measure of pleasure from the way the men's mouths dropped open. "I refuse to be part of this—whatever you call it."

"Miss Speer." The lieutenant pushed back from the table, his chair scraping loudly on the wooden floor, and rose, bringing him close to eye level with her. He yanked off his glasses. "You can either answer my questions now, in private, or later, in public."

"I'm not on trial, Lieutenant. I can't be forced to say anything I don't want to."

"Watch it, young lady." What she could see of Sinclair's neck was rapidly turning red. "You are making assumptions about the law when you know nothing about its workings."

And he did? "I'm leaving." Determined to present a calm exterior, she kept her voice low and steady. "You can't keep me here."

"You can't—" Suddenly the lieutenant clamped his lips together. His attention was now riveted to a spot behind her.

"Jessie. Get the hell out of here."

Daniel. She would know his voice in her dreams. Despite the upheaval inside her, she slowly gathered her skirt and stepped away from her chair. She dipped her head just the slightest bit at Lieutenant Sinclair and his companions. "You may be right," she said calmly. "I might be ignorant of the way the law works. However, I came of my own free will. I have decided to leave, of my own free will."

With her breath caught deep in her chest, she turned and faced Daniel. He stood with one hand gripping the door latch. The other rested at his waist, less than an inch from his knife.

No one spoke. Slowly, so that Lieutenant Sinclair wouldn't think she was fleeing, she slid past Daniel and waited for him to close the door behind them. He took her elbow. Together they descended the stairs. As they reached the ground, a low, heavily laden wagon pulled by a team of oxen jerked past.

"What are you doing here?" she whispered when she could make herself heard.

"I had business with Captain Sutter. I heard about Keseberg. I saw you go in there."

He had business with Captain Sutter. Surely he'd known he'd be coming to the fort when she left him yesterday. Why hadn't he said anything? Sudden anger, in part backlash from what she'd just endured, surged through her. "And you thought I needed rescuing? I needed that once, Daniel. No longer. I don't need a protector." *Protector.* How weary she was of the word. "Do you understand?" The words lashed around her; she didn't try to stop them. "It's my life. I will live it. Me. Only me."

Daniel's features darkened. He'd already taken his hand from her elbow. Now he stepped back. Still, she felt his presence. "That's what you think I'm doing?"

"Aren't you?"

She expected a quick denial; she didn't get it. Instead, Daniel's fingers curled inward toward his body, leaving her confused as to his thoughts. She didn't regret her outburst. Still, why had she been able to control her temper around Lieutenant Sinclair and not with Daniel?

A sound above distracted her. The sudden change in Daniel, the way his body became hard and alert, momentarily forced her thoughts off everything else. The lieutenant, flanked by his aides, stood on the small landing.

Lieutenant Sinclair had drawn his pistol. It was aimed at Daniel's head.

"Get away from her, Bear."

Slowly, his body radiating barely suppressed fury, Daniel did as he was told. His hands had turned into white-knuckled fists. Jaw clenched, eyes black as midnight, he stood staring up at Sinclair.

"What are you doing?" Jessie demanded. She wanted, needed, to touch Daniel. He'd been so many things—the man who'd carried her out of hell, a rider of man-hating bulls. Now he stood before an armed man, as taut and ready for battle as any wild animal. He might see himself as helpless. She sensed only his hard-won self-control, challenge, the sense of danger. "Did you hear me?" she demanded. Somehow, although she was aware of nothing except Daniel, she kept her gaze trained on the lieutenant. "I asked you what you're doing. Drawing a weapon on an unarmed man—"

"He's carrying a knife."

"A knife against a pistol," she scoffed. "How brave you are."

"Jessie," Daniel hissed. "Don't."

"Don't tell me that!" Her entire body trembled, and yet she felt in total control. Lieutenant Sinclair had drawn a weapon on Daniel. How dare he! If he fired— "I will not have him treat you like a criminal," she told Daniel. "You did nothing wrong by coming in. You had every right."

"You didn't think that a minute ago."

Jessie glanced at Daniel. For the briefest of seconds, laughter touched his eyes. Then he again looked like a man both trapped and free and her heart swelled.

Beside her, Daniel warred with the insanity that had brought him here. Yesterday he'd nearly told her he would be coming to the fort, but then he'd touched her and felt her warmth and known that only a fool would thrust his hand into a fire twice. He'd conduct his business and leave without seeing her. For her sake if not for his, it had to be that way.

Then he'd heard that she was being asked to answer questions about Keseberg. He couldn't let her go through that alone.

Only, she hadn't needed him to protect her after all. Quite the opposite; she was now glaring up at an armed man.

He forced his fingers to relax and stared at the lieutenant. "If Miss Speer wants nothing to do with me, she has only to say the word. Until then, she, not either of us, will speak for her."

"The likes of you has no business being around a lady."

"My only intention was to make sure she wasn't being forced to do something she didn't want to. She has amply proven that isn't the case." He flexed his fingers, careful to keep his hands away from his knife. Lieutenant Sinclair wasn't known for having a hot temper, but their exchange had attracted a great deal of attention. If the man thought his reputation might be at stake, it was impossible to say what he might do. Besides, Daniel had no doubt that his death could be easily justified. He wasn't afraid of dying, but he wasn't going to let it happen in front of Jessie.

When the lieutenant continued to stare at him, the pistol shaking slightly as the man's anger vented itself, Daniel made a dangerous and yet, he believed, necessary decision.

Keeping his movements slow and measured, he placed his hand on Jessie's elbow. She could have jerked away. He would have understood if she had. Instead, she remained within easy reach.

"We're going to walk away," he whispered to her. "You and me together."

"All right."

Side by side, slowly, they turned their backs on the lieutenant. Then, mindful of the eyes on them, he released her. When he spoke, it was in a voice that carried. "If I'd known you were determined to handle this situation on your own, Miss Speer, I would not have bothered you."

"Bothered?"

"Just because you had need for me once doesn't give me call to interfere in your life. I hope you will accept my apology."

"Daniel?" she whispered. "What are you doing?"

"You will," he went on in that unnaturally loud voice, "accept my apology, won't you?"

"Daniel. Don't."

He couldn't let her speak his name again. If she did, his resolve would desert him. By now, they'd crossed the compound and reached the door to her room. He didn't have to look around to know they were still the center of attention. What happened now, his actions, could make or break her reputation. Despite his inner turmoil, he stepped away from her. "You were right to call me to task. I should not have stepped in where I wasn't wanted or needed. Miss Speer, I have completed my business here. I will not be bothering you again."

She stared up at him with eyes so filled with unrest that it was all he could do not to crush her to him. If only he hadn't kissed her, leaving would be easier. But leave he must. For her sake. He bowed elaborately, not trying to deny the impact her nearness had on him. "Miss Speer, good-bye." Then, quickly, softly: "If you need me, Narcisco and I will be camped where Flathead Creek flows into the Sacramento."

"Flathead?"

"The moon is full. You'll be able to find me."

"I—"

"Don't say a word." Dragging his eyes off her, he started toward his horse. "Not a word, Jessie. Come only if there's no other way."

CHAPTER 11

Silent, Jessie watched Daniel ride away. He should have been an actor. No one but she knew that what he'd said to her, his formal demeanor, had been an act. The anger and passion he'd shown before they stepped outside had been the truth—not his unemotional and public leave-taking.

Why?

The eyes of so many were on her. Although no one had moved, it felt as if they were coming closer. Careful to keep her movements slow so they might think she was unaffected by what had happened, Jessie let herself into her room. The moment she did, she was sorry. The confining space she'd barely been able to suffer became even smaller. Yesterday when she'd ridden out to find Daniel, she'd felt at home. In truth, thinking about exploring the rich Sacramento Valley from one end to the other was what it took for her to fall asleep these days.

Maybe if Daniel hadn't come here today, she wouldn't be fighting the walls that surrounded her.

But if he hadn't, she wouldn't know about this side of him.

Come only if there's no other way.

When Captain Sutter entered his room, Jessie waited a few minutes before crossing from her end of the courtyard to his. In the light cast by the candle burning on his dresser, she could see him sitting in the chair he'd brought from his home in Sweden, his head bent over a book. She knocked, wondering if anyone was watching her.

When he opened his door, she saw that he had removed his boots. Except for that, he was still dressed as if ready to receive visitors. She took note of his new but dusty uniform, wondering if he wouldn't prefer more casual attire.

"Miss Speer." He smiled expansively and welcomed her in. "How are you? I'm sorry my duties have kept me so busy that I haven't been a more attentive host."

"I'm the one who should be apologizing." She closed the door so their conversation couldn't be overheard. "I've imposed on you long enough. I'm sure you have other needs for the room you were so kind to let me use."

Captain Sutter waved off her words, then indicated she was to use the chair he'd just vacated. He sat on the side of his high bed. Flanked by the deep red fabric that served as a canopy, he looked even more imposing than he had when he asked her in. She shouldn't feel awed in his company. From what she'd heard, he was barely able to keep ahead of his creditors. Maybe—the thought gave her courage—he needed any amount of money, no matter how little. She folded her hands in her lap, careful not to clench them.

"I love this land," she began. "The richness of the soil—"

"Ah yes. You come from farming stock, don't you? So, tell me, have you seen my wheat fields?"

Jessie told him she had. Then, although she wasn't sure how he might interpret her words, she mentioned that she'd recently come across his herd of cattle. "They looked so fat and sleek and not nearly as wild as I'd been told." *Except for the one Daniel rode.* "The grass here agrees with them."

He sighed. "If only I can keep the Spanish and Walla Wallas from stealing them. Miss Speer, you didn't come to listen to my problems. What can I do for you?"

Heartened by his generous words, Jessie told him about the land she'd found, land that would be right for her purposes. "From the moment my family decided to come to California, I've dreamed of having my own farm. If you have need for that particular acreage, I will look for something else. But having a stream there would make watering my crops an easy matter."

Captain Sutter had been smiling at her much as an indulgent father smiles at a child. Now the corners of his mouth straightened. "Are you getting married, Miss Speer?"

Despite the instant knot in her stomach, she assured him that marriage wasn't on her mind. Then, without giving him time to interrupt, she went into her farming background in great detail. "I know I can make it work," she finished. "I have the seeds and the know-how. All I need is the land."

"By yourself?"

How many times would she have to answer that question? Smiling confidently, she explained that she intended to clear and till just enough land for her own use this year. If she was successful, she planned to at least double the size of her garden next year. "I know you've met with only limited success in growing the vegetables you need," she hurried on. "With everything that demands your attention and the need to concentrate on a wheat crop, it isn't possible for you to tend to everything. I might be able to supply some of what you need. In fact, if I hire some Indians to work for me, I know I can."

"You have the money?"

Jessie thought she saw something glitter in Sutter's eyes. "I can pay a reasonable amount for the land. Certainly I expect to do that."

Sutter didn't speak. Instead, he stared at his feet as if fascinated by his dirty socks. After a long minute during which it was all Jessie could do not to shake him, he focused on her. "Miss Speer, I am a reasonable man, one who knows there are many ways to live. I am surrounded by all manner of people and would not pretend to try to tell them what to do."

"I'm glad to hear that."

"But you aren't an Indian who has spent her entire life here. A civilized woman, one who has been educated and used to a certain standard of living—you have no idea how hard this land can be on a body."

She did. Her father had seen to that. "If I fail, it's my failure, Captain. I wouldn't hold anyone, especially you, responsible."

"Wouldn't you? That is refreshing to hear. Tell me, Miss Speer, if the Walla Wallas run you off the land or you can't make a go of your crops, will you be back at my gate asking for refuge?"

"No. No."

"Are you sure?"

"I won't fail," she told him. What else could she do? Give up? Throw herself on some man's mercy? "Chief Narcisco of the Maidu has promised that his braves will watch after me." She didn't mention that the offer had come from Daniel. "With them nearby, I don't foresee any problems with the Walla Wallas. The land I want to buy isn't far from the Larkins, the people who took the baby I was caring for. They've never had a moment's trouble."

"Miss Speer, I've never done business with a woman, never entered into a contract with her."

Why not? Were women some inferior breed? "I'd like to be the first," she said with all the confidence she could muster. "I have every reason to believe the arrangement will work out well for both of us."

"And if it doesn't—"

Although she wanted to fill the silence with argument, she waited him out.

"If it doesn't, it will fall on my shoulders that I jeopardized your safety, and maybe your life."

You wouldn't be thinking this if I were a man. "I'd never place any blame on you. This is something I want to do." *Something I have to do.* "I'll accept all responsibility."

"Miss Speer." Sutter sighed. "How old are you?"

She winced. "Twenty. But I've—"

"Twenty. Only twenty."

Jessie leaned forward, not surprised to find she hadn't succeeded in stopping her hands from clenching together. How could she help it? "I intend to pay you handsomely."

"Pay?" His eyes narrowed. "If you were married, we would already be shaking on the agreement."

"Married? The money is mine."

"Miss Speer, this is no land for a woman alone. I understand Raymond Sage is most fond of you. Become his wife and our conversation will have a much different outcome."

No! "If—if I were married, you'd sell me the land?"

"With clear conscience, yes."

"But because I'm not, you won't?"

"It's never been done, Miss Speer." Sutter shifted, obviously eager to have the conversation over. "In all my years and travels, I have never heard of a woman owning land by herself. I will not be the one to turn against tradition, what exists for valid reasons."

The only reason was that men like Sutter refused to see women as equals. But if she tried to shake sense into him, she'd never get him to listen to her. With her emotions barely in check, she stood on numb legs. "Thank you for your time, Captain. If you don't mind, I have one last question."

He sighed, then smiled. "Of course."

"Is the land for sale? If you and I were able to work past your objections, would you sell it to me?"

"That isn't the issue, is it, Miss Speer? My objections stand. But for argument's sake, yes, every acre I don't have in production has a price on it."

Jessie honestly didn't remember walking out of Sutter's room. His soft accent remained in her mind—a gentle echo at odds with his refusal.

Unable to force herself to walk back to her room, she stared up at the darkening sky. Daniel was out there somewhere. Tonight he'd sleep under the stars. He was doing what he wanted with his life, wasn't he? Why couldn't it be the same for her?

Her throat felt ragged. Tears were so close; if they broke free, they'd overwhelm her. All she wanted out of life was earth to call her own. Was it so much to ask?

Her attention drifted to her hands. Her father had called

them a man's hands. Even when the strength in them had kept food on the table, he'd ridiculed her for not having long, white, tapering fingers—hands that would catch a man's eye.

No. These were not, would never be those kind of hands.

She could succeed; she would.

The moon, blue-hazed, spun its magic over the valley and made it easy for her mare to follow the river to where Flathead Creek fed into it. She'd had to wait until she'd helped the Buckhalters clean up after the evening meal before leaving the fort. She'd been aware of eyes on her as she rode through the gate. She was certain she would be the subject of many conversations.

She didn't care.

She'd gone less than a mile when she heard the wolves. Because their night song had always been part of her life, she didn't cringe from the sound. Instead, she felt comforted by it. If this were her land, if she'd coaxed the soil to grow her crops, there would still be room for wolves and other creatures on it. True, she'd have to contend with hungry deer, but if she surrounded her garden with corn, the deer should be stopped by the stalks' dry rustling sound.

Did Daniel know about corn? Had he ever sat out on a hot summer night and listened to it pop and snap as it pushed toward the sky? If she told him about the joy she felt when the first green tips of what she'd planted burst through to the surface, would he understand?

Maybe not.

The wolves, calling to the moon, distracted her. She listened, trying to sort one sound from another. She thought she had isolated the deep howl of the dominant male. Was Daniel like that, the dominant male?

Shocked by her thought, she tried to concentrate on the progress her mare was making and what she'd say to Daniel when she found him. But the wolves weren't done with her. The deep-throated male, full of himself, would hold the younger wolves at bay. If they dared to challenge his authority, he would teach them respect with teeth and claws.

Daniel didn't need teeth and claws. He'd disarmed Lieutenant Sinclair's anger with his intelligence—and maybe with his reputation.

Chief Narcisco had been stretched out on his back, staring up at the stars. Now, although he hadn't said a word, hadn't moved, Daniel knew he was no longer relaxed. Acting on the Indian's silent warning, Daniel tried to dismiss the howling wolves so he could concentrate on the other night sounds. After a moment, he caught the soft thud of an approaching horse. He and Narcisco exchanged a look.

Daniel had only a moment in which to ask himself how long ago he'd learned to be alert to danger before he relaxed. Whoever was approaching was making no attempt to hide.

Jessie?

He'd told her where he'd be if she needed him. But she'd seen him helpless in the face of a weapon. Did she understand or did she think him a coward?

Jessie?

Had she come looking for him because she had no choice?

Or because she wanted to see him?

After glancing over at Narcisco, he sat up and waited for her to come closer. She sat her pinto easily, a woman who'd never feared a horse. Nothing in her demeanor gave him any hint that she would rather spend the night surrounded by guards and cannons than out here with the wolves.

With him.

"Daniel?" She drew on the reins, stopping her horse a dozen feet from where he was sitting. He'd taken off his shirt so he could mend a tear in the neck. Warmed by the fire, he hadn't bothered to put it back on. "Daniel."

"I'm here, Jessie."

Narcisco grunted, then turned his back to them. Daniel ignored his friend. Whatever the Indian thought of this, he would let him know, eventually.

She slipped off her horse. It was then that he realized he'd never seen her use a saddle. The thick hair she'd despaired of earlier was pulled into two practical braids. She reminded him of an Indian.

"You said I could come to you if I was in trouble."

He didn't remember putting it to her quite like that, but the words didn't matter. "What is it?" If they'd been anywhere else and anyone but Narcisco had been with them, he wouldn't have pointed to his blanket, indicating she could sit there. But they'd slept with their bodies touching so they could keep Elizabeth alive.

For a moment she simply stared at the spot next to him, then walked over and folded herself down on it. The firelight glinted off something at her waist. When he looked closer, he saw that she carried a knife. He nodded at it.

"This is an uncertain land, Daniel. Uncertain times. Only a fool would fail to know that."

"I'd never call you a fool."

"No? Thank you."

She was looking at him—probing, really. If she'd taken her eyes off his and indicated that she was aware of his shirtless state—maybe affected by it—he would have touched her. Held her against him. He sensed something building inside her, but was unable to concentrate enough to learn anything of her emotion.

Did she know how beautiful she was? If he told her that he'd fallen asleep thinking about the strength in her slim body, would she be taken aback? She was twenty, a woman. Certainly she knew the effect her high, full breasts and long, work-tempered limbs had on a man.

But maybe she didn't. Otherwise wouldn't she have known better than to sit so close to him?

"Daniel? After you left, I talked to Captain Sutter."

"Did you?" He was right. Her mind wasn't on him. "What about?"

She told him of the conversation, quickly, the words pouring from her as if she wanted to be rid of them. "I couldn't think of anything that would change his mind, nothing except—"

He waited her out, wishing he'd been there to watch her confront Captain Sutter.

"Daniel . . ." Without taking her eyes off him, she reached into her dress pocket and pulled out the leather pouch she'd brought down off the mountain. "I need your help."

He thought he knew what she was going to say, but for a moment he couldn't concentrate on that. *I need your help.* No one had ever said that to him. He'd never wanted to hear the words—not before today, tonight, from her.

"What can I do?"

Narcisco grunted; Daniel ignored him.

"Captain Sutter doesn't believe women should own land."

"Doesn't he?"

"He's wrong."

"I know."

She'd already opened her mouth, ready, he knew, to voice her next argument. Unprepared for his agreement, she could only stare at him. Before, he'd thought her body beautiful. Now he knew that her eyes were the most incredible things about her. "Why?" she whispered.

"Why do I think Sutter's wrong?"

She nodded.

"Jessie, my mother supported herself and me by breaking horses all over Texas. When she was done with one, there wasn't a horse anywhere who was better at working cattle. She had no man to lean on, none to fight her battles for her." Aware of how close he'd come to the reason he'd fled Texas, he paused. Someday, maybe, he'd tell Jessie about that. "I was raised by a woman who feared nothing and no one. She broke and trained horses. You farm."

"Then ..." Jessie licked her lips. The gesture stopped Daniel in mid-breath. "Then you understand why this means everything to me?"

He was beginning to. He wished he knew more. "Jessie, I told you to come to me if there was anything I could do." He touched the worn bag she still held toward him.

"You'd take this? Buy the land for me?"

She made it sound so simple when he knew it was far from that. For an instant he wanted to tell her no, that he wouldn't be a part of her maybe endangering her life. But if any man had tried to tell his mother that, she wouldn't have listened. Jessie wouldn't either.

Without saying a word, he took the bag from her and emptied its contents on his blanket. He sorted through the coins, then met her waiting eyes. "It isn't much, Jessie."

"It's all I have. It'll be enough. I'll make it enough."

He didn't doubt her determination, or her desperate promise to herself. Still, he had to make sure she understood what he was trying to tell her. "I've heard Sutter bargain with others for land. If he holds true to what he's done before, it'll take most of what you have just to buy the acres."

"I already have a horse. I don't need a plow, just a strong stick—I'll need a cow for milk."

"What about a cabin?"

"It's all I can do to be inside for a few minutes. I'll sleep outside, near my crops."

His mother had spent more of her life sleeping under the stars than with a roof over her head. Still, the thought of Jessie surrounded by nothing but this untamed valley made him hesitate. "What about winter?"

"By next winter I'll be a wealthy woman. I'll sell my carrots and onions at unheard-of prices because I'll be the only one with a crop."

He liked it that she could joke. "What will you do with your wealth? Hire someone to build you a cabin?"

"Maybe I'll build my own fort."

He didn't for a moment believe that. "The captain will ask why I want to buy land. If I try to tell him it's for me, he'll know I'm lying."

"Once it's mine, I don't care what anyone says."

"That's not what I'm talking about. Sutter knows I'm not one for settling down. He'll guess I'm speaking for you. He might say no. In fact, he probably will."

He thought she might wilt under his words, but she didn't. Instead, she ran her hand down her braid. "I've already thought about that. But—" Her eyes flickered away from his, then fastened on him again. "If you told him we were getting married— He said if I was Raymond's wife— Daniel, I don't know what else to do!"

Her agony exploded inside him. "If folks think we're getting married, you won't be able to hold up your head."

"I don't care."

He couldn't believe that, but he guessed that she was so focused on what she'd come here for that she'd blinded herself to the consequences of an alliance with him. "I do. You're planning on spending the rest of your life here. You'll have to face people."

"Daniel. We won't be getting married. They'll—maybe they'll think we changed our minds."

"And maybe they'll think we conspired to lie to the captain so you could get the land."

"Maybe."

"And you don't care?"

He knew she was going to shake her head even before she did. "If I told you no to this," he asked, "what would you do?"

She picked at the money between them. "I don't know."

He was already sorry he'd asked the question. Instead of telling her that, he picked up the coins and slowly put them back in the bag. He felt her searing eyes on him, but until he'd come to terms with himself, he couldn't speak. He didn't want her out there alone, vulnerable. At least his mother had had him—first a child in need of her and later a young man capable of working side by side with her. Knowing Jessie was safely in the fort, he'd been able to go on with his life.

He couldn't do that any longer.

"He'll be at the fort in the morning?"

She nodded, her eyes hot coals.

"Let me talk to him alone. The captain and I understand each other, at least a bit."

"Oh. If . . . You'll do it? Ask for me?"

"Yes." He didn't for a moment believe that the silent Indian nearby was sleeping. It didn't matter.

Jessie had come to him.

The moonlight bathed her. He stared at her hands and wondered if she knew how incredible they were. Hands like that—small and soft-skinned next to his—should be pampered. She should have a wealthy husband who didn't want her to lift a finger. But to her, that incredible mix of muscle and bone was simply one of the tools she must have if she was going to survive.

Still, he could spin a dream of what those same hands would feel like on his flesh.

He'd caught her hand before giving himself time to judge the right or wrong of what he was doing. He had to tell her to leave, that he'd see her tomorrow after he talked to the captain. But he couldn't let her go—yet.

"If you have a house, what would it look like?"

"What? Daniel, I don't care about that." She was staring at their hands. She'd made no move to remove hers from his.

Neither did he. "What do you care about?"

"What?"

"Besides land of your own, what do you want?"

He expected her to shrug off his question. If she had been the one to ask him, he wouldn't have said anything. At least he didn't think he would.

"I don't know." She sounded wistful. "For almost a year now there hasn't been time for anything except selling the farm, traveling, trying to stay alive. It's hard to think of anything else."

"You have the time now."

He felt her hand move. Still, she did nothing except flex a finger so that he wasn't holding it as tightly. "Maybe I don't want to think."

Because that would force her to dwell on what she'd endured? He didn't believe that was it; she was too brave. "Why not?"

By way of answer, if that's what it was, she rested her free hand on his cheek. Need, so powerful it took his breath, flamed inside him. But she wasn't a woman to be taken on the ground by some man turned animal. Feeling his way, he laid his hand over hers and pressed her fingers more firmly against his cheek. He hadn't shaved since yesterday. Was his beard too rough for her skin?

No.

The wolves had been howling without interruption since the moon rose. There was a pulse to the sound, a rising and falling like the beating of a heart. He wondered if the wolves' song sounded the same to Jessie.

"I—" She drew away, yet didn't try to pull free. "I have to leave."

"I'll go with you."

"No. No. I don't want to take you from your sleep."

Didn't she know that he wouldn't be sleeping tonight? Because he didn't know how much longer he could keep his hands off her if she went on touching his cheek, he released her. Her fingers slid off him, drawing out the leave-taking until he thought he might go crazy with it.

"Jessie, listen to me. If I don't go with you, I'll spend the night wondering if you made it back safe. Believe me, this is easier."

"You'll worry about me?"

He couldn't believe she had to ask. Maybe she needed to hear him say the words. "I care about you," he whispered. As the words drifted from him, he had the fleeting thought to grab them and try to shove them back inside himself. The thought died. He might know nothing about how a man spoke to a woman, but he could speak out of emotion; in truth, he couldn't do anything else. "We shared something that'll stay with us for the rest of our lives."

"I know."

The wolves almost swallowed her words, but even if he hadn't heard her, he'd seen her mouth move.

Her tempting, kissable mouth.

The devil take Narcisco. Jessie had come to him for something only he could give her. He wanted only one thing from her.

He wasn't sure he'd done all the reaching. Maybe she'd put an end to half of the distance that separated them. If so, if she wanted and needed this as much as he did . . .

"Jessie. Jessie." He spoke with his mouth against hers.

She said nothing. Her body had begun a dance so faint that if he hadn't had his arms around her, he wouldn't have known it. He felt the same unease, the same mystery.

Her hands might be strong and capable, but her mouth was for losing himself in. As he drew her even closer, his heart pounding, he caught the faintest scent of lilac.

Jessie. Although he wanted to hold her against him until the moon had completed its journey, he forced himself to draw back a few inches. The fragrance faded. Because he still had his hands on her arms, he felt capable of dealing with the loss. What did she think of him? She must know why he'd left Texas, at least the story folks told and retold. Was she afraid of him?

No. A woman afraid wouldn't have ridden out at night to look for a man, and she wouldn't have told him of her dreams, and asked him to help her make them come true.

"Daniel? What—"

He didn't want questions. Questions might put an end to what they were experiencing. Before she could finish whatever it was she was going to say, he drew her close again and tasted of her. Again the night air brought the scent of lilac. The call of wolves.

Take her back to the fort? Later. After he'd had enough of her soft lips and his body had stopped humming.

If that ever happened.

CHAPTER 12

Three days after Daniel rode back to the fort with her, Jessie gazed out at her land. This morning the sun was so bright it hurt her eyes. Birds, more than she could count, hopped over the ground, reinforcing her belief that the earth was well populated with earthworms. It seemed as if the oaks here were a richer green than elsewhere, that the breeze smelled sweeter.

Daniel had told her she'd chosen well.

When her mare jerked against the reins, impatient to test the new grass, Jessie slipped off the multicolored back and removed the bridle. She sank to the ground and leaned her back against a dark trunk. After sniffing at her, the mare turned her attention to eating.

This was hers! Even now, with the all-important paper in her possession, she found that almost impossible to believe. Daniel had been right; purchasing ten acres at Captain Sutter's inflated prices had taken most of her money. She'd already talked to one of the farming families about buying a milk cow and would be picking it up in a few days.

Tomorrow she'd begin cutting into the earth with a hoe and pointed stick. By the end of the week, God willing, she'd have planted the first of her seeds.

And then . . .

Jessie pushed herself to her feet and began marching off the boundaries of her land. She couldn't hear the wolves today. Not long after she'd left the fort, she'd spotted an elk. She'd heard that the great, graceful creatures were plentiful, but this was the first she'd seen.

Did Daniel ever stop what he was doing to stand and marvel at an elk?

When her mare began trailing after her, Jessie stopped walking and turned to rub a soft nose. "Are you lonesome? Don't worry. I'll take good care of you."

The mare blew out a warm breath.

"Captain Sutter knows Daniel bought the land for me. I'm sure he does; he just doesn't care so long as folks don't think he sold direct to a woman. The way the Buckhalters looked at me when I told them—they don't understand. They just don't understand."

Obviously satisfied with that explanation, the mare went back to eating. Jessie stood watching her, feeling the sun's heat seep into her back. She lifted her head and took another deep, rich breath.

Wonderful!

After years of wanting something to call her own, wonderful!

"Thank you, Grandma," she whispered. "Thank you for your gift."

The mare ignored her. After shaking her head at the animal, Jessie went back to pacing off her boundaries. Counting didn't take up all of her mind. She remembered clinging to Daniel after he'd told her he'd approach Sutter. She remembered the long, mostly silent ride back to the fort with him. He'd insisted on staying outside while she went in for the rest of the night. He didn't want folks to see them together. Knowing an argument would accomplish nothing, she'd started to leave him. Then—then she'd reached for him and he'd gripped her shoulders and although they were both on horseback, their mouths met.

"I wish he was here."

The mare lifted her head, chocolate eyes serious.

"I can't help how I feel. Do you understand? Both our names are on that piece of paper. I paid for the grass you're eating, but I couldn't have done it without him."

She reached out, this time brushing a white forelock away from the big, bright eyes. "I wish he was here. I think."

The oxen pulling the laden cart plodded slowly, obviously not the slightest bit interested in hurrying their task. For the first mile, it had been all Daniel could do to keep from urging the animals on. Now, however, he'd accepted the pace.

Beside him, carpenter James Marshall rose in the saddle to ease his seat. "Do you believe what they say about those New York Volunteers sailing into San Francisco any day? Captain Sutter says there isn't going to be any fighting for them to do, that whether he likes it or not, they'll be stationed at his fort."

Daniel shook his head. "Where will he put them?"

"All he talks about, with me anyway, is how he needs lumber so he can begin building Sutterville. Maybe he'll send the soldiers there."

"They aren't his to direct." Daniel glanced over at the tall, handsome man who'd come to California about the same time he had. "How is he going to get the lumber?"

"By building a sawmill. He wants me to find a site."

"Not around here. There isn't enough timber."

"No." James pointed east, toward the distant foothills. "Up there. Right now, he has all he can think about worrying about the Walla Wallas. I ran into a couple of them the other day. They're still grumbling that Sutter lied to them, saying they'd be paid for serving in Fremont's army. They weren't. I heard Sutter gave them some horses to calm them, but they haven't yet left for up north."

"I've seen the horses. They're broken-down nags."

"True."

"They're not going to leave until someone satisfies them."

"That's what your friend, Chief Narcisco, says? I know he isn't a Walla, but he must know how they think."

Narcisco had expressed his concern that the Walla Wallas would continue to stir up trouble simply because that was their nature. Jessie was out there alone and unprotected.

As James continued to talk about how he intended to build the sawmill once he'd found a proper site and Sutter's guarantee that he'd give Marshall the necessary men to get the work done, Daniel's thoughts stayed with Jessie.

She'd nearly cried when he told her that the land she wanted was hers—theirs. He almost reminded her of that, thinking she needed to hear that she wasn't as alone as she must think. But he hadn't been able to shake off the look on Sutter's face when he'd told the captain he was going into partnership with Jessie Speer. "You? Her? She's too good for you, Bear."

True.

At least he could make sure she had a roof over her head.

As they crested a low hill, Daniel looked out at Jessie's land. With the sun beginning to fade, the greens, browns, and grays of grass and tree were less distinct. He could understand why she'd fallen in love with this place. A body needed to be surrounded by color, by space, by quiet.

He spotted her on her hands and knees, a thin furrow of nearly exposed earth stretching out behind her. She'd said it would take several days to ready the rows. She'd worked faster than he'd thought.

"There's nothing like a woman for making a nest," James observed. "You were right. She isn't afraid."

"No. She isn't."

At that moment, Jessie scrambled to her feet, probably because she'd heard the approaching wagon. She stood facing them, her hand raised to shield her eyes. She still wore one of the dresses Mrs. Buckhalter had given her. Although he was too far away to see what she had on her feet, he guessed she would be wearing the moccasins. The land made her look small. It surrounded her, almost swallowed her.

The Walla Wallas were on the move. He had to tell her that.

"There." James pointed to a level spot touched by a large oak's shade. "That's the best place for building."

Daniel didn't take his eyes off Jessie. Because she was walking toward him, he guessed she'd recognized him. She still looked too slight for the task she'd given herself, but he could see strength in her eyes, her hands, her surprisingly broad shoulders.

"Daniel. Mr. Marshall. What are you . . ." It seemed as if it took a long time for her to take her eyes off him and focus on the wagon, but maybe that's what he wanted to think. "What is this about?"

"I want to try to change your mind about sleeping outside," Daniel said. He'd spent a long time after purchasing the cull lumber planning his argument so she couldn't refuse his offer. Now, seeing the way some of her hair had come loose from its braids and now fanned out around her face, he could only grasp at bits and pieces of what remained in his mind. "Just because it's spring, doesn't mean it's not going to rain again. You don't want to wake up in the middle of the night soaking wet with no way to get dry."

"You—" She pointed at the wagon, settled her eyes on him again. "You brought the lumber here for that?"

"Yes."

"I don't understand." She wiped her hands on her skirt, then wiped them again. "Where did you get it?"

Not *I don't want it*. Daniel took that as a good sign. "From a farmer who decided to move on to Monterey. He gave me this for next to nothing." He'd already told James that that was what he was going to tell Jessie. Still, he held his breath, afraid James might betray him.

"Almost nothing?" Jessie looked skeptical.

"Let us do it, Jessie," he pressed his point. "You can't really want to stay out here all alone without even a decent place to sleep. No way to cook or bathe in private."

He saw it in her eyes. Privacy meant as much to her as space did. Seizing on that, he explained that James Marshall had told him that with a little help, they'd have the cabin up in a couple of days. "Narciso said he'd be by tomorrow. He has to. Otherwise he'll have to take my place with the cattle."

Jessie chuckled at that. He followed the musical sound as it floated away. When she said nothing, he dismounted and began leading the oxen over to the spot James had indicated. Still, he held his breath, thinking that at any moment she'd tell him she didn't need or want his help.

"It's beautiful out here," she said.

James agreed with her, speaking easily about how it shouldn't be hard for her to keep her garden watered. She told them she'd seen an elk the other day and was concerned that the elk and deer might get to her plants before the corn dried into a tall, shaking wall. "A body has to be patient to farm," James observed as he began unloading lumber.

"So does a carpenter." Jessie stepped close to the wagon and ran her finger over a board. "I can't believe that farmer didn't sell this to Captain Sutter. Surely he has a need for it."

"Perkins was in a hurry to get on his way." Daniel stumbled over the words, not looking at James. "He was happy to get anything."

James grunted. Jessie glanced at him, then, wiping her hands again, stepped closer to Daniel.

She'd been out in the sun all day. It had been good to her, bringing out a few freckles on her nose and cheeks. He loved the way her hair shone and wished he knew how to ask her what she did to make it look like that. Her body seemed just the slightest bit fuller than when he'd told her about purchasing the land a week ago. He guessed that she was finally settling into her usual weight.

That would help her, keep her strong for what she wanted to do.

"I have a little food," she said. "Some stew Mr. Buckhalter gave me. I need to get some dried meat, maybe salmon from the Indians. The least I can do is offer you dinner."

He should say no. She should keep what little she had for herself. But he'd seen her pride; she wouldn't accept charity. He told her they'd join her once the wagon was unloaded; then, because looking into her eyes made him forget why he'd come here, he grabbed as many pieces of lumber as he could get his hands around and pulled.

By the time Daniel and James finished unloading, it was nearly dark. Because she'd hollowed out a place for a campfire and lined it with rocks her first day here, Jessie had a fire going when they joined her. She wanted to give them a proper meal, but she hadn't had time to do any cooking of her own. When James scooped into his bowl of stew, she knew she didn't have to worry about satisfying the carpenter.

"What do you think of the wolves?" James asked. "Do they keep you awake?"

"Not really." Jessie sat down to Daniel's right, despite everything they'd shared, suddenly shy about being near him. "I've been so tired that I can barely stay awake past dark."

James indicated the few rows she'd plowed and pulled the rocks out of. "The soil's about right, isn't it? Not too dry."

"Just right. You sound as if you know something about farming." Why wasn't Daniel saying anything?

"Not really," James told her and then went on to explain that he was a naturally curious man who took note of everything going on around him. With a little prompting, he launched into a discussion of how he was going to build her cabin—boards set in place over a log frame, an opening in the split-stave roof for a chimney so she could have a sheet-iron stove if she wanted one, a bed set up on forked branches driven into the ground. She tried to concentrate on what he was saying. Certainly, as the picture in her mind grew clearer, she began to yearn for what he had in mind.

But Daniel was staring into the fire. His features had been painted in a million hues of red and orange, what wasn't illuminated by the low flames trapped in the night. She wondered if he regretted coming to see her. No. She didn't think it was that. After all, if he hadn't wanted her to have a place to stay, he wouldn't have gone to all this trouble.

What then was he thinking about? Her?

She hoped so. At the same time, just the idea of being the object of his attention made her uneasy. There were only a handful of women in California, and most of them either married or too young to be interested in such things. She wasn't vain; just the idea almost made her laugh. Still, she couldn't help but wonder what Daniel saw when he looked at her.

If he wouldn't so much as look at her tonight, why had he accepted her hospitality?

"From what I hear, he's going forth with his suit, but there isn't anyone who thinks he should."

Jessie started, struggling to remember what James had been saying. Something about Keseberg. She nodded, hoping that would be enough.

"As long as he doesn't want anything more from you."

Daniel had spoken to her. The wonder of that made more of an impact on her than his words. Still, she remembered to nod at him, hoping she wouldn't be asked to contribute anything more.

James filled what would have been silence. "Keseberg

has been trying to ingratiate himself with Sutter. Folks think he's unbalanced. Whatever he did or didn't do, I'm not going to be the one to judge."

Jessie was glad to hear that. Despite what Keseberg had put her through, she had only sympathy for the man, who'd been badly injured, first when a large splinter became lodged in his foot and then when he cut himself with his axe. She said so.

"You're incredible," Daniel said softly.

"Incredible?"

"You don't hold a malicious thought toward anyone, do you?"

Jessie wasn't a saint; she'd never thought of herself as one. "I try not to. Hating is a terrible way to feel."

"Hate? Some folks live by it, even if they have to lie to keep it going."

What was he talking about? She longed to ask, but she couldn't make him say anything he wasn't ready to. "I don't think there's many people like that," she said, hoping he wouldn't fall silent. "Most just want to live their lives as best they can."

"I know." After a moment, he gave her a rueful smile. "You're tired, aren't you?"

She hadn't given it a thought. Now that she did, she realized that her arms and legs were fairly trembling with fatigue. Her face felt tight and dry from all those hours in the sun. "I've been lazy too long. I've forgotten what a full day's work feels like."

"You needed the rest. And you need it now." He stood and walked over to where he'd dropped his rolled blanket. He began spreading it out on the ground.

She nearly pointed out that he would be sleeping on rocks, but certainly this wasn't the first time he'd done that. She felt bad sleeping on the mat of leaves she'd collected for herself, but she didn't have enough to share.

If Daniel slept with her, they'd make room for both of them on the soft, sweet-smelling mattress.

Slept with her. What was she thinking?

Still, she couldn't force the image away. She'd heard her parents making love, and a few days ago Margaret had told her that there were more important things than getting a full night's sleep. Still, what she knew of what happened between a man and woman was limited to snatches of whispered conversation and her mother's embarrassment the few times Jessie had tried to bring up the subject.

She was twenty. She should know more.

The truth was, her body wanted to know more.

Narcisco and three other Indians showed up while Daniel and James were marking out the cabin's boundaries the next morning. Although Jessie hung around, wanting to help, James reminded her that she needed to get her seeds planted as soon as possible. Still, she worked with one eye on the seemingly never-ending task of covering up her precious seeds and the other watching in awe at how rapidly the cabin was going up.

It wasn't large, probably not quite twice as big as the one she'd stayed in at Fort Sutter, but this was hers, made not from cold adobe but from wood that still smelled of pitch. She didn't have a stove and wasn't sure when she could afford to buy one, but just the idea of being able to attend to her personal needs without worrying that someone might see made her glad that the work was going as rapidly as it was.

She was concerned that she wouldn't have enough to feed everyone, but Narcisco produced a large leather pouch filled with smoked salmon and enough acorn-meal cakes to last a week. The men worked until dark; then, after dinner, the Indians slipped off to sleep under an oak while Daniel, James, and she spread out as they had last night. She woke once to replenish the fire. In the gloom, she sensed that Daniel was looking at her. He didn't say anything and his silence unsettled her more than any words could have.

Late the next afternoon, James told her to carry her oak-leaf bed from near the firepit into the cabin. She placed the boughs on the rough lumber affixed to the forked branches, laid her blankets on top, and stood back.

"My home." The words sprang from her without conscious thought. "It's really my home."

"Is it what you want?"

Jessie turned around. James and Daniel had accompanied her into the cabin for her final inspection. Now only Daniel remained.

Like the other men, he'd gone shirtless for most of the day. She told herself she should be immune to the impact of his sun-touched body by now. She wasn't.

"It's wonderful. Thank you. I—" Daniel had brought greased paper for a windowpane, but she didn't want to shut out the light. Through the open window, she heard the Indians moving away.

"I still don't know why you did it," she whispered. "With everything you have to do . . ."

"You really don't understand?"

He hadn't moved. Because she was staring at him, she knew he hadn't so much as tightened a muscle. Still, the power she'd always sensed in him seemed to reach out and touch her. She should pull away from that invisible draw. Although the wind shouldn't be able to reach her here, she felt it—or something—along the sides of her neck, down her spine, touching her where a man had never touched her.

Had he built this place for her because he felt the same things she did?

On legs that seemed to have lost all feeling, she slid closer until she thought she could see the pulsing of his heart through flesh and muscle.

"Thank you." The words ended; she didn't close her mouth.

Slowly, so slowly that she almost cried out from need, he lifted his arm from his side and touched his fingers to her lips. "You're welcome."

Was she expected to say anything? She hoped not; she didn't care. She drew his finger into her mouth, loving the taste of him. Suddenly shy, she thought to lower her eyes, but he'd thrown an invisible rope around her, holding her to him. She did the only thing she could put her mind to. When she pressed her palms against his chest, he drew in his breath, the sound sharp and wild.

He snaked his free hand over her shoulder, around to her neck, up into her hair. She felt strands being drawn between his fingers, and then he was pressing against the back of her head, bringing them even closer.

She didn't fight. When he pulled his now damp finger out of her mouth, she left her lips parted.

The distance remaining between them slid off into nothing. Her body felt as if thunder rumbled through it. There was only one way to still the sensation, or make it more powerful—by tapping the thunder's source.

The other times they kissed, there'd been a gentleness to him, a near shyness. None of that remained. Instead, she felt herself being crushed against him, her breasts flattened so she nearly forgot that they weren't one and the same.

Daniel. Daniel! You frighten me. I frighten me.

The thought was drowned out by the thunder. She clenched her arms around his neck, standing on tiptoe to make the contact complete. He breathed; she breathed.

He'd folded himself down around her, holding her so tight that the next breath was nearly impossible. She didn't care.

Daniel. Daniel.

Something had changed about their kiss. She concentrated, filled with wonder and excitement over what he was doing. He'd parted his lips and touched his tongue to her. For a moment she didn't understand; then she did. Because she wanted him as much as she wanted and needed air, she gave him entrance. She felt her chest expand, surprised that breathing was so easy after all.

And then he pushed past her teeth and she forgot to let the air out. Her arms had gone numb—numb and shaking at the same time. She searched through her mind, the journey ragged and fragmented. What had happened to her body? All the feeling that should be in her limbs seemed centered in her belly. And lower.

Daniel.

When had she brought her tongue to play against his? Was she too bold? It didn't matter. Daniel had surrounded her; he was her.

She felt—the man part of him had become hard. It pressed against her, momentarily frightening her. She tried to draw away.

"Jessie, don't. It's all right."

"All right?"

"Those things happen to a man sometimes, when he's with a woman he desires."

Woman. Desires. His words stripped fear from her. A thousand questions about what it meant to be a man slid through her, but her body's needs stood in the way of voicing any of them. She wanted to be held tight and secure against him, wanted to explore what was happening to her. *Daniel. I want*— Want what? She barely understood, only that he and no one else could supply the answer.

One moment his fingers felt like butterfly wings on her temple. The next he pressed his mouth so firmly against hers that she nearly cried out. No matter what his gift, she wanted it. And, although no one had ever told her how such things were done, she knew how to give him pleasure.

And yet—fingers pressing into the back of his neck, her belly against him, mouth open and willing—there was more.

She couldn't say when he'd begun to draw away from her. It had happened so gently, so gradually, that she'd been able to ignore it. Now he stood looking down at her with his hands clamped around her arms, keeping her fast before him. She looked up, knowing her mouth hung slack, unable to do anything about it.

"Daniel? What?"

"You are so innocent."

"No," she protested. "No. I'm not."

"I'm not talking about running a farm or surviving a mountain, but when it comes to other things—"

"Tell me. Show me."

"Show you." The words came out a groan. "Don't tempt me. Don't ever do that."

Tempt. Was she capable of that? "Why not?" If he hadn't been holding her, she would have molded her body to his.

"Because I'd lose myself in you. Jessie, Jessie—I'm sorry."

She was free. She hated being free. "Sorry?" she mouthed, aching with the need for his touch.

"I shouldn't— Jessie, I'm not good for you."

"Stop it!" Anger washed through her. She wanted to strike out, slap away the words, then lose herself in him again. "I'm the one to decide that, Daniel. Only me. You've done nothing except be kind to me."

"Kind?" He laughed at that. Then, before she could tell him to stop laughing, he reached out and ran his fingers through her hair. She leaned into him, her fury now mist. She felt and saw his body shudder as if waging a battle within himself.

He lost. Or maybe he'd won. Her arms went around his waist. She felt her body melt into his inch by inch. Now his hand was at her throat, finding the top button on her dress, releasing it. He looked down at her, asking with his eyes. She did the only thing she could, arched her spine toward him. The buttons came free one by one, a slow, lightning-filled dance.

When his roughened fingertips touched the flesh over her collarbone, she shuddered. Her body had turned into fire-touched liquid. *Daniel. Daniel!*

He brushed aside her undershirt, covered a breast. It seemed to expand to fill his palm. A man's hand on her breast. Daniel's hand on her breast.

What was happening to her?

Afraid now to meet his eyes, she ducked her head. She'd seen his hands grip a bucking rope as he rode a wild bull. Those same hands had held a baby. Tonight—holding her—she knew fully what they were aware of.

He slid thumb and forefinger slowly down her breast until he caught the tip. He held her, owned her, simply because two fingers were on her body.

A sound, half moan, half something she'd never heard

before, escaped from between her lips. Fascinated, she listened as it slowly faded into nothing. This close to her, his features had become indistinct. Still, she thought he was smiling.

Smiling. What a wonderful thought.

That faded, replaced by sensation. Her body had never felt like this, and yet it didn't frighten her. She wanted to bury herself in the liquid power that seemed to flow between them. She wanted to touch Daniel in an intimate way and learn if she could do to him what he'd done to her.

Maybe she already had.

Made bold by that thought, she ran her hand inside his doeskin shirt and flattened her palm against the base of his throat. She shifted her weight slightly so she wasn't quite so close to him. She didn't want to leave him. No. Not that. But she had to see what was in his eyes.

What she found in the night-darkened depths made her catch her breath. For this glorious moment, she could see into his heart—see the human being beneath the powerful exterior.

He wanted her. Needed her.

Then, as if he'd realized how much of himself he'd given away, he took a step of his own, breaking contact.

"Jessie." His fingers now hung in the air. "Jessie. I have to leave."

"No."

"Yes." He overrode her plea. "You're not ready for this. When you give yourself to a man, it shouldn't be an outlaw."

I don't care. Don't you know that? But her brain echoed with the word *give*; she said nothing. Instead she nodded, the gesture automatic and painful.

"I'll be leaving now. The Maidu will look after you. You'll be safe."

Don't leave, her brain screamed. Still, she nodded. When he turned and walked out the door, she stood where he'd left her, heart hammering, body hot and weak, the word *give* still echoing.

A moment later he reappeared. In his hand he held both a rifle and powder horn. "Do you know how to shoot?"

She could only nod at his question.

"Good. Don't ever let yourself be far from them."

"I—won't. Where are you going?"

"To meet up with the cattle. It's better this way, Jessie. When I'm around you, I forget myself."

"So do I," she told him, not lowering her head. "You be careful now, please."

"I will. And you—you do the same."

"How—long before you'll be back this way?"

"Maybe a week."

A week. She didn't know how she felt about that.

CHAPTER 13

Three days later, after finishing with her final row, Jessie rode to Sutter's fort. Using one of her two remaining coins, she bought flour, salt, jerky, and a handful of tallow candles. Her intention had been to complete her business as rapidly as possible so she wouldn't be gone any longer than necessary. But as she paid for her purchases at the dry goods store, she caught snatches of conversation and stayed long enough to be assured that the long-awaited agreement between the United States and Mexico had taken place. Now that the war was over, all folks wanted to do was settle the land. However, as Daniel had told her, the Walla Wallas were still around.

From what she heard, Captain Sutter still had done

nothing to turn Sutterville into a town, aside from marking a few boundaries near where the American and Sacramento rivers joined. Although some folks laughed at Sutter's grand plan, others said that as soon as he had enough lumber, the project would begin.

Those words caught Jessie's attention. Lumber was at a premium. If that was the case, she couldn't imagine a farmer practically giving his supply to Daniel. How much had Daniel paid?

Had he considered the expense worth it?

She didn't have the answer. All she knew was that a part of her had felt hollowed-out since he left, and yet she needed to be alone—to see if she could turn her dream into reality.

She dropped by the kitchen hoping to see the Buckhalters, but they were so busy cooking for a hungry group of soldiers that they barely had time to acknowledge her presence. It seemed to her that their smiles were a little reserved, the conversation perfunctory. She wondered if they'd heard about her cabin and knew who had built it.

After the noise and activity at the fort, her cabin seemed strangely silent. Thankfully, someone dropped by every day, members of Narciso's family, neighbors, a man in pursuit of his horse—a horse he now called by unrepeatable names. When she wasn't visiting, she spent the days clearing more ground for the mounds squash needed and then planting. Once that was done, she began preparing stakes for the pole beans to climb. Although she didn't have to go at the pace she'd set for herself, she knew she wouldn't be able to sleep if she didn't work her body until it demanded its due. Even so, her nights were filled not with dreams of seeing her garden ready to harvest but Daniel.

The dreams were unsettling, not at all gentle.

One afternoon five days after she'd been to Fort Sutter, Jessie looked up from her work to find she was being watched. Because of the distance between her and the half-dozen mounted Indians, she couldn't tell much about them—just enough that she knew they weren't Maidu. Remembering what she'd heard about the Walla Wallas, she reached for the rifle Daniel had given her and held it cradled in her arms. The Indians continued to regard her. Occasionally a horse moved, and she caught the sound of unshod hooves pounding against earth.

Finally, one of the braves lifted a hand as if to salute her. Then, one at a time, they turned and rode away. Five minutes later Jessie set down the rifle and wiped her sweating hands on her skirt. The birds were still singing. She could hear her mare and the milk cow tear at grass. But except for those sounds, the valley was silent. Too silent.

She wished she lived closer to Elizabeth's new family. She wished Daniel had left her more than a rifle.

Daniel reached Jessie's land at dawn. He'd ridden half the night—ever since a passing settler told him the Walla Wallas had been spotted near the farms that bordered the Sacramento River.

He'd been a fool to leave her alone. Still, even though he knew the Maidu couldn't keep an eye on her all the time, he'd managed to convince himself that she'd be better off alone than with him around. He could no longer tell himself that.

When he spotted the outline of her cabin, he let out his

breath in a long, slow whoosh, only then realizing how long tension had kept him breathing shallowly. She'd left her pinto tethered between the cabin and her garden. The milk cow dozed near one of the oak trees, also tethered. He remembered that she'd told him she wanted to build a small corral before her vegetables pushed through the ground. If there was any way he could get his hands on the necessary wood, he'd do it for her.

The pinto lifted her head and whinnied. Although he hated the thought of waking Jessie this early, it might startle her less to hear her horse than suddenly be aware of a man at her door. The pinto whinnied again; a few seconds later the cabin door opened and Jessie, wearing a shapeless nightgown, emerged. She held the rifle he'd given her.

"Jessie," he called. "Jessie, it's me."

"Daniel." Her free hand went to her throat, and he hated himself for having scared her that way. "What are you doing here?"

He waited until he'd dismounted before answering. "The Walla Wallas are about. I wanted to make sure you were safe."

"Are they causing trouble?"

"If the man I talked to can be believed, they scared a boy who'd gone after water. Chased him all the way home." He tried to keep the words casual. "They haven't been bothering you, have they?"

She chewed on her lower lip. "They were here yesterday. Just watching."

"Damnation. I'm sorry. I didn't mean to say that." She'd propped the rifle against the side of the cabin and folded her arms under her breasts. Surely she'd realized by now that she wasn't dressed for greeting company. But maybe she didn't think of him as company. "They're sure to have noticed you're alone."

"I know."

I know. Her courage never ceased to amaze him. "I wished there was something I could do about that."

"You can't. Daniel, I knew there might be trouble with the Indians."

"And that didn't scare you?"

"It worried me some." She gave him a fleeting smile. "But I'm a stubborn woman."

"They're a warlike tribe," he pressed. Still, her words rang in him. Fear, he decided, meant different things to her than it did to most folks.

"Then I'd better always be armed."

"That's not enough." He shifted his weight, aware of just how tired he was. "One rifle against God knows how many of theirs."

"What do you want me to do?" she challenged. "Give up?" Before he could answer, she hurried on. "I've been out here for better than three weeks now, living in the cabin you put up for me. Why, if you want me to leave now, did you do that?"

Because a cabin was the only thing I could give you.

She'd cocked her head, waiting for him to answer. When he said nothing, she went on. "I thought about it. Right after I saw them yesterday, I thought about packing up what little I have and taking my horse and cow back to the fort. But if I did, all I'd think about was how my vegetables were doing."

He knew that. He only had to look into her eyes to see how alive she became when she stood on land she'd claimed.

"If you're dead, you'll never be able to harvest those vegetables."

She recoiled. Still, she didn't look horrified. "I've faced death before. I know what it looks like."

"I know you do."

"I'm not afraid of it."

I am. For you. Damn it, he didn't want to care like this. He had, once. That time he'd had to watch his mother die. "I admire your courage, but I don't want you risking your life again. Is there anything wrong with my thinking that?"

"No." The word came out a whisper. "No," she repeated. "I don't want to be shot by some Indian. After what I've gone through, I don't want my life to end like that. But . . ." Her eyes, which had been so dark that he couldn't see into them, brightened. "When I came to you after folks started talking about the cannibalism, Narcisco said something I haven't forgotten."

He waited, wondering whether he would respect or hate his friend for his words.

"He said that life is a gift from the spirits. That the spirits decide who lives and who dies, and when. I'm going to live, not worry about when it might end."

He opened his mouth, whether to agree or not he couldn't say. Her presence distracted him. He couldn't look at her, her tousled hair, slim frame under the bulky nightdress, bare feet, competent hands, without wanting her.

But there was more to her than a tempting body.

She reminded him of another woman. The woman he'd nearly lost his own life for.

"By all rights, this land is part mine." The words ran out of him, swirling while he waited for them to make sense to him. "I could say I've decided to stay here with you. I would be within my rights."

"Daniel—"

"But I won't. Not now. I just want you to think about that. You've been out here for days, alone—"

"Not completely alone. I've had company. Neighbors."

"But alone at night."

She nodded. "I refuse to be run off my land."

"I know," he said as, once again, the image of another woman swam through his mind.

"I hope you do." Although she was whispering, he heard the strength in her voice. "I want to live the way Narcisco does. To put my life in the hands of the spirits, in God's hands." She waved her hand to encompass her surroundings. "The thought of losing this . . ."

"I understand."

She was looking at him as if she wanted nothing more than to believe him. Still, her eyes warned that if he disagreed with her, she wouldn't change for him. She couldn't.

She was so much like his mother.

"I want you to make me a promise." He dropped the reins he'd been worrying and stepped closer. When she stood her ground, he took her hands. "That you don't do anything to make the Walla Wallas angry. Narcisco says they're just curious about farmers and it's Sutter and Fremont they're mad at. If folks leave them alone, they'll get their fill of watching."

"Do you believe that?"

"If I thought it was that simple, I wouldn't be here."

She nodded, her eyes still on their hands. "But you can't make me leave."

"No."

"And you can't stay here."

"Would you want me to?"

She didn't shake her head. She didn't say yes. "As long as I can remember, all I've wanted to do was farm." Her voice trailed off at the end, making him think she was talking more to herself than to him. "Sharing acorn mush with Narcisco. Having Elizabeth stay here for a few days.

Harvesting my garden and taking the proceeds to the fort. Getting the land ready for winter, not having to think about anything more than that. Only, it isn't going to be like that."

Although he wanted to tell her he wished he could change that for her, he held silent.

"I have to choose between my stubborn desire to have a farm and sleeping safe. I've already made that decision."

He knew she had. Maybe he should tell her that because he'd been raised by a woman like her, he'd known what she was going to say. But this decision was about her, not his mother. "I'll talk to the soldiers."

"I'd appreciate that."

Although his head warned him to leave, his heart wouldn't let that happen. He drew her toward him, slowly, allowing her all the time she needed if she wanted to break free. Instead, she stepped closer, her eyes now locked with his. The wolves had been howling all night, but in the last few minutes they'd stopped. Now he caught the sound of frogs croaking. He hoped they made that sound often. They might make her feel less alone.

Alone? Her mouth had softened. He took it, covered it, wrapped his arms around her and held her close. Although his body beat with the need that overtook him every time he saw her, he lashed that need into submission. She deserved to be treated like a lady. An intelligent, independent woman.

Daniel stayed until midafternoon. Although he'd protested that he shouldn't use her bed, she pointed out that probably no one knew he was here. And even if they did, she didn't care. Finally, his lids sagging in fatigue, he'd collapsed. After a couple of hours, he got up and helped her place flat rocks in front of the cabin door as protection against the upcoming dust of summer. She'd asked him to stay at least through the evening meal, but he'd wanted to take a look around to see if he could spot the Walla Wallas.

Now, trying to fall asleep, all she could think about was his good-bye kiss and his whispered promise to make her world as safe as possible. The comforting thought spilled over into her dreams. Then sometime during the night she woke suddenly, remembering little about her nightmare except that the Walla Wallas were part of it.

She dragged through the morning, but by noon, buoyed by the unexpected sight of a doe and her twin fawns, she regained her optimism about life. If the warm weather held, the first of her crops would be poking through the soil in another day or two. Daniel, despite his duties, had concerned himself with her life. With him not that far away, her nightmare—whatever it had been about—surely wouldn't become reality.

She'd just taken a drink from the watertight basket Narcisco had given her when the pinto stamped her foot, her neck arched in anticipation. Wondering if it might be Daniel, she pushed her hair back from her face and straightened her dress. She didn't recognize any of the seven horses coming her way, but there was no mistaking Raymond's straight carriage.

Mixed emotions assaulted her. She was eager to hear anything Raymond might tell her about the goings-on at the fort, but she doubted that he'd come here to pass on rumors. The soldiers he'd taken up with were casting speculative looks at her land. Why Raymond had anything to do with the unkempt bunch she couldn't begin to guess. Obviously they accepted him as their leader.

Leaving the others behind, Raymond came closer. "I heard *he* built you a cabin" were the first words out of

Raymond's mouth. "Jessie, you must know what people are saying."

She didn't care. "You're looking good," she said, hoping to distract him. "This weather must agree with you."

"Well enough." He touched his hand to his reddened forehead. "I've always burned in the sun." Ignoring the others, he slid out of the saddle. "I can't believe what you've accomplished."

"It's coming along. If I'd waited any longer, I'd have the devil's time keeping enough water on things. This way there'll be decent roots by the time it gets hot."

He nodded, but she sensed that he really hadn't heard what she'd said. He wore a vest and starched shirt, looking out of place next to the men who wore a sad assortment of military uniforms. She watched as he scanned his surroundings, his lips thinning when his eyes rested on her cabin. She almost asked what he thought of the workmanship, then thought better of it. "Is that what you and the others came out here for, to see what I've been doing?"

"In part." His eyes flickered to her face. "You've chosen well. I've heard any number of settlers say that this is some of the richest land around."

"Did they?" Her farm was no better than a half-dozen others. If it produced more, it was because of her skill, not the soil itself.

"And that they'd pay handsomely for it."

She laughed. "Now that I've done the work."

"True." He tried to smile, but his eyes gave him away. "Land that's already been planted, with a cabin on it to boot—you could come close to doubling what you paid for it."

She glanced at the others. They were intent on the conversation. "Maybe I could."

"Think what you could do with that." Raymond's head

came up. He looked at a spot just above her forehead. She might have a smudge of dirt there, but she didn't think that was it. "What we could do with it."

"We?"

He indicated his companions. "My business associates and me. I worry about you. This is a dangerous place for a woman alone to be, especially now with the Walla Wallas causing trouble. The Feather River has much more to offer."

Jessie couldn't help but feel sorry for Raymond. Whatever he'd come here to tell her wasn't easy. She supposed she could have said something to help him relax, but ever since he'd used the word *we*, she'd been uneasy.

"Sutter has a salmon fishery there. Not as productive as it could be because he's had to leave it in the hands of the Indians, but if I was to run it for him with the help of my associates . . ."

"I'm happy for you, but what does this have to do with me?"

"Did I say that?" He glanced back at his friends. His mouth twisted upward. They smiled back at him but said nothing.

"Not in so many words." To the east she could see a faint wisp of smoke drifting into the sky. Her neighbors there, a young couple and both their mothers, must be smoking meat. Had they taken note of her visitors? She hoped so. Being alone out here with them had her on edge.

Raymond pulled his lips together. "I've given it a great deal of thought, Jessie. A great deal of thought. I worry about you. I know how independent-minded you are, but after what we endured together—" He fastened his eyes on her. "You understand, don't you?"

She nodded, half believing his sincere words, half wondering what he would say next.

"I'm certain you do. There's a bond between us. Something that will never be wiped away."

"No. I don't suppose it ever will."

"I can't forget that, Jessie. That's why I'm here. To ask you to continue what we had."

Her stomach knotted. She wanted to tell him to leave, that she didn't want to hear anything he might say. How was it possible for so many horses to make so little noise?

"I have the know-how to make the fishery into a success Sutter never envisioned. And the manpower." He indicated behind him. "The return would far outweigh anything you might gain from selling your vegetables."

Jessie blinked, then fought to keep from blinking again. She forced herself to concentrate on Raymond and ignore the others. "You're asking me to sell the farm so you'll have the necessary funds to get started?"

He didn't look as if he was ready for her to say that. Still, after a moment, he nodded. "I wouldn't suggest this if I didn't honestly believe my associates and I could turn the fishery around. All we lack is the necessary capital."

"You're asking me to move to the Feather River?"

"In good conscience, it's the only thing I could do. Once you no longer have this . . ." He pointed at the cabin as if it were a pile of rubble to be burned. "You would have to return to Fort Sutter and I know how you feel about taking charity there."

"And you think I'd rather be with you?"

"It isn't as if we'd be alone, Jessie." He pointed at the closest rider, a short, stocky man with a badly scarred upper lip. "There are several shelters. You'd be safe."

She suppressed a shudder. The way the men were looking at her made her feel dirty and apprehensive. One was missing several teeth. Yet another looked as if he hadn't bathed for years. They reminded her of stray, hungry dogs. "Safe?"

"It has to be a worry for you." Raymond sounded like a patient father explaining the night to a frightened child. He kept his voice loud enough that his companions could hear every word. "To be alone like this, never knowing when trouble might strike. You know how I felt about this from the beginning, but you were determined to give it a try. Now that you have . . ." Once again he smiled his understanding-father smile. "Ah, Jessie, there's no shame in admitting that this life is too hard for you."

It was the only life she'd ever wanted. Didn't he know that? "You think someone would pay good money for crops that are still under the ground?"

"I'm certain of it. I've made inquiries. We could have you ready to move before the end of the day."

That was enough! Raymond was trying to take her life out of her hands. "I can't! I won't. Raymond, please, I understand you're concerned." She had to be careful not to say anything that would let Raymond or the others guess how vulnerable she felt. "I appreciate it. But selling, buying into a fishery—never."

"I can't believe I'm hearing this."

Weary of the argument, yet knowing it wasn't over, she waited him out.

"If I am capable of leading these gentlemen, then surely I can handle the simple selling of a parcel of land," he continued. "I will not be treated as if I'm coming to you hat in hand."

"That wasn't my intention. This farm is all I have. You know that."

"If you'd listened to me months ago, you could now be a wealthy woman. Extremely wealthy."

If I'd dug the Allsetters' coins out of the snow. "I didn't have the strength. It was buried so—"

"I would have done it, if you'd told me where."

She'd been about to tell him that they'd had this argument before when she noticed that all six men were leaning forward, a new intensity on their features. What had Raymond told them about the Allsetters' money? Maybe that it had been a vast sum? Was that why they were "loyal" to him? "Captain Sutter's the one who wants the fishery increased," she said, determined to change the subject. "Isn't that for him to finance? Isn't it enough that you would be working for him? Daniel—"

"Daniel! Don't mention that outlaw's name in my presence again."

Jessie clenched her teeth but said nothing. If they started arguing about Daniel, she might never get Raymond and the others to leave. She was trying to think of a way to point out Sutter's responsibility toward the fishery when Raymond cut through her thoughts. "I came to you because I thought you'd have a sense of responsibility, of obligation toward me."

"Obligation?" The moment the word was out of her mouth, she regretted it. Why had she given him an opening?

"Obligation." He spat the word. "I saved your life, Jessie. Who hunted for you? Who, no matter how sick it made me, provided Elizabeth with what she needed to stay alive? Can you stand there in front of these men and deny that?"

You ate it, too. No. She wouldn't bring that up again. "I am grateful. You know I am."

"But not grateful enough to see that I'm able to support myself and give honest employ to hardworking men."

When had she become Raymond's keeper? "The game

you shot, I'm the one who prepared the meat. We're even, Raymond. We worked together doing what had to be done. I didn't ask for your help with my farm. I never thought to burden you this way."

"No. You didn't." Raymond stabbed a finger at the cabin. "You got *him* to do it."

"He offered." Why was she arguing? What went on between her and Daniel was none of his affair.

"Offered?" Raymond sneered the word. "And how did you pay him for his generosity? Don't." He held up his hand, stopping her. Behind him a couple of the men guffawed. "Don't try to deny it, Jessie. Everyone's talking about you and that outlaw."

"Are they?" she demanded as seven pairs of eyes narrowed at her. "Or are you and your 'friends' the only ones?"

"You know the answer to that. If *he* comes around anymore, you will have ruined your name."

She didn't care about that. Did she? Squaring her shoulders, she faced Raymond. Still, she kept an eye on the others. "He came, with James Marshall and some of the Maidu. They built the cabin, all of them. No law was broken."

"Law? What about propriety, Jessie? Has he even told you why he had to flee Texas?"

No. She hadn't asked and he hadn't offered. But then, she'd never told him what living with her father had been like. For her and Daniel, there was only today, only . . . "It was a long time ago."

"You don't know, do you? He's kept that from you."

She wanted to yell at Raymond that that was between her and Daniel, but if she did, Raymond would only use it against her. "I don't want to fight with you. We shared something once, but I have to take care of myself; I want to. I don't want to be beholden to any man."

The man with the scarred lip snorted. Raymond stared him into silence. "It's too late for that."

She thought to argue away what Raymond had said, but before she could form the words, sudden exhaustion spread through her. "You're going to think what you want. Nothing I tell you will change that."

"You don't care about your reputation?" Raymond asked.

"I just want to be a farmer." She straightened her spine. "I can't satisfy everyone's dreams. If I gave you and your men what you're asking for, I'd become beholden to you. I can't do that. I won't."

"It wouldn't be like that if we were married."

"Married?" She could barely get the words past her lips. "I don't love you. You don't love me."

"Love?" He glanced over his shoulder, then focused on her again. "I admire you. Isn't that enough?"

"No, Raymond, it isn't."

"I can't change your mind, can I? You're going to hold on to this." He swept his hand over her land.

She nodded.

"And this comes before everything else."

Again she nodded.

"And I'm not part of it."

She didn't move. He knew the answer to that.

"I feel sorry for you, Jessie." He spoke through thinned lips. "You're going to dry up here. You'll become a slave to this land. You already are."

"If I am, it's my decision."

"Tell me that again in a year or in two years when you realize you have nothing in life except a garden."

CHAPTER 14

The day after Raymond came to see her, the first of her plants poked through the ground. Jessie knelt before the tiny yellow-green miracles and cried. If only Daniel could see this. He might understand her tears, and the joy of bringing life to the soil.

But he wasn't here.

She saw regular soldiers from the fort almost daily, and the Maidu came around even more often than that. Sometimes she sensed that she was being watched. After her confrontation with Raymond and his "associates," the prickling along her spine made her uneasy because the soldiers and Maidu always stopped long enough to see how her garden was progressing. Three days running, the

Maidu showed up not long after dawn, dragging poles behind them, and built a small corral for her horse and cow.
She pressed for an explanation of where the wood had
come from, but all they told her was that it had been cut
on Maidu land. She suspected Daniel was behind it.

On a moonlit night a week after Raymond's visit, Jessie
spent several hours reading in the Bible she'd borrowed
from the Larkins. The verses conjured up memories of being read to by her mother. Still, she wasn't able to quiet
her restlessness. She needed more to do, more land to till,
more something. Finally, though, she lay down and drifted
off to sleep.

*She wasn't alone. Someone had stepped into the cabin.
He barely fit; his size dwarfed the space, made it impossible for her to think of anything except him. He took a step
toward her, growing larger, pulling her toward him without
a word being said. His hands were at his side. She
couldn't see into his eyes, couldn't tell what he was thinking. But she moved toward him; her heart thudded, sounding like Indian drums. She wanted to run, to order him
from her place. But he'd taken over, and she wanted those
arms reaching toward her. Taking . . .*

A scream, sharp and terrified, sliced her free from the
dream. She bolted upright, then grabbed for the rifle, the
separate movements nearly merging into one. Another
scream ripped the air. Suddenly so cold she had to clench
her teeth against the tremors assaulting her, she scrambled
to her feet. In the dark, she couldn't find her moccasins.
All that mattered was the powder horn Daniel had given
her.

Another scream—this one more bellow than whinny.

"No!" She yanked on the cabin door and stumbled outside. "No!"

Moonlight washed over her world. Because she'd turned

toward the corral, she saw that first. The logs on one side had been torn down, but neither pinto nor milk cow had made any attempt to escape. Instead, they cowered, rump to rump, in the far corner.

A mounted Indian pressed his animal forward. His hand, holding some kind of weapon, was upraised. Then he drove it down. The cow bellowed, lost her footing, splayed on the churned ground. Her legs kicked, once, twice, fell still. A moment—another blow—and the pinto collapsed on top of her.

"No!" Rage, so heavy there was no room for fear, exploded inside Jessie. She sprinted toward the corral. Rocks tore into her bare feet; she ignored them. "No! Damn you, damn you, you can't do that!"

The Indian in the corral whirled his horse around to face her. The moonlight caught his features, seared them into her brain. Walla Walla!

He wasn't alone. Two more mounted Indians moved out from under an oak. She heard one yell something. What did she care? They'd killed her animals, her companions, her livelihood. Her hands were steady as she rapidly loaded and aimed her rifle. The explosion nearly knocked her to her knees. An instant later, she began loading again.

She didn't have time to finish the act. The Indian who'd murdered her animals sagged sideways and started sliding off his now plunging horse. But the others were galloping toward her, yelling, the sounds touching her spine with ice.

Not sure whether she'd screamed or not, Jessie whirled and raced away, still gripping her weapon. Her feet burned; she tripped, righted herself, tripped again. She headed, not toward the soft earth she'd exposed, but to the slight hill that stood between her and her closest neighbor. After she'd covered about fifty yards, her right foot slammed into something. This time she couldn't ignore the sharp pain. Brought up short by her own body, she whirled to face her attackers.

Only, she hadn't been followed. She dropped to her knees, gripped her foot until the pain subsided, then began shaking gunpowder into the rifle muzzle, her hands still.

The moonlight told the story.

She'd left a number of coals glowing in her outdoor firepit. The two Indians who'd remained on their horses had grabbed tree branches and plunged them into the fire. As she watched, one Walla Walla threw a burning branch inside her home. The other raced around to the far side of the cabin and threw his flaming brand onto the roof. Whooping, they galloped toward each other. One lifted his fist in her direction and shook it.

She saw the flames building on her roof, saw the glow beyond the cabin window.

He'd set her bed on fire.

"No! Damnation, no!"

But, although she felt capable of killing the two with her bare hands, she knew it was too late. The cabin's interior fairly exploded, smearing harsh red over the landscape. Her throat felt as if it had been gripped by huge, cruel fingers. She staggered, caught her balance, sobbed.

The Indians had turned from the cabin and were galloping over to the corral where their fallen companion lay. She watched as they dismounted and knelt in the dirt. Had she killed him? Did she care? *No!* Why? Shouldn't she care about the taking of a human life?

She had only to hear the sound of her dying cabin, to stare at the motionless animals in the corral, to know the answer to that. The Walla Wallas had taken two lives. She'd reacted out of instinct.

The cabin was fully engulfed when one of the Indians grabbed the loose horse as the other Indian lifted the mo-

tionless body onto the broad back. Then the two re-
mounted and raced out of the corral. Once again fists were
raised in her direction.

She didn't care. As long as they didn't come after her,
she didn't care.

She had to do something. What? After a few minutes,
instinct took over and she began walking. Walking away
from the crackling screams of her dying cabin.

Because she was barefoot, she guessed it would take her
several hours to reach her closest neighbors. But before
she'd traveled—stumbled—little more than a half hour,
she heard pounding hoofs. For a moment, she thought the
Indians had returned for her. But when she heard a man
call her name, she realized that Mr. Larkin had come looking for her. She stood and waved, catching his attention.

"They burned it, didn't they?" Mr. Larkin asked after
dismounting and grabbing her shoulders. "Your cabin.
That's what I saw."

Jessie nodded, for a moment wanting to bury her face in
the young man's chest. But, although she felt as if her
heart had been ripped from her, she didn't cry. Couldn't.
"There were three of them," she explained. "They killed
my animals. I watched them. I shot one of them. The
others—they set fire to . . ."

"Come home with me," Mr. Larkin offered gently. "We
can't do anything until morning."

It was still morning when three families gathered outside the Larkin cabin. Annie Larkin had given Jessie a
skirt to wear over her nightgown. She wore cracked old
leather boots. Her feet ached from the unaccustomed con-
finement. But what could she do? She'd lost everything,
even her moccasins.

She listened to the angry conversation about demanding

better protection and insisting that the Walla Wallas be made to return home. When someone asked her a question, she managed to speak a few words. Otherwise, she merely nodded when one of the men told her to mount up and go with them to Fort Sutter.

Dimly, she sensed that things weren't right with her mind, but every time she tried to think, what she'd seen last night washed over her until she was afraid she'd start screaming. Annie Larkin had told her it was all right if she cried. In fact she would feel better if she did. But she didn't know how.

Or maybe the truth was, she was afraid to let go.

No sooner had she passed through the gates than one of the Indian guards touched her boot. "It wasn't Maidu," he said in halting English. "Maidu would never attack."

"I know," she reassured him. Her voice sounded flat and unused. Had she said anything during the ride here?

Daniel.

Oh God, how she needed him.

Someone took the reins out of her hands and helped her off the borrowed horse. Propelled by her neighbors, she went with them to see Sutter.

"We're farmers, not soldiers," Mr. Larkin told the captain. "I've got three little children. If the Walla Wallas attack, my family doesn't stand a chance."

An involuntary shudder slashed through Jessie at that. She didn't try to still it. She looked down at her hands knotted into the faded skirt. Captain Sutter, his accent sounding thicker than she remembered, asked how many Indians were involved. She answered, explaining in that same dull voice that she may have killed one of them.

"Did they come after you?"

She shook her head, feeling dizzy. "They were busy setting fire to my cabin."

"I'm sorry, Miss Speer. Truly sorry. I've been hoping to avoid trouble with the Walla Wallas. They had no cause . . ." He motioned to the aide at his side. "Find Captain Kern and tell him his presence is needed. Now. The man simply must take control. I can't do everything." After the aide left, Captain Sutter launched into his complaints against the former topographical engineer who was now, supposedly, the fort's ranking officer.

Jessie couldn't concentrate. She'd been out in the sunlight for days now, working while sweat pooled on her forehead and ran down her back. This room with its single window felt so cold, was so dark. Despite herself, she thought back to winter. For months she'd seen nothing except snow and a shadowy hovel no better than a bear's den. Once she'd been rescued, she'd spent weeks at the fort, biding her time until she could be free.

She'd tasted freedom. Touched her dream.

And now Indians with mischief on their minds had taken both freedom and the dream from her.

She was on her feet before she realized what she'd done. Although all conversation ceased and people stared at her as if she'd taken leave of her senses, she couldn't force herself to sit back down. "I have . . . Margaret Buckhalter. I have to tell her."

Annie reached for her, but she shied away. Repeating that she wanted to find Margaret, she stumbled out of the room. As she'd done a few weeks before, she stood at the top of the stairs looking down at the fort. The weather had changed, taking with it those who'd been trapped here all winter. Still, she imagined what this place would look like in a few months when this year's pioneers reached California.

She couldn't go back to living here. She couldn't!

Her vision had cleared, focused on one horseman, al-

most before she became aware of who he was. He rode a
high-headed stallion, his hands firm on the reins. Although
the horse shied and pranced, the rider's attention wasn't on
his mount.

Because she knew who he was, she knew who he was
looking for.

Ignoring her still tender feet, she hurried down the stairs
and dodged around a couple of men. She opened her
mouth to call out. Before she could speak, he turned toward her, then vaulted out of the saddle.

"Jessie, I'm so sorry."

The tears that had been threatening for hours rose like
a wave inside her. "I couldn't do anything to save them.
Or the cabin. Daniel . . ." She reached for him, not caring
who saw or heard. She *had* to feel his arms around her.
"I'm so sorry. After all your hard work, what it cost
you—I couldn't stop them."

He crushed her against him. "You're apologizing to
me?" She felt his body shudder, felt his lips in her hair.
"Don't. That's not what matters."

"But you worked so hard."

"It's your land, Jessie, your dream."

He understood. That's all that mattered. She tried to take
a breath; it came out a sob. But he had her in his arms,
holding her, letting her cry. She tried to look up at him, to
ask him to help her make sense of the nightmare, but her
tears blurred the world. Blurred him even.

"Don't try to talk," he ordered. "Just cry."

That she could do. In truth, she couldn't do anything
else. After hitching his horse, he led her out of the fort,
down off the hill, toward the tree-shaded lake where soldiers sometimes camped. She didn't think anyone was
staying there now but couldn't make herself care enough
to find out. Her body felt as if it might break, shaken as

it was by the agony inside. If it hadn't been for Daniel's arms, for his silent understanding of what she needed, she might have started to scream. Instead she cried.

Finally: "It hurts. I don't want it to hurt anymore."

"I know. Jessie, listen to me. There's no way around the pain, no way of making it go away. But soon you'll have to think about starting over."

Over? She couldn't put her mind to that. "How—did you hear?"

He said something about Narcisco having brought him the news at dawn, but she couldn't put her mind to what must have gone through him when he heard. She almost asked where he'd been, what duties he'd left, how he'd known to come to the fort, what he'd felt when he saw her place, but those were simply whirling thoughts. She hurt too much to try to make sense of them.

"Jessie." He tugged lightly on her hand. "Sit down. You're limping."

Was she? She stared at her foot, puzzled by the strange boots. Then, when he pulled again, she crossed her legs and collapsed on the ground. He knelt before her and began to remove the boots. "What are you doing?"

"I want to see what's wrong."

"Oh. All right. Daniel, they were dead, weren't they?"

He knew she was talking about her livestock. "Yes," he reassured her. "I don't think they suffered much."

"You didn't hear them." She shuddered, tearing him between tending to her feet and holding her again. But even though her swollen eyes made his heart ache for her, he knew that her time of leaning on him was coming to an end.

She'd been brought to the fort by other settlers. She'd been meeting with Captain Sutter, but for whatever reason, she'd walked out of the room. He couldn't say what she'd been thinking, whether she knew where she was going when she spotted him.

He didn't care. She'd let him hold her. Let him see her tears.

He touched a thumb to her instep. She winced but didn't try to pull free. "You ran barefoot, didn't you?"

"My moccasins." Fresh tears glittered in her eyes but didn't break free. "They're burned."

"I'll get you another pair."

"Will you, Daniel? What about a horse? A milk cow. Can you build me another cabin?"

Although she'd thrown the words at him, he knew she wasn't angry at him. If she hadn't believed, deep down inside, that he'd accept her the way she was today, she wouldn't have said what she had. "If that's what you want."

She blinked. "You can't," she whispered. "There isn't enough timber."

"It can be had. Brought up from Monterey. For a price."

"A price? I don't have any money."

She did, miles and miles from here, but he knew she wasn't ready to hear that. Not yet. He lowered her foot and started in on the other boot. He could hear her breathing, see the moisture in her eyes. Her left foot had sustained a nasty-looking cut. He guessed that she'd been so in shock that she hadn't noticed her injury, hadn't mentioned it to the Larkins. Leaving her, he walked over to the pond and dipped his shirttail in it. He knelt before her again and began washing the cut clean. "Did you see your place this morning?"

She shook her head. "We didn't come that way. I didn't want to. All my work, my dreams, a lifetime of dreams . . . I don't have anything." She spoke without emotion.

"Nothing?" he prompted, laying himself open to attack. "It's not that bad, Jessie. You have something left."

"What?"

Me, he wanted to say. "The land itself. Your crops. They didn't take that from you."

"Worthless land. I kept my shovel and hoe inside."

He winced at that but forced himself to think beyond her too-calm words. He could sympathize with her, but she'd been surrounded by sympathy since last night and those well-meaning gestures hadn't restored her spirit. Risking a great deal, he tried another approach. "And you can't tend your plants without a hoe, can you?"

"No."

"You have to have a plow. You can't dig another row with anything as crude as a stick."

Her head came up. She glared at him.

"Narciso can give you more baskets so you can carry water to your plants, but you wouldn't want to do that, would you?"

"Daniel! Stop it."

"Stop what?"

"What you're doing." She looked confused and angry. At least she no longer looked as if her heart had been ripped from her.

"I'm not doing anything," he lied. "You told me you'd lost everything. I'm simply agreeing with you."

"Are you?"

"Yes." He whispered the word. Then, after releasing her foot and clamping his fingers lightly around her ankles, he went on. "You don't have a roof over your head. You—"

"It's more than that," she interrupted. She paused then, but he didn't try to fill the silence. "You lost something, too. All your hard work, the money you spent getting me the lumber."

So she knew about that. "I can always build another cabin. But I have to ask myself, what for?"

She stared at him, teeth clamped over her lower lip. She seemed unaware that he was holding her ankles.

"What for?" he repeated. "Like you said, the land isn't worth anything. Without you there, the plants will shrivel up and die. Maybe they'll be eaten by wild animals, but that shouldn't make you feel too bad. At least something will make use of your crops."

"Stop it."

He waited her out.

"I know what you're doing, Daniel. You want me to argue with you. But I won't."

"Why not?" he asked gently.

She pulled her lower lip between her teeth again, released it, took a deep breath. "Because you're right."

He wanted to hug her to him and whisper words of encouragement. But because he believed she needed more time with her emotions, he held off. Still, he couldn't stop himself from leaning forward, his hands moving from her ankles to her calves. "Right?" he prompted.

"I haven't lost everything. I have my garden."

"But it won't last long if you're not there to tend it."

She started to nod; the movement ended with a shudder. "What's wrong?" he asked.

"The way it looks right now, I don't know if I can go back."

"Not now," he agreed. "No one expects you to do that until the army has dealt with the Walla Wallas."

"That's not it." She was staring at his hands, her body still.

"Not it?" he repeated.

"My animals. Daniel, I can't look at them."

He gave her legs a quick squeeze. He felt the muscles

under his hands bunch and tighten. "I'll take care of that, Jessie."

"Thank you." Her eyes teared again. Her calves remained tense. "Oh Daniel, thank you."

She drew her legs up against her body, leaving his hands with nothing to hold on to. Then she wrapped her arms around her knees, hugging herself. He noticed that her fingers now massaged where he'd been tending to her a few seconds ago.

"I don't want to do it. Oh God, it's the last thing I thought I'd ever do."

How could a woman say something so softly and yet have it make this much of an impact on him? "Don't want to do what?" She couldn't leave her mouth parted and vulnerable like that, not if she didn't want him to cover it with his own.

"Go up there."

He'd been studying her hands, her mouth, trying not to think about how slight she looked in the oversized shirt. But her words were a plea, pulling his attention to her eyes.

"You won't be alone." He held out his hand. After a moment, she stopped gripping her knees and extended her fingers to him. They felt icy. He caught them in his palm and closed his fingers around her. Then, without asking whether she wanted it, he took her other hand and began warming it. "I'll go with you."

"You—will?"

Didn't she know it couldn't be any other way for him? "I don't want to push you, Jessie. I know how hard this decision is. But it's the right one; the only one."

"I know." She sounded as if the words hurt her. "I've been thinking—right after the attack, I didn't think at all. I couldn't. But then, maybe it's the human spirit. Maybe

I'm just as stubborn as my papa said. I can't give up on my dream. It's the only one I have."

He hurt for her. A body should have more than that reason to keep going. His—he stopped. What were his reasons? "It's a good dream," he said, because he couldn't think of anything else.

"Is it?" Now she sounded angry at herself. "I don't know what else to do. I have to have a horse. And a cow. Even if I sleep in a tent, I have to have the animals. But without the means to purchase them—" She pulled her hands free and waved them in the air. "I could work for Captain Sutter or for the Buckhalters, but . . ."

"Even if they can pay you, it would take a long time to earn the kind of money you'll need. Jessie, I will not let you live out there in a tent."

Her mouth twisted. "Why not? It wouldn't cost as much to replace a tent."

"You deserve better."

"Do I? Daniel, do you know why I can't work for the captain or the Buckhalters?"

"Because you wouldn't have enough time to tend to your own garden." He knew it went beyond that, but the words were for her to say.

"That too." Again she pulled her knees against her body and held her legs in place by locking her arms around them. She didn't seem to remember that he'd been trying to warm her. "I'd have to live at the fort."

"Yes. You would."

"Surrounded by people. And noise. I didn't know how much I hated the noise until I was on my own land."

He studied her, wondering if she might start crying again. But although her eyes glistened, her features remained calm. "I need space around me. And I need silence."

He already knew that about her. "There's silence on the mountain."

"I know." She straightened and took a deep breath. "I know."

"I just want you to think about that. I'll be with you, but there's no way I can stop the memories."

She nodded, then crossed her legs under her. She leaned forward and rested her elbows on her knees. "I've been trying to tell myself that I'm lucky. Most folks here barely have enough to keep body and soul together. I have more money than I ever dreamed I would. I—I used to."

"You have another chance, Jessie."

When he spoke her name, she blinked and focused on him. For a moment she said nothing, only stared at him as if she was truly seeing him for the first time today. "You understand me," she whispered. "So well."

Did he? "I knew you needed someone to talk to."

She shook her head at that. "Not just someone, Daniel. You. You're the only one who truly understands me." Again she shook her head. "I'm sorry. I'm going on like a child with a broken heart."

He almost told her that she shouldn't apologize for her emotions, no matter what they were. But he held back.

"I don't know what I'm going to be like when we get up there. Just thinking about it makes me want to run away. But I can't."

He knew that; they both did. "You'll get through it."

"Are you sure?"

"You got through last night."

She stared without blinking, letting him know that she was turning what he'd said around in her mind. After a moment, she pulled her skirt up and uncovered her feet. She touched the cut he'd cleaned, then frowned. "I don't remember when that happened."

"I think it's going to be all right. It isn't too deep."

"Thank you. For cleaning it. Oh Daniel, I'm such a mess! I can't even think to look after my own health."

"Don't." His voice held a hard note. He swallowed and tried again. "Don't expect the impossible of yourself, Jessie. No one can come through what happened to you without feeling as if they'd been kicked by a mule."

Her mouth lifted. He held his breath, wondering if he might get a full smile from her. "Kicked by a mule. That's what it feels like." She sighed. "When? When should we go?"

Instead of answering, he stood and then helped her to her feet. He led her slowly to the edge of the pond and indicated she might want to soak her feet in the clear, cool water. She plopped unceremoniously onto the ground and again yanked on her skirt, reminding him of a child unaware of her body.

He was aware, so much so that he filled the air with talk about getting a member of Narcisco's family to look after her garden while they were gone, how he'd have to prevail upon Narcisco to take his place with the cattle. Narcisco would agree, he reassured Jessie. There'd be a price to pay, probably helping Narcisco break the yearling horses.

All the time he spoke, he kept his eyes on Jessie's legs.

"You're so good, Daniel." She spoke with her eyes on him. "Without you I'd be lost."

He didn't say anything.

CHAPTER 15

Daniel disappeared into Narcisco's house for the moccasins Narcisco's daughter Misha had made for her. Still unable to enter what seemed more like a cave than a house, Jessie waited outside.

"It is a good thing Daniel has me as a friend," Narcisco said. "A less generous man would not do what he has asked."

"I know." Jessie smiled to let Narcisco know how much she appreciated his generosity. As soon as she and Daniel were under way, Narcisco would leave for the cattle herd. The young brave who'd fallen in love with Misha was already at the farm tending her garden. "If there was any other way, I wouldn't have asked Daniel to go with me.

But I can't do this alone." Her last words seemed to hold suspended in the warm spring breeze.

"I do not begrudge my friend his generous offer. Jessie, it takes a brave woman to do what you are going to. But Daniel would say I have changed if I do not make him think he will be in debt to me for a long time."

What a wonderful friendship the two men had, she thought. They teased each other mercilessly. And yet underneath the joking words ran a rock-solid relationship. She guessed that each would lay down his life for the other.

Daniel emerged from the smoke hole. He walked toward her, broad shoulders squared for the task ahead of him. He was clean-shaven, but he hadn't cut his hair for months. It drifted, thick and black, down the sides of his face, roughening him, turning him into a mountain man in her mind.

His walk—she couldn't ignore the sure strides, the powerful thigh muscles working under their deerskin covering.

His eyes—even with the bright sunlight wiping away the shades and planes of his features, his eyes continued to bore into her.

Did he have any idea what had been going on inside her when he led her away from Fort Sutter last week and gave her the solitude she needed? Not only that, he'd tended to her feet.

Tended to her feet!

No. It had been much more than that, a reawakening of emotions she thought she'd lost when she watched her cabin burn. All he'd had to do was wrap his fingers around her ankle and she found her way out of her tears—and into awareness of him.

Awareness.

How was she going to survive all that time alone with him?

He handed her the moccasins, then watched, silent, as she yanked off the hated boots and slid her feet into soft leather. She smiled up at him, then stood quickly so she wouldn't risk having him touch her. Acting on impulse, she cocked back her arm and flung one of the boots into the bushes. The second followed a few seconds later.

"Wonderful!" She grinned at Narcisco. "Please tell Misha how much I appreciate this."

"You told her already."

"I know," she told the chief. "But she deserves to hear it again. I hoped I'd be able to tell her myself."

Rolling his eyes skyward, Narcisco shook his head. "My daughter said she was going for a ride this morning. Not asked, said. I know where she went."

"Can you blame her?" Jessie teased. "Vaca is a handsome young man."

"Handsome!" Narcisco snorted. "When he was a child, he chased the dogs around the village. Twice they fell into my home."

Jessie laughed at that, struck by the realization that this was the first she'd laughed since she spotted the doe and fawns near her place. She turned to tell Daniel how good it felt to feel like this again, but he was walking away from her. She stared after him, as intrigued by the way his muscles meshed into a whole as she'd been when he came toward her.

"You can trust him."

Startled because Narcisco had read her mind, she tried to tell the chief that she was only anxious to be on her way.

"I say it again, Jessie. You can trust him."

"I—never thought I couldn't."

"Maybe you are the only pale skin to think that."

"If I am, then I feel sorry for them."

"It is the way he wants."

Jessie could no longer divide her attention between what Daniel was doing and what Narcisco was saying. She would be with Daniel for days; now might be the only time she could talk to his friend. "Why doesn't he want anyone to know what kind of man he is, how gentle . . ."

"This is not a gentle place, Jessie. Many die. Half of those who started here with you are now dead."

She nodded.

"Years ago Daniel lost the only person he has ever loved. He told me what happened, but those words should come from him."

"I know. I wasn't asking."

Narcisco glanced over at Daniel. "They call him a murderer, a man who would shoot another in the back."

"I can't believe that."

"That is because you owe your life to him."

"It's more than that. When I look at him, hear him talk, I know I'm with a decent man."

"And you feel the way my daughter does when she gazes at Vaca."

Jessie had seen Misha's dark, lovesick eyes. "Me? Oh, no. She's smitten, Narcisco. Do you know what smitten means?" Because she'd never experienced the emotion, she had to dig for an explanation the chief might understand. "A woman—and a man, too—is smitten when she can't remember to do her chores and forgets her parents because all she can think about is a certain man. I'm not like that, not at all. When I see Daniel . . ." He was walking toward her; she kept her eyes off him. "I have no idea where you got a notion like that."

Narcisco's chuckle told her what he thought of her denial. But he was wrong, she thought as Daniel mounted his horse, his thighs pressing against his deerskin pants. Misha was thirteen, a shy, giggling girl who couldn't sit still long enough to learn how to weave a gift basket decorated with feathers and shells. Jessie had tried to tell Misha how important it was to keep weeds from choking out her vegetables, but Misha would rather chase rabbits with Vaca.

Certainly she'd never chase rabbits simply because that was what Daniel wanted to do.

No more than three feet away, Daniel leaned forward to shake Narcisco's hand. Then he straightened; the hard muscle at the side of his neck tightened, then disappeared beneath tanned flesh as he turned toward her. "You're ready?"

No. I don't want to do this, go up there. "Yes."

Because they'd left a little after dawn and kept to a steady pace, they reached the base of the foothills by nightfall. Jessie hadn't said anything about the pace she wanted to keep. In fact, other than to respond to his few questions, she hadn't said anything. Even when he pointed to a bull elk in the distance, she'd only nodded and watched until the huge animal disappeared into the trees.

He was going to have to spend days, nights with her.

While he built a fire, she tended to the horses. He watched her out of the corner of his eye, thinking that she carried herself more like an Indian than a white woman. Although she still wore clothes that were too large for her, their bulk didn't completely hide her lean, strong form. Or maybe the truth was, his mind would have been able to imagine what was beneath her clothes no matter what she wore.

She leaned down and picked up his horse's hoof. The stallion, determined to eat, tried to pull away. She followed his movement, keeping her shoulder against his, talking quietly, firmly. Finally she released him, patted his side, looked up at the emerging stars.

"It's beautiful, isn't it?" he asked.

"Incredible. I don't know how anyone can ignore the sky." She raised her hand as if trying to reach a star. A few seconds later, her hand dropped back by her side and she walked toward him. "All the time I was growing up, that was one of the things I loved most. Sitting outside at night watching the stars come out."

He'd carried a fallen log near the fire so they could sit on it. He waited, wondering if she'd settle herself beside him. "By yourself?"

"Sometimes my mother would join me, but not very often. At night, when she didn't have work to do, she'd read in her Bible." Jessie glanced at the log, at the fire, at him, at the log again. Finally, sighing a little, she gathered her skirt and lowered herself. She was maybe six inches away. "My mother took a great deal of comfort from the Bible. I found my peace in the stars."

He wanted to tell her about his mother, about a brave, half-wild woman who'd shown her son that nothing mattered as much as freedom. But Jessie had gone into her own past, and he didn't want to distract her from that. "Peace?" he prompted. "Was that hard for you to find?"

"Not really. I don't know." She turned toward him, the firelight shimmering in her eyes. "As long as I can remember, I've been restless. I loved the farm. I don't mean for you to think I didn't. But it was Papa's farm, Papa's land. Sometimes he made me think it was his air I was breathing. At night . . ." She went back to looking at the sky, which had now exploded into a thousand distant lights. "At night I'd listen to the silence and think about what it would feel like to be an eagle free to fly wherever he wanted. Did he reach the stars? That's what I'd ask myself. If I was an eagle, could I fly to the stars?"

His mother had said essentially the same thing. For her, freedom waited on the back of a strong horse.

"Daniel, have you ever wanted to fly?"

Her question pulled him out of the past. No one had ever asked him that. Until tonight it had never occurred to him that someone would care. "Not an eagle." Now that he'd made the decision, or the decision had been made for him, he wanted to tell her everything about himself. But, aware that he was peeling himself away layer by layer, his voice remained a whisper. "I don't care that much about flying, Jessie. But that bull elk we saw today—that's what I'd like to be."

"An elk. Why?"

"Because he's so proud of who and what he is." Was this him talking, laying himself open to her? "He has everything he needs, strength, speed, keen hearing, the ability to fight if that's what it takes."

"I saw a deer once who'd been killed by a bear." She, too, was whispering, slowly folding and unfolding her hands in her lap. "Maybe a bear can't bring down an elk, but an elk isn't without enemies."

"No one is safe, Jessie. Not even a bear. He might be attacked by another bear, or by man."

"Man. With his rifles and arrows."

He nodded, his attention split between her profile, the flames, the sky. "But an elk lives by his wits. And when he passes by, those who see him are touched by his presence."

"That's what you want, to be noticed?"

"No." He spoke with his heart, not knowing how she'd brought him to this point, not caring. "I'm so in awe of those great creatures. Maybe that's why, if I wasn't who I am, I'd want to be one."

"Have you ever wanted to be someone other than who you are? Would you want to be rich, powerful?"

She was looking at him; he couldn't ignore her. Did she know that her eyes had been touched by the night, that nothing was left of her features except ebony shadows tinted with firelight? "No. I've never wanted to be anyone except who I am."

"Even if that means you had to flee Texas?"

"I did what I had to to stay alive. And because there was nothing to keep me there. Because of what you've been through, I think you understand."

He felt his heart beating; maybe he felt hers as well. She didn't speak. Instead, she took his hand, and he didn't need to hear a word from her. When she laced her slender, strong fingers through his, he brought their intertwined hands up to his mouth and kissed her knuckles.

He heard himself breathe. He knew he'd heard her quick intake of breath. His body, the man part of him, wanted her beneath him, opening herself to him. But he was more than that. He was also heart and soul. His heart needed to beat in time with hers. His soul—he didn't know what his soul needed, only that with what she'd said tonight, he'd come closer to understanding that than he ever had before.

She was asleep. Daniel turned on his side and faced her from across the fire. The next few days were going to be hard on her. He didn't want to ever forget that, to let his awareness of her stand between him and her need for his support. Narciso had offered to accompany them, but he'd turned down the invitation. Even when Narciso reminded him that he might ruin her reputation if anyone found out where they'd gone together, he told his friend it was a chance he was willing to take.

Jessie needed time with her emotions.

And he wanted this time alone with her.

He'd started to move onto his back, hoping to become comfortable enough that he could fall asleep, when his stallion suddenly stomped his hoof. Instantly he tensed. The stallion let out a shrill whinny. Jessie stirred. He sat upright, cocking his head, listening for something, anything.

The stallion, which had been sleeping a moment ago, again hammered his hoof against the ground. Silent, he slipped out of bed and reached for his rifle. With his free hand, he grabbed the powder horn and headed barefoot toward the horse.

Jessie's mare, too, had come alert, her breath wheezing in the night. Between bursts of sound, he listened.

Then he heard it, distant hoofs landing on packed earth. So they weren't alone out here. It could be settlers, soldiers, even Walla Wallas.

For the next half hour, he sat cross-legged near the horses, listening, taking his cue from the stallion. Although the animal paced and pawed for several minutes, he finally settled down. Still, Daniel continued to strain, certain that the faint sounds came from horses forced to keep their distance.

Jessie woke first. Where she was and what she was doing here came to her slowly. Even before the where and what made sense, she remembered last night.

He'd kissed her knuckles. That's all.

She pushed the bedroll down off her shoulders and lay with her hands folded under her head, watching the day grow in strength. She didn't have to look at Daniel to know he was still asleep.

Last night he'd let her see inside him. After that, how could she not know everything about him?

Not everything, she reminded herself. The admission brought her not disappointment but anticipation. They would be together, just the two of them, for days. In that time maybe he'd no longer be cloaked in mystery.

Was that what she wanted?

The crickets had begun their song before she went to bed. Now their vibrating voices had been replaced by the croaking of frogs.

Frogs. Crickets. The sound of horses tearing at dew-wet grass. Daniel sleeping a few feet away.

She slid out of bed and walked barefoot into the trees so she could find privacy. As she returned, her gaze fell on the moccasins she'd placed by her bedroll. Perhaps in a moment of whimsy, Misha had wound several white owl feathers into the design. No matter how many pairs of shoes she might have in her life, she would always remember the moccasins with the owl feathers. The moccasins Daniel had known she wanted.

He stirred, pulling her away from her thoughts. She watched, aware of the swift way he left sleep behind. When his eyes opened, they were clear and bright, aware.

"Did you just wake up?" he asked.

"A few minutes ago."

"Hm." He looked around, his attention on the plains they'd crossed over yesterday. "How did you sleep?" he asked after a minute.

"Fine. I've been listening to the frogs."

He stood up, seeming to do it without having to first brace his body with his arms. "They're noisy. Do you want a fire?"

Although she felt slightly damp and cool, she shook her head. Cold, she'd learned last winter, went far deeper than this slight discomfort. She asked if he thought they could cover as much territory as they had yesterday, aware that he hadn't taken his eyes off her. Did he regret any of last night's conversation?

She hoped he didn't, because she would never want to take back a word, or gesture.

"It should be fairly easy going," he told her. "There'll be some climbing, but hardly enough for the horses to notice. Tomorrow we'll get into the mountains."

Tomorrow. The mountains. She nodded and sat down so she could put on her moccasins. He hadn't moved; his eyes were still on her and she knew she didn't have to tell him what she was thinking.

Daniel wanted to tell himself that he'd only imagined last night's unsettling sounds, but he couldn't. Years of not being able to take freedom for granted had done that to him. But, he reasoned, just because someone had been out there didn't mean their safety was at risk. Even if it had been the Walla Wallas, surely they knew that their unprovoked attack on Jessie's farm had roused everyone's wrath. Another incident and they'd face much more than an order to go home.

Most of the time Jessie rode behind him, making it hard for them to carry on a conversation. That bothered him. If he could hear her voice, maybe he'd know more about what was going on inside her. When he mentioned the mountains, he'd seen raw fear in her eyes. He had seen her shove her fear into submission almost as soon as it emerged, but he knew her battle wasn't finished.

Because the horses had traveled without stopping to eat yesterday, he called for an hour-long break when the sun was high in the sky. While the horses grazed, he and Jessie sat at the edge of a creek eating sweet cakes and dried salmon. She filled her time trying to count the thin-legged water skippers that ran over the water's surface. Her hands lay in her lap as she leaned forward, concentrating. Although she'd braided her hair this morning, they'd passed through enough brush that a number of strands now trailed down the side of her face.

She looked so pensive, so lost in herself.

Even when he told her that it was time to mount again, her eyes remained thoughtful. Their dark depths told him something else: for now, at least, she had her fear under control.

That night they bedded down in a manzanita thicket with a seemingly unending mass of evergreens ahead of them. This time he looked after the horses. Many women, he knew, would have waited for the man to go in search of firewood, but a few minutes after she disappeared in the thicket, he heard his axe thudding against wood. When she emerged, her arms were full of dead limbs.

She dropped her load and turned to regard him. "It smells wonderful here. So clean."

"What you smell is pitch."

She gave him a look that said she didn't need the obvious pointed out to her. "Last winter I couldn't smell the pitch. It was too cold. That's what I smelled, the cold."

"What does summer smell like?"

"Heat." She smiled. "The sun baking the grass and dirt. Do you know what I love the most? The smell of hay just after it's been harvested. And roses." Her voice took on a wistful tone. "Mama and I each had our own rosebushes. We used to argue over whose had the most beautiful flowers. One of hers—the yellow in it would put the sun to shame."

She'd been slowly swinging the axe. He took it from her and set it down. Together they went about clearing a space between two boulders and soon had a small, hot fire going. Dinner was a repeat of last night. Because they'd followed the creek, they were able to clean up after their meal. Daniel watched, barely able to contain his amusement as she knelt beside the creek, trying to wash her face and arms without getting her moccasins or dress wet. Standing, she placed her hands on her hips and glared at him. "You men don't know how easy you have it. No one looks scandalized when a man does something undignified."

He could have told her that if folks knew that just the two of them had come up here, she would lose more than her dignity. But she already knew that. Besides, despite her best intentions, the hem of her skirt fairly dripped water.

"Why do they do it? Women dressing to please other women?"

"What are you talking about?"

He gave her a look designed to let her think he'd spent a great deal of time coming to this conclusion when in truth this was the first he'd set his mind to it. "The way women dress. Corsets of all things. How can any woman stand a corset?"

"I don't wear the silly things."

He couldn't help grinning. "And why not?"

"Because it's like trying to walk in leg irons."

She had a point there. At least from what little he knew about corsets, she did. "Then why do they do it?"

"Because, because—oh, I don't know. Mama did. Papa insisted on it. He said a man wants to be able to span his woman's waist."

Daniel glanced at Jessie's waist. Whether he could span

it or not he couldn't say. But he wanted to try. "Your father didn't insist the same of you?"

"He tried. One time when he got all worked up about it, I threatened to run away."

He would have loved to see her standing up to her father. "And that made him back down?"

"Yes. If I'd left, he would have lost his hired hand."

Daniel paused long enough to place another branch on the fire. "Where would you have gone?"

She reached down, grabbed her skirt hem, and squeezed. The gesture pulled the fabric from around her ankles, exposing them. He tried not to look.

"I would have hired myself out to a farmer down the road. He needed someone to tend his orchard."

"Just like that?"

"No. Not just like that. But I would have done it, and Papa knew it. It would have shamed him."

He absorbed that bit of information. "What do you know about orchards?"

"Enough. One growing thing isn't that different from another." She shook out her skirt, making it easier for him to concentrate. "Daniel, thank you."

"Thank you?"

"For coming up here with me."

He wondered if she knew how incredibly hard it was to keep his hands off her and how every moment he wondered if he would succeed the next. "I saw how you looked when your place burned down. I couldn't do anything then."

"You had to listen to me cry." She sat on the rock closest to the fire and spread out her skirt so it could dry. Tonight, probably because they were near the creek, it seemed as if the frogs and crickets were battling each other. "I've never cried like that before," she said. "Not even when my mother died."

He didn't know what to say. When his own mother died, there hadn't been time for tears, barely time for a scream that came from a place so deep and dark inside him that it frightened him. "Don't think about that now. You'll be able to start over."

"I hope so."

"The army's rounding up the Walla Wallas. They might well be gone by the time we get back."

"I wasn't thinking about that."

She'd hunched forward, turned so he could no longer see into her eyes. He wished he wasn't standing so far from her. "What were you thinking about?"

"Other things. Daniel?"

He waited.

"Daniel, last winter when you were encouraging me to keep going, did you truly believe what you were saying?"

"I said a lot of things, Jessie."

"I know." She spoke into the fire. "And without those things I think I would have died."

He didn't agree. He'd seen her will.

"Even now, sometimes I think about what we endured and don't know what kept us alive."

She was talking this way because tonight, here, the memories had begun to close around her. He wanted to tell her that and warn her that they might get worse. Instead he stepped away from the fire and began spreading out his bedroll—as far from her as he could get and still feel the fire's heat. As he worked, he felt her eyes on him and hoped she wouldn't ask why he hadn't come near enough to touch her tonight.

"I wonder if I'll ever be able to go inside Narcisco's house."

"If you don't, he'll understand."

"I hope so. He's a wonderful man. Daniel? Did you think we were going to die?"

She'd changed too fast on him. He needed to concentrate on what being this close to her was doing to him. But she'd asked a question that deserved an honest answer. "Maybe."

"But you came anyway."

"Yes."

"And when Mr. Reed wanted you to go back up with them, you did that too."

"Yes."

Although he'd been looking out at the night, he knew when she stood and started toward him. Her skirt made a faint whispering sound. Despite the frogs and crickets, he heard that.

Then he felt her shoulder against his and the weight of her head as she rested it against him. He wasn't going to touch her; he wasn't. But somehow his arm went around her and he made a shelter for her. He still studied the way the night cloaked the trees.

"You're a rare man, Daniel. Not many will admit it when they think they're going to die."

"If they don't, then they're fools."

"Maybe they just don't want to face certain things."

He'd never thought he'd stand in the wilderness with his arm around a good and decent woman while they talked about what went on inside a person's heart. Now it had happened, with Jessie.

Even with the fire at his back and Jessie beside him, a sliver of dread shot through him. Although he'd put better than a thousand miles between himself and his past, there was no guarantee that past hadn't followed him. If it found him, would it find Jessie as well?

Thinking not enough, thinking too much, he slowly drew her around in front of him and cupped her chin. She stood there with her breath coming in quick, slight bursts, her body trembling like a storm-touched aspen.

When he covered her mouth with his and felt her breasts flatten against him, he stopped thinking of anything except her.

It was only much later that he put his mind to anything else, not because he wanted to, but because he had no choice. As he'd done the night before, the stallion suddenly drove his hoof against the ground. The sound instantly swept Daniel's mind clean of everything except caution. But although he strained to listen, the crickets made it impossible for him to hear what the stallion had.

CHAPTER 16

Although they'd been climbing over rocks and through snow since a little after dawn, Jessie knew the pounding of her heart had very little to do with exertion and too much to do with walking back into a nightmare.

All day the terrain had been familiar. When they had left the horses the day before yesterday and strapped packs onto their backs, she had concentrated on that. She'd been grateful when Daniel pointed out the signs of a changing world—the melting snow, new pine needles, spring wild-flowers poking through the ground where the sun had already put an end to the snow. She'd pointed out an eagle to him and then teasingly informed him that he'd fright-ened the eagle because he looked like a grizzly.

But they'd gone through the pass and she could make out the peak she'd spent last winter staring up at.

Suppressing a shudder, she concentrated on plowing through the snow. He was alert to their surroundings, uneasy even, which only increased the strain on her nerves. From what she could tell, it hadn't snowed since the last of the survivors were brought down. The individual tracks they'd made had been erased by wind and sun, but the long, thin depression in the snow remained.

Daniel, who was leading the way, paused and turned to look back at her as he'd done so many times during their climb. "Are you all right?"

"Yes. I was just thinking—looking at the tracks and remembering."

"If we'd waited a month or so, more of the snow would have melted. The landscape would have changed."

"I just want to get this over with."

When she'd faced what her options were without money, she'd known she had to come back here. Only, knowing they were approaching where she'd spent the winter was the hardest thing she'd ever done.

Daniel must have retraced his steps while she'd been lost in thought. Although the trail was too narrow for them to walk side by side in comfort, he took her hand and drew her beside him. "It's going to be all right, Jessie. I can't take the memories away, but I'm not sure I should try."

"I know," she reassured him. "I can't pretend last winter didn't happen. I think the nightmares will only start all over if I do. But . . ." She took a deep breath, her eyes on the peak. "It's so hard."

"Do you want to talk about it?"

Talk? Wasn't that the same as wanting to relive the nightmare? Still, she was glad he'd asked the question. "People do incredible things," she whispered. "Things you never think they're going to. Like my mama coming to California. Trying to reach California."

"She was a brave woman."

"Was she? I don't know. She always talked about how hard living with my father was. When I was a child, I wondered why all she did was talk. I wanted her to leave and take me with her. Then I got older and realized there wasn't anything she could do. She hadn't brought anything to her marriage. She was beholden to my father for everything. At least she believed she was. But she couldn't keep it all bottled up inside her. She needed me."

Jessie lowered her gaze. Looking at Daniel was easier than studying the peak. "It wasn't the same for me. Maybe because at an early age I realized I could till the land and grow enough food to support myself. Maybe that's why I survived last winter, why I found a way to make sure I wouldn't have to live at the fort—or marry a man so I'd have a protector."

She gave him a quick, slight smile, hoping he'd understand whatever she said. "I wouldn't be alive now if it hadn't been for you. I don't ever want you to think I believe different. But I'm not helpless the way Mama was." She took a deep breath. Although she needed Daniel's warmth, she didn't lean against him. If she did, she'd be putting a lie to a lifetime of independence. "Maybe I can deal with what I went through, what's going on inside me now, because I'm proud of myself."

He hadn't done anything to indicate he thought they should be moving on. Although she wasn't sure whether what she was saying made any sense, she needed to get the words out.

"Mama wasn't proud of herself. Papa did whatever he wanted because she never once stood up to him. Instead, she came crying to me."

"Maybe she didn't have a choice. You said it; if it wasn't for your father, she wouldn't have a roof over her head."

"I know. But he couldn't have run the farm without us. Mama cooked his meals, washed his clothes. She was as good a wife as she knew how to be. He always had his way in bed. Even when she was sick or hurting, she never refused him." Jessie had never imagined telling a man about that part of her parents' marriage, but it seemed easy with Daniel. "I told myself I didn't want to talk about what's going on inside me now, but I'm talking anyway."

"I would rather have you do that than be silent."

He was *so* good to her. Nothing like her father. She pointed a finger at the peak. "The mountain fills me up inside. Looking at it, sometimes I can't think of anything else. If I'm quiet, that's why."

"Fills you up inside?" He looked slowly around. "Are you ready?"

She wasn't, but when he started walking again, she kept pace with him. To her relief, there were only a few harmless white clouds in the sky, and although it would get cold once the sun set, right now she barely needed her coat. A couple of times Daniel pointed out deer and bear tracks, proof that life had returned to the mountain. The sound of squawking birds had replaced last winter's ceaseless wind.

If she'd been able to stop the memories, she would have enjoyed the day.

They passed by the Donner cabin without stopping to look into it. When it was covered by snow, she hadn't given thought to how insignificant it appeared surrounded by endless mountains. Now, with the warped lumber roof exposed and the whole cabin listing to one side, she was in awe of the resourcefulness of those who'd survived in it.

Not all had.

Daniel placed his arm around her shoulder. "It's over," he whispered. "For those who survived and those who didn't, at least it's over."

He was right, thank God. "I wonder how long the shelters will stand. When this year's settlers come over the mountains, will they see this and know what happened here?"

"I'm certain they will."

Last winter she hadn't had the strength for the trip from the Donner cabin to hers. Now it took little more than a half hour. The wind no longer ruled her world, no longer assaulted her senses. She was aware of color, white snow, blue sky, the brown-tinged peaks.

Still, with every step, she felt more and more of the past encircle her. How could she help it? Yet, strangely, she no longer wanted to flee. Instead, with Daniel beside her to give her his strength, she faced a thousand memories.

"At least he died quick," she said of her father. "No matter what kind of man he was, I wouldn't have wanted him to suffer."

Of her mother: "Near the end, I don't think she knew what was happening. I'm grateful for that."

Then: "Sometimes the sun shone. I'd sit outside and feel it on my face and take strength from it. During those times I believed, deep down inside, that I'd survive."

Finally, because she wanted to be done with the remembering, she told Daniel how she felt when she first saw him stumbling toward her. "I told myself you'd come to save me. That my prayers had been answered. I called it a miracle. Then I got scared and thought maybe I'd just dreamed you were here."

"Did you think about how hard the trip down would be?"

She turned her attention from Daniel's deep, dark eyes and stared off into the distance. The snow, which she'd come to hate, looked so beautiful today with the sun glinting off it. "Not until we got started. I couldn't put my mind to that."

"If you had, maybe you would have stayed."

"Oh no! No matter what, I had to leave."

They'd crawled around a sharp-edged boulder. She took a step, thinking to head toward the small flat space below the rock, when he stopped her. Blinking, she realized why.

Directly ahead stood the crude structure she and Raymond and the others had hurriedly erected where the oxen mired down. As the storm built, they'd quickly dismantled the wagon so they could use the wood and canvas for a shelter. Even the wheels were gone, having been used for firewood. There might be a few leavings buried under the snow, but she forced herself to face the fact that maybe nothing remained of the long journey to this horrible place. Barely aware of what she was doing, she clutched Daniel around his waist and pressed herself as tightly to him as she could. Only a thin layer of hard-packed snow remained on the roof, and the top one-third of the sides were exposed. From where she stood she couldn't see the opening.

"Is this what you expected?"

"It seems small. We worked so hard to build it. I thought it would be larger."

With his hand on her shoulder and her arm tight around his waist, they stepped a few feet closer. Again she took note of the sky—the beautiful blue sky. "It's sturdy. At least it's that." Her throat felt as if it might close up.

"It might stand for years, Jessie. Reminding everyone who passes by of what you survived."

"It might." She stepped forward, trying to concentrate on pulling her feet out of the snow, controlling her heart's hammering. There, to the left and slightly above the cabin, was where she'd laid her parents to rest. Wordless, she pointed.

"I know. I wish I could make it different for you."

Because the sun seldom reached that spot, only a little snow had melted. There was nothing to indicate that anything except rocks were there. "You can't. No one can. I—couldn't give them a decent burial."

"You did what you could. Don't think beyond that."

"It's hard not to."

"Jessie?" He waited a moment, then went on. "Is there anything inside you need?"

His voice was so gentle. His side a warm mountain to take refuge against. "The Bible."

"Do you want me to go in with you?"

"Yes." She looked up at him, held the gaze. "Yes. Please."

After slipping off his pack and helping her out of hers, Daniel led the way around to the front of the cabin. The blanket had been shredded and torn away from the opening so that only a few tattered threads clung to splinters.

She wrapped her arms around her middle, then reached out and touched the damp wood. "It is sturdy, isn't it? I was proud of what we'd accomplished. Does that sound crazy? I hated it and yet I was proud of it."

"No. It doesn't sound crazy."

His voice was all it took. After taking a deep breath, she ducked her head and stepped inside. Except for the light that came in the opening, nothing illuminated the cavelike interior. She shuddered; no wonder she couldn't go into Narcisco's home.

Still, this had been her world; something of her remained here. After a minute she walked over to where she'd slept and reached for the family Bible. Clutching it to her, she returned to Daniel's side. By then her eyes had become accustomed to the gloom. His presence dominated the room, giving her strength. Did she want that, want to be so dependent on him? The question frightened her; she cast it away. "It's so small," she whispered. "So incredibly small."

"It did what it needed to."

"Yes." She wanted to say more, to explore her emotions, but they were so deeply tangled inside her that she couldn't sort one from the other. With the Bible still pressed against her, she walked from chair to stove to where Elizabeth had slept. She trembled, yet didn't ask Daniel to make the emotion go away.

How could she possibly stand here and not be affected?

"There are things here people can use," Daniel said, his voice low. "The stove and tools, the clothes. If travelers see them—"

"If someone needs a stove, I want them to have it."

"If those who speak ill of what happened here could see this place, they'd understand what desperation is."

His words drew her back to his side. Instead of clinging to him, she showed him the front page of the Bible, where her grandparents and great-grandparents had written their names. "I didn't think of these when you asked if I wanted to take the Bible down with me. I knew I didn't have the strength, and I couldn't ask anyone else to."

"I'm glad you have it now."

She believed him. He knew so much about her, cared.

Did she want that? Did she have a choice? "Did—you ever have a family Bible?"

"No. Jessie, is there anything else you want?"

She had her memories; that was all that mattered. "No," she told him and then headed toward the door. She was still shaking. It helped to have the Bible pressed to her. It helped even more to sense Daniel behind her.

She waited until they were outside before speaking. "For so long I tried not to think about this place."

"You don't feel that way anymore?"

"No." The breeze smelled clean, new. Early-evening shadows had begun to slide down the peaks, but she no longer feared the coming night. It was spring, the time that had always meant life on the farm. "Because coming here has made it real."

"You don't mind that?"

If she'd had any alternative, she wouldn't be here. But she'd done it; she'd had the courage. Daniel had been part, a large part of it. "No," she told him, although the answer was much more complicated. "I think I needed to see it. To remember other things."

"What other things?"

She couldn't answer him, not until she'd made herself admit why she'd been able to step inside what had been more prison than home. Until she'd faced his role in what and where she was today. "I don't know, Daniel." Turning from him, she took a minute to study her surroundings. The cabin was nestled into the mountains, protected from the worst of the wind by jagged rocky spires with snow blunting much of their starkness.

She pointed at two peaks, one much shorter than the other. "Mrs. Allsetter called them dog ears. She said they reminded her of a dog she once had with one ear that never stood up." After a moment, she again pointed.

"Over there is where I set up my snares. Raymond said it was too close to us, that the animals wouldn't come there. Besides, all the squirrels were hibernating. But I liked walking out there, being by myself."

"You never caught anything?"

"No. Still, I kept coming right up until the end."

He gently took the Bible out of her hands. After placing it on top of his pack, he returned to her. "Do you want to spend the night here? I could build a fire in the stove."

She only had to look around to know the answer. She'd been able to step into the cabin because Daniel was with her, but she couldn't possibly stay in that confined space, where memories might crawl too close. They could sleep outside.

Or could she?

"No." Her throat felt as if she'd wrenched the word from it. "Please. Things are different at night. Without the sun . . ."

"You don't have to explain. It's going to be dark in a couple of hours. If we're going to make it back to the pass, we can't stay here much longer."

She was grateful for his gentle reminder. Still, because she would never again have a reason to come here, she couldn't make herself move yet.

"What is it?" The question was spoken gently. "Do you need to say good-bye first?"

"I already did. When you and I walked out of here, I told my mother I loved her."

"You're going to be walking away again."

He knew her better than she did. The thought occurred to her that she ought to thank him, but she wasn't sure she trusted herself to speak. Turning away, she made her way to the slight hill where she'd buried her mother. For a space of time she didn't try to judge, she stood looking at

he smooth expanse of snow, remembering not the day her
mother died but a farm girl's childhood, her mother sew-
ng new dresses for her as she grew, gentle guidance in the
art of bringing life to the earth, shared delight at the birth
of a calf or lamb.

"You'll like the summer here," she whispered to her
mother. "The animals are returning. When the snow melts,
here'll be wildflowers. Do you hear the birds? They're
beautiful, so beautiful and free." Then: "Dad? I hope you
find some measure of peace here. I just wanted you to
know, I'm all right."

Eyes misty, she swiveled and faced Daniel. He stood
lightly downhill from her, his dark eyes regarding both her
and their world. Daniel. He'd become so much a part of her.
Did she want that? Was it too late for anything else?
Maybe someday they'll make a shrine of this place."

"Maybe."

He hadn't moved, hadn't invaded her space. Now that
he'd said what she needed to to her parents, she was ready
to rejoin him. It seemed that a little of the deep intensity had
left his eyes, but maybe she needed to believe that.

"We have one more thing to do."

"I know." She wanted to touch him, yet didn't. From
the moment they started out, she'd been aware of him. But
this time was for gathering memories, squarely facing the
past, accepting what couldn't be changed, not questioning
Daniel's place in her world. Silent, she headed toward a
smooth-sided boulder.

"Mr. Allsetter didn't have the strength to walk," she told
Daniel. "But his mind was as sharp as ever. After I dug,
I told him his coins were safe where I'd placed them, but
he called me an innocent and naive child and ordered me
to dig deeper. He wasn't satisfied until I'd brushed the
now smooth so no one could tell I'd been digging."

She dropped to her knees and began scooping. Becaus
the snow had packed down, she was afraid it would b
dark by the time she found Mrs. Allsetter's beaded leathe
pouch. After a minute, she stopped, thinking to put on he
gloves. That's when she sensed more than saw Danie
coming toward her. Without saying a word, he began dig
ging with Mr. Allsetter's shovel. After backing out of hi
way, she sat on the snow, watching.

He made movement look easy. Although she'd seen hir
so weary that he could barely hold up his head, sh
couldn't imagine him slowed by age or infirmity. A ma
like that would be impossible to forget.

Finally he'd cleared a space some three feet across an
nearly four feet deep. He lay on his stomach and continue
digging by hand. With a grunt, he reached down as far a
he could, then straightened and handed her a cold, sogg
lump of leather.

Caught in memories of that day, she turned the pouc
over and over in her hand. The threads holding the bead
in place had rotted. Tiny, still bright pieces of color fell t
her lap.

She picked up a tiny bead, remembering. "Mrs. All
setter told me she bought this from a Plains Indian, a littl
boy. The next day he came back with his horse piled wit
blankets and baskets, trying to get her to buy everything
Finally she gave him some hard candy."

"Open it, Jessie."

He was right. The slender thong felt as if it had melte
into the rest of the leather, but she finally managed t
make an opening large enough that the coins fell out. The
landed in her lap, scattering the beads. She picked one u
and held it in her hand, warming it, then counted the res
It came to a little more than the amount her grandmothe

ad given her, enough to buy lumber to rebuild and an-
ther horse and maybe two cows.

"It's a goodly amount."

Daniel's comment pulled her away from her thoughts. She
ried to hand him several gold pieces, saying he'd earned
hem and more, but he shook his head. "It's yours, Jessie."

"But everything you've done, I want to pay you back."
Want to feel less beholden.

"I don't need the money. You do."

"But ..." His look stopped her. Whatever his reasons
or coming here with her, money wasn't one of them. She
ad to respect that. "The Allsetters never told me how
nuch money they had," she told him. "They said that if I
idn't know, I wouldn't have to lie if someone asked me."

"If Raymond asked you."

"Yes." One by one, she placed the coins back in the
ouch, then stood. Together they walked back to where
ney'd left their packs. He'd already added her Bible to his
oad, making her wonder where her mind had been while
e was doing that. After tucking the pouch into the middle
f her bedroll, she handed the pack to Daniel so he could
elp her into it. Then she did the same for him, reaching
p to place the straps over his shoulders. Her fingers had
urned numb from handling the coins, but one touch of his
hirt and she felt warm.

Today, in addition to everything else, she owed him for
varm fingers.

"Tell me," he said after he'd swung around to look at
er. "Are you ready?"

She should stop looking at him, take in her surroundings
ne last time, make her decision based on that.

Instead she found it in his eyes.

"I'm ready, Daniel. There's nothing here for me."

CHAPTER 17

Jessie's moccasins made no sound as she walked behind him. Yet Daniel didn't need to hear or see her to know everything about her. He'd half expected her to falter at the last, but, although her mouth had pinched and her eyes became deeply shadowed, she'd done what she'd come here to accomplish.

Now they were nearing the pass and she matched his slow, easy pace.

She was a woman for the mountains. If he hadn't been afraid he'd reveal too much of himself, he would have told her that. *You face the wind. You don't turn from it. You accepted nature at its rawest, lived with it.*

What would she say and think if he told her that? She

might call him crazy, insane. And if she did, she would be right. Being around her made him feel as he never had before, taught him the deepest meaning of the word admiration.

And maybe another word.

"Jessie, it's going to be dark soon. I want to cut some firewood before that."

"I'll help."

Would another woman say that? Because they had only one axe between them, he went off in search of dead branches while she hollowed out a place in which to build the fire. When he returned, she had already gotten out their food. While he got the fire going, she used the axe to hack off a number of branches so they would have pine needles to sleep on.

She dropped cross-legged onto her blanket and bent her head over her Bible. Her fingers, both competent and incredibly gentle, moved lovingly over the faded signatures. He watched, seeing reverence in her touch. He concentrated on her profile, seeking to understand her emotions.

Instead he saw the smooth line of her neck, soft strands of dark hair sliding over her cheek. Her back was gently curved; her slim arms hung in a straight line from her competent shoulders.

He'd never looked at a deer without being in awe of nature's graceful design. Jessie Speer carried that selfsame grace.

And he felt lost.

Despite the inner voice that shrieked a warning, he moved closer and settled himself beside her. Looking over her shoulder, he read. More than names and places and dates of birth had been written down. One note from Jessie's mother made mention of twins born when Jessie was a year old. "They were too little, their births too difficult. Luke and Lach. I loved them so."

He pointed. "I didn't know."

"Mama hardly ever talked about them. I don't know what happened when she was giving birth, but she never carried another child after that. Papa blamed her."

"For the babies dying?"

"For so many things." Jessie sighed and looked over at him. "I never understood that. Why would he even think to blame her for a poor crop or when one of the cattle died? She said he was always that way. That's all—that he was that way." She covered her mother's words with her fingers. "Did he ever love her?"

"She shouldn't have stayed with him."

"She had a child to raise."

"So did my mother. But she ran."

When Jessie blinked, Daniel realized what he'd said. For a few seconds he sat unmoving, listening to the words echo inside him. He'd never told anyone that, not even Narcisco or Salenack.

But Jessie had trusted him with so much of herself.

"My parents never married, Jessie."

"Never married. I'm sorry."

She hadn't recoiled from him. But had he expected her to? "Sorry? Why?"

"You never knew your father, did you? You should have had that."

"No." He turned his attention to the campfire; at least he tried to. "From what my mother told me of the man, I'm glad I didn't. Otherwise I might have killed him."

"Like you killed that other man?"

He felt as if he'd been slapped. They were supposed to be talking about their mothers, not murder.

"I'm sorry." Her voice was soft, too soft for his anger

to have anything to work against. "I understand your not wanting to talk about that. But you know so much about me."

"Some."

"Some? Do you think it's right that I have no secrets from you and yet I know nothing about you?"

He wanted to tell her he didn't know nearly enough about her, but this wasn't the time for that. "Some things are best left alone, that's all."

"Don't do this to me, Daniel."

Her words wrenched him from his study of the fire. For the second time in a few minutes, he looked into her eyes, and found not accusation but a silent plea. Before he sat down beside her, all he could think about was how much he wanted her. Now want had become need—the need to trust himself to another human being. To her.

"I didn't murder anyone, Jessie. I shot him; if I had to do it over again, I wouldn't change anything. But it wasn't murder."

"Why?"

"Why wasn't it murder?"

"No." She shook her head, freeing even more strands from the loose braids. "Why did you do it?"

Once again she'd cut through to the heart of things. If he could, he would have gone back to staring into the fire. But Jessie's eyes held him. "Because he was killing my mother."

"Oh, God." Her hand snaked out, slow, mesmerizing. She gripped his hand with fingers so strong he wasn't sure he could break free. "Daniel, I'm so sorry."

Something had begun to well up inside him, years of emotion freed by nothing more than a touch. A look. Gentle words. "She'd gone to him for her pay. He'd hired her to break some horses. He kept after her while she was working, trying to get her to go to bed with him." For a heartbeat, he stumbled over the words. Was Jessie too innocent to hear this? Never mind. He'd come too far to think about sparing her. "It wasn't the first time. My mother was a beautiful woman, dark, slender. But after my father, she didn't have much use for men."

"How old were you?"

"Seventeen. Old enough to know what I was doing. I never regretted it. I want you to know that. My mother and I both believed that a person looks out for himself. If someone does right by you, you do the same to them. But some people you never turn your back on."

She'd been gripping his hand so tightly that his fingers had begun to throb. But before he could think to put an end to the pressure, she released him, then began stroking his fingers. He followed the sensation up his arms and into his body.

"Is that what happened?" she prompted. "Your mother had turned her back on this man?"

"No. But he was bigger, stronger. I told her I'd go with her to get her money, but she wanted to face him on her own." When had he freed himself from her eyes? He didn't know, didn't know anything except that he was now staring at their hands. "I was at the same ranch, helping with branding. I heard her scream."

"Oh, Daniel, I'm so sorry."

"I broke down the door, ran into the house. A couple of the rancher's hired hands tried to stop me, but— They were in the bedroom. He'd dragged her in there. When I— She was on the bed, bleeding. He had his hands around her neck. She was still fighting, still trying to breathe." He closed his eyes, thinking of nothing except that day and Jessie keeping his hands warm. "She looked at me. I saw her fear, her pain. She was pleading to me to help her."

"What happened?"

How long had he been silent? It seemed as if the words were barely out of his mouth, but seconds, maybe minutes must have passed or she wouldn't be prompting. With his eyes still closed, he continued.

"I ordered him off her. He had a pistol near the bed. I grabbed it. He saw me. Then—then he broke her neck."

"Oh, God."

Rocking slightly now, he let the rest of the words spill out. "I knew what he'd done. The look in her eyes—the dying I saw in them— I fired. He fell over her and I shoved him off."

"In the back. You shot him in the back."

"I'd do it again, Jessie."

"I know." Her whispered words touched him, ran over his flesh, reached his heart. "But that's all folks talk about—that you shot him in the back."

"Because he'd just killed my mother and I was seventeen years old and I'd just lost the only person I'd ever loved."

"Daniel. Daniel." She spread her arm over his shoulder, rocking with him. "You were trying to save her life. Didn't you tell folks that?"

He laughed, unable to keep bitterness out. "Have you ever heard of Albert Perkins?"

"Perkins?"

"He was the governor, Jessie. I killed his son."

"Oh, my God."

"I ran. I knew that if I stayed there, I was as good as dead. Worse than dead."

"Worse?"

"I heard, from his foreman, that he wanted me to spend the rest of my life in prison. His prison."

"But you're here. You're safe."

The tremor in her voice pulled him out of himself. She was scared for him; no one ever had been before. "Because folks here are more interested in keeping themselves going than taking me back to Texas. But Albert Perkins has made sure that everyone believes I murdered his son in cold blood. If he can't get his hands on me, at least I'll be an outcast."

"You aren't an outcast to me."

Her words stopped him. He knew that; hadn't she already shown him that she trusted him? But to have her say it . . . "What folks think of me, they'll think of you."

"It's too late for me to worry about that. You gave me reason to trust you long before I knew who you were. That's all that matters."

It wasn't. She had to know that as well as he did. But he didn't want to talk about that, or anything else, now. It must be awkward for her to keep her arm stretched around him. Concentrating on that, he took her hand and drew it down so that it rested on his knee. Then he covered her fingers with his.

She'd become part and parcel of him even before they began talking. This touch, this coming together, made it even more so. "Thank you for telling me," she whispered.

I had to. I wanted to. "I wished I could have spared you."

"Why? Because your mother's death was too violent for my innocent ears? Daniel, surely you know me better than that."

He did. And yet he didn't know her at all. "Maybe it was me I wanted to spare."

"Maybe. Daniel, your father. Did you ever know him?"

He shook his pounding head. He wanted to tell her that he'd done all the talking he could for tonight, but after what he'd already revealed, this little bit shouldn't be so hard. "He was Mexican. A wild vaquero, she said. She was seventeen, in love with a wild, handsome, cruel man. Then he ran out on her and when her family learned she was with child, they threw her out."

"How could they do that?"

"They did." He shrugged. "But she survived. And she taught me that a person only has himself."

He thought she might argue, tell him that a person must trust his fellow human beings, but she didn't. Instead, she turned her attention to the fire. "I wonder if she was ever lonely," she whispered.

Jessie couldn't say how long they sat side by side watching the fire. She thought she'd be content to remain like this for hours, at least until Daniel had distanced himself from the day that had changed his life. But when they stopped talking, she started listening to what was happening inside her.

Daniel made her feel alive.

More than alive, she acknowledged when he left her to throw more branches on the fire. The moon was full tonight, a cool, gentle light that spread its spell over the snow and cast Daniel's features in magical shadows. So his father had been Mexican. She wondered if he knew how much of the man he carried in his midnight eyes and hair. If his father had looked anything like him, she could understand why his mother had fallen in love with a wild vaquero.

What had their loving been like? At seventeen, Daniel's mother must have been full of herself and her budding womanhood. When she met a man who tapped her senses and body, she would have lost her heart to him.

That passionate coupling had resulted in a son as wild as any mustang.

What was happening to her?

In a desperate effort to find distraction from her thoughts, Jessie opened her Bible and hunched over it. But it was too dark. She couldn't read.

Daniel had finished with his chore. Now he stood with his back to her as he looked out at his surroundings. She could see nothing of him except shadows.

It was enough.

They were the only two people in the world. Nothing else existed—nothing except ... She smiled. If she stopped listening to the words in her head, she could hear wolves, an occasional owl. The wind. But the wolves and owls didn't care about the humans who'd joined them in the mountains, and the wind did what it wanted.

If she could do what she wanted, what would it be?

Run, a voice answered. *Run and never stop running. Walk out onto the snow and keep on walking until I reach the moon.*

Reach for Daniel.

He'd turned around. How long he'd been staring at her she didn't know. She could only pray he didn't know what she was thinking.

But maybe she wanted him to.

"Are you tired?"

Tired? Never. "A little."

"If you want to go to sleep ..."

"No. No. Not yet."

He left his post by the fire, becoming larger, darker as he drew nearer. "Jessie?"

"W-what?"

"You're a beautiful woman."

Did he feel it, too? He must; why else would he say that? "I—don't know what to say."

"You don't have to say anything."

Good. She needed to lick her lips, but if she did, he'd know she was coming apart inside. He stood over her, a mountain. There'd been a time when she hated the mountains; she could never hate him.

His hands—she saw them extend toward her—watched fascinated and trembling. Those hands had kept him on a bull's back and gently held Elizabeth. She'd felt them on her breasts and knew what they were capable of doing to her senses.

Did she want that?

How could she not?

"Jessie."

All he'd done was speak her name—nothing for her to respond to. But his hands were still stretched toward her. She reached for them. He clamped his fingers around hers. Pulled her onto her feet, to him. When she breathed in, she sucked his warmth deep into her chest. Wearing a doeskin shirt, he reminded her of a mountain man. The offspring of a wild Mexican and a restless horsewoman.

That man, that frightening, exciting man, stood before her.

"Daniel?"

"You know what I want, Jessie. I think you do, too."

"Yes." The word hung between them. It was too late to take it back, but she didn't want to. She should say more than that. Surely there were words women used when they wanted to be with a man.

But she'd never been with a man.

He released her hands. They felt cold and lonely. Then he pressed his palms lightly against her cheeks and heat poured through her. She tried to look into his eyes, but his face was cast in night. What he thought and felt came to her not through his eyes but in his touch.

Covering his hands with hers, she smiled; he could feel that even if he couldn't see her.

"Are you afraid?"

"Of you? Daniel, no."

"Of what's going to happen?"

How could she be afraid of something she'd never experienced? But she carried the memory of her mother crying in the bed she shared with her father. "I don't know. I want—I don't know what I want."

"I'll show you."

He'd do that for her? Because she couldn't bring herself to speak, she drew his hand around to her mouth and covered his palm with soft kisses. When she released him so she could wrap her arm around his waist, his fingers became feathers that teased at her lips. She traced the touch from skin to bone to blood. Three fingers; that's all he used. They heated her entire being.

Feeling bold and needful, she ran her tongue between his fingers. His body straightened, quick, letting her know what her simple touch had done to him. Then, just as quickly, he caught her around the waist and pulled her hard against him. She felt her body shudder and turn liquid. On legs that felt both numb and on fire, she matched his pressure, his demand.

Her hands were trapped between his arms and body. She could have pulled free, but she'd never been controlled by a man before. It was an experience she wanted and needed to explore. Still, she could reach him with mouth and lips and teeth. How she knew he would suffer her teeth clamped over his lip she couldn't say. But he possessed her body. She could have this small measure of control.

Then he drew free and covered her mouth with dozens

of rapid kisses. She swam before them, drowned in them. Became heated under the assault.

She pressed herself so tightly against him that her back ached with the effort. But deep inside her, so deep that she'd never felt that place's existence before, a fire raged. Only Daniel could reach it, tap it, put an end to it.

He begun unbuttoning her blouse. Her back and waist where his hands had been felt suddenly cold. Rough fingertips touched her throat and she forgot the loss. Trembling, needing him to help her retain her balance, she somehow managed to spread her legs enough that she could keep her feet. Still, she had to keep reminding herself to lock her knees.

The unfastening was done. She should have concentrated on that, listened to her body's response. She would, next time.

When he leaned forward in an attempt to look into her eyes, she ran her hands into his hair and drew him even closer. His breath, hot and quick, slapped her lids, lashes, cheeks. Then, somehow, they were kissing again and he was pulling her dress off her shoulders all at the same time. Night air scraped at her flesh, but he spread his hands over her and held it at bay. Slowly, so slowly that it nearly killed her, his fingers inched downward, finally covering her breasts. She'd made herself a camisole from scraps of cloth one of the fort women had given her. Now she hated the garment because Daniel's fingers were on that, not her. Still, warmth invaded her.

Invaded? No. She wanted this.

"Jessie. Lift your arms."

She did, becoming aware of her nakedness inch by inch. She sensed more than saw when he let the undershirt drop onto the ground beside her discarded dress. In the night air, her nipples instantly hardened. Daniel caught one between thumb and forefinger and drew it outward. Although he'd made her flesh warm again, her nipples remained hard.

Had he done that to her?

When he lowered his head and took her breast into his mouth, she had her answer. Buried deep and warm and moist inside him, she felt her breast swell even more. She wanted to tell him that, wanted to thank him. But when she opened her mouth, all she could do was suck in cold mountain air.

It didn't help. The ache, the wonderful, exciting, terrifying ache inside her still pulsed.

Still grew.

"Jessie. You're shaking."

Was she? It didn't matter. She wanted to tell him she needed her breast in his mouth again. Instead, she waited as he yanked off his shirt and pulled her against him.

Locking her knees no longer worked. She felt herself sliding, sliding, sinking down onto her blanket. He came with her, somehow never losing touch with her. Although she gave a half thought to remaining seated, he pressed gently against her shoulders She felt the scratchy blanket against her back; one leg remained curled up under her.

He was leaning over her, sitting beside her with his hands braced on either side of her. She didn't know where to put her hands. On him. Yes. She could grip his shoulders and a little strength would remain in her.

What did it matter?

She felt his fingers at her waist again, then the slow drawing down as he pulled her underskirt over her hips. She thought she lifted her hips to help, but maybe she lacked even that much strength.

Her moccasins—the moccasins Narcisco's daughter had made for her. *You can trust him,* Narcisco had told her.

She knew that.

"Jessie. Jessie."

"Daniel."

Reaching blindly, she wound up gripping his forearms. They bunched and hardened under her fingers. He leaned closer; she saw his shadowed form become larger, felt the heat from his body. Lips parted, she waited.

Nothing. Startled, she blinked, trying to find him in the dark. He'd pulled free, left her fingers with nothing to cling to.

And then, and then, he touched his mouth to her belly and her body knotted. Ache became throb and she knew without anyone ever having told her what he would do to make her body stop pulsing. To feel satisfied.

"Jessie? It's all right?"

"Don't leave me. Please. Don't leave me."

He wouldn't. She didn't need to say that. But words, thoughts, feelings built inside her and she had no control over them. Once again she reached for him. This time she touched his chest, fingers searching until she placed her thumb over his nipple. Like hers, his was hard.

Hard.

That's how she felt inside, hard and hot and alive.

He pulled back again. She reared upward, watched wide-eyed as he stood and yanked off his pants. Firelight and moonlight caught him, outlined him. Revealed everything. *Mountain man.* The words ran through her mind, filled it.

The wolves sang to the moon. The wind still whistled and shook its way through the trees. She felt as if she might be spirited off by the wind. Then Daniel dropped back down beside her and knew she was rooted to him.

"Don't be afraid."

Afraid? "I'm not."

"I'll be gentle. I'll try."

She didn't care. Her body didn't want gentle. There was only one way to let him know that. Not caring that he might think her wanton, in truth wanting him to think that of her, she wrapped her arms around his neck and arched upward to press her breasts against him. Then she fell back, bringing him with her. Still, he managed to catch himself before she was crushed beneath him. She felt blanketed by his weight and warmth.

When he touched his tongue to her throat, she again arched her body toward him. From her throat he traced a slow, damp trail down her body, leaving her breasts, ribs, waist, belly on fire.

Her body spasmed, spasmed again. He started to laugh. The sound turned into a groan. His breath danced over her and her groan matched his.

After a moment, she clamped her hands over his shoulders and pulled him toward her. His mouth sought hers, but she wasn't content with that. As another deep-rooted groan built inside her, she stabbed outward until she found his hips. His naked hips. Never, never had she imagined herself touching a man in his most private places. But her body no longer belonged to her. Her temple throbbed; she could only breathe in short bursts that did nothing to clear her head.

She didn't care. Thinking? That was for another time and place. The male part of him was already so swollen she could barely span it, but she didn't recoil.

She wasn't afraid of Daniel, would never be afraid of him.

Acting without conscious thought, she ran her finger

over the tip of his manhood. He shuddered, shuddered again.

"Jessie? I can't wait much longer."

For what? No. She wouldn't let him think she was that ignorant. If she did, he might think she wasn't ready for him.

And she was.

"Now Daniel. Now."

He twisted so she had to release him. The night wind slapped at her flesh, and she started to reach for him, needing him between her and the night. But his hand now lay on her inner thigh. With his fingers, he made her spread her legs. Then he—then he slid a finger inside her and she rode with him. Died and came back to life because he was inside her.

Pressure. Yes. She felt that. Wet. She was so wet. On fire.

His finger. Where had it gone? No! She needed something of him inside her. Needed—

He was on top of her, his knees spreading her even more. She felt his body slide down over hers, felt him settle himself within the cradle of her legs.

Between her legs, inching past barriers she only dimly understood. Filling her—oh—filling her. Pain. Sharp. Quickly gone.

And then him. Over her. In her. Becoming her.

And her becoming him.

On fire.

The fire building.

Exploding.

Him showing her the way to exhaustion, peace.

"Jessie? Jessie? Are you all right?"

How long had they lain like this? Hours, maybe. He'd

left her long enough to throw blankets over them. Then he'd cradled her against him and she'd fallen asleep listening to his heart. Feeling as if she held it in her hand.

Maybe it was he who held her heart.

"Jessie? Are you all right?"

She didn't know.

CHAPTER 18

When Jessie moved away and scrambled to her feet, Daniel watched her though half-opened eyes. Her quiet still bothered him, but he didn't know how to ask her to explain herself.

If she said anything, he would feel compelled to do the same.

It was easier to reach for his clothes and slip into them, watch as she dressed. She didn't try to hide her nakedness behind a blanket, didn't turn her back modestly to him. Neither did she look at him.

"Jessie," he said as he jammed his feet into his moccasins. "We don't have to hurry. If you want to go at a slow pace . . ."

She picked up the coin-laden purse and tied it around her ankle. "I have to get back to my crops."

Or away from me? Nodding, he began rolling up the blankets. When he spied a long, dark strand of hair, he held it up to the morning light. She'd given herself to him last night. Become a woman in his arms. He wanted to thank her for the gift, to let her know how much that meant to him.

But the words remained clogged in his throat. Instead, he released the hair and watched as it drifted to the ground. He couldn't offer her a life of safety. As long as she wanted and needed her farm, she would face risks. He could live there with her; the possibility rambled through his head. But no matter what she now believed of him, he still wasn't a fit companion for her. He couldn't ask her to marry him.

She was an earth-tied woman. He'd never wanted anything except to be free to move about.

"I swear," he whispered to her mother's memory, "as long as I live, I'll put her life first. I'll do what's best for her."

The words surprised, even shocked him. Still, he felt no desire to take them back. He *wanted* to assume responsibility for Jessie.

After a quick, silent breakfast, they packed up their belongings and began the long climb down. Daniel had nothing to look at except the ground ahead of him. A thousand times he caught himself on the verge of turning and asking if she regretted last night. Again and again he told himself that her unashamed nakedness this morning had been proof enough that she didn't. Still, she said nothing as the hours stretched on.

After crawling around a rocky ledge and finding a narrow, nearly level strip of ground, he stopped and waited for her. "Rest a few minutes," he told her. "You don't want to get back home so weary that you can't do anything."

With a sigh, she dropped cross-legged to the ground and leaned forward, resting her elbows on her knees. "My poor legs. For days I've been asking them to climb a mountain. I don't think they know how to go down."

He sat next to her. "Maybe it isn't just the climbing that's made your legs sore."

"No. I don't suppose it is. Daniel?"

He waited.

"You haven't said anything about last night."

"Neither have you."

She smiled, then let the gesture drift away. "I guess I didn't know what to say. The woman I was last night? I don't know her."

"I think you do."

She blinked, then focused on him. "What do you mean?"

Although he'd taken her hand a half-dozen times during the morning so he could help her, he felt shy about doing that now. Still, he didn't want to talk without touching her. "What we did, it's natural. My mother never apologized for giving herself to my father. She said that what happens between a man and a woman is God's will."

"I . . ." She turned her attention to their intertwined hands. "I wish I'd known your mother. Daniel, what I felt last night—what you did for me—I never thought it would be like that."

"You didn't?"

She shook her head. "My mother kept me ignorant. I didn't even know what questions to ask."

His throat tightened. After giving himself a moment to

test the wisdom of what he was going to say, he spoke. "Was it what you thought it would be?"

"More. So much more."

More. "My mother said women need more out of loving than a man does."

"Maybe she's right. I don't know." She straightened and fixed a steady gaze on him. "Daniel, I might be carrying your child."

"I know" was all he could say. This morning he'd promised her mother he'd do what was best for her.

"But maybe not," she whispered. "Maybe—the first time . . ."

"Maybe not the first time."

He saw her mouth spasm and wondered if she'd been hurt by his words. "I'll do right by you. I promise."

"You do?"

She might not have known anything about what happens between a man and a woman, but she certainly was no child. "Jessie." He squeezed her hand. "If you have my baby, I'll be there for you. I won't leave the way my father did. That I will promise you."

She nodded. The gesture went on a long time. "Thank you."

They were still high in the mountains when they stopped for the night. Because the wind had picked up, almost as soon as she stopped walking Jessie felt the cold. Daniel had chosen a small, deep pool of water and immediately started fishing. She stood watching him as a thousand emotions swept through her. Strange, she hadn't been embarrassed bringing up the possibility that she might be with child. She'd told herself it was because she faced life straight on. But now, studying his broad, competent back, she knew it went far beyond that. When he told her he'd be there for her, she'd already known that.

Did she want that?

Her mother had spent her life surrounded by a man. Did she want the same?

She didn't know she was pressing against her stomach until her fingers cramped. She folded her arms over her middle and went on looking at Daniel. With him beside her, she'd put last winter's nightmare to rest. Another man might have taken advantage of her, but when they came together last night it was because she'd wanted, needed him.

Whether she carried his child, whether he could keep his vow to be there for her, she had no regrets about one thing.

A child. His child.

Daniel's excited cry silenced her thoughts. Grinning, she reached him just as he pulled a silver-sided fish out of the water. "How wonderful! Can you imagine what a meal of something besides dried meat will taste like?" Before he could say anything, she pulled her knife out of her waistband and hurried off in search of a green branch to cook the fish on.

By the time she returned, he'd gutted and cleaned the fish and was pulling together dried leaves to start a fire with. She got out several acorn-meal cakes and set them near the fire to heat. Teasing, she told him he should get back to fishing so he'd have something to eat himself.

"I so appreciate your fishing skill. I intend on enjoying every bite."

Daniel eyed the large fish, then leveled a stern look at her. "I believe, Miss Speer, that this is my fish. If there's a fin left, I'll be happy to split it with you."

"Will you? I'm the weaker sex, Mr. Bear. Without this

meal I will probably waste away to nothing before morning."

"I'm sorry to hear that." He splayed his hand over the fish as if measuring to see if it lived up to his expectations. "I've enjoyed your company. I'll miss it."

"The only thing you're going to miss is this meal," she informed him. When he cocked an eyebrow at her, she snatched the fish out from under his fingers. The moment she clutched it to her, she knew she'd made a mistake. She might be starved, but a raw fish wasn't what she had in mind. Daniel clamped his arms around her and pulled her tight against him.

"Unhand my fish, Miss Speer."

"I will not, Mr. Bear."

"Oh, I think you will."

She'd never told him she was ticklish. How he'd— "Stop it!" she gasped. She twisted in his grip, half laughing, half yelling. "Stop it! Now!"

He ran his hands lightly up her sides and into her armpits. "When you unhand my catch."

Although she battled for control of the fish for the better part of a minute, finally, in an attempt to distract him, she tossed it under a nearby tree. "There!" she gasped. "Have your old fish. See if I care."

He locked his arms around her again. "You have sorely tested my patience, Miss Speer. Don't think I'm done with you."

"What—do you have in mind?"

"What? Drawing and quartering, for starter." His fingers inched upward from her waist, finally settling over her breasts. "Tarring and feathering once that's done."

She should tell him that being tarred and feathered after he'd drawn and quartered her didn't make any sense. But his fingers were too gentle, too practiced, and her body too ready. Sighing, she settled against him and rested her head on his chest.

He pressed the heel of his hands under her breasts, pushing them upward, reading them for his fingers' sensual, yet gentle assault. Groaning, she sought his lips. He bent over her, then sealed his mouth against her. "Jessie," he whispered into her. "Jessie."

Daniel.

This time when he took her there was no unspoken question, no slow guidance. She felt his urgency and responded by fairly ripping off his shirt and pressing herself to him. His breath coming as rapidly as if he'd spent the day running, he vised his arms around her now bare back and buried his face in her hair. She tried to control her own breathing, tried to make sense of the wild urgency that consumed her. But how could she? This wild, magnificent man wanted to make love to her and she needed him more than she'd ever needed food or water.

"Jessie. It's all right. I'll—do—you'll be safe."

He was trying to tell her there were things he could do to keep her from carrying his seed, if that hadn't happened already. But she didn't care. Didn't care!

"Daniel, I need you, all of you."

"But—"

"No." She slammed her word over his. "All of you. Please."

By way of answer, he clamped her arms against her side and held her, her body shaking, as he traced her from throat to breasts with his tongue, setting her on fire.

"Daniel! Please!"

"You want me?"

"Need. I need you."

"No regrets?"

Regrets were for people who could think. How could

she care about tomorrow or the rest of her life? "I need you. Now."

He unfastened the drawstring on her underskirt so quickly that she didn't know what he'd done until he began pushing it down over her hips. She stepped out of it, feeling free.

It was her turn. She took a moment to press the heel of her hand against his belly. He sucked in his breath; she stayed with him. When, following his lead, she touched her lips to his nipple, the groan that came from him sounded as if his lungs had been ripped apart. Only half believing that she was doing what she was, she yanked on the thong that held his pants in place and ran her fingers over his hipbones.

Again he groaned.

She could do this to him? She could control this powerful, brave outlaw!

"Daniel? I need you. Inside me."

A rock bit into the back of her right leg, but for several minutes Jessie's mind felt too numb for her to put it to anything as complex as moving. Daniel lay over her, his hot body slicked with sweat. Half-conscious, she flicked her tongue over his chest and tasted salt. He sucked in his breath, then fell quiet again.

They'd made love. Twice. The first time they'd come together like a mare and a stallion, biting, grabbing, demanding. The explosion inside her head and body had built so quickly that all she remembered was him entering her before lightning struck. The second time—even now she could barely believe there'd been a second time. But even before her breathing returned to normal, he'd taken her breast into his mouth and she'd wanted him again. "Time, Jessie. I need a little time," he'd whispered. She'd given him that, a few minutes at least during which she stoked his arms and chest and legs, slowly bringing her fingers closer and closer to his manhood. Then she opened herself to him and they held on to each other and she felt as if she was slowly dissolving into him.

She wondered if she'd ever get enough of him.

When she realized she hadn't escaped the rock's bite after all, she slid out from under the weight of Daniel's arm and leg and lay looking up at the sky. She'd begun to shiver. In a moment she'd have to move.

In a moment.

But for now, she could bury herself in the wonder of needing another human being, him, this much.

The wonder and fear of needing.

Daniel said nothing as he went about cooking the fish. Once again Jessie had retreated into silence, and he didn't know how to break through it. He chided himself for his lack of self-restraint; then, because it was too late to undo what they'd done, he put recrimination behind him.

She was beautiful, all grace and downy skin. He couldn't look at her without wanting her. She'd told him she wanted him, all of him, not careful, half-loving. He'd believed her because that was what he wanted to hear.

If she turned from him, at least he would always have tonight. And last night.

"Jessie? It's ready."

"Thank you." She waited until he placed the fish on a rock and then broke off a hot, flaking piece. He watched as she popped it in her mouth, chewed, swallowed, licked her fingers. He wanted her again.

"It's all right?"

"Fine. Wonderful." She reached for another piece, then glanced up at him. Her gaze wavered, held. He saw or

sensed the battle inside her and couldn't think of a thing
to do except wait her out. "I don't know what to say," she
whispered. "I didn't know that was going to happen, that
it was possible to feel like that."

"I didn't either."

Her eyes begged him to say that again. He did. "When
you touched me," she said, "I didn't know my body. I
didn't know it was possible to feel that way."

"Neither did I."

"I—want to believe you. I need to." She held the fish
inches from her mouth. A flake fell off, but she didn't notice. "To want something that much . . . It scares me."

He didn't want to hear her say that. And yet, hadn't
there been a part of him that only wanted to run from her?
"I don't have any answers for you, Jessie," was the best he
could give her.

"I know you don't." She glanced down at her fish, then
brought it a few inches closer to her mouth. "Maybe you
never will." She sighed. "Maybe neither of us ever will."

Her words played through her mind for fully half of the
night, but at last, weary of reaching for that illusive and
nameless something, she fell asleep with Daniel stretched
out on the opposite side of the campfire. Twice dreams
woke her, but she couldn't remember them. Finally, a little
before dawn, she got up and threw a few dead pine boughs
over the coals and blew on them until they sprang to life.
When Daniel sat up, she smiled at him but said nothing
about what they'd discussed last night. Neither did he.

That afternoon they came across their horses, still on
their long tethers. After transferring their belongings, Jessie swung onto her mare's back and leaned forward, pat-
ting the animal's neck. Daniel's stallion, obviously weary

of having his movements confined, was harder to control. She waited while he let the high-strung animal run.

"It's a good thing we came back when we did," she observed as the stallion continued to prance, now making her mare snort and fling her head. "Another day and he would have found a way to free himself, or injured himself trying."

Daniel nodded but didn't say anything. He seemed to be studying his surroundings more than he had earlier in the day. Maybe he was on the lookout for Walla Wallas.

When a jackrabbit sprang out of the bushes and ran just in front of her horse, the mare reared and tried to run. With a firm hand on the reins, she managed to bring her under control. Then she watched as Daniel, perched high on the stallion's back, fought to keep his animal under control.

After a couple of minutes, he guided his horse closer to hers. "He isn't usually this hard to handle. I wish I understood what's gotten into him."

She indicated their world of rolling hills and low-growing oak trees. She pointed at a swath of wildflowers. "It's spring. They're feeling it."

"Maybe. I've been thinking. Talk to James Marshall. If anyone knows where there's lumber, James does."

"I've already thought of that. Is he at the fort? I wouldn't know where to go to look for him."

"He might still be looking for a site for the sawmill Sutter wants. Until then—"

It sounded like a sharp, heavy clap. Jessie opened her mouth, a question already on her lips. Daniel jerked straight, then slid gracefully off his horse and landed in a tangled, motionless heap near the prancing hooves.

She screamed; while the sound still echoed, she urged her horse forward, forcing the stallion away from Daniel.

Ignoring everything except him, she catapulted herself onto the ground.

"Jessie!"

The hard cry swung her around. Standing inches from Daniel, feeling like a mother bear protecting its cubs, she faced the three men riding toward her. Daniel didn't move.

"Jessie. Don't touch him."

Raymond! What was he doing here? Although nothing made sense and questions crashed through her, she dropped to her knees and bent over Daniel.

His eyes were closed, his body without the energy that had kept him, and her, alive last winter. Unmindful of the blood running down his forehead, she pressed against his temple until she found a pulse—quick and erratic. Her hand trembled; she hated her weakness.

"Jessie. Get away from him."

With her hand still on Daniel, she spun toward Raymond. He was flanked by two of the men who'd come to her farm earlier. He looked at and through her at the same time, his eyes unfocused. "What have you done?" she screamed. "You shot him!"

"Get away from him."

"No."

She'd begun probing through Daniel's hair, trying to find the source of the bleeding, when powerful fingers clamped her arms and she was hauled to her feet. Although her arms were turning numb, she tried to wrench free. She had to get back to Daniel! He needed her.

"Jessie, stop it!"

Grunting, she heaved away from Raymond. His fingers bit into her flesh; his nails tore long gashes in her sleeve. She was free! Free!

No, not free. Before she could think what to do, he grabbed her throat and squeezed. Fighting the white-hot pain that came from being robbed of breath, she began kicking and scratching. Somehow she managed to clamp onto his cheek and squeezed with every ounce of strength in her body.

She could breathe! She sucked in air. Something plowed into the side of her face and she stumbled backward, barely keeping her balance. "What are you doing? Raymond, stop!" she screamed.

He hit her again. She managed not to lose her footing. Still, the pain forced her to stop fighting and start thinking. Raymond was advancing on her. Without turning to look at them, she knew the others had moved behind her, cutting off her escape.

"What do you want?"

Spittle bubbled at the corner of his mouth. "The money."

Money. He'd shot Daniel for money? "You're talking crazy." Her jaw throbbed. Then, although she knew she shouldn't take her eyes off Raymond, she glanced down at Daniel. He still hadn't moved.

"Crazy," Raymond echoed. Eyes still unfocused, he took another step toward her. When she backed away, she collided with one of the horses. She wanted to shove the animal out of the way and run. She knew she had to stay, for Daniel.

She looked over her shoulder at the soldiers. The one with the badly scarred lip stared down at her, his eyes void of life. "How can you let him do this?" she demanded. "He—" She indicated Daniel. "He's done nothing wrong."

"He's a killer."

"That's a lie. You don't know him."

"The way you do?" Raymond's eyes became slits. "He's taken you to his bed, hasn't he? You don't have to tell me. All I have to do is look at you to know."

Jessie didn't believe him. What she must look like was a terrified, yet determined woman, not one who'd spent the night with a man. "Are you part of this?" she demanded of the scarred man. "If he's dead, I'll make sure you're charged with murder."

"There'll be no murder charges, Jessie."

The way Raymond spoke her name spun Jessie back around. When she tried to swallow, pain shot through her throat. She could feel her cheek swelling. "How are you going to prevent it, Raymond?" she challenged. Maybe it was the pain and fear. Maybe it was seeing Daniel like this. Either way, nothing mattered except trying to make sense of this nightmare. "Are you going to shoot me too?"

"I don't have to."

His cold, heavy words chilled her. If she'd had any thought that she might be able to draw on her past relationship with Raymond, that died. Whether he hated her because she'd refused to marry him or because he'd found her with Daniel—or because his ordeal last winter had finally snapped him—didn't matter.

Found?

"How did you know where we were?"

"I followed you. What else could I do? A man can't be destitute. He's got—got to have a way of keeping body and soul together." He kicked out, his boot thudding into Daniel's side. Daniel groaned, setting Jessie's heart to racing; he was still alive! "Followed you and then waited for you to come back down. Where is it, Jessie? Where?"

He was asking about the money. Her future and independence. "I don't have it. I couldn't find it."

"You're lying." He inched closer. "I know you, Jessie. You wouldn't have gone back up there if there hadn't been so much it was worth any risk." He kicked at Daniel again. "Tell me. Now!"

"Stop it!" Mindless to any danger to herself, Jessie lowered her head and slammed into Raymond. He fell back, grabbing for her at the same time. She managed to wrench free.

Run! But she couldn't leave Daniel. She wouldn't. She reached for the knife at her waist. By the time Raymond righted himself, she'd pulled the weapon free. She faced him, knowing how pitiful a weapon the knife was against the men's rifles. But the others hadn't dismounted. They seemed content to watch the fight between her and Raymond.

Raymond? She didn't know this man.

His legs widely splayed, breathing deeply, Raymond stared at her. "I don't want it like this between us, Jessie. I thought we had something special."

Special? Horrible was more like it.

"You wouldn't be alive if it wasn't for me." He wiped the corner of his mouth. "Why are you turning against me?"

Without taking her eyes off him, she indicated Daniel. "You shot him."

"To save you, Jessie." He ran his hand over his eyes. "He would have killed you for the money."

How wrong he was. "Why didn't he do away with me up on the mountain?" she challenged. Why was she arguing with Raymond? The only thing that mattered was escaping his clutches and taking care of Daniel. "Once I'd dug up the money, why didn't he take it and leave me there?"

"You have it. I knew it."

Anger surged through her as she realized what she'd given away. An instant later, she cast off the thought. It didn't matter. Despite the risk, she turned from Raymond long enough to look at the two who'd accompanied him here. "Can't you see what he's doing? He—just shot a man who did nothing to him."

The deformed man shrugged. "It's more money than I've seen in my life. My share—a man does what he has to." Chilled, she faced Raymond again. Out of the corner of her eye, she saw Daniel's fingers twitch. *Oh God, please. Help him.* "I trusted you, Raymond. And now—now you're willing to turn me over to them?"

Something flickered in Raymond's eyes, but she didn't understand what it was. When he opened his mouth, she waited for him to speak. Instead, he took a step toward her. She tightened her grip on the knife. "Don't do it," she warned. "It isn't worth your life."

"Not my life, Jessie."

"What are you saying? That you'll kill me?"

He blinked.

"Is that what you want?" she pushed. "What you're willing to do so you'll have some money?"

"Some? A king's ransom. You wouldn't let me have what's mine by rights."

"Yours by rights? How can you say that? Daniel—folks will find his body too. How are you going to explain that?"

Raymond flicked his tongue over his lips, then blinked. "I'll say I came across Daniel as he was attacking you. I shot him trying to defend you. But it was too late."

Jessie felt shock. Did Raymond really think folks would believe Daniel had murdered her after taking her up and then back down the mountain? But, because of Daniel's reputation, maybe. What—

Daniel stirred. The movement splintered her thoughts. "Do you want my blood on your hands?" she asked the two without looking at them. "Are you willing to kill just so you—so you can . . ." She couldn't finish.

They said nothing.

Her mind raced with what she should do next. Would another plea to the men convince them that they'd joined Raymond on an insane mission? No. They'd let him lead them and the others for weeks now. Obviously they believed whatever he told them. Could she remind Raymond of how she'd looked up to him when he put Elizabeth's and her needs before his?

Before she had time to answer her questions, Raymond jerked his head at the soldiers. "Get her. Now."

Leather squeaked. She heard boots hit the ground. A scream surged through her, but she refused to give it life. She felt the men on either side of her. Ignoring them, she speared a look at Raymond. "You're insane! This is insane!"

"I'm after what's mine."

You're wrong! The man on her left stepped closer. She swung the knife around, stabbing at him. She felt the tip hit something, but before she could concentrate on that, she was grabbed from the other side. Her breath coming in a ragged hiss, she whipped the knife in that direction. Again her weapon found something to bite in.

Then something slammed into her and she hit the ground, the side of her head striking it with such force that her vision became shards of light. Again she took a ragged breath. Nothing mattered except staying alive. Fighting. Reaching Daniel.

She saw Raymond's boot, turned her head to avoid the blow. Her hand holding the knife exploded with pain, then turned numb. She felt the weapon slip out of her fingers and grabbed for it with her good hand.

Raymond kicked her again. She felt her back bow from pain. Ignoring her injured wrists, she glared up at him.

Shouldn't she be terrified? Why this anger—this white-hot anger? "Damn you, Raymond. Damn you to hell!"

He kicked the knife away, then nodded at the two men. She felt their hands circle her wrists. Pain slashed through her; a sob tore at her throat, broke free. "Damn you!"

"What's this, Jessie?" Raymond dropped to his knees beside her. He clamped his hand over her jaw, forcing her to look at him. "Such words coming from a lady."

"Damn you."

His fingers ground into her flesh. She clenched her teeth, determined not to cry out again. Again her vision blurred, and she fought, bucking in an attempt to free herself from the three men.

"Give it up, Jessie."

He was right. But what was she going to do? Surrender to these animals? "Go to hell."

He slapped her, the force of his blow jamming her lip against her teeth. She tasted blood. Strangely, she wanted to thank him. Now she knew what Raymond was capable of if she angered him enough. Blinking back tears, she focused on him.

"I don't want to hurt you, Jessie."

Could she believe him? "What do you want?"

"The money that's rightfully mine. All of it." He began digging at her waist, ripping off the leather thong that held the knife pouch.

Go to hell. No. She didn't dare say that again. "It isn't yours."

A smile, thin, not extending to his eyes, contorted his features. He yanked at her blouse, tearing off buttons. He pressed down on her rib cage. "Jessie. Jessie. Don't you think, under the circumstances, that I'm the one in a position of determining ownership of all that money?"

Bile rose in her throat. She dragged in a deep breath,

fighting to remain calm. His hands continued their upward march, popping more buttons as he went. Finally he spread his hands over her breasts and flattened them. She winced. One corner of his mouth twitched. "The money, Jessie. Where is it?"

Despite her anger, she could do nothing except tremble as he exposed her breasts to him and the now heavy-breathing men. She wanted to scream, to beg, to curse. But Raymond had become an animal. She wouldn't join him there.

He cupped a breast. "You'll learn to like this, Jessie."

"Never!"

"Maybe not." He frowned. "But you'll learn to accept it." His fingers tightened. "If you want to stay alive, you'll let me do what I want."

Never!

He ran his hands down her sides, fingers probing. "Do you understand what it means to be helpless? To have to do what I say, when I say?" Without waiting for an answer, he ground the heel of his hand into her belly. "It didn't have to be this way, Jessie. If you'd said yes when I asked you to marry me, we wouldn't be here today. You wouldn't have made me angry."

Was this what it was all about? He was consumed by the need for revenge? Whatever had made her think she knew him? His hand inched lower. Hating her helplessness, she struggled to free her wrists. "What's the matter, Jessie? Is it not being in control? Well . . ." He brought his face inches from hers. "Now you know what you did to me. Making me beg for what's mine."

"It wasn't—" When he clamped his hand over her jaw, she bit down the rest of what she was going to say.

"I've thought about this for a long time. Thought about

precious little else." He ground his mouth against hers. "I could kill you. Right now." Again he kissed her.

She wanted to bite him. To feel the knife in her hand and bury it in his chest. But she couldn't! She managed to turn her head and avoid him. "Don't. You're not . . ."

"Today I don't have to ask. I can take."

She waited him out, hands and wrists numb. Hating. Terrified.

He rocked back on his heels, his eyes fastened on her breasts. "Where's the money? Tell me and maybe I'll let you live."

"Go to hell."

The words earned her a fist in her midsection. She gagged, fought the hands that held her on the ground. Somehow Raymond smiled and frowned at the same time. She ordered herself to lie still, to wait.

He stood up, stared down at her. Then, moving slowly and deliberately, he picked up her knife. "You don't want to die, do you?" He took another step. "Not out here. Like this." Another step. "Not at my hands simply because you wouldn't answer my question." One more step. "That's all it takes. Cooperate and you can live."

She turned from him and squeezed her eyes shut. What came first, fear or hate? Maybe they were the same.

"Look at me, Jessie."

She did. He stood over Daniel, knife pointed downward. "What's his life worth?"

CHAPTER 19

"Don't! Please. I beg of you."

Raymond turned back around. "Don't?" he questioned. "You've forced my hand, Jessie. What else can I do?"

"Take the money. I don't care. Just don't kill him."

"Don't kill him." Raymond's mouth tightened. "You don't understand, do you? No one does. All my dreams—" With his free hand he jabbed at the men who held her to the ground. "I hold your life in my hands. His too."

With his words, her body went limp. "Raymond, please. He hasn't done anything to you."

"He took you from me."

"Took? I'm not a piece of property."

"You became his lover."

Could he see it in her eyes? What did it matter? "Raymond, I'm begging you. Leave him alone."

He dropped to his knees beside her. "I don't want it like this between us. I never did. But I *have* to have that money. Without it I'm lost." Leaning forward, he gripped her ankles. As he did, his fingers circled the pouch. Frowning, he pushed her skirt away. "What is this?" he asked after tearing it off her ankle. "You didn't trust him? You felt you had to keep it on your person?"

Her hands throbbed. When she swallowed, she again tasted blood. From where she lay, she couldn't see Daniel. She tried to listen for his breathing, but her attention had to be on Raymond. He loosened the fastening and let the coins drop to the ground. His eyes bulged, then narrowed. "Where's the rest?"

She didn't speak.

"There's more. There has to be!"

The scarred man turned to stare at the pile. "It's enough for a stake, a damn good stake. Why the hell do you think we're here?"

"You're here because I told you to," Raymond shot back. "What about the others? I've made promises."

"You deal with them. All I want is my cut."

The other man nodded agreement, then indicated Daniel. "He's comin' round."

Jessie swiveled her head, desperate to see Daniel. But Raymond was in the way. "Raymond, don't become a murderer."

Raymond frowned. She prayed she'd gotten through to him. He ordered the men to release her and hauled her to her feet. She tried to pull her clothes together, but her fingers were numb. Standing made her light-headed; it was all she could do to keep from grabbing Raymond for support.

Daniel still lay crumpled on his side. His wound continued to bleed.

"You aren't a killer, Raymond." She kept her voice low, under control. "You're desperate, that's all. You didn't know what else to do."

"Desperate? You don't half understand. You shouldn't have refused me. Do you have any idea what it's been like all these months, taking charity from Sutter? Having plans, great plans, but no way of putting them into action. Nightmares." He ran a shaking hand over his forehead. "All those nightmares."

"Nightmares? I'm sorry."

"Folks want to know why you didn't marry me. I know what they're thinking, that I'm not man enough to hold you. After what I did for you . . ."

Raymond wasn't making sense. But if listening to his ramblings would spare Daniel's life, she'd do that. Feeling had crept back into her fingers. They now felt on fire. Still, she pulled on the ruined fabric and covered herself as best she could. Daniel's right leg straightened a few inches, but other than that and his quick, shallow breathing, he gave no sign that he was alive.

Daniel! I'm sorry. So sorry.

Without taking his eyes from her, Raymond leaned over and picked up the coins. After counting again, he placed them back in the leather purse. As he did, the others followed his every move, grumbling that the time had come for them to be given their share. Raymond ordered them to shut up, that he was in charge. If the men started fighting among themselves, would that help her and Daniel?

"He won't live." Raymond indicated Daniel. "A few hours, wolves, they'll take care of him."

Jessie screamed a silent denial but said nothing. When Raymond again fastened his attention on her, she felt deep sorrow for the man he no longer was. "What are you going to do?" she managed despite her swollen lips.

"Leave him." Raymond jerked his head at his henchmen. "Get her horse. Tie her to it."

Shards of sound and movement reached Daniel. He struggled to make sense of it, but his head pulsed with pain. He had no idea how long he'd been on the ground when he heard the sound of retreating hoofbeats. More minutes passed. Finally, spurred on by fear for Jessie, he fought his way to the surface. Through filmed vision, he saw that he was alone.

He remembered talking to Jessie and then something slamming into his head. He'd heard her cry out. He was sure of that. Raymond's voice was in there somewhere. He had the vague sense that there'd been other men but how many he couldn't say.

Despite the constant throb inside his brain, he managed to pull himself to a sitting position. Except for his stallion, he was alone.

Jessie. Where was she?

With Raymond.

Raymond. Why had he taken her?

Twice he tried to stand. Both times his strength deserted him. Finally he forced himself to crawl on hands and knees to his stallion. When he reached for the animal, it shied away. Groaning, he sat with his head hanging, thinking—trying to think. He ran his hand through his hair. He looked at his hand. It was dark with blood.

Who had shot him?

He tried to whistle, but the effort made his head throb more than crawling had. Jessie was with Raymond. He couldn't stay here—couldn't . . .

Reaching the nervous stallion seemed to take hours.

When he wrapped his hand around the trailing rein, the animal jerked, but he held on, teeth clenched down over a groan.

Could he mount? Could he see well enough to follow the hoofprints that told him which direction Jessie and the men had gone?

Jessie with men—men who'd shot him.

"Be still, please." He mouthed more than spoke the words, aware of little except the need to keep the stallion near him. By gripping a front leg, he managed to stagger to his feet. He clamped onto the mane, then looked up, up at the back that seemed more insurmountable than the mountain ever had.

After a moment he forced his legs to bear his weight. But when it came to leading the stallion to a rock he could use to lever himself onto its back, he couldn't remember how to walk.

"Please."

The stallion swung his head around toward him. A powerful shoulder bumped into him and his feet gave way.

The ground. Hard.

Standing again? How?

Because her hands were tied in front of her, Jessie managed to keep her torn blouse in place. She rode directly behind Raymond, who held her mare's reins. The two silent men brought up the rear. The hours stretched on. By the time the sun dipped down over the horizon, her lip was so swollen she couldn't shut her mouth. With every breath, her thoughts scattered back to Daniel; she couldn't help him.

Maybe she couldn't help herself.

When Raymond led the way to a creek clogged with

blackberry bushes, she wondered vaguely what he had in mind and why he hadn't simply killed her and Daniel.

Maybe because there was still a shred of decency in him.

Raymond dragged her off the mare. She staggered and caught her balance. The movement dislodged her blouse from around her shoulders. When she reached for it, he grabbed her hands. "What call do you have to be worried about modesty when he's had you?"

Although his words hurt as much as his blows had, she refused to let it show. "Raymond, what happened to you?"

"What?" He jutted his chin at her; his hot, sour breath assaulted her nostrils. "A man can only take so much. Then it doesn't matter anymore." When she said nothing, he shrugged and pushed her toward an oak half-swallowed by blackberries, giving her a few seconds of necessary privacy. Alone, she made a vow to do as Raymond wanted. She wouldn't anger him. That way she *might* stay alive. Might be able to help Daniel. Otherwise . . .

Raymond dragged her back to where they'd left the horses and ordered her to sit. He quickly retied her wrists so they were behind her now and then lashed her ankles together. She lay on her side, watching, thinking, praying, as the three men went about setting up camp for the night.

One of the men pulled a jug off his horse, took a deep swallow, then handed it to his companion. Although they had plenty to eat, none of the three offered her anything. At least Raymond held a tin cup to her lips so she could drink. When, because of her injured lip, she spilled some of the water, he merely shrugged. Without giving herself time to test the wisdom of what she was saying, she told him she was glad Elizabeth hadn't seen him today.

"She doesn't care about me. Neither do you. I'm looking after myself. From now on, I'm only looking after myself."

She touched her tongue to her lip, then winced. When she shifted her weight in an attempt to find a more comfortable position, he watched, eyes empty of emotion.

What had happened to him? Keseberg had lost his mind last winter. Raymond had come through the ordeal untouched.

Or had he?

"I don't want to hate you," she whispered.

"I don't care."

He turned from her and walked over to where the others were drinking. He grabbed the jug and took a deep swallow. "You'll get your cut," he told them through thin lips. "I promised; I keep my promises. But not until I've got it straight in my head what I'm going to do."

"You start drinking and you'll never get anything figured out."

"Shut up! If it wasn't for me vouching for you with Sutter last month, both of you'd be in the brig. You want me to keep quiet about what happened with that little Indian gal, don't you?"

Both men cussed Raymond, then passed the jug around again. Body aching, Jessie lay unmoving, watching. A few minutes ago she'd fought to reach what remained of the Raymond she'd known. Now, like him, she no longer cared.

A whisper of fear pulsed through her, but she couldn't keep her mind on it long enough to think about what might happen to her if the men got drunk enough. Was Daniel alive?

A prayer bubbled up inside her. She gave it silent voice. He had to be alive! If he wasn't, what was her life worth?

The question struck her with the force of a blow. Her

fear for him, her desperate prayer—she wouldn't feel this way if he was simply the man who'd taken her up a mountain and shown her how to face her worst fears.

Raymond was right; Daniel was her lover. Only, it wasn't dirty the way Raymond tried to make it sound.

It couldn't be. She loved him.

Love.

No. Love made a woman vulnerable.

Loud laughter cut through her thoughts. As she watched, Raymond placed the neck of the bottle in his mouth and tossed his head back. Again and again he drank. Each time he did, his laughter became louder, harsher, and he looked over at her with dead eyes.

Finally one of the men crawled over to his bedroll and sprawled out on it. The other staggered to his feet and attempted to grab the bottle from Raymond. Raymond shoved him away. Cursing, the man sat back down and stared into the fire. For the better part of a minute, Raymond stood, swaying. Then, bottle still in hand, he walked over to her.

"Raymond. Please, think what you're doing."

He shook off her words, then, nearly losing his balance, plopped beside her. He started to lift the bottle to his mouth again but wound up setting it down instead. "I didn't want to kill him," he muttered. "You made me. Going off with him like that, sharing yourself, the money with him instead of me. What was I going to do? Stand there like a whipped pup while folks laughed at me? A man can't do that and hold up his head." He lifted her skirt just enough that he could see the ropes around her ankles. "A man's got his pride. Certain things he's got to do."

When he reached for the bottle, he almost fell over. Grunting, he straightened and slid closer. With one hand still on the ground to support himself, he yanked at her top until he'd exposed her breasts. Jessie shuddered and clamped her teeth together. No matter what he did to her, she wouldn't be dragged down to his level.

"You don't want me, do you? I can see it in your eyes, Jessie. See everything in your eyes—even in my dreams. Dreams? Bad enough to wake me up screaming." He squeezed her breasts. She blinked rapidly so he couldn't see that he'd brought tears to her eyes. "What's a man to do?" He swayed, released her long enough to right himself, then shoved against her, knocking her backward. "What's a man going to do? Got to hold his head up."

"What dreams?" she made herself ask. "Tell me about them."

"Shut up." He reared back to hit her, but she jerked away in time.

With her hands knotted behind her and her feet tightly bound, she could only move a few inches at a time. He laughed and kept after her. Struggling against the churning in her stomach, she forced herself to speak. She had to find the man buried under alcohol and twisted thoughts, somehow. "Are you going to kill me?"

"Kill?" He dragged his mouth off her. "Kill? No."

"You'll have to."

He blinked, blinked again. His eyes remained unfocused. "I'm no killer."

You tried to murder Daniel. Maybe you succeeded. "You can't keep me here forever. Those men, they're soldiers—they'll have to go back to the fort. They'll tell what happened."

"I'm paying them not to. There's things I know about them that'll keep their mouths shut."

"If they get drunk, or start boasting, they might forget."

Raymond's gaze slid from her eyes to her exposed throat and breasts. Head throbbing, stomach rolling, she fought down her reaction. His mouth worked, but seconds passed before he spoke. "You'd rather be dead?"

She ignored the question. "I'll tell Sutter what happened. He'll go after Daniel, bring—bring him back."

"Bear's dead. Wolf bait."

No. Please. "Don't you see what you're doing," she managed. "If I'm alive, there's no way you can keep me silent. They'll hang you."

"Hang!" Raymond spat out the word. He reached for her again, then seemed to forget what he was doing. "For killing Bear? Never. They'll call me a hero."

"No they won't," she pushed. "It'll be your word against mine. There's only one thing to do. Cut me loose. Go back with me to find Daniel." She paused, watching Raymond to see if her words had made an impact. She couldn't tell. "If he's alive, if you help me get him to a doctor, I won't tell anyone what happened. Otherwise . . ."

"Otherwise, Jessie?" He wiped the back of his hand over his mouth. His lips flapped, then he belched. "What you going to tell them? That I killed Bear? And had my way with you?" Again he reached for her. This time he gripped torn fabric. "No one's going to believe you."

While she waited him out, he slid closer. With his leg digging into her hip, he began tracing a rough finger from her throat downward. She clamped her eyes closed, then opened them. No matter what, she didn't dare stop thinking.

"I'm a respected—respected businessman. Sutter likes me. You—you fooled him so you could get your hands on some of his land. Like some hermit, you lived out there in that cabin Bear built for you until the Indians burned it down. Then—" He ran his forefinger over her navel, cackled. Belched. "Then you went off with Bear." He leaned over her. "Folks won't listen to you."

Was he right? She needed time to search for the answer, but Raymond wasn't giving her that. He seemed fascinated by her stomach. His dirty fingers prodded at her flesh. His breath quickened. Every time he breathed out, she smelled whiskey. No matter how hard she tried, she couldn't keep herself from flinching.

Please. No.

"Been a long time. Need—need a woman."

No!

"Need you, Jessie. Jessie. Beautiful woman." He rocked forward, planted his thin lips on her middle. She felt his wet tongue and turned her head to one side so she could draw in cold night air. *No. Please!*

"Keep you safe. With me. Folks, they'll think I'm looking after you. Call you crazy Jessie, that's what they'll do." He raked his teeth over her flesh. "You need me— need me taking care of you."

"No!"

"No?" He reared back. In the firelight, his eyes turned a million shades of red. "No. You don't ever tell me no." He swayed, then looked around. She watched, not breathing, as he reached for the bottle. After a couple of tries, he picked it up and took another drink. Then, one side of his mouth lifted, he extended the bottle to her. "You ever tasted whiskey, Jessie? Makes a man want a woman. Maybe—maybe does the same for a woman."

When he jabbed the bottle at her, she clamped her lips together. Red. And black. His eyes were that color. They seemed to widen, then narrow. Now they were nothing but slits. She watched him sway again. He tried to set the bottle down, but before he got it to the ground, he pitched forward and landed on top of her.

She counted, ten, fifteen, twenty. When Raymond still didn't move, she managed to roll out from under him.

Then, with her face buried in grass that smelled of wet earth, she started crying.

The night lasted forever. The ropes bit into her wrists and ankles and the cold air made her shiver. Still, she was grateful for Raymond's snoring. As long as he slept, she was safe.

She didn't want to think about what he'd said, spent hours denying that she'd heard the words. But when the crickets stopped making their sound and the land began to take on a silvery hue, she gave up the battle. Raymond had been drunk, but his words still made terrible sense.

Despite everything she now knew about him, he was a confidant of Captain Sutter, respected for his intelligence and business sense. She'd done everything he'd accused her of—insisting on living alone in the wilderness, taking charity from a man everyone considered an outlaw, going back to a place of nightmares with him.

Everyone would think she'd lost her mind.

Maybe she had.

With a loud grunt, the younger of the men lurched to his feet. He staggered about for a moment trying to put his boots on, then sat on a rock and finished the task. He glanced at her. His mouth fell slack, but he merely kicked at his companion. Cursing, the other man sat up. They began arguing, but Jessie didn't care what they said or did as long as they left her alone.

After a few minutes, the second man walked over to where Raymond was sprawled beside her. "Didn't get too far last night, did he?" he observed. He jabbed Raymond in the side. "Don't you worry, missy. That'll change once he sobers." He nudged Raymond's shoulder.

Raymond let out a string of oaths. With one hand pressed against his forehead, he pushed himself into a sitting position and looked around. "We can't be stayin' here all day," the young man said. "Burkham and me, we gotta get back. You staying here with the missy? Iffen so, you owes us, now."

Raymond belched, then turned his attention to Jessie. Not breathing, not moving, she waited. "You'll get your pay when I say you do." He swung his head toward the man, then groaned. "Damnation, I feel like I'm going to die. I want to talk to the two of you. About what you are and aren't going to say."

"Fur enough money, we'll call you king."

Raymond started to laugh, then groaned again. "How do you drink that stuff? It'll kill a mule."

"You gotta get used to it. Look Sage, you know we're flat broke. We need—"

"Don't tell me what you need. I'm running things."

When Raymond untied her ankles and hauled her to her feet, she cried out. Something—regret?—flashed through his eyes, but she was beyond caring. Last night she'd tried to reason with him, tried to find the man she thought she knew. No more.

He spun her around and untied her wrists. He told her to use the bushes and she staggered off, knowing she couldn't possibly run with her legs throbbing the way they were.

He was waiting for her when she stepped out from behind the bush. The others were already mounted, keeping a goodly distance from Raymond. The scarred man, Burkham, announced that they were out of meat and he was going to follow a deer trail he'd spotted. When Raymond nodded, he began loading his rifle. Jessie tensed, wondering if Burkham might be thinking to use the weapon on Raymond. "Don't even think it," Raymond warned. "If anything happens to me, who do you think

Sutter's going to blame? He's seen us together enough and you're not near as upstanding as I am." After a moment of tense silence, Raymond jerked a finger at her, ordering her to come to him. She nearly gave into the voice that shrieked at her to run. But she was barefoot. They'd overtake her before she got more than a few feet.

Hating herself, she approached Raymond. "No one will believe you, Jessie," he said. "Don't ever forget that."

Just then one of the soldier's horses let out a sharp squeal. She heard the sound of hooves pounding on packed earth, wrenched free of Raymond, and stared.

A man was racing toward them, his body bent low over his mount.

Daniel's stallion. Daniel!

Before the men could move, Daniel charged straight at Burkham, yanking the rifle out of his arms as the scarred man tried to avoid a collision. Daniel swung the weapon toward Raymond. "Get away from her!" he ordered.

His breath a sharp hiss, Raymond stared. His arms were at his sides, his body looking so tense that Jessie thought it might snap. "Damn you."

"Yeah. Damn me. You—" He jerked his head at the other men. "Get out of here if you want to go on living."

Raymond ordered the men to stand their ground. Burkham shrugged. "You ain't holding the rifle, Sage. He is." Despite Raymond's continued oaths, they slowly, carefully turned their horses around and urged them away. Jessie stood only a few feet from Raymond and watched the two disappear from sight. The shock of seeing Daniel alive and well plus her still numb legs made it impossible for her to concentrate on walking.

No. Not well. Daniel's wound was bleeding. He was leaning forward now, bracing himself against the stallion's neck with his free hand. He kept blinking.

"Daniel? Are you all right?"

"I will be." Eyes narrowed, he concentrated on Raymond. "I don't want to have to kill you. Get away from her, Sage. Now!"

Raymond stabbed a glance in Jessie's direction. Instead of doing as he'd been ordered, he took a step toward her. She slid away.

"Damn it! Leave her alone!"

"I don't think so, Bear." Raymond snaked out a hand and grabbed her sleeve. "How good a shot are you in your condition? Are you going to risk killing her?"

Jessie managed to put a few inches between herself and Raymond, but she couldn't feel her knees and her feet seemed three times their normal size. "Daniel?" she whispered. "I—can't."

She felt Raymond grip her forearm. Desperate, she focused on Daniel. He tried to jerk himself upright, then sagged forward again, the rifle sliding downward. "I mean it, Sage," he whispered hoarsely.

"Go to hell."

As if the world had slowed down to wait for her, Jessie watched, helpless, as Daniel struggled to level the rifle. She tried to jerk free. Raymond vised his fingers into her, cutting off circulation. Then she felt something cold and sharp jab her side. Startled, she swung her attention toward Raymond. Too quickly for her to react, he jerked her against him and pressed his knife to her side.

"Now what, Bear?"

"Damn—damn . . ."

Once again the world slowed down. Daniel blinked, jerked his head upright, blinked again. The rifle began slipping from his grip. She wept for him, willing strength back into his body.

But he'd spent himself. He slid almost gracefully off the

stallion, landed on his knees, and pitched forward, the rifle thudding against the ground.

Daniel lay in a crumpled heap, bringing back yesterday's horror.

"Daniel! Daniel!" Only when she felt the knife nick her flesh did she stop fighting.

"That's better." Raymond sounded as if he'd been running for hours. "Do what I say and you'll live."

A thousand words clogged her throat, but she said nothing. The wrong word might push Raymond over the edge. As long as he held her, he couldn't hurt Daniel. Couldn't kill him, if he wasn't already dead.

But Daniel wasn't dead. As she watched, praying, Daniel pushed himself so that he now rocked on his knees, eyes boring into Raymond's. "Don't kill her," he hissed. "Whatever you do, don't kill her."

Raymond shoved her closer to the fire, keeping distance between himself and Daniel. "You aren't giving the orders, Bear. Stay where you are and she'll be all right."

"The hell—" Daniel reached for the rifle. At that instant, Raymond pressed the knife so tight against her throat that it again drew blood. "Don't!" Daniel hissed. His eyes filled with hate, he held his hands high for Raymond to see. "Whatever you do, don't hurt her."

When Raymond tried to lean down and hold on to her at the same time, she realized he was reaching for the length of rope that had been left there. He was going to tie her again. And then—then he'd kill Daniel.

Gathering strength from somewhere outside herself, she shoved her body back and against Raymond. He grunted; the knife again nicked her throat. He staggered, clutching her ruined dress as he struggled to regain his balance. She whirled toward Raymond, barely aware that she was all but naked from the waist up. He'd caught himself, was ready for her. She shoved the heel of her hand up under his chin and into his throat. His eyes bulged. She heard him try to suck in air.

The knife. She had to grab it!

Before she could focus on the desperate task she'd given herself, he slashed at her. She ducked, feeling air on her exposed arm. "I'll kill—" He shuddered, mouth sagging open.

For an instant Raymond locked eyes with her. She read shock, fear, pain. "Jessie," he groaned. "Help me." The knife slid from his fingers, and he reached for her, looking like a tired, frightened boy.

Then he pitched forward. Without thinking, she braced herself to hold him. But he was too heavy. She couldn't stop him from falling to the ground.

A knife handle protruded from his throat.

His hand inched forward, weakly circled her ankle. "Jessie."

Sobbing, she turned toward Daniel. He was trying to push himself to his feet, trying and failing. She looked down again, then met Daniel's eyes.

"You killed him. Oh God, you killed him."

CHAPTER 20

Nothing had ever looked as good as the high, stark walls that surrounded Fort Sutter. "We're there," Jessie whispered to Daniel. "Hold on. Please."

Slumped over his stallion, Daniel said nothing, but then he'd barely spoken for the rest of that horrible day and night as she prodded the weary horses onward. Daniel was hurt. She had to get him to help.

And then, maybe she'd fall apart.

From the sun's position, she guessed it to be almost noon when she guided Daniel and the horses through the open gate. Ignoring the curious looks, she headed for Captain Sutter's office. When she dismounted, her legs gave out and she sank to her knees in the dirt. Tears were so close. She wanted just two things in life; Daniel to be healthy, and then to be able to sleep.

She felt strong hands on her shoulders and looked up. One of the Indian guards stood over her. "We care for him, Miss Speer. You rest."

"I can't." The words came out a sob; she clamped down on the sound. "He needs a doctor." She blinked and took in her surroundings. Two other Indians were easing a limp Daniel off his horse. "Please. Don't hurt him."

The Indian who'd been comforting her helped her to her feet. She walked over to Daniel and pressed her hand along the side of his neck. He lifted his head and for a moment his eyes cleared. "You're going to be all right, Jessie."

"I don't care about me. You're the one who was hurt." *Only, seeing you hurt is tearing me apart.*

"I'm—all right."

He wasn't. His flesh felt frighteningly hot. Alarmed, she looked around. It seemed as if dozens of people were watching them now. Still, other than the Indians, no one had offered a hand. Why? Surely these so-called decent, God-fearing men and women weren't afraid of a wounded man.

"Please." Her throat felt raw. She swallowed and tried again. "Please. He needs help."

After a moment of strained silence, a man dressed in black pants and a too-tight black vest stepped forward. John Marsh. Some folks said he was a doctor. Others weren't sure. As long as he helped Daniel, she didn't care. Although her legs threatened to give out on her, she hurried to him and grabbed his arm. Slurring her words, she explained that Daniel had sustained a head wound and had been drifting in and out of consciousness since then.

Dr. Marsh pointed toward the sickroom, a dark, spare

enclosure she'd never entered. With her hand at her throat, she watched the Indians help Daniel inside. She started to follow, but Dr. Marsh stopped her. "You're out on your feet, Miss Speer. You're going to wind up looking like him if you don't get some rest."

"I don't care. I have to help him."

Dr. Marsh grabbed her arms and propelled her away from the curious onlookers. He spoke in a low voice. "Listen to me, young lady. I'll tend to him. You take care of yourself."

"He's burning up."

"He's got infection. A lot of my colleagues would be bleeding him, but I've never seen that help. What he needs is to be cooled down with well water. That and decent food."

"Decent food?" Remembering what she'd eaten while living at the fort, she winced. "He has to have more than bread and meat."

"I agree, but it's going to be hard getting him the vegetables he needs. Surely you've seen the state of Sutter's garden."

"Vegetables? I can get him that, from my farm."

"Miss Speer, you're not up to it."

She agreed with the doctor. But if she didn't take responsibility for getting Daniel something nourishing to eat, maybe he'd die. After all they'd been through, she *couldn't* let that happen to the man who meant everything to her. "I got this far; I'll make it the rest of the way. I'll be back as soon as I can."

Dr. Marsh's eyes narrowed. "You are a stubborn woman, aren't you? At least agree to one thing. A few hours one way or the other isn't going to make that much difference with Bear. Pace yourself so I don't wind up with two patients."

Jessie didn't have the energy to argue with that. Besides, Dr. Marsh was right. Right now, rest was more important for Daniel than food. Although every step made her head pound, she slipped into the sickroom. The two Indians who'd brought Daniel inside had him on a bed and were already loosening his clothing. His eyes were at half mast, unfocused. "You're going to be all right," she whispered. "I'll be back as soon as I can, with decent food."

"Jessie, don't."

It seemed as if she'd been waiting a lifetime simply to hear his voice. Why then did she feel like turning and running? "Don't what?"

"Bother. Look after yourself."

"When you've been tended to."

He reached out his hand, and she placed hers in it. His fingers felt hot, still strong. His eyes cleared. "I'll be all right." He indicated the Indians. "You go see the Buckhalters. They'll take care of you."

She wanted to be taken care of, to have someone explain to her why she felt like screaming. Most of all she needed to understand how Daniel had come to mean so much to her and why that terrified her. "Later. You come first."

He gave her a wry grin. "I heard Dr. Marsh call you stubborn. He's right. Jessie?" His voice dropped to a whisper. "I'm sorry. I didn't want to have to do what I did. I hope you believe that."

He was waiting for an answer. Only, she couldn't give him anything. "I need—time."

"Time?"

"To think."

His eyes continued asking questions, but he remained silent. Jessie was grateful for that. Still, maybe if he had spoken, she would have been forced to explore her churning, overwhelming emotions.

"I'm tired," she whispered. "I don't know what I'm thinking."

Once again his eyes spoke for him. He didn't believe her. "You're all right? He didn't hurt you?"

Although she'd already explained that Raymond had passed out before he could do anything to her, she told him that again. "Good, good," he whispered, making her wonder what he remembered of yesterday. "Jessie? Please let someone take care of you."

"What I need is for you to be well. Daniel . . ." She leaned over him and touched her lips to his forehead. "Thank you."

"For saving you from Raymond?"

He'd whispered his question. No one had heard. Why then did she feel so cold? "For being there when I needed you. Up there."

"The mountain? That's not what's eating at you. I see it in your eyes."

She drew away. With an effort she forced herself not to press her hand to her eyes. "No. It isn't."

An hour later, Jessie rode away from the fort, feeling as if she'd left part of herself behind. Although she'd had a little to eat and had cleaned up as best she could, her body still trembled. Exhaustion, she told herself as the swaybacked old gelding she'd borrowed plodded toward her farm. An Indian had given her a doeskin shirt to wear. If it hadn't been for his act of kindness, she would have had to go begging to the Buckhalters.

Right now, despite her need to watch over Daniel, to hear the sound of his voice, she needed even more to be alone.

To understand herself.

The afternoon wasn't hot, but she could feel summer in the air. The valley grass had already lost some of its bright new green coloring, and the oaks were putting out fresh leaves. If Vaca had been diligent about tending her vegetables, a few could be picked. The beans, peas, and beets wouldn't be full-grown, but they should have enough sustenance to help Daniel.

Daniel.

Room to think.

Daniel.

No matter where she tried to take her thoughts, even if she willed her mind to be quiet, everything came back to Daniel.

She'd seen him kill a man. Yes, Raymond had been capable, even ready to end her life. He'd shot Daniel; Daniel had acted to defend her. But . . .

Last winter had been filled with death. The dream of coaxing life from the land, her land, had kept her alive. Not long ago the Walla Wallas had tried to take her farm from her, but she hadn't given up. She'd climbed a mountain so she would have the means to keep the dream going, so she could devote herself to renewal.

In an instant Daniel had ended a life.

What was she thinking? Nothing mattered except helping the man she loved regain his health.

And then? Oh God, then what?

How could she possibly make sense of how much she loved Daniel and how that love, that vulnerability, had changed her?

When, finally, she spotted the charred remains of her cabin, she moaned aloud. The sound echoed, died away. No. She wasn't going to think about what she no longer had. She didn't dare. Because she'd forced herself to touch

Raymond long enough to retrieve the money purse, she had the means to rebuild her life.

Life.

Her life. Daniel's life. Their lives. Together?

But their being together had already ended in tragedy.

Why couldn't she think?

In desperation, she focused on her surroundings. Vaca wasn't around, but she could tell he'd been diligent about watering and weeding. He'd left a pine-bough bed under the oak she'd thought would shade her cabin this summer. After dismounting, she staggered more than walked over to the bed and dropped to her knees on it. She needed to wander through her garden and decide what she should take back to Daniel.

But she was played out. "Pace yourself," Dr. Marsh had said. She had no choice but to obey him.

As she stretched out on the bed, she became aware of the gentle hum of insects. Songbirds were in the oak, and if she listened hard enough, she could, or thought she could, hear the stream.

Soon she'd do what she'd come here for. Soon she'd get back on the tired old horse and return to Daniel so she could gift him with her garden's young harvest.

First she had to sleep.

It was nearly dark when Jessie finally roused herself. Through the gloom she could see the horse grazing a few yards away. It was a comforting presence, the only one she wanted. The air was warm enough that she wouldn't need a campfire for several hours, if at all. Good. She wanted to pick all she could before it got so dark that she couldn't see.

She nearly cried with joy when she saw the fragile green row of lettuce—would have except that she was afraid she couldn't stop if she started. Instead, she sat to one side of the row and popped small, sweet leaves into her mouth. Already she felt as if she'd barely closed her eyes instead of having slept for a couple of hours. The peas and beans bore little resemblance to what they would look like in a month, but the tiny sprigs tasted wonderful. She didn't eat much—just enough to assure herself that Daniel would have something nourishing.

Daniel.

He was all right, Mr. Marsh had said. In no danger of dying. Thank God. As long as he was alive, she could face anything.

Couldn't she?

As the sun set, she half walked, half staggered over to Vaca's bed and sat with her back propped against the oak. She sent out a silent message to Daniel. *I'll be with you tomorrow. You'll get well. Then we'll* . . . She didn't know what came after that. Didn't know how to begin searching for the answer.

The old horse came over and sniffed, then wandered off again. When the stars came out, she stared up at them. How long had they been there? Forever, her grandmother had said. Before God made man and woman. Although her mother and grandmother had never questioned what the Bible said about God creating the world in six days, she'd wondered if maybe there were different ways of looking at days.

The Bible . . .

Suddenly, she clutched her stomach and rocked forward. Oh God, the family Bible was gone! After Raymond forced her onto her horse, he'd gone through her belongings. Except for a few pieces of smoked fish, everything had been scattered about. Then she hadn't thought about anything except to pray for Daniel's life.

Now she cursed Raymond for what he'd done.

She continued to rock herself, too weary to battle what was going on inside her. For days, it seemed, she'd been filling up with tears. She hadn't had time for them, hadn't dared let down her guard. But now, knowing she might never again see her mother's most treasured possession, unsure and overwhelmed and afraid of Daniel's place in her tomorrows, nothing mattered except release.

Tears rolled down her cheeks and soaked her deerskin shirt. She sobbed and shook, hurting too much to care whether she might be losing her mind.

Alone. She felt so alone.

They were all gone, her parents and grandparents, the Allsetters, little Elizabeth. Raymond had turned into someone she didn't know; she'd watched him die.

Daniel. What was Daniel to her?

Did she dare ask him to be her everything? *Yes!* her heart moaned. But only a few hours ago she'd thought him dead. That possibility had nearly killed her. She never wanted to hurt, to feel that kind of fear again. To forget what it felt like to hold herself separate and free from a man—from Daniel.

Morning. She tried to give the word definition, but it kept slipping away. Although she'd managed to sleep most of the night, she still felt exhausted. At least her tears had ceased. As long as she refused to listen to the questions in her heart, she would survive.

She had things to do today. Daniel needed decent food, and now that she'd seen her crops, she could leave the farm long enough to spend the time she needed to with Daniel.

Needed, not wanted. Maybe wanted.

Want? To feel his arms around her, to have him whisper

that her fears were for nothing and that just because she'd lost loved ones before didn't mean it would happen with him.

Loved one? Is that who he is? Can he possibly keep such a promise?

Sick of questions, she cleaned up at the creek, collected her vegetables, and mounted her horse. If Daniel was still feverish, she would go in search of some herbs. Otherwise, she would help him eat, tell him that Vaca had done a man's job. Then she would begin rebuilding her cabin, taking strength from her land.

Maybe Daniel wouldn't look too deeply into her eyes and she wouldn't have to lay herself open to him.

Although she was anxious to see how Daniel was, she allowed the stiff old gelding to plod along at an untiring pace. She took comfort from the soft thudding sound his splayed hooves made. The birds were out again today, as were a large number of squirrels who'd staked a claim on the oaks. She should be like them, content to run along tree branches, scolding anyone who dared come too close. Squirrels didn't think, didn't worry about anything except nuts.

When the gelding pricked up its ears and snorted, she felt an instant of panic. But this wasn't the other day when her horse's nervous movement had been followed by a rifle blast and the horrifying sight of Daniel falling to the ground.

A rider was heading toward her. Before he'd come close enough that she could make out his features, she recognized his sturdy frame. She lifted her hand in greeting but waited a few more minutes before calling to Narciso.

"Have you come to check up on Vaca?" she asked. "He isn't here, but he's done a wonderful job."

"Jessie, you did not stay with Daniel."

"I couldn't." After spending so many hours tangled in her thoughts, surprisingly, she found it easy to explain to Narcisco that she'd needed some time by herself. Then she asked if he'd seen Daniel.

"I tried last night after I received word that he was at the fort."

"Tried?" She felt her stomach tighten. "Is he sicker?"

"The braves who were tending him say not. Jessie, he is not with Dr. Marsh."

"Why not?"

Narcisco kicked his horse forward until he was close enough that he could take her hand. "He is in jail."

Jail! She'd seen the damp, cavelike room under the stairs, smelled the stale, musty air coming from it. "No. Why?"

"He has been accused of murder."

"Murder?" Pulling her hand free, she pressed it against her forehead.

"Raymond's body? Didn't Daniel tell them what happened?" What made her think folks would believe Daniel Bear?

"I do not know what Daniel said. Or what has been said against him." Narcisco spoke softly. "That is why I came looking for you. So you can try to make them listen to the truth."

Jessie pushed her horse as fast as it would go. She was barely aware of Narcisco beside her, yet was grateful for the company. When they passed through the fort's open gate, he pointed unnecessarily to where Daniel had been taken.

"What should I do?" she asked in a tone she didn't recognize. "I'm sure they won't let me see him."

"Sheriff McKinstry will know. You have to talk to him."

Silent, Jessie led the way across the open courtyard. She reined in her horse at the foot of the stairs that led to where Keseberg's hearing had been held. Back then she'd thought she'd never again have to concern herself with the fort's legal matters, that she'd be allowed to live her life in peace.

How wrong she was.

"You have thought this over?"

Brought up short by Narcisco's question, she could only stare back at him. Although she'd barely taken note of her surroundings, she felt eyes on her. Surely everyone here knew that Daniel Bear had been arrested for the murder of Raymond Sage.

They all thought of Daniel as a killer. Except for her and Narcisco and a few Maidu braves, they must all believe that he deserved to be kept behind that heavy door.

That justice would be served by his hanging.

Justice?

"They don't know the truth. I do." Daniel was several hundred feet away. He couldn't hear her, but was it possible that he sensed her presence? *I'm here. I'll find a way to free you. Try . . . Please believe that.* Her promise, maybe hollow, swirled around her, trapping her.

"You will have to tell them that you were with Daniel."

She stared at Narcisco. "I know."

Narcisco didn't move or speak, but his eyes mirrored the desperate determination she felt. They said something else—that she was risking a great deal. Maybe everything.

She knew that, but Daniel had given so much of himself to her. How could she do any less for him?

Leaving Narcisco to tend to the horses, she dismounted and started up the stairs. She had no way of knowing whether the sheriff or anyone else was up there, but a man's fate would soon be settled. Those charged with enforcing law at the fort had to be concerning themselves with that.

Before she could decide whether to knock or simply walk inside, the second-floor door opened and she faced not Sheriff McKinstry but Lieutenant John Sinclair. His eyes narrowed, then flickered to what was going on behind and below her. Turning, Jessie saw that the courtyard had filled with people, all of them watching her.

She should have stayed out on her farm.

What was she thinking! She might be all that stood between Daniel and death.

"You must know why I'm here," she said. "The charges against Daniel Bear? They're false. The truth—"

"The truth will be decided tomorrow, Miss Speer."

"Tomorrow." She clenched her hands by her sides. "I want to testify. I insist on it."

"You know what you're doing, do you?"

Narcisco had asked her the same question. She felt Daniel's friend's presence behind her, but didn't take her eyes off Sinclair long enough to look at him. "I don't have a choice. Who is accusing him?"

By way of answer, Sinclair pushed the door all the way open. In the ill-lit room she spotted the two men who'd accompanied Raymond. She spun toward Sinclair. "Them? You're listening to them? The things they did . . ."

Sinclair frowned, his heavy eyebrows seeming to merge into a single line. "They brought in Mr. Sage's body, with Bear's knife still in it. I'm on my way to speak with the captain so I can properly prepare for tomorrow's trial."

Tomorrow's trial. She pointed at Daniel's accusers, surprised at how steady her finger was. "Did they tell you that they were with Mr. Sage because he'd promised them money—money that's rightfully mine?"

"I'm afraid I am not at liberty to discuss anything of what they've told me."

Not at liberty? She spoke through clenched teeth. "If you'd listen to me now, there wouldn't be a need for this travesty of justice."

"Travesty? Miss Spear, Mr. Bear is being accused of the cold-blooded murder of a highly respected man, a man you owe a great deal to."

"I owe even more to Daniel." Although her words hung in the air, exposing her, she didn't want to take them back. All she had to defend Daniel with was the truth. She stared past Sinclair at the two silent, sober-faced men inside. In their eyes she read a hungry, almost desperate determination. Did they really believe that with Daniel gone, nothing stood between them and her money? They must. Why else would they be doing this? "When will the trial begin?"

"Directly after breakfast."

Feeling sick, she nodded. Daniel's fate would be decided in a few hours. "I'll be there. I trust I will be allowed to testify."

"If that's what you are determined to do. Certainly we intend to give Bear a fair trial."

Fair? It was his word, and hers, against two men in Captain Sutter's employ, Raymond's body with Daniel's knife in it.

Sinclair was waiting for her to leave. She had no choice but to follow Narciso back down the stairs. Halfway to the ground, her legs turned weak from fear. Would anyone believe her? If they didn't . . . As she looked out at the crowd, she spotted Margaret Buckhalter. She stared at her, needing reassurance, support, something. Margaret stared back, shook her head, then turned her back on her.

She felt more alone than she had out on her farm yesterday.

"Please, can I see him?" she asked Sinclair. She sounded lost. "Just for a minute. I brought food for him. He's hurt; he needs to be taken care of."

"Miss Spear, if he's found guilty, it won't matter whether he's injured or not, will it?"

From where he sat behind the massive door that held him prisoner, Daniel heard the murmur of voices. Although he couldn't understand what anyone was saying, he recognized one of them. Jessie.

He shifted position and wrapped the blanket the guards had given him more securely around his shoulders. Although his body felt hot, he couldn't stop shaking. His head pounded, making it nearly impossible to think.

Again Jessie's voice reached him. She should be out at her farm, encouraging her beloved plants to grow. Using her rightful money to build a decent place to live. Buying a horse. A cow. Maybe cloth for bright new dresses. Instead, who and what he was had brought her back here.

Damn it, she deserved better than him—a man who could come to her open and honest. A man folks would approve of. A man—

What had they told him? That he'd hear everything he had a right to tomorrow. That then his fate would be decided.

Tomorrow. That's why she'd returned.

No! Damn it, he wouldn't drag her down into hell with him. Somehow . . .

If he'd walked away from her when he should have, she wouldn't be here, pleading for his life as he knew she would. But she'd meant too much to him and he'd stayed. He'd allowed their lives to tangle together.

Tangled. Like his mind.

The voices faded away and after a few minutes, he gave up straining to hear. Although the dirt continued to chill him, he felt too weak to do anything except curl up and lie back down. The stale air had made him sick to his stomach. It took every ounce of self-control not to let the relentless dark strip him of what little sanity he had left.

Jessie. Sunlight.

His arms ached with the need to hold her. *For you, anything. I promise.*

CHAPTER 21

Jessie spent the night in the blacksmith's tack room. Perhaps she could have prevailed upon the Buckhalters to extend her their hospitality, but she needed to be alone with her fears, her prayers, the promise she might not be able to keep. Because both she and Narcisco had been relentless in their questions, she knew Daniel's accusers had told Captain Sutter that Daniel had, without provocation, attacked and killed Raymond.

According to the story circulating throughout the fort, Daniel and Jessie had surprised Raymond and the others while the three men were out hunting. Yes, Raymond should not have accused Daniel of ruining Jessie's reputation by being with her, but how could a responsible man such as Raymond Sage do anything less? There'd been no call for Daniel to stab Raymond, none at all. As for Daniel's wound—Raymond had gotten off a hurried shot before Daniel's knife struck him down.

Only a man as brazen as Daniel Bear would have marched into the fort, expecting to be taken care of. What unspeakable things he'd done to Miss Speer no one would say, only that many now doubted her sanity. Why else hadn't she gone running to the sheriff the moment she was free of Bear? Any other young woman would have been frantic to defend her reputation.

Her reputation when Daniel's life was at stake?

When she heard people begin to move about, she brushed her clothes and hair clean of straw and went in search of Narcisco. She found him stalking away from Daniel's cell.

"They will not let me see him," the bleary-eyed chief explained. "I told them that a man who has not yet been condemned has a right to eat. They said his needs are being looked after." Narcisco spat the last words. "My friend will die in that hole."

"Oh God, I know!" The words burst from her before she could think to stop them. Now they hung in the air, terrifying her. *Daniel! I'm here! I'll—what?* "What is he thinking?" Her question made her shiver. Fear forced her on. "How horrible it must be for him, sitting there, not knowing what's happening."

"Stop," Narcisco warned. He gripped her arms and held her firmly. His eyes were heavy with understanding. "Making yourself sick is not going to help Daniel. Only one thing might. The truth." He looked as if he didn't believe his words. "You have decided what you are going to say?"

She nodded, barely. If he thought she'd spent the night

planning her words, he was wrong. Every time she tried to do so, her thoughts centered on Daniel.

Daniel rode wild bulls. He would rather sleep on the ground than under a roof. If he was sentenced to prison ... No. Prison wasn't for a man like Daniel Bear. Found guilty, he would hang.

If he did, they might as well kill her, too.

At his guards' prodding, Daniel climbed the stairs and stepped into the sparsely furnished hearing room. As before, Lieutenant Sinclair sat behind the rough-finished table, flanked by Governor Kearny and Consul Larkin. Captain Sutter sat at the far end, looking removed from the proceedings. The room overflowed with onlookers.

He didn't care. There were only two people he wanted to see. Narcisco leaned against a wall. Jessie, looking dwarfed by his friend, stood beside him. The others had left them alone.

Although his guards were trying to get him to sit in the chair that had been placed in front of the table, he couldn't drag his eyes off her.

She looked haunted.

Lieutenant Sinclair pounded on the table with an axe handle. The sound set his head to throbbing and silenced the room. He barely listened as the lieutenant read the charges against him. What did it matter? He'd killed Raymond. He'd do it again if Jessie's life was at risk. Barely aware of the guards flanking him, he leaned back, trying to clear his head. The room felt hot and close; it smelled of unwashed bodies. He could barely breathe.

The men who'd been with Raymond spoke first. The one with the badly deformed upper lip did little more than nod to reinforce what his companion said. The other faced not Sinclair but the packed room. As he told it,

Raymond had felt compelled to speak his mind when he found Daniel and Jessie together. What was he doing with that man? Didn't she care anything about her reputation? Before Jessie could reply, Daniel had ordered her into silence. Jessie's life, he'd told Raymond, was no longer his concern. He, Daniel, had taken responsibility for that. The words—lies—filtered into Daniel's mind, then escaped before he could make sense of them. Only one thing mattered. Jessie.

"He boasted about it," the sometime soldier finished. "He told Mr. Sage that he and Miss Speer had recovered a great many things from the mountain and were now well set. Grave robbing, that's what Mr. Sage called it. Mr. Bear took exception."

Grave robbing. The words buzzed throughout the courtroom. Daniel longed to look over at Jessie to see her reaction; he didn't. When the sound subsided, Sinclair asked the man why he and his companion hadn't tried to render Mr. Sage assistance. They couldn't, he explained. Mr. Bear had ordered them off at gunpoint. Obviously Miss Speer had received rough treatment at Bear's hands. Her clothing was shredded.

"That's not true," Jessie burst out. "It's a lie!"

"Miss Speer," Sinclair ordered. "I must insist that you wait your turn."

Despite the crowd and the buzzing in his head, Daniel swore he could hear Jessie breathing. His body feeling like a frayed rope, he sent her a silent promise. *Whatever it takes, I won't have you dragged down with me.*

After a few more questions, the witness was dismissed. Judging by the many whispered comments, Daniel guessed that no one in the room doubted that what the man had said was the truth. Why would they? He wore the uniform of the United States Army, while Daniel Bear—Daniel almost laughed at that. He knew what his reputation was worth.

He thought he would be ordered to testify next. Instead, he heard Jessie's name being called. Only when she came to stand to the left of the table did he let his gaze settle on her. The table, the tribunal, the crowd, all that dwarfed her. Someone had given her a doeskin shirt to replace the ruined one. He wished these righteous people could have seen her with Sage's knife at her throat, that they'd been there when Sage leveled a gun at him.

But would it make any difference?

In a strained yet strong voice, Jessie said that the man who'd spoken ahead of her had lied. A ripple of disbelief ran through the room. Unblinking, Jessie looked around. For an instant, she locked eyes with Daniel. He saw nothing in them to remind him of the precious nights they'd spent in each other's arms.

Why should they? Since then her life had become hell—because of him.

Jessie spoke sparingly, yet passionately. Daniel followed most of it; if only he could shake himself free of the web wrapped around his mind. Daniel, Jessie said, had *not* attacked Raymond as had been testified. Rather, Daniel had been gunned down before either he or she knew Raymond was around. When she fought to stay with Daniel, she was tied and forced to leave with Raymond. "Raymond was after my money, money Daniel helped me recover. Something must have happened to Raymond's mind. He—he frightened me."

Again the room buzzed. Daniel shut his eyes, wishing with every ounce of strength in him that he could take Jessie out of here and spare her this.

"Daniel saved my life. He did the only thing he could."

When the crowd quieted down, Sinclair began his questions. Jessie wasn't denying that she had spent several days with Daniel? She didn't deny that they'd made the climb for the purpose of bringing down money that belonged to people now dead? Jessie answered, her head held high. It wasn't, she continued, the way they were trying to make things sound. The money had been given to her by the Allsetters. She was only retrieving what was rightfully hers. With Daniel's help, because she couldn't do it alone.

Then she wasn't denying she'd been with Daniel for a number of nights?

No. Jessie turned toward Daniel, her head still high. No. But that wasn't what this hearing was about.

The questions went on, Sinclair and the others questioning Jessie's version of what had happened, Jessie staying with her story, eyes boldly meeting her questioners'.

Daniel felt his chest tighten with fear, with love that hit with a force stronger than any bullet. Did she know what she was doing, risking everything for him? *Jessie, hear me. I'll go to my grave loving you.*

Finally, her voice worn thin from repeating herself, Jessie was dismissed. When his guards started to haul him to his feet, Daniel shook himself free. For a moment he thought he might pass out but willed himself to stand erect. *Her life. That's all that matters.* Ignoring the attention focused on him, he turned toward Jessie and Narcisco. The message in Narcisco's dark eyes was clear. White man's justice wasn't for the likes of Daniel Bear. Or Jessie Speer. Jessie, too, met his gaze. He read determination and a fierce pride. No matter what she'd done to her reputation, she had resolved to speak the truth. As for how she felt about him—that she kept to herself.

He was glad. It made speaking easier.

"I've got only a couple of things to say," he began in a

voice he didn't recognize. "First, what you heard from those so-called upstanding men about how Sage died is a bald-faced lie. He shot me before I even knew he was there."

Sinclair and the others leaned forward but said nothing. He didn't care. They would believe what they wanted. That wasn't what mattered. "As for Miss Speer—I never knew it would come to this."

"Come to what, Mr. Bear?"

"That she'd lie for me."

He didn't want to glance at Jessie. He wasn't going to. But something pulled him around. He found her features contorted with disbelief. Fighting off the impact of that look, he went on. "I might not have much of a reputation here. I know that. But I'm not going to hide behind some woman's skirt."

"What are you talking about?"

He paused, drawing out his answer, praying he could find the right words. Others might believe he was wrestling with what passed for his conscience. But it was much, much more than that. With his next words he would destroy what existed between him and Jessie. He had to. The rest of her life depended on it.

"I forced her to go with me."

"Daniel, no!"

Ignoring her, he plunged on. "I fear the experience has unhinged her. Forcing her to look at her parents' graves was more than she could take."

"It seems, Mr. Bear, that your consideration for her welfare has come a little late."

"It was never my intention to hurt her that way. But when she told me what had been left behind . . . I have nothing, little more than a horse and bedroll to call my own. I'd saved her life. Why shouldn't I be rewarded?"

He expected Jessie to say something, but she remained silent. The room was so quiet that he could hear the blood pulsing in his temple. That and Jessie breathing. "She fought. I wouldn't let her go. But I never . . ."

"That's not true. Daniel . . ."

"Look at her," he implored, fighting the fog that swirled around him. "If any of you were her, would you have willingly gone up that damnable mountain?"

"No!" Jessie's cry rang in the room. "Daniel, why are you doing this?"

So you won't be dragged down with me. Don't you understand that? "She's a lady, a true lady. Whatever else I might be, I do not force myself upon women. Miss Speer, I beg your forgiveness. That's all I can do, ask for your forgiveness."

She started toward him, but Narcisco stopped her. "Jessie, don't," Narcisco warned. "Let him do what he must."

"Must? He's going to hang! Please, someone, listen to me."

"No." Daniel's voice was low, sounding in control when he felt himself falling apart inside. "Miss Speer, please, think what you said about going willingly with me. It didn't happen that way. I hit you. Don't you remember that?"

"Hit me? Never. Oh, God—"

Wrapping his arms tightly around her, Narcisco lifted Jessie off her feet and marched through the crowd and out the door. Daniel caught the sound of Jessie's sobbing breath, then nothing.

When the door closed, he turned back to the tribunal. No one would ever know that his heart had gone with her. That nothing mattered except saving her. That he loved her more than he loved life. "Mr. Sage shot me first," he continued, his throat raw. "When he left, taking Miss Speer and the money with him, I went after them. I killed Mr. Sage defending Miss Speer's life. It's the God's truth, even if no one believes me."

"Let me go! Damn it, let me go!"

"No. Jessie, listen to me. Let it be."

Jessie wrenched free, then sagged against Narcisco. "Why?" she moaned. "Why did he say what he did?"

"For you."

She knew that. She had from the moment Daniel opened his mouth. But hearing Narcisco say the words made her head throb and her heart ache with fear and love. "He's condemning himself. If they think he kidnapped me, they're not going to believe the truth about how Raymond died."

"I know."

The defeat in Narcisco's voice pulled her out of herself. She pushed back her tangled hair and tried to straighten the oversized shirt. "What . . ." She took a deep breath. It didn't help. She sucked in more air. Fear rushed in to overwhelm her. "What's going to happen to him?"

"They'll hang him."

"No." Although she knew what he was going to say, her voice caught. She tried again. "No. I can't— Narcisco, there must be something—"

"What? Jessie, they will not listen to you."

"Listen? I'm done talking." She gripped Narcisco's arm, too scared to try to hide anything from him. "Please. You have to help me. I can't—I can't let him die. Without him—" *Without him I'm nothing.*

Was this what love had done to her? Made her willing, ready, determined to risk everything for him?

Yes. Even though she didn't want that, *yes.*

Daniel, dead?

No! Not as long as she lived.

* * *

Night. Jessie felt it surround her. She couldn't remember what she'd done after folks started filing out of the hearing room. One look at Daniel had told her what she both needed to know and feared most of all. He'd been found guilty. With Narcisco standing beside her, she'd watched as the guards returned Daniel to his cell. Just before he disappeared into the dark, cold room, he'd turned and faced her. Because he was deep in shadows, she couldn't read what was in his eyes.

It didn't matter.

She'd talked to Narcisco. She remembered that. After all the tears, the fear, had been set aside, she'd forced herself to think. To plan.

Now, her heart thudding as loudly as it had when she was in the hearing room, she approached Daniel's cell.

"Miss Speer." The guard stepped out of the darkness. "What are you doing here?"

"I—I have to talk to him."

"Talk to him? After what he did to you?"

"You don't understand." She pulled herself straight and faced the guard squarely. "He's going to die tomorrow, isn't he?"

The guard nodded. "Don't think about that, Miss Speer. He's getting what he deserves, but you don't have to concern yourself with it."

"No." She shook her head, then blinked to keep from becoming dizzy. "He has something of mine. I need it back, tonight, before—before . . ."

"Something of yours? On him?"

"My mother's wedding ring." She almost gagged. Still, she gripped his arm and swayed toward him. "This has all been so horrible. So horrible. I didn't know where else to turn." She held his gaze, hating herself, yet knowing she had no alternative. "I— He took it from her grave. It's all I have of her. Please, you understand, don't you?"

The guard peered into the night behind her, then, when she swayed away, let her brace herself against him. "You stay here, Miss Speer. I'll get help. We'll make sure he returns it to you."

"No." She made her voice quaver. "That isn't necessary. He'll—I know he'll give it to me."

"He's a cold-blooded killer."

Killer. How she hated the word. "He took pity on me today." She let her head hang forward and rested it on the man's chest. "What he forced me to—it was a nightmare. I thought I was going to go crazy. Maybe I did. But . . ." She gripped the guard's arm more firmly. "He must regret what he did to me. He said he did. You were there today, weren't you?"

He nodded.

"It was awful. I felt so alone. You—do you have any idea what that feels like?"

"I don't—yes, of course, ma'am."

"Thank you." The guard was little more than a youth, looking uncomfortable in his ill-fitting uniform. Narcisco had told her that he usually tagged after the Indian soldiers and seemed not the brightest of men. "If I ask, I know he'll return the ring to me."

The guard glanced over his shoulder at the cell. "He hasn't said a word since we put him in there."

"Because he's filled with regret. And—and because he's thinking about dying. A dying man has no need for a woman's ring."

Again the guard looked at the cell. "I'll get it for you, ma'am, have him shove it under the door."

Jessie took another deep breath. She kept her fingers wrapped tightly around the man's arm. She hated herself for what she was doing, and yet she had no choice. "No. Please," she pressed. "I want to talk to him. I have to. You'll be right here, making sure I'm safe."

"Talk to him? After what he did?"

Still gripping the man, she stood as tall as she could. "I can't go through the rest of my life never understanding why—don't you understand? How can I put my life back together if I don't confront him?"

"He might hurt you."

"Hurt me?" She made herself laugh. "Why would he? He's going to die tomorrow. You have a weapon. He's un-armed and sick."

She could hear the guard sucking on the inside of his lip. She waited him out, praying she'd said the right thing.

With a grunt, the young man pulled a battered pistol from his belt and proudly showed it to her. "You let me go in first, Miss Speer. I'll make him stand by the wall. Then you tell him what you have to, but I don't think he's going to say anything."

Maybe he wouldn't. Jessie thanked the man, then waited while he unlocked the heavy door and stepped inside. Because she'd been standing in the dark for several minutes, she could make out the guard's shadow and beyond that the figure of a man sitting on the earthen floor. *Daniel!* No. She didn't dare react.

"Miss Speer," the guard called after a minute of whispered conversation. "You come stand just inside the door. I'll be right beside you, watching him. You don't have to be afraid of anything, not as long as I'm here."

"Thank you. Oh, thank you." Jessie began shaking before she was fully inside. It was so cold, so evil-smelling. How could anyone stand to be in here?

But Daniel didn't have a choice. This was where he was destined to spend the last night of his life.

"Daniel. Daniel Bear." Ignoring the guard, she stepped toward the sitting shadow. "You must know what I came for."

Silence.

"You took something from my mother."

Silence.

"Something I want back."

"I don't know what you're talking about."

Daniel's voice sounded as if he hadn't spoken for weeks. "Her wedding ring," she said around the wall of emotion in her throat. "You—I saw you go over to what was left of her and— Don't make me say it."

"I don't have her ring, Jessie."

Jessie. Oh, Daniel. "Don't lie! After everything you've done to me, everything you made me endure, don't lie now." She slid closer and leaned over him. Even sitting, he seemed too large, too powerful to be contained by these walls. Seeing him trapped made it possible for her to continue. "You spoke the truth earlier today. Owned up to what you did. Why can't you . . ." She jabbed her finger at him.

"Get out of here, Jessie."

Jessie. "No. Not yet." She jabbed again, this time poking his shoulder. He tensed. Despite the gloom, she could feel his eyes boring into her. "I will *not* let you hang with my mother's ring on you." She kicked out, striking his ribs.

Without saying a word, he pushed himself to his feet. The guard hissed a warning and hurried to Jessie's side. Daniel stood with his hands hanging by his sides, looking down at her.

"Now." She held out her hand. "I want it, now."

"Jessie—"

She didn't give him time to finish. Her hand snaked out,

catching him a glancing blow on the side of his face. He reacted by grabbing her wrist and shoving her away. She caught her balance and dove at him. "Now!" she shrieked. "For God's sake, give it to me!"

"Miss Speer—"

She felt rather than saw the guard beside her. He held the revolver aloft, unsure what to do with it. Hating what she had to do to him, she pushed free of Daniel and reached for the guard's wrists. She felt her nails bite into his flesh, shoved her weight into his.

"Daniel! Run!"

For what seemed like forever, Daniel didn't move. She continued to struggle with the guard, praying. Another shadow briefly filled the open door; a deep voice repeated her command.

Then Daniel was gone.

Praying now for forgiveness, she released the guard's wrist and dug her nails into his cheeks. He cursed, trying to free himself. She hung on. Seconds, maybe a half-minute later, he tore her off him. He shoved. She felt herself land against the rough-finished wall. The breath was knocked out of her; it was all she could do to keep from collapsing.

Through blurred vision she watched as the guard clamped his hands over his raked flesh. He swayed over her, looking confused and betrayed.

I'm sorry.

Daniel was free. Narcisco and several of his braves had prepared for his escape. They'd get him out of the fort, take him someplace safe.

Good-bye, Daniel. Good-bye.

CHAPTER 22

Two weeks after she'd helped Daniel escape a hanging rope, Jessie woke from a restless, dream-trod sleep to the sound of her horse's nervous pacing. With her blanket still over her, her body cushioned by the leaves that made up her mattress, she listened.

Had Daniel returned?

No. He didn't dare.

When she heard approaching hoofbeats, she slipped out of bed, grabbed her few belongings, and ran for the trees. When she'd tried to purchase a horse from Captain Sutter, he'd informed her that her actions had forced him to wash his hands of her. She'd made it possible for Bear to escape. He would lose all credibility with a very angry military if he continued to help her. Finally she'd purchased a horse from Narcisco, who hadn't given up trying to talk her into living with his family.

She couldn't. She desperately needed time alone.

But she wasn't alone.

Aided by the moonlight, she watched as two horsemen came closer. They first rode aimlessly around her burned-out cabin, then approached her garden. She held her breath, terrified they might destroy it. Instead, after wandering up and down its edge, they headed toward the corral where she'd kept her horse since the mare had discovered how tasty carrot tops were.

"She's here. She's got to be. She wouldn't leave her horse."

"Miss Speer. Miss Speer, we know you're out there."

That voice. It belonged to one of the men who'd been with Raymond when this nightmare began. What had they called him, Burkham?

"I think you know what we're here for, Miss Speer. Sage said it wasn't a fortune, but it's sure as hell more money than we've ever seen."

Not moving, she remained pressed against the ground. If the men separated, they'd eventually find her. And then . . . She could give them what they'd come for, but what if they weren't satisfied with that? She'd be alone with them, helpless.

Once again destitute.

No!

"It won't do you any good to hide, Miss Speer. After what folks are saying about you being unhinged and all, even if you told that we'd come a-visiting, who'd believe you? It'd be your word against ours. And we all know who folks believed during Bear's trial."

Unhinged. A woman who helped a convicted killer escape. Sutter had turned his back on her. Margaret Buckhalter and Annie Larkin avoided her. Only Narcisco was left, but he'd been banned from the fort because of his suspected role in Daniel's escape.

Daniel! What happened to what was good and right and wonderful between us on that mountain? Oh, Daniel—

"It doesn't have to be the way it was with Sage. If you're nice to us, we'll be nice to you. For a while." Burkham wheeled his horse around, came closer.

The men roared with laughter. Shaking, she hugged the ground. She'd told Narcisco that she needed space, the sky overhead. Time to think about Daniel and what seeing him that last time had done to her.

Now that need might kill her.

"Tell you what, Miss Speer. I'm guessing you can hear me. Probably looking at me and my friend this minute. I'm giving you something to think about." He urged his horse back over to the garden. "These here plants mean a lot to you, don't they? Maybe more than money."

The other man's laughter shattered the night quiet. "What's it going to be, Miss Speer?" he asked. "It won't take more than a few minutes for us to push those plants of yours back where they came from. If you don't want that to happen, you'd better show yourself. Hand over that purse."

Never!

Before she'd done more than lift her head a few inches, thinking to tell them that, sanity returned. Even if she did as they were ordering, what was to prevent them from ruining her crops? And killing her.

"We ain't patient men, Miss Speer. For months now Sutter's been promising us decent wages. Sage, he wasn't no better. We can't live on promises. Now, thanks to what you've got, we don't have to."

Her heart screamed a denial. They couldn't treat her this way. They couldn't!

But who was going to stop them? Crying silently, she grabbed the leather pouch, her knife, and began inching away. Her body rang with the sound of laughter, pounding hooves. Still she kept crawling, crying.

The pounding went on forever.

"No. Do not try to speak. Drink first."

Too weak and heartbroken to argue, Jessie did as Narcisco urged. She sagged against the brave, only vaguely aware of the hours she'd spent fleeing what should have been her home. Her safety . . . a refuge.

"I couldn't stop them," she whispered when she finally stopped drinking. "Short of shooting them—I couldn't do that. Oh, God, I couldn't."

"I know."

"There's nothing left. I didn't have to see. I know. Nothing's left."

"Jessie, be quiet. Talk later."

When Narcisco's daughter handed her a warm acorn-meal cake, she bit into it. Although she tasted nothing and barely remembered how to chew, she knew she needed food in her stomach. She'd spent the night and much of the morning making her way to Narcisco's camp. For too long she'd thought of nothing except the sound of horses being driven back and forth over what she'd planted and nurtured.

Over her dreams. A lifetime of dreams.

Finally her mind had rebelled. If she wanted to stay alive and sane, she had to think of something else.

But what? Other than taking refuge with Narcisco, what?

"He has to be told."

He. Daniel. Jessie focused on Narcisco. "You know where he is?"

"I can find him."

Did she want that? Did she want anything else? "He can't do anything. It's too late."

Narcisco dropped to his knees beside her. "You saved his life. He has not forgotten that."

He wouldn't. But if she turned to him now, it would be because she was helpless and scared and sick at heart. She'd lean on him as she did when he took her back up the mountain—before everything shattered between them. "He'd be risking his life by coming here."

"He already has."

It took a moment, but finally she made sense of his words. "He hasn't left? I thought—you said . . ."

"You heard what you wanted to, Jessie. You needed to think that he was where he would be safe. But he is an honorable man. He could not leave you alone."

Not alone. When everyone else had turned their backs on her, Narcisco and his family had remained.

But they didn't love her, not the way he—not the way she . . . "Where?"

"I will bring him here."

Did she want that? Clenching her hands so tightly that her nails dug into her palms, she listened to her heart. Did she want anything else?

Despite his sense of urgency, Daniel went by Jessie's farm first. When he saw what remained of her garden, he nearly bellowed in rage. She'd left during the night. Maybe she didn't know how bad it was.

But she had to.

Because there was nothing he could do to repair the damage, he threw a rope over her mare's neck and rode away. Leading the still nervous animal, he headed toward Narcisco's camp. Although his route wouldn't take him near the fort, he kept his eyes on the horizon, alert.

If he'd stayed near her, he could have prevented this.

Maybe. And maybe he'd only have gotten himself killed, risked her life even more.

What could he say to her? The question had been with him from the moment Vaca told him what had happened. In truth, he'd thought of little except her since she'd set him free.

He could thank her. Tell her he admired her courage and daring. He'd tell her she shouldn't have, because if she'd let him hang, she might not be an outcast herself.

But he hadn't wanted to die. There were too many things he hadn't yet told her—nights he needed to spend in her arms.

His mind still whirled as he approached Narcisco's camp. She sat near Narcisco's home, watching as a child tried to show her how to use a bone whistle. Someone, maybe Misha, had braided two strands near her temple and then pulled them back, leaving most of her hair free to reflect the afternoon sun. Free? He would risk a great deal to be able to give her that.

As he came closer, she lifted her head, stared at him. He stared back. This was the face that had haunted him since he fled Fort Sutter, the eyes that dominated his dreams. Because he didn't know what to say, he simply dismounted. The child had scrambled to her feet and was staring at both him and Jessie. Jessie stood, the movement both graceful and labored. She wore a simple doeskin dress that ended at the knee. He didn't think she was aware of her body.

"Daniel. You look better."

How long had it been since he'd heard her voice? Only a few days; it felt like forever. "Jessie? I saw."

"My farm?"

He nodded. Neither of them had moved. Did he want to? Could he not?

"What does it look like?"

"Not ..." No. He couldn't lie to her. "There's almost nothing left."

"Nothing?" She swayed slightly, then caught herself by wrapping her arms around her waist. Eyes unfocused, she glanced down at her bare legs, then back up at him. The child slipped away.

"I'm sorry." *More sorry than I've been about anything in my life.*

"Gone." The word trailed off. "All of it, gone?"

He didn't care whether she wanted to be touched by him or not, whether he might lose what little was left of his heart by holding her. She shouldn't have to go through this alone. Leaving the horses, he stepped closer. He was afraid she'd shy away, but she seemed locked within herself.

When only a foot separated them, he held out his hands. She stared at them, kept on staring. Finally she laid her cold fingers on top of his. Still, she didn't collapse against him. He honored that.

"Some of the plants can be salvaged. With care, they'll grow. You can ..." He stopped. Even if her garden could be reclaimed, she couldn't stay there. She'd become as much of an outcast as he was—because of him. "I'm so sorry," he whispered. "It would have been better if I'd never met you." The words tore at him.

Her eyes focused. "If we'd never met, I'd be dead."

She was right. "You should have left me to hang," he amended. "If you had, this wouldn't have happened."

She shook her head. "It doesn't matter, Daniel."

No. It didn't. He wanted to ask her what she was going to do now, but before he could think how, her eyes gave him the answer. She was deep in shock. She had no idea what to do with the rest of her life.

"Jessie? Listen to me, please."

Her gaze remained on him, but she didn't speak. Although he'd wrapped his fingers around hers, hers remained cold. Damn it! He didn't care what anyone, she included, thought. She needed to be held.

And he was the only one who truly knew why.

Still, as he drew closer, he did so slowly enough that she could jerk away if she wanted. She didn't. He enveloped her, held her against him. He felt her body shudder. She seemed so small, so helpless.

He wanted to give her everything.

He could only give her his strength to lean against.

"I can't cry," she whispered into his chest. "I want to. I need to. But it won't . . ."

He waited with his lips touching her silken hair and his body wanting hers, waiting for the release she needed. When it didn't come, when she simply let him support her, he truly knew how little he could give her.

There was only one thing.

"Jessie. Listen to me, please."

"W-what?"

"I was with James Marshall when Vaca found me. James has decided on a site for the sawmill, in the hills several days east of here. He wants me to work with him. It's going to take months to get the mill ready."

"Is it?"

She sounded as if none of this concerned her. "There'll only be a handful of men there, all of them carefully chosen. They won't care who I am."

"I'm glad."

"And they won't care who's with me."

Her head came up. She leaned far enough away that she could look into his eyes. "What are you saying?"

"That I want you to go with me."

"Go? Leave my farm?"

"For now." He hurried the words. "You can't stay there." *You don't have a farm, not now. Maybe never.* "You know that, don't you?"

She didn't answer; she didn't shake her head.

"You could stay with Narcisco; I know he wants you to. But I don't think it's right for you. You can't live at the fort."

"You want me to leave my farm? Live in the mountains?"

"Foothills really, not mountains," he explained. He wasn't sure, but he thought she'd begun to shake. Why wouldn't she? Last winter she'd lost everything except her life. This spring she'd started over again. Only, now that had been taken from her.

Because of him.

"I'll be there, Jessie. Me and James. You'll be safe. You still have your money. When the time's right, you'll decide what to do with it. At least you have the means to support yourself. That's one thing you didn't have to give up." *Maybe the only thing.*

"I—" She blinked. Her eyes glistened. "I can't farm in the mountains."

He almost repeated what he'd said about the sawmill being built in the foothills, but maybe she was right. Seeds—even if she could get her hands on any—might not flourish there. "We'll find something," he promised, although she was the one who had to find another dream to guide her.

"My land, I can't abandon it."

Her desperate plea tore at him, scared him because this wasn't the Jessie he knew. He couldn't change things for her, give her back what she once had. Somehow he had to make her understand that, even if it meant weathering her rage. Her blaming him. "Jessie, I didn't want to leave Texas. But I did because I had no choice. It's the same for you."

She tried to pull free. Before he'd done more than hold on to her, her tears spilled over. She didn't seem to know she was crying. "I was so scared for you," she whispered. "When I thought they were going to hang you— I've never felt fear like that."

"Never?" God, he loved her!

"I don't ever want to be scared like that again." The life went out of her voice. She looked at him with dull, wet eyes. "To care like that again."

He felt sick. *Jessie, what are you saying?*

"I—won't let it happen." She started shaking her head, leaving him without taking a step. "It hurts too much."

CHAPTER 23

The air smelled of pitch and pine needles when she needed to fill her nostrils with the scents of earth, prairie grasses, onion starts. She needed to see for miles, not have hills rising up in all directions to block her view. To feel surrounded by trees.

Jessie repositioned herself on her rock and absently dug her nails into a moss-filled crevice. After a minute she forced herself to focus on a team of oxen dragging a massive log into place near the gravel-bottom creek. Sweat soaked both the oxen and men working on the mill, giving her a sense of work being done. Purpose. Was she the only one without that essential element?

When one of the gentle Mormons who worked for

James gave her a shy nod, she stirred herself and nodded back. She'd spent the morning baking bread, taking pleasure in the simple task. Although the men were a goodly distance from the wood-slab table where the loaves were cooling, they'd discovered that there'd be a treat tonight.

Why shouldn't she bake? She had little enough to do with her time.

In the distance, Daniel and James began crossing the broad, shallow creek, coming her way. She tensed, then forced herself to relax. In the five days she'd been there, Daniel had barely had a moment for her. Either that or he'd deliberately left her alone. That wouldn't change today.

The afternoon he brought her here, he'd set up an army tent for her on a rise overlooking the mill site. Thankful for anything to call her own, she kept her belongings there—the doeskin dress Misha had given her, the Allsetters' coin purse, her knife. During the day she walked, exploring the hills, tiring herself, trying to think.

Her thoughts always went back to her ruined farm, never ahead to the rest of her life.

Life? She didn't have one. Didn't know what she wanted.

Because thinking only brought on another headache, Jessie concentrated on James and Daniel. They were engaged in serious conversation, their attention divided between each other and their horses' progress. It seemed as if they were always together, the great task of building a sixty-foot-long mill consuming them.

Good.

Before the men left the stream, Jessie slid off her rock and walked over to where the camp cook, Caroline McBride, had just added more wood to the open fire. Caroline, the only other woman at the mill site and wife of one of the workmen, acknowledged her presence with a quick smile. "I hope my boys are behaving themselves. I keep telling them to stay out of the way, but you know how curious they are."

Jessie explained that Matthew and Joseph were fishing. Since they spent more time splashing water on each other than watching their lines, she wasn't sure how successful they'd be. She picked up a battered spoon and stirred the stew. Even with so many trees around to cast shadow, the air felt uncomfortably hot. After a minute, she backed away.

"I'm going to let the fire go down," Caroline said. "I was hoping to tender the meat a little more, but this heat is doing me in. So, is the log they brought in today going to be long enough?"

"It looks like it. I still can't believe how big a sawmill needs to be. The workmanship—I'm in awe of what they're accomplishing."

Caroline touched her arm. "You don't know how much it warms my heart to hear enthusiasm in your voice. You've been so quiet."

Jessie couldn't deny that. Because it hurt so much, she'd told Caroline only a little about what had happened to her farm. Caroline had never been to Fort Sutter, knew nothing about her or Daniel. All she cared about was feeding the men and looking after her family. As for farming, it wasn't something she'd ever wanted to do.

Jessie offered to keep her eye on the stew while Caroline went to check on her young sons. From where she stood, she could still see the men. Using an assortment of pulleys and rope, they managed to wrestle the latest log into place and began securing it with wooden pegs, working in water all the while since the stream's current would turn the huge water wheel that powered the vertical saws.

It wasn't a farm. For the mill to produce, trees had to be cut.

Stop it!

She'd cried out her tears. It was time to go on.

Only—

Again she tried to shake herself free of her thoughts. She was here, for how long she had no idea. Both she and Daniel were, she prayed, safe. That's what mattered.

But she needed more than baking bread and stirring stews and endless walks. She needed to stick a shovel in the earth and find rich soil, not rocks and tree roots. She wanted to stop thinking about what she'd lost and be free of nights filled with Daniel's presence. How?

When she heard a horse approaching, she stirred herself. Talking to someone, anyone, about anything, was better then living inside her head.

Only, that someone turned out to be Daniel. Although she wanted to turn her back on him and the memories that stalked her whenever she saw him, she held her ground. He held up a spindly seedling with a few clumps of dirt clinging to the roots and tiny, drooping branches. "It's an apple tree, Jessie. At least it will be."

"Apple. Where did you get it?"

"From a farmer passing through. He'd broken down. James and I fixed his wheel. He paid me with this."

She stared at the pathetic little tree. It would die if it wasn't immediately placed in the ground. She glanced at Daniel, thinking to tell him that. But he wasn't wearing a hat and the sun was high overhead, letting her see deep into his eyes.

He held himself apart from her.

Why shouldn't he? What they'd had, what they'd started—those things no longer existed. She had nothing but this moment, this hour. She couldn't offer herself to him as a complete, competent woman. He had an important task to accomplish, men depending on his leadership, a life to rebuild.

"Jessie, are you listening to me? The farmer was in San Francisco some two weeks ago when a ship arrived laden with fruit seedlings. He bought as many as he could afford."

"Did he?" Daniel had shown her the tiny tree. Didn't he have somewhere else to be?

"He said they'll grow here. That a person could have an orchard."

Orchard? With Daniel looking at her, she could barely concentrate on the word. "I suppose that's possible."

"I've watched you trying to work with the ground. It isn't what you need for your garden, is it?"

"No. It isn't."

"I wish I could make it different."

"Please stop talking like that. I don't blame you."

He stared unblinking at her. "Don't you?"

Damn his hard questions. "We can't change what happened."

"I know." He carefully set down the seedling. "At least you're free to go where you want here. No one bothers you."

"No. They don't. Caroline's a good woman. Strong and resourceful."

"Like you."

Maybe once. She couldn't say anymore. Still, she pointed at the bread. "The men are grateful for anything I do. They're good to me."

"But they're not much like you. Their religious beliefs . . ."

"It's all right."

"Is it? You need someone to talk to, to feel you belong here."

"Why?"

Her question seemed to take him aback. "Because this is where you live, Jessie."

"Do I? I'm a farmer, Daniel. It's the only thing I've ever wanted to be. But here—"

He continued to stare. "Are you thinking of leaving?"

Where would she go? How could she possibly face a life without him in it? Didn't he know she needed those answers before she could decide anything? "I don't know what I'm going to do, Daniel. But . . ." She indicated the seedling. "It has to be my decision, not something you chose for me."

"Jessie—"

"I mean it," she interrupted. "Raymond, the men with him, the Walla Wallas, they all tried to take my life from me. Maybe they succeeded." She lifted her head, wishing she understood herself—and how she felt about the man standing before her. "I need to put me back together."

His eyes darkened. She thought he might be reaching for her, but the gesture stopped before she could be sure. "I don't know how to help you mend yourself."

Her head started pounding. Still, she made herself go on facing him. "I'm not asking you to. I'm the only one who can do that. I know one thing about me. I need freedom. To be proud of myself."

"To not be beholden to a man."

How well he knew her. "Yes."

Was it possible for his eyes to get any darker than they already were? She felt suspended before him, exposed, vulnerable.

"I know what you're thinking," she hurried on. "That I

can't say I'm not beholden, not after everything you've done."

"Done? Jessie, if I'd stayed out of your life, you wouldn't have lost everything."

No. That wasn't true. Or was it? "If you hadn't gone up the mountain with me, hadn't confronted Raymond, you wouldn't have faced a hanging rope." She raked her hands through her hair. "Why are we doing this? Going over what can't be changed? Don't you understand, Daniel? I need to find me. That's all I can think about."

"By yourself?" He glanced at the discarded seedling.

"By myself."

He seemed to recoil at the words that had caused her so much pain to say. His mouth worked, but although she waited him out, he remained silent. She wanted to bury herself against him, lose herself in him. Instead, she fought the emotion, held it at bay. "If I don't make my own decisions," she whispered, "there'll never be a real tomorrow for me."

"Tomorrow?" He leaned over as if to pick up the seedling again, then straightened. "If you want it, it's yours. If not . . ."

Two days later she stood looking at her handiwork, as she'd done more times than she could remember since poking it in the ground. Because she'd braced the trunk with a thick branch, the apple seedling stood straight and tall. After the planting, she'd gone in search of the farmer Daniel had gotten it from. Although the man didn't have any trees to spare, he'd reassured her that more starts were due to arrive in San Francisco within the month.

An orchard?

Maybe.

But if she bought enough trees for a real orchard, she wouldn't have much money left for anything else.

With an angry shake of her head, Jessie walked away. She'd promised the two McBride boys that she'd take them to a fox den she'd spotted the other day. That's what she needed to concentrate on, not the questions in her head and heart. Because Caroline had told the boys they couldn't leave until they'd finished their arithmetic lessons, Jessie wandered down to the mill site. James was on the raised platform where the sawing of logs would take place. He gestured, indicating she could join him. Gathering her skirts, she climbed the stairs. "It feels so sturdy," she told James. "And the view . . ." Shading her eyes, she looked out at her surroundings. From up here, she could see everything of the hazed hills far beyond the stream. She could hear an axe biting into wood, water rushing over rocks, a crow calling. The sweep of trees extended to the top of the gentle, rolling hills and beyond, endlessly green. Endlessly alive. "It's beautiful."

"It is."

James's simple words caught her attention. She swung around toward him. "You searched for this place a long time. You've chosen well."

"Not well enough for Daniel."

"Daniel?" She forced herself not to close her eyes. "What do you mean?"

"He's restless and uneasy with himself. Maybe he's going to leave."

Leave? "He-he hasn't said anything to me. How can he even think that? He's safe here. Someplace else—"

"He'll never truly be safe, Jessie. Not as long as . . ." James paused, his attention drawn to something in the distance. She followed his gaze and saw two horsemen approaching. From this distance she couldn't tell who they were.

"James?" Eyes still on the men, she gathered her courage for the question she needed to ask. "Has he said anything about me?"

"Only that he hopes you find peace. And that his being here might stand in the way of your finding that."

Was he right? She tried to answer her question but couldn't. "Where is he?" she asked.

"Hunting. He shouldn't be gone much longer."

The men had stopped to talk to Mr. McBride. Mr. McBride pointed toward the hills. She turned back toward James. "How can he think of leaving? You need him."

"I've told him I'll understand, no matter what he decides to do. You aren't the only one looking for something."

No. Of course not. Why hadn't she thought about that? Because she'd been in shock. In truth, she still felt wounded.

Maybe she should tell Daniel she didn't want or need him around anymore, free him to follow his own star, to put his past—and her—behind him. Away from him, she might—might what?

When one of the workmen who'd been standing in the creek called up to James, asking his advice, Jessie stirred herself and climbed down off the mill. For a moment she stood with her fingers on a hand-hewn timber, remembering. Her first day here she'd watched Daniel hack a precise notch into this very timber so it now fit securely in with the others. When she didn't believe herself capable of a single thought and tears were a heartbeat away, she hadn't taken her eyes off him until he'd finished his task. His strength, skill, patience, pride had held her attention.

That and the way his body worked and moved and obeyed.

He can't leave! I need him!

Let him go. I don't ever want to need anyone again.

When the oldest McBride boy called out to her, she headed toward their small, half-finished cabin. Her legs felt wooden and her head seemed about to burst. *Daniel, gone?* She, no longer beholden to him. No longer feeling a part of him.

Free.

Lonely.

The boys were chattering about how they were going to try to sneak close enough to see the newborn foxes without disturbing them when Jessie noticed that the two strangers had finished their conversation and were heading toward the hills where Daniel had gone to hunt. She hoped they wouldn't frighten away the game.

Strangers? Uneasy, she continued to stare, but they were so far away that she couldn't make out their features. James was hip deep in water, wrestling with something. If James wasn't concerned, she shouldn't be either. Just because James had reminded her that Daniel would never truly be safe . . .

Fool. Daniel tried to cast off the word, but it returned screaming at him. *Fool!*

When his stallion slid down an embankment, he gripped the animal's side with his knees. Still, he nearly fell off. How could it be otherwise? A man with his hands tied behind him was all but helpless.

Fool.

The man with the scarred lip glanced over to make sure Daniel was still on horseback, but didn't slow the pace. "It's gonna be a fast ride, Bear," Burkham said. "Lieutenant Sinclair's still all worked up about you getting away, but he's not going to be staying at the fort much longer. That reward money he's offering—we want to git our hands on it afore he spends it on something else."

What did he care? Daniel ground his teeth together, anger nearly overriding his need to think.

Ten minutes ago he'd been bending over a deer carcass, preparing to lift it onto his horse's back. Then, suddenly, Raymond's former henchmen had ridden out of the trees, their rifles trained on him. He'd almost run.

But he didn't want to die. Not this way.

For the second time since the men hoisted him onto the stallion, he tested the bonds around his wrists. Maybe, given hours in which to work, he might be able to free himself. If not, he'd be returned to Fort Sutter and a hanging rope.

What was it like to die? He didn't want to think about that. Still, helpless, he couldn't put his mind to anything else. He'd seen death. Sometimes it came quick, a merciful end. He could hope for that. Other times—

Being dead meant no longer watching a sunrise, never seeing an eagle take flight.

Never telling Jessie how much he loved her.

Jessie.

"How'd you find me?" he asked.

"How? By puttin' things together. We knew you weren't with that injin friend of yours. When Miss Speer disappeared, we figured you'd taken her somewhere. You'd been hanging out with Marshall. Maybe, we figured, you'd taken her wherever Marshall was gettin set up. We was right."

A reward. For money, these two would do anything. They were heading straight for the mill site, obviously be-

lieving no one would stop them from taking a wanted man
to justice.

Were they right? Did anyone except Jessie care what
happened to him? Jessie? God, she would see!

His hands had gone numb by the time they reached the
stream and began crossing it. He concentrated on remaining on horseback, his attention riveted on the clearing
ahead. The Mormons had stopped working and were
watching, some of them still holding on to their tools. He
tried to spot James, his head fairly screaming with the
question of how much, if anything, James might risk for
him.

Then he saw Jessie.

She stood at the creek bank, her skirt trailing in the
shallow water. He'd never seen her body tenser, her eyes
darker. *No! She shouldn't see this.*

But she had.

As they came ashore, the men tried to ride around her.
She shifted position, placing herself directly in front of
them. "What are you doing here?" she demanded in a tone
filled with spirit and fear. "You have no right—"

"We've got every right, missy." Burkham jerked his
head at Daniel. "He's a wanted man."

"Because you lied."

"Jessie," Daniel warned. "Don't—"

Her glare stopped him. "What do you want me to do,
Daniel?" she asked. "Let them leave with you? I can't do
that. I . . ." She grabbed his stallion's reins, all but jerking
them out of Burkham's hands. "Why?" she demanded.
"Why would you come this far for him?"

"There's a bounty on him."

She blinked but didn't let go. "You'd let an innocent
man die, for money?"

"Folks don't think he's innocent, missy."

"We know why, don't we?"

"Jessie," Daniel hissed. "You're wasting your breath."

"It's my breath to waste. Go on, Daniel, tell me to turn my back on you."

I can't. Surely you know that. "It isn't your concern."

She looked as if he'd slapped her. Her eyes, so large and dark that he felt as if he could climb into them, stared back at him. Her mouth had gone tight; the white around her knuckles spread. "Not my concern?" She spoke so softly that he could barely hear her. "You saved my life. I'll never forget that."

"I hope you never do." The words were out of him before he could stop them. What did he care what anyone heard or thought? This might be the last time he ever saw her. If so, at least she would hear the truth from him. "Everything that's happened between us? Jessie, I'd do it all over again."

"You would?"

"Yes." He whispered the word, hoping his eyes were saying what was in his heart. "Oh, yes."

Her eyes filmed over. She blinked, stared at him for a length of time he couldn't, didn't try to judge. Then, shoulders squared, she turned toward the two men. When he saw her nostrils flare, he would have laid down his life for her—if he hadn't already. "How much is the reward?" she asked.

When the man told her, Jessie sucked in a deep breath. "That's a considerable amount."

"Sinclair's an angry man. He says his reputation is at stake. But the lieutenant's been known to change his mind, especially when money's coming out of his pocket. That's why we're in a hurry."

"Why you'll sell your souls."

"Whose soul?" Burkham challenged. "Seems like that's

what you did when you hooked up with Bear. Look missy, we can't stop you from going back to the fort, begging for Bear's life if that's what you've got a mind to do, but folks didn't listen to you before. They're not going to now."

"No." Jessie looked at Daniel again. "No. They're not."

"Then—" Burkham pushed his horse forward a step, stopping when the horse's nose was only a couple of inches from Jessie. "Then you'd best be letting us go. Unless you think those religious folks—" He indicated the gathered Mormons. "—are going to take up arms to defend a convicted murderer."

"Let you go?" Jessie barely whispered the word. Daniel took note of her knotted hands, the way her mouth had gone completely white, eyes that had turned into midnight. "Let you go?" she repeated.

"Jessie." Daniel barely got the word out. Would he ever say her name again? "You can't stop them."

Instead of saying anything, she slowly turned to take in her surroundings. As she brought her gaze back to him, an errant breeze caught her loose-flowing hair and whipped it around her face. She didn't bother to brush it away. Instead, she stood with her legs widespread, fingers now relaxing, head held high. Her eyes were still night-dark. "How long will the money last you?" she asked. "Will it be enough that you can sleep nights?"

"More'd be better."

"Yes. I'm sure it would."

Daniel fought to concentrate, to understand what Jessie was thinking. But he'd never seen her look more beautiful. And he'd never been more afraid, not of losing his life, but of losing her.

"We don't want to run you over, missy. But if you don't move . . ."

She didn't. Instead, after a few seconds, she bent down,

lifted her skirt, and began removing something from her ankle.

Suddenly Daniel understood. "Jessie, don't!"

She ignored him. Straightening, she held the leather pouch aloft. Eyes bright and bold, she shook a number of coins into her hand. She held them so the men could see. "That's what Sinclair's offering, isn't it?"

The men nodded, eyes riveted on the money.

Jessie shook out a few more, then turned so that the Mormons could see what she'd done. "I'm offering you more, in front of witnesses."

"Jessie, don't!"

A few more coins landed on the pile. "Like you said, Lieutenant Sinclair might change his mind. If I were you, I'd take this, now, and leave."

"You're offering—"

Jessie swiveled around to face the second man. "I'm buying Daniel's freedom." She upended the purse. Three more coins fell out.

"Jessie . . ." The line of her neck—had she ever looked stronger?

"Yeah?" Burkham leaned forward in the saddle and tried to reach for the money. Jessie jerked back. "Wait a minute," he ordered. "Are you going back on your word?"

"I'm telling you to untie Daniel and let him ride away. Then you'll get your money."

Instead of saying anything, Burkham reached for his pistol. But before he could pull it free, James called out a warning. Daniel looked over at James, wondering why he hadn't noticed his friend picking up his rifle. Several of the Mormons carried their axes at the ready. "Do what she says," James ordered.

Keeping his movements slow, Burkham backed his horse up so he could reach Daniel. He leaned forward and yanked at the knots. Daniel felt his arms fall free and winced at the sudden pain. He couldn't take his eyes off Jessie, didn't want to.

She stepped back several feet, drawing the two men with her. So slowly that he had no doubt of what it cost her, she started to hand the money to Burkham and his partner.

"Jessie! Don't!"

"Don't, Daniel?" She swung toward him, her body still rawhide strong. "I won't let them hang you."

"Because you think you owe me something?" He sucked in air, clearing his thoughts. She wouldn't have a single coin left. "I won't—"

"Not because I owe you."

There, in her eyes, the answer. The dark that had made it impossible for him to know what was going on inside her faded, became morning. He saw—love. For him. Her raw, honest gift rocked him to his soul. Still, he had to try to make her understand. "Jessie, for God's sake, without that you'll have nothing."

She stretched out her hand again, this time letting the coins drop into the man's palm. "Without you, I am nothing."

Jessie waited until the men had ridden away under the watchful eyes of James and the others before looking at Daniel again. She winced at the rubbed flesh around his wrists, then waited as he jumped down off his stallion. He stood before her, a mountain. Strong and free. Awed. Awed? By what she'd done?

Didn't he understand?

"Jessie." He laid his hands on her shoulders. "What you've done . . ."

What did she care whether anyone saw them? "What did I do? I only gave them money."

"Your farm . . ."

Her farm? Although she concentrated, she couldn't make sense of the words. Land or Daniel's life. The decision had been simple. She'd never regret it. "I don't care. When I thought—when I saw—I don't care."

She thought he might ask her to explain herself further and knew she couldn't. Instead, he traced a finger over her cheek, sliding a strand of hair back where it belonged. "I don't know what to say."

Neither did she. But maybe—maybe she didn't have to. A sound, a voice had come to life inside her. It built, overwhelming her. There was only one thing she could—wanted to do.

The back of his neck felt almost hot. She pressed her palms against the heated flesh, absorbing it. He was looking down at her, his mouth soft. Soft and inviting. Impossible to ignore. She answered with her lips, her fingers now in his hair, leaning toward his.

He enveloped her and let her listen to the beating of his heart.

"No one has ever done anything like that for me," he whispered a long minute later. "I still can't believe— Jessie, if you ever regret—"

"Never. Earth under my feet or you in my life. That's the decision I had to make. I know what I need, now."

"Me? In your life. Oh God, Jessie . . ."

Jessie what? Instead of asking him to say more, she pressed the tips of her fingers against his temple. His blood pulsed inches from her. She tried to see into his eyes but they were standing too close. She felt his breath on her hair. She thought to smile; the gesture felt newborn, shy. Somehow bold.

"Jessie," he whispered. "I love you."

"Love?" The word seemed to fill her. Tears stung her eyes, but she fought them off. She could cry later. Right now she couldn't be anything except as honest as he'd been. "Daniel, when I thought I'd lost you— I spent my whole life believing that I needed to be independent. But I was wrong."

"Wrong?"

"It wasn't that at all. Without love—Daniel? Daniel. I love you. I just didn't know it. No." She shook her head. "That's not true. I was afraid to admit to myself how much I love you. I thought love would make me vulnerable, weak, unable to stand on my own. I was wrong."

"Jessie . . ." His breath whispered across her face. "You are an incredible woman. I've never seen you look as strong as you do today."

I've never felt stronger. "Thank you. Thank you."

When he didn't speak, when she felt herself being pulled against him, she told him thank you again, not with words, but with her body.

Her heart.

EPILOGUE

Jessie sat waiting for Daniel, a blanket wrapped around her shoulders. Although it was afternoon, the January sun held little warmth. She could have gone into the cabin they'd built during the fall, but the air smelled so sweet and clean, the green of the forest looked so rich, that she couldn't bring herself to leave it.

Daniel had been with James since dawn, but he'd promised he'd be back in time to help her spread more leaves around the base of the three dozen apple seedlings she'd planted with the money that Daniel had earned working for James Marshall and that the Mormons had paid for her tending to their clothes. Just thinking of the way Daniel went to the little orchard every few days to see how the trees were thriving made her smile. He might never take to farming the way she did, but he was beginning to understand.

For Christmas she'd carved him an apple from a length of manzanita wood, explaining that until the trees reached maturity, he would have to be content with a wooden apple. Staring at her handiwork, he'd informed her that she'd given him a chunk of firewood, a rather ugly one at that.

Pretending indignation, she'd told him he had no appreciation for her craftsmanship and she'd like to see him do better. With one hand tied behind him, he'd retorted. Not if both McBride boys helped. Their "argument" had turned into a wrestling match, which quickly turned into something else. The thought of that something else made her forget the cold.

"Your daddy's a rare man," she told the tiny presence inside her. "Life has special meaning for him. He's going to make a good father, don't you worry none about that. He can hardly wait to be able to hold you, to tell you how Mommy and Daddy met. When you get older, he'll teach you how to break horses and . . ." What if they had a daughter? It made no difference. Daniel would place his daughter on the back of a horse just as he would a son.

The baby kicked. She looked up, hoping Daniel would hurry. He'd felt the baby move twice now; the look on his face as he held his hands over their child made her want to weep with love for him.

"Maybe we'll stay here," she continued. "Maybe, once James no longer needs him, he'll want to move on." Her eyes strayed to the orchard. "It's all right," she whispered. "As long as I'm with him—"

"Jessie! Jessie."

For an instant her heart skittered. Then she relaxed. From what she'd heard, Lieutenant Sinclair, Captain

Sutter, even Sheriff McKinstry didn't have the time or energy to look for Daniel these days. As long as he stayed away from the valley, he was safe. "Up here." She stood and waved to catch Daniel's attention. "You're late. I thought you were going to—"

"I know what I was going to do, Mrs. Bear." Daniel hurried closer. When he reached her, he held out his hand. In it was a small, flat, shiny nugget of some kind.

"What's that?" she asked when she realized Daniel wasn't going to say anything.

"You can't guess? James and I found it a little while ago, at the tail race. I hit it with a hammer. It flattened out instead of breaking. There's more tests we have to give it but—Jessie, this might well change our lives."

She took the nugget from him and held it up to the sun. It felt heavy for its size, and the color . . . "Daniel?"

"Gold, Jessie."

"Gold?"

"Maybe enough to buy you all the land a strong horse can travel through in a week."

She laughed and hugged him, catching the baby between them. "Oh, Daniel, I don't need that. Just you."

"Just me?" He leaned away, looking so serious that for an instant it frightened her. "What if I can buy every seed and seedling that comes off a ship, and can hire folks to plant and tend your garden, a garden bigger than Fort Sutter?"

"A garden larger than the fort? That'll never be." She tried to pull back. He wouldn't let her. "Besides, what would I do with all that land? I'd never have a moment away from it. I don't want that."

"Why don't you, Jessie Bear?"

"Because—you know the answer to that. All I truly need is you. You've shown me that."

"Me?" He whispered the word into her ear, sending a shiver throughout her. "Me? When?"

"Now." She laughed, feeling free and loved and in love. "You, Mr. Bear. Now." *Forever.*

ADVENTURES IN ROMANCE FROM TOR

BESTSELLERS FROM TOR

☐ 51195-6 BREAKFAST AT WIMBLEDON $3.99
          Jack Bickham Canada $4.99

☐ 52497-7 CRITICAL MASS $5.99
          David Hagberg Canada $6.99

☐ 85202-9 ELVISSEY $12.95
          Jack Womack Canada $16.95

☐ 51612-5 FALLEN IDOLS $4.99
          Ralph Arnote Canada $5.99

☐ 51716-4 THE FOREVER KING $5.99
          Molly Cochran & Warren Murphy Canada $6.99

☐ 50743-6 PEOPLE OF THE RIVER $5.99
          Michael Gear & Kathleen O'Neal Gear Canada $6.99

☐ 51198-0 PREY $5.99
          Ken Goddard Canada $6.99

☐ 50735-5 THE TRIKON DECEPTION $5.99
          Ben Bova & Bill Pogue Canada $6.99

Buy them at your local bookstore or use this handy coupon:
Clip and mail this page with your order.

Publishers Book and Audio Mailing Service
P.O. Box 120159, Staten Island, NY 10312-0004

Please send me the book(s) I have checked above. I am enclosing $ _____
(Please add $1.25 for the first book, and $.25 for each additional book to cover postage and handling.
Send check or money order only—no CODs.)

Name _____
Address _____
City _____ State/Zip _____
Please allow six weeks for delivery. Prices subject to change without notice.